A STORY BY
JONATHAN AUXIER

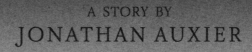

AMULET BOOKS

NEW YORK

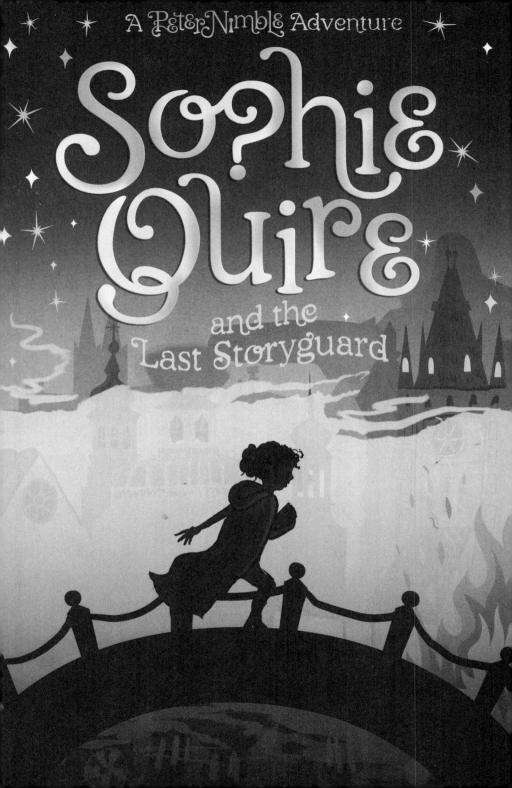

A Peter Nimble Adventure

Sophie Quire

and the
Last Storyguard

For Mary
*In good sooth, my love,
this is no door.
Yet it is a little window,
that looketh upon
a great world.*

Library of Congress Cataloging-in-Publication Data
Names: Auxier, Jonathan, author.
Title: Sophie Quire and the last Storyguard / by Jonathan Auxier.
Description: New York : Amulet Books, 2016. | Series: A Peter Nimble adventure ; [2] | Summary: "Twelve-year-old Sophie knows little beyond the four walls of her father's bookshop, where she repairs old books and dreams of escaping the confines of her dull life. But when a strange boy and his talking cat/horse companion show up with a rare and mysterious book, she finds herself pulled into an adventure beyond anything she has ever read"— Provided by publisher.
Identifiers: LCCN 2015039272 | ISBN 9781419717475 (hardback)
Subjects: | CYAC: Books and reading—Fiction. | Magic—Fiction. | Adventure and adventurers—Fiction. | BISAC: JUVENILE FICTION / Action & Adventure /General. | JUVENILE FICTION / Fantasy & Magic. | JUVENILE FICTION / Mysteries & Detective Stories.
Classification: LCC PZ7.A9314 So 2016 | DDC [Fic]—dc23
LC record available at http://lccn.loc.gov/2015039272

Text and chapter illustrations copyright © 2016 Jonathan Auxier
Title page illustrations copyright © 2016 Gilbert Ford
Book design by Chad W. Beckerman

Printed and bound in U.S.A.
10 9 8 7 6 5 4 3 2 1

Amulet Books are available at special discounts when purchased in quantity for premiums and promotions as well as fundraising or educational use. Special editions can also be created to specification. For details, contact specialsales@abramsbooks.com or the address below.

ABRAMS
THE ART OF BOOKS SINCE 1949
115 West 18th Street
New York, NY 10011
www.abramsbooks.com

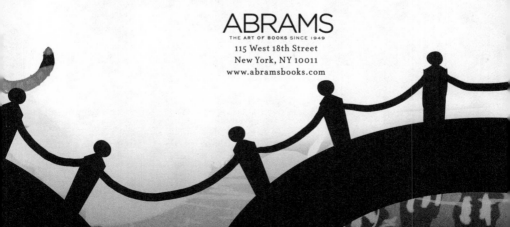

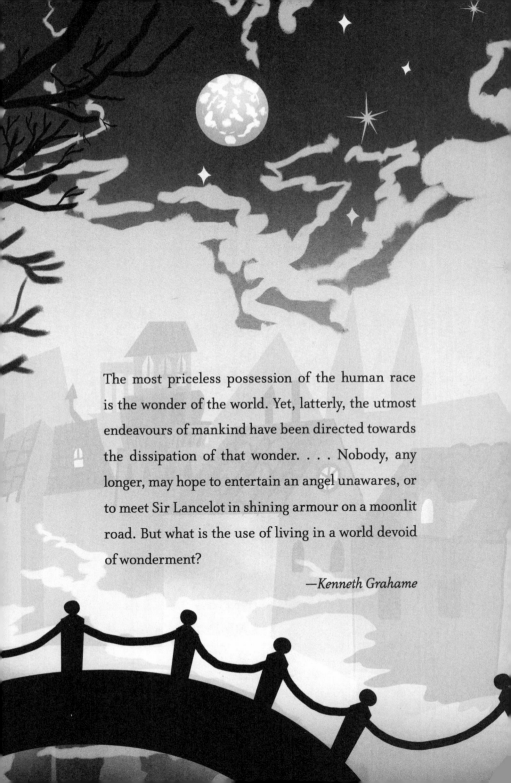

The most priceless possession of the human race is the wonder of the world. Yet, latterly, the utmost endeavours of mankind have been directed towards the dissipation of that wonder. . . . Nobody, any longer, may hope to entertain an angel unawares, or to meet Sir Lancelot in shining armour on a moonlit road. But what is the use of living in a world devoid of wonderment?

—*Kenneth Grahame*

Contents

PART THREE
WHERE

PART FOUR
WHEN

Sophie Quire

and the
Last Storyguard

PART ONE

WHO

It has often been said that one should never judge a book by its cover. As any *serious* reader can tell you, this is terrible advice. *Serious* readers know the singular pleasure of handling a well-made book—the heft and texture of the case, the rasp of the spine as you lift the cover, the sweet, dusty aroma of yellowed pages as they pass between your fingers. A book is more than a vessel for ideas: It is a living thing in need of love, warmth, and protection.

Few people have ever understood this fact so well as Sophie Quire—a twelve-year-old girl with chewed fingernails, pigeon-toes, and a disturbingly intelligent gaze. Sophie loved books beyond reason. Indeed, she loved them more than she loved the world around her. It was the very thing that made her unique, until it made her *dangerous*. But we are getting ahead of ourselves, which is also dangerous. So light a lamp and find a comfortable chair, and I will tell you her story.

✦   ✦   ✦

It was a crisp, windy morning in Bustleburgh—perfect weather for burning books. Thin trails of smoke rose up from chimneys all across the city, raining down flecks of burned paper. A small bell rang above the door as Sophie Quire stepped out from her father's bookshop and into the cold street. She shivered, breathing in the sweet, ashen air. People had taken to burning their old storybooks in their fireplaces to ward off the autumn chill. The smell would have been lovely if it weren't so disheartening. She watched as embers drifted past her and wondered: Were any of those books hers?

Her gaze moved to the door of the shop. Tacked to the lintel was a handbill someone had posted in the night:

NO NONSENSE!
All citizens are compelled to attend the
annual Pyre Day ceremony on the twenty-seventh
of this month, storybooks in hand.
Join your fellow Bustleburghers
as we cast off the shackles of childish superstition and
boldly march toward a modern, sensible tomorrow!

Sophie tore the poster down before her father could see it. As if either of them needed reminding about Pyre Day.

She wondered what this latest celebration would mean for her father's bookshop, which specialized in the very sort of "nonsense" that the city seemed determined to destroy. Her father tried to follow the newer fashions, stock only certain types of more improving literature, but what if that wasn't enough? Where would the two of them go if the shop closed altogether? She threw the poster to the ground and pulled her hood over her tangle of black hair. She couldn't waste her time wondering *What if*—she had work to do.

Sophie ran through the city, keeping to the smaller streets whenever possible. It was just after dawn, and Bustleburgh was quiet but for a few dockworkers and beggars and sentries finishing their night rounds. She kept her head down as she ran, her hood pulled low over her eyes so as not to attract notice. Most people in Bustleburgh were pale—so pale, you could almost trace the blue veins beneath their skin. Sophie, on the other hand, had dark skin and darker hair, which made her feel like an outsider. These features she had inherited from her mother, who had been born on an island far beyond the continent. Sophie had asked her father the name of the island many times, but her father—as with all questions regarding Sophie's mother—remained maddeningly silent. She sometimes wondered if he even knew the answer.

Sophie passed the inner canal, the academies, the counting-houses, the courts, and even the entrance to the crypts, where her mother had been laid to rest twelve years before. Sometimes, when Sophie felt particularly alone, she would sneak down and visit those forgotten depths.

She continued moving in the direction of the Pyre grounds, which lay just beyond the river. At several points in her journey, she had the sensation of being followed. She even once thought she heard footsteps echoing somewhere behind her, but when she paused to listen, she heard nothing. "You're just being a worry-weevil," she muttered to herself as she ran down a narrow staircase that led to the eastern shore.

Sophie, however, was not being a worry-weevil, for at that very moment someone *was* following her every step—stopping when she stopped, running when she ran. The reason she did not see this someone was because she did not think to expand her view above the streets. If she had, she might have glanced toward the rooflines. And in doing so, she might have noticed the slender figure of a boy crouched behind a chimney, attending her with keen interest. The boy wore a threadbare riding coat and a salt-stained tricorn hat. He clasped in one hand the strap of a canvas satchel, and in the other what appeared to be a very sharp harpoon, its silver point flashing in the early-morning light.

Where Sophie went, the boy followed, hopping silently from roof to roof as easy as you please. And if Sophie had managed to spy this acrobatic pursuer, she would have been struck by one thing above all else:

The boy was wearing a *blindfold*.

✦   ✦   ✦

Sophie cut a wide path around the docks until she reached the ancient stone bridge that connected Bustleburgh to the rest of the hinterland empire beyond. She ran past the Wolves of Dawn—a pair of massive lupine gargoyles that towered over the Wassail River. It was said that these stone beasts had defended the city from invading armies in ages past. She was half surprised not to see NO NONSENSE! signs looped around their necks. She petted the rightmost wolf paw as she passed, for luck.

Rows of modern gas-burning lamps lined the sides of the bridge, their flames creating an eerie, flickerless glow that reflected off the river far below. On the opposite shore was a clearing encircled by a high stone wall that had been constructed to cut off travel to and from the Grimmwald, a dangerous forest that loomed just beyond the city. Two guards stood at attention at the iron gates, muskets propped against their shoulders. Rising up behind them was the Pyre of Progress—an enormous mountain composed not of rubble but of *books*.

Bustleburgh, you see, was a city in the midst of a great transformation. For centuries, she had been home to myriad wonders and oddities—creatures and artifacts one might expect to find in fairy tales or nursery rhymes or any number of ballads. In recent years, however, the common folk had become leery of this heritage, and they began to suspect that these stranger elements were in some way holding them back from progressing into the modern world. And thus the No Nonsense movement was born.

For as long as Sophie could remember, every autumn brought a new vote about what type of "nonsense" to burn next. First it was fairy fruit. Then it was any object forged by dwarfs. Then it was any object that talked. Then it was alternative medicines and certain baked goods. Then it was (puzzlingly) windup toys. Then it was clothes that were too bright or flamboyant. Then it was any good imported from a foreign land. Then it was anything deemed too old—tapestries and paintings and spindles. Now, at last, it was storybooks.

For months, guards had been raiding libraries and schoolhouses, gathering up storybooks of all kinds for the annual Pyre Day ceremony. When that day came, Sophie's bookshop would also be purged. Of course, sensible things such as reference books and scientific periodicals would continue to be sold, but anything silly or frightening or fantastical or the least bit entertaining was to be summarily burned. Many people in Bustleburgh giddily predicted that this would be the largest Pyre to date. As if that were a thing to celebrate.

Perhaps you have heard the famous bit of wisdom about how the making of an omelet requires the breaking of eggs? This philosophy, while technically true, does not account for the fact that omelets are universally disappointing to all who eat them—equal parts water and rubber and slime. Who among us would not prefer a good cobbler or spiced pudding? Sophie often thought that Bustleburgh was not unlike the omelet maker who, having grown obsessed with his task, had decided that all eggs everywhere must be broken at any cost. While she acknowledged the convenience of living in a modern city, she wasn't sure it was worth the destruction of so many wondrous things . . . especially if those things included books.

Keeping her head down, she snuck off the bridge and approached the edge of the wall. She found a place where the stone had crumbled away to create a hole big enough for a twelve-year-old girl. She wriggled through the gap and pulled herself to her feet.

Sophie dusted off her frock and gazed at the pile of discarded storybooks. Through the early-morning mist, she could see a row of guards unloading wagons of more books near the front gates. A few more guards were distributing stacks of Pyre Day announcements.

Sophie crept toward the nearest wagon and crouched behind its back wheels. She then stood on tiptoe and peered into the bed. She was always surprised to see what sorts of books had been thrown out—often she found stories she remembered selling in her father's shop. She removed a heavy old book and inspected the cover: It was a tattered collection of tales about Saint Martin the Bruin King. At one time not so long ago, every child in Bustleburgh would have known these stories by heart; now they were consigned to the Pyre. A few pages were torn, and the spine was a bit frayed, but the damage was nothing that couldn't be repaired.

She reached back into the wagon and found two more interesting books: a slim volume of hinterland nursery rhymes and an annotated treatise on temperaments of the constellations. "Hello," Sophie whispered. "I'm taking you home." She gingerly wrapped the books in her cloak.

"You there!" a voice cried from the gates.

Sophie looked up to see a guard pointing straight at her. He was fumbling with a whistle on a chain around his neck. Clutching the books, she raced back toward the wall as fast as her feet would carry her. A sharp whistle split the air as guards stormed after her, shouting, "Stop, thief!"

Sophie wriggled back through the narrow hole, tearing her cloak on the edge of a rock. She ran onto the bridge, the books tight against her chest. She kept her eyes fixed on the crumbling stone buildings at the far end of the opposite shore: If she could just reach Olde Town, she could easily lose her pursuers in its alleys. She was nearly to the other side when she saw two uniformed men appear at the foot of the bridge—night sentries returning from their rounds.

"Stop her!" the guards from the Pyre cried.

The sentries heard the cry and rushed to block her path. "Halt!" they called, lowering their muskets like spears.

Sophie very nearly ran straight into the points of their sharp bayonets. She collapsed to the ground, gasping for air. The two guards from the Pyre joined their compatriots, and now Sophie found herself surrounded. "On your feet," the one who had first spotted her said, jabbing his bayonet to show he meant business. "Drop the nonsense."

Sophie stood, but she did not let go of the books. She cast an irritated glance at the giant wolf statues towering over the bridge. *So much for good luck.* She edged toward the stone railing, briefly wondering if she might be able to swim to safety. She was a strong swimmer, but the stone walls along the river were too high to climb— between the current and the temperature, she would probably freeze before getting to the docks. And even if she did survive, the books would not.

A fifth man approached from the direction of the Pyre. "At ease," he said in a sinewy voice. Sophie peered out from her hood to see a rail-thin man wearing an immaculately tailored blue coat and wielding a polished ebony walking stick that clicked against the cobblestones.

The soldiers stepped back and saluted the man. "I-I-Inquisitor Prigg," said the first guard, clearly nervous. "I didn't know you were up and about this early."

"Progress never sleeps," he said coolly. "And neither do I." Inquisitor Prigg was known far and wide as the architect of the No

Nonsense efforts. He undertook this task with a zeal that seemed almost superhuman, documenting every single object that went onto the Pyre. The man stepped in front of Sophie, who kept her head down. "Let's have a look at our thief." He lifted Sophie's hood with the tip of his cane.

The guards, seeing Sophie's dark skin, all stepped back. "A foreign spy!" one of them cried, drawing back the flintlock of his musket.

Prigg's lip curled in a look of pure disgust. "Your imagination is outstripped only by your stupidity. What spy would waste her time with storybooks?" He grabbed Sophie by one wrist and peered at her hand. "Note the calluses on the inside of her thumb and forefinger, indicating needlework. Observe the dried ink in the beds of her fingernails. And in the tips of her hair . . ." He leaned close, sniffing some clumpy strands that had fallen loose from Sophie's braid. "Wheat paste." He let go of her hand and stood back. "She works for the bookseller in Olde Town. Quire, I believe."

Sophie was shocked to learn that this important figure knew about her father's shop, but then, Inquisitor Prigg seemed to know everything about everyone.

"The bookseller probably put her up to it!" one of the guards said. "You—girl!" He poked his bayonet at Sophie. "Does your master know what you're doing here?"

This was a common mistake: Sophie so little resembled her father that few people knew they were related. "You can't charge me with anything," she said. "The ban against storybooks doesn't begin until Pyre Day."

"And what a glorious day that will be," Prigg said in a tone of genuine relish. "But the books were stolen from *our* Pyre, which *is* a crime." He removed a small notepad from his breast pocket and began writing. "You are hereby charged with trespassing and destruction of city property."

"*Destruction?*" Sophie said. "You're planning to burn them."

"The fine is five dulcets—"

"Five dulcets?"

"*Per book.*" Prigg gave a prickly smile and continued writing. "If you cannot pay that fine—"

"You know I can't," Sophie said. "That's more than the shop makes in a month." She could feel a flush of hot anger spreading across her face, and she briefly considered what the fine might be for shoving Inquisitor Prigg over the side of the bridge.

"Very well." He put his book away. "To ensure you pay this sum, you shall be confined to the High Dudgeon until the debt is discharged." He nodded to the guards, who marched toward her.

Before Sophie could respond, two of them had seized her by the arms and lifted her off her feet. The stolen books fell from her hands and onto the ground.

"Stop it!" she cried, pulling against their grips. "Help!"

Sophie did not know why she called for help at that moment,

for there was certainly no one nearby who could hear her plea, but words, as you know, sometimes have a way of slipping out. And to her profound surprise, no sooner had she called *Help* than an answer came—

"LET HER GO!"

CHAPTER TWO

DEEDS *of* DERRING-DON'T

"Let her go!"

The boy's words echoed in the still morning air. His voice was as cold as steel and twice as sharp. The blindfold around his head prevented him from seeing the scene below, but he could hear well enough. He fought back a smile, listening to the sounds of confusion as the guards tried to figure out who had just addressed them in such a bold manner. He heard their breathing change as they all slowly peered up toward him.

"Who on earth . . . ?" he heard the girl say.

The boy adjusted his grip on the crown of the high lamppost that he was perched upon, the gas flame hissing steadily beside his face.

When he was certain he had their attention, he raised his silver blade and pointed it directly at the man they had called the Inquisitor, whose wig reeked of perfume. "I'm not going to ask again."

The Inquisitor rapped his cane on the ground—ebony, from the sound of it. "Get down from that lamp this instant!" he shouted. "Climbing city property is expressly forbidden."

There was a rustle of black cloth as the boy leapt from the top of the lamppost. In one fluid movement, he opened the flap of his burgle-sack—and out sprang a mangy, catlike creature with four hooves and a wispy horse tail. "Tally-ho!" the creature snarled as it careened through the air, hooves swinging.

The boy hit the ground with a roll and sprang to his feet, his blade poised at the Inquisitor's throat. "Is this better?" he asked.

Now, at this point, it might be wise to pause our scene and better describe our blindfolded rescuer. The cleverest among you will likely have already guessed that this strange boy was, in fact, the famous Peter Nimble—Vagabond King of the unmapped seas and Greatest Thief Who Ever Lived. As for his furry companion—why, that was none other than Sir Tode, knight errant and storyteller laureate of the kingdom of HazelPort. For the moment, let us be satisfied to know that Peter Nimble had been following this particular girl for nearly a week and had no intention of losing her to any Dudgeon, High or otherwise.

He removed his hat—a handsome tricorn with a great white

feather he had purchased at a bazaar in the Freckle Islands—and offered Sophie a gallant bow. "My lady."

By now the guards had dropped the girl and were turning their muskets on him. Peter concentrated on the sounds of their footsteps, listening as the men shifted their weight and moved to encircle him. He knew his own weapon was not impressive: It was a short blade with an oddly shaped edge. But what it lacked in reach it made up for in strength and sharpness. And, unlike an ordinary sword, this blade could never be knocked from his grip. "Leave the girl here, and go on about your business," Peter said to the Inquisitor. "I don't want to hurt anyone, but I will if I have to."

"Are you threatening a public officer?" the man said.

Peter shook his head. "I don't make threats."

"Guards!" the Inquisitor cried, drawing a needle-thin sword from his cane. "Arrest this interloper!"

The men charged for Peter, who gave an irritated sigh. "I warned you." So saying, he leapt into battle—his blade raised. The fight was too close for long muskets, and so the guards were forced to take jabs with their bayonets. Steel clashed against steel, one boy against four trained soldiers. This, however, was no ordinary boy. Peter Nimble was as fast as any fighter who had ever lived, and no sooner had he struck a blow to his right than he managed to spin around and parry on his left. Whenever one of the guards tried to strike Peter from behind, Sir Tode was there to deflect him with a well-placed head-butt or bite to the rump. It was a dance they had performed a hundred times over the past two years as they roamed the map in search of adventure. One that rarely ended well for their enemies.

Peter sliced and stabbed at his opponents, taking special care not to hurt the girl, who was scrambling across the ground to retrieve her fallen books. She was shouting something at Peter, but he couldn't take the time to listen. "Just stay down, my lady!" he called, hopping deftly onto the rail of the bridge.

The girl kept yelling, and it took Peter another moment to realize that she was not screaming out of fear, but out of rage. "Stop it!" she shrieked, pushing through the guards to meet him. "Stop it, *right now!*"

Peter wasn't sure why the girl would interrupt her own rescue, but he could tell she was serious. "If you insist!" He took one final leap toward his enemies, spinning his body like a dervish as he moved among them, his coat flying out behind him. This was a befuddling trick from his thieving days, and when he had finished moving, he had all four of their muskets slung over his thin shoulder.

The guards stared at him, unarmed and dumbstruck. Peter allowed them a moment to absorb what had just happened before saying, "Boo!"

All four guards screamed and ran along the bridge toward the Pyre. Sir Tode, not being one to pass up a good chase, clopped after the men, snarling and snapping at their heels.

"Cowards," Peter said, tossing the guns off the side of the bridge. They hit the water with a satisfying splash. He turned to the Inquisitor, who had remained at his post, still clutching his blade. "I suggest you follow your men . . . unless you're wanting a duel."

The man did not say anything for a moment. Peter could hear his tense breathing, his teeth grinding, his heart racing—it sounded as if he were genuinely considering the offer. "Blind rogues and hooved cats?" He wasn't talking to Peter but to the girl. "I'm sure the city council will be very interested to learn of the company you keep, Miss Quire." He shoved his blade back into the sheath of his cane and retreated to the shore.

Peter brushed a bit of dust from the brim of his new hat and fit it over his head at a rakish angle. He turned to the girl and flashed a winning smile. "Well, that was fun."

Now, Peter Nimble had performed a number of daring rescues in his career, and while every one was a little different, the reactions were generally the same. As a rule, most people seem to appreciate being rescued by dashing strangers. Most people, perhaps, but not Sophie Quire.

"Are you insane?" she shouted, her voice hoarse from screaming at him. "You nearly killed those men!"

Peter almost fell over as she wrenched a book out from under his boot. He listened as she riffled through the pages, as though inspecting the book for damage.

"And what were you doing up on that lamppost, anyway?" she demanded. "Were you following me?"

Peter stepped back, caught off guard. "I . . . um . . ." Obviously he had been following her. People didn't just spend their mornings climbing lampposts for the fun of it. But to hear her describe the activity, you would think it was the worst thing in the world. "In case you forgot," he said finally, "I just *rescued* you."

"Rescued me?" The girl got right in his face. She was radiating indignation like a furnace. "I was going to have to pay a *fine* . . . Now I'm party to attempted murder. Who knows what they will do to me, or my father? One word from the Inquisitor and we'll be on the street or worse—and it will all be thanks to you!"

Peter opened his mouth but closed it again. He could feel his whole face flushing with anger, or perhaps embarrassment—he wasn't sure which. All he knew was this was *not* what he had planned. "I . . . I was only trying to help," he said, inching back.

"Next time, resist the urge." The girl yanked her cloak over her shoulders with a dramatic flap. "And if you're going to throw something into the river," she added, "why not start with that ridiculous hat? You look like an ostrich in mourning." With a dramatic heel, she turned away and ran toward the road.

"Oh, yeah?" Peter called after her. "Well, you look like an ostrich in . . . in pyjamas!" But it was too late. The girl was already out on the streets. Peter did not know why he'd yelled the remark about pyjamas—which, even he had to admit, was a rather weak retort; he was only aware of wanting to have the last word.

He remained on the bridge, listening to the sound of the girl's footsteps as she ran between two stone buildings. If he concentrated, he could still make out her heartbeat, pounding hard against the books clasped to her chest. A part of him wanted to call her ugly—which was a serviceable insult for most occasions—but he didn't actually *know* what she looked like. He could, of course, remove his blindfold and look at her, but he knew from experience that that was a bad idea. So long as he was blindfolded, the world could be full of a million swirling possibilities, but the moment he looked at a thing, it was irrevocably reduced.

Peter Nimble had spent the first ten years of his life blind. All that had changed, however, when a mysterious benefactor named Professor Cake had magically restored his sight with a pair of emerald-green eyes. At first, Peter was overjoyed by this miraculous gift. But miracles, as you probably know, often come at a price. Suddenly the Greatest Thief Who Ever Lived found himself a little less *great*. He could still smell and hear and feel things well enough, but not the way he once had. His sight restored, Peter Nimble had become . . . *ordinary*. It did not help that whenever people looked into his eyes, they reacted with hushed awe. Perhaps it was the unusual green color? Whatever the reason, the effect only made Peter feel like more of a fraud. And so, for now, the blindfold remained.

He came to attention as Sir Tode returned from his chase, his small horse hooves clopping merrily against the stones. "I say!" the creature exclaimed, out of breath. "Nothing like a bit of heroics to get the vitals flowing! Though I could have done without that bayonet to the rump." He stopped next to Peter and peered about. "Er, where's the girl gone?"

"Back to the shop," Peter muttered. *And good riddance*, he thought. He snatched the hat from his head and ripped the feather from the band, silently cursing the merchant who had sold it to him.

Sir Tode seemed not to notice the boy's mood. "A bit younger than I expected," he said, scratching behind his ear with one hind hoof. "We're certain she's the one?"

"That's her, all right." Peter knelt down and opened the mouth of his burgle-sack. "We should go."

The knight clambered into the bag and made himself comfortable. "Not a bad introduction, I'd say. Getting the girl's assistance should be good as done—seeing as how we saved her life." He gave a knowing chuckle. "In my experience, damsels are more than willing to help the heroes who rescue them."

Peter set his jaw, recalling the sting of the girl's parting words. "She might not be your typical damsel." He fastened his coat and stepped into the fog.

THE BOOKMENDER *of* BUSTLEBURGH

S ophie's father was waiting for her when she finally reached the bookshop. "You are late," he said, not looking up from his work. "We opened our doors half an hour ago—what if a customer had come?"

They both knew that this was a highly unlikely scenario, given how few people set foot in their shop these days. "I'm sorry, Papa." She closed the door and removed her cloak. If her father noticed the torn hem or the mud on her apron, he chose not to say anything. "I was . . . slowed down a bit on the way home," she said.

Sophie had spent the entire journey home mulling over her encounter with the blindfolded boy. A part of her felt bad for being so ungrateful, but every time she pictured his cocky grin, she felt a new wave of anger. The boy could have gotten himself killed, and it would have been her fault. It was one thing to read about sword fights in a story, but to see clashing blades in front of her was altogether more horrifying. She shut her eyes, trying to banish the memory from her mind, and turned back to her father.

Augustus Quire sat hunched over his desk, working sums into a ledger that stubbornly refused to show a profit. "I would ask what business drew you out of bed at so early an hour, but I suspect I do not want to know." He absently tried to drink from his mug of tea, which he had long since emptied.

Sophie set the three rescued books on the counter in front of him. His pen stopped. "Again, Sophie?" He did not ask where the books had come from. He did not need to. "How many times have I warned you about this?"

"I couldn't just leave them there to burn." She ran a hand over the worn cover of the topmost book, the collection of Saint Martin tales; it was embossed with a picture of a roaring bear. "They deserve better than the Pyre."

Augustus removed his spectacles and massaged his temples. "You sound like your mother." This was something he often said to her, and she never quite knew if it was meant to be a compliment.

Sophie's mother had died when Sophie was still an infant. The circumstances of her death were a complete mystery to Sophie, being something her father refused to discuss. "It's troublesome luck to trouble the dead," he would always say, citing an old hinterland proverb. The only memento of her mother Sophie possessed was a silver necklace on which hung a round sleigh bell. The curious thing about the bell was that, no matter how much Sophie shook it, it never seemed to make a sound.

Sophie studied her father, who was now gazing past her to the empty workbench at the back of the shop. Augustus Quire was the sort of man who looked old beyond his years. His hair was thin, his movements were deliberate, and he never raised his voice. Indeed, many customers assumed he was Sophie's grandfather. That or her master. Sophie had learned from neighbors and old customers that her father had once been quite different—an avid reader who could recite lengthy passages verbatim from every book he read. Sophie often tried to picture what he had been like in those days, but some things were beyond even her imagination.

"You shouldn't worry about me, Papa," she said, resting a hand on his shoulder. "Most of those guards can barely tie their laces."

He blinked, as if startled from a dream. "It is not the guards who frighten me." He replaced his spectacles. "You are a smart girl. But even smart girls can get into trouble. These are dangerous times we live in, led by dangerous men." He was, of course, speaking of Prigg. For as long as Sophie could remember, her father had feared the day when the man might direct his attention toward them.

"The shop will be fine, Papa," Sophie said, inching back. "Even after Pyre Day, we can just sell other kinds of books."

Her father waved a hand. "I do not worry for this shop. What is the point, even, of a bookshop in a city that no longer reads stories? To lose this place would be a disappointment. But to lose my daughter?" He fixed his eyes on her, and Sophie wondered for a moment if he had somehow learned about her capture on the bridge. "That would be more than I could bear."

That he might one day lose his daughter was a constant fear for Augustus Quire. His every conversation, even over the smallest things, seemed to return to this subject. Sophie grabbed her father's hands in her own. She knelt, saying, as she often did when he was in this state, "I will never leave you, Papa. Never."

Her father smiled, though not in a way that said he entirely believed her. "You have books to mend," he said, and returned to his own work.

Sophie stepped into the small inventory room, which doubled as her workshop. Stacks of scavenged books, all in various stages of disrepair, lined the floors and furniture. In a far corner sat her mother's workbench. She clasped the bell hanging from her neck, as she often did when thinking of her mother.

Sophie's mother had been a bookmender named Coriander whose work carried her to every corner of the map. How she had ended up in Bustleburgh married to Sophie's father was, like everything else about her, a mystery. Longtime customers would occasionally relate memories of her when they visited the shop. They said that she was a quiet woman, graceful in her movements, but that there was a sort of sadness in her face, even when she smiled.

Sophie sat and studied the condition of the books she had saved from the Pyre. They had all three of them been trod on during the fight on the bridge and were nearly beyond repair. Pages were torn down the middle, corners were crushed in, entire spines flattened, and muddy boot-prints embossed the covers. "Let's see what we can do," she said as she lit a lamp and set to work stripping the casing of the first book. Sophie had no formal training in bookmending, but she had learned a great deal from practice and careful study of the repaired books her mother had left behind.

"Welcome home," she whispered to the collection of Saint Martin stories, now resting coverless atop a scratched copper plate. She gently turned the screw of her vise until the pages were secure. She removed a pot of paste and a spool of binding thread from a drawer beneath the bench and set to work repairing the spine. First she cut the old thread from the spine and pulled apart the signatures. Then, working carefully with a brush, she cleaned dirt and grime from the cracks between the pages. "Stay calm," she said. "It'll only sting a little."

Sophie had learned long ago that books were temperamental creatures that must be coaxed back to life. A careless stitch could shift the pages and weaken the binding. Likewise, the spine would not square without proper exercise. Over time, she had discovered that the best way to repair a book was to first *know* it. And so she made a practice of reading every word of every book she repaired. It was slow going, of course, but the end result was worth it. Books she repaired were not just readable—they were transformed. The print seemed to shine brighter. The pages would lie flat, opening to just where you had stopped reading. The spine would call out to you, begging to be taken off the shelf. Not that anyone in Bustleburgh would ever care. But Sophie cared, and that, perhaps, was enough.

Sophie adjusted her reading lamp and ran her fingers over the title page. Her heart beat faster, thrilling at the prospect of reading a new story—a story that might for a moment transport her beyond the walls of the bookshop to a world filled with bear kings and trickster frogs and wicked trolls and a thousand wonders besides. She turned the page, wishing that she could escape to the lands described in such stories. But no sooner did she think this than a rush of shame swept over her. She already had a home.

She looked at her father, who sat hunched over his desk, scribbling in his ledger. Sophie closed her eyes and quietly renewed the promise she had made to him that day and countless days before. "I will *never* leave you, Papa." Even as she said this, the promise sank to the soles of her feet, like an anchor plunging into cold water—

Never. But what Sophie Quire did not know—what she *could not* know—was that her promise would very soon be broken.

CHAPTER FOUR

A CURIOUS OFFER

The next morning, a notice from the Inquisitor's office appeared on the front window of the shop: Sophie Quire was being charged with destruction of property and assault of a civil officer, for a total fine of thirty dulcets. This, of course, was more money than her father could ever hope to pay, and he would likely have to sell the shop to cover the expense. It seemed that Quire & Quire Booksellers was finally in its last days.

"Do not torment yourself, my child," Augustus said upon seeing the citation. "With Pyre Day so near upon us, we were not long for the world anyway." He was right. The entire town was abuzz with excitement over the upcoming celebration. What few customers they had were only coming to buy storybooks so that they might have something to personally cast onto the Pyre of Progress. With every book she sold, Sophie whispered, "Good-bye," knowing that she was very likely sending that story to its fiery death.

Sophie wondered what might be next for her and her father. She wished they could escape to some more tolerant part of the world, but she knew her father was too frail for such a journey. They might find refuge in the Grimmwald beyond the river, but that was a dangerous proposition: Every day, it seemed another story reached town about innocent people being attacked by highwaymen or strange beasts that lived in those woods. Laws had recently been changed to allow children as young as six to work in the mills by the river (apparently childhood was also nonsense), and she hoped that this meant that she could find work alongside her father. Then, at least, they could still be together.

✦ ✦ ✦

"Here you are, Madame," Sophie said, returning a repaired book to one of her more loyal customers—a striking woman who went by Madame Eldritch, though Sophie was fairly certain that this was not her real name. Madame Eldritch had thick auburn hair and porcelain skin. She came in from time to time with books for Sophie to repair. The books were always quite old and written in languages that Sophie could not understand. "I took the liberty of remarbling the endpapers to match the gilding on the spine," Sophie said, handing her an ancient volume dedicated to the mysteries of beekeeping.

Madame Eldritch inspected the volume as a jeweler might inspect a ruby. "The girl has her mother's touch," she said.

Sophie lowered her head to conceal her smile. This was something the woman often said, and it brought Sophie no end of pleasure. "You're very kind, Madame."

Madame Eldritch counted out an assortment of old coins from different lands—overpaying, as she always did—and pressed them into Sophie's palm.

Sophie watched as the woman glided toward the front door, which her father had opened for her. Sophie had long observed that Madame Eldritch had a somewhat stupefying effect on men, including her father. Today, however, was different. Augustus Quire was sober-faced as Madame Eldritch reached his vicinity. "Madame?" she heard him say in a muted tone. "I'm sure you have noticed that we have been cited by the city. We have appreciated your patronage over the years . . . but I'm afraid after Pyre Day we can no longer afford to be seen servicing a more . . . *eccentric* clientele." He lowered his head. "I'm sorry."

The woman nodded. "As am I." She turned back to Sophie, who was still watching from the counter. "Farewell, little bookmender," she said. "Perhaps you will one day find a world more appreciative of your gifts." The shop bell rang behind her as she stepped out the door.

Madame Eldritch's parting words echoed in Sophie's mind for the rest of the afternoon and into the evening. She wondered what the woman had meant about finding a different world. Something about the words made Sophie think of her mother.

✦ ✦ ✦

Night soon came and, with it, closing time. This was Sophie's favorite part of every day, for it meant she could work without fear of interruption from customers.

"Not too late," Sophie's father said as he kissed her head, and then shuffled upstairs to their apartment above the shop. Sophie settled into her place at the workbench, carefully mending books that would be cast into the Pyre before the month's end. This thought made her feel less like a bookmender than an undertaker—dressing corpses for a funeral.

It was just after midnight when Sophie heard the bell ring in the front of the shop. This surprised her, because her father usually locked the door before going upstairs. "We're closed," she called, sliding off her stool and walking onto the main floor. The shop was empty but for the shadows. "Hello?" she called, stepping closer.

A voice sounded in her ear. "Did you miss me?"

Sophie shrieked, staggering backward and tripping over a seven-volume set of *Villanelles Fantastique* she had left on the floor.

She looked up to see the boy with the blindfold standing over her, grinning like a goon. His ugly pet cat was crouched beside him, looking similarly amused.

"Sophie?" Her father's voice sounded faintly from upstairs. "Are you all right?"

"I'm fine, Papa!" she called, scrambling to her feet. "I just saw an ugly pest in need of squashing."

"Do you greet all your customers that way?" the boy asked, leaning against a wall. "I can see why your shop is struggling."

"Our shop is closed, you trespassing oaf," Sophie said. "That's why the door was locked."

"As if a lock would stop me." The boy cleaned his fingernails with the tip of his silver blade.

"I see you've come armed." Sophie scowled at the curved weapon. The very sight of the thing made her sick with the memory of the fight on the bridge. She wondered how much blood that edge had spilled in its lifetime. "If you're planning to rob us, you should know that we haven't any money."

"If I were robbing you, you wouldn't see me." He tipped his hat, which Sophie noted with some satisfaction had lost its silly feather. "I'm sorry if my silver hand offends your delicate sensibilities . . . but, you see, it can't be helped." He pulled back his sleeve to reveal his right arm.

Sophie understood at once why he had never sheathed his

weapon. The blade was a part of him, the hilt attached directly to the stump of his wrist. A dull metal cap concealed most of the wound, but around the edge of the cap she could make out ugly red scars.

Sophie stared at the boy. "What . . . What happened to your hand?"

"You know what they say," he said. "The bigger the scar, the better the story. I lost it in a duel." He swiped the blade through the air, and it responded with a sharp, singing noise. "My opponent lost a lot more."

There was a bite of truth behind his boast that made Sophie quaver. "You would brag about killing a man?"

The boy's smile disappeared. "The man deserved it. Besides, a good weapon can be useful—as you learned yesterday on the bridge."

Sophie, who up to this point had been secretly impressed, regained her sense of indignation. "You'll be pleased to know that Prigg cited me this morning," she said, resting her hands on her hips. "We're going to lose our shop, and it's all thanks to you."

"You were going to lose your shop anyway, if those posters all over town are to be believed." He knelt down and scratched his cat behind the ears.

Sophie noticed for the first time that the boy's pet was no ordinary cat—or at least no cat she had ever before seen. For starters, it had hooves instead of paws. Also, its ears were entirely the wrong shape. And it had a *mustache*. "What kind of pet is that?" she asked, inching back.

"He's not a *pet*," the boy said. "He's a knight."

The creature clopped toward her and bowed his head in a manner that could only be described as chivalrous. "My lady," he said in a gravelly voice. "It is a pleasure to make your acquaintance."

Now, I do not know your opinion about talking animals, but Sophie's opinion was that, even if they existed, they did not exist in places as dull as Bustleburgh. The discovery of one such creature now filled her with an amazement she could scarcely describe. She turned toward the boy, her mouth agape. "Did . . . did it just talk?"

The creature sniffed, placing a hoof against its chest. "If by 'it' you are referring to me, then *yes*."

Sophie covered her mouth. "It did it again!"

"Of course he can talk," the boy said. "It's getting him to shut up that's the trick." While this was, on its face, a mean thing to say, it was clear from his manner that the boy and the creature shared a great fondness for each other—the sort of jocular camaraderie Sophie had often read about but never herself experienced.

Sophie knelt down, peering closely at the animal's face, which she now realized was only *slightly* like a cat's. The creature seemed at once familiar and completely new to her. She had spent a lifetime reading books filled with different magical beasts, but none of them quite like this. It was almost as if several different creatures had been basted together with invisible thread. "I've got it!" She snapped her fingers, running to a bookshelf. "You're a *chimera*."

The creature blinked, his mustache twitching. "I beg your pardon?"

"A chimera!" From one of the shelves, she drew a favorite bestiary entitled *The Seas Beyond the Sea* and flipped to the corresponding entry. "It says right here: A *chimera* is a creature who is made from parts of different creatures. Like a griphon or a pigfrog." She turned back to him. "Let's see now . . . there's plenty of cat in you—that's obvious enough—but those hooves and ears are equine . . . so there must be some horse in you. But there's something else, too. Your eyes and mustache . . . why, they almost make you look *human*." She snapped the book shut. "I've changed my mind. You're not a chimera at all. I think you're a normal person who's transformed himself into a ridiculous creature." She covered her mouth. "Well, not ridiculous, just . . . *unusual*."

At these words, the creature preened with visible pride. "You do me a kindness, my lady. It is a pleasure to meet someone who can see me for who I truly am."

"And it's not like he did it on purpose," the boy said. "He was hexed by a hag a long time ago."

"It's an interesting story, actually," the creature said, settling down onto his haunches. "Some years back, I was on a quest to find this maiden who, for a variety of reasons, had refused to tell me her name, when . . ." What followed was a lively, if lengthy, tale involving the maiden, several competing knights, a greedy duke, a sleeping hag, a noisy alley cat, and a jousting tournament whose prize was to be a new pair of seven-league boots. ". . . and before I knew what was happening, the old hag wagged a dishrag out her window and—*poof!*—my horse, the cat, and I were all combined together into the form you see before you today. I've been roaming the earth thusly ever since."

Sophie listened to his story, unsure whether she was meant to laugh or cry. "Did you ever try looking for a cure?"

The creature made a curious face. "Hexes are tricky things. They can only be undone by the one who cast them. We did recently have a rather promising lead on her whereabouts, but she seemed to have moved on by the time we got there." If Sophie had been paying more attention, she would have noticed that Peter turned away at this moment.

"No matter!" the knight said with obviously forced cheer. "After two hundred years, I've grown a bit attached to these old hooves. Besides, if the unhexing had worked, we might not be here, talking to you." He took a step closer. "The truth is, Sophie Quire, we've traveled a very great distance to find you."

"Find *me*?" She stared at these two visitors, each more strange than the other: a hook-handed boy in a blindfold and a talking cat-horse-gentleman thing. She stepped back, holding the bestiary close. "Who are you?"

"My name is Sir Tode. And my companion here is Peter Nimble."

The boy tipped his hat with the end of his blade. "Perhaps you've heard of me?"

Sophie was very pleased to report that she had not. "Peter *Nimble*? Sounds like something from a misremembered nursery rhyme." She was closer to the truth than she realized. "I suppose you've come to sell me magic beans?"

"*You're* a magic bean," he muttered by way of a comeback. She saw the boy's ears go bright red, which gave her no small degree of satisfaction.

"All right, you two!" Sir Tode said, clearing his throat. "We weren't sent all this way so you could bicker like a pair of hedge imps."

"Who is it that sent you?" Sophie asked.

Sir Tode made a face as though he might have divulged too much already. "I'm afraid I can't tell you that," he said. "Peter and I were entrusted with a book—a very special, very old book. One in need of repair."

Peter reached into his bag and removed what looked to be a thick folio wrapped in oilcloth. He held it out for her. "We were instructed to bring it to the Bookmender of Bustleburgh."

The Bookmender of Bustleburgh.

The words moved through Sophie like an unexpected breeze.

She tucked a loose strand of hair behind one ear. "You want a bookmender." Had he told her they were looking for a flying porcupine, she could not have been more surprised. These two strangers had traveled countless miles, all to find a bookmender— to find *her*.

But no, she realized just as suddenly. They were not looking for her. "The bookmender doesn't live here anymore," she said softly. She clasped the silver bell hanging around her neck.

The other two exchanged worried looks. "Perhaps we weren't clear . . ." Peter said. "*You* are the bookmender."

"I'm not," she said. "The bookmender was my mother, and she died a long time ago." She walked past them before they could see her face, which was burning with shame. She felt like a fool for thinking that someone might have been searching for *her*.

"Hold on just a minute." Sir Tode trailed after her. "We were told we could find the bookmender at this shop."

"Whoever told you that was wrong."

Peter released a rueful chuckle. "The person who told us that is *never* wrong." He held the book out for her to take.

Sophie eyed the parcel but did not touch it. There was something about it that made her heart clench, then flutter the way it did when she looked straight down at the river from the top of the bridge. "What's the book about?" she asked.

"There's one way to find out." He stepped closer. "Maybe you're not *the* bookmender, but you *can* mend books. We've seen you in that room back there—night after night—repairing discarded stories."

Sophie warded off a shiver. "How long have you been following me?"

"Long enough," Peter said, stepping closer still—so close, he was nearly touching her. "Please. I can't let him down."

Sophie couldn't possibly fathom what *him* he might be referring to. She studied the boy's face; his expression was difficult to read through the blindfold. It wasn't fear she saw, exactly, but something close. Her eyes fell on the Inquisitor's citation, which was pasted to the front window. The sight was like a bucket of icy water on her heart. Whatever this mysterious book was, it could only lead to more trouble for her and her father. "I'm not my mother," she said, opening the shop door for them. "I'm sorry."

The boy looked as if he were about to object, but Sir Tode rested a hoof on his boot. "We cannot force her to help us." He lowered his head, clopping outside.

Peter sighed and walked toward the door. He paused on the stoop. "I know what it's like to think you're not allowed to do or be a certain thing," he said, more kindly than she expected. "To feel guilty for wanting more." For a moment, it was as if he were looking straight at her—even with the blindfold. "Wanting more out of life isn't something to apologize for, Sophie Quire. I hope you figure that out before it's too late." So saying, he tipped his hat and slipped into the night.

Sophie closed the door. She sighed, staring at the dusty bookshelves, which leaned inward as if to smother her. A sinking dread crept over her. What if she was mistaken? What if that book really had been meant for her? And even if it wasn't, wouldn't her mother have wanted her to fix it? Didn't the book deserve to be read?

"Wait!" she cried, pulling open the door. "I changed my mind!" She ran outside into the cold night, searching the alley in both directions—

But Peter Nimble and Sir Tode were gone.

Her stomach clenched, and a cold sweat formed on her brow. An extraordinary opportunity had been offered to her, and she had refused it. And for what? Pride? Fear? How many stories had she read in which ordinary people had their lives changed by mysterious strangers, and she had just chased two of them away. "You're a fool, Sophie Quire," she muttered, walking back into the shop and locking the door.

She was still chiding herself when she reached her workshop and settled back into her chair. But when she lifted her eyes to the workbench, she very nearly cried out with shock—

For there, sitting before her, was *the book.*

CHAPTER FIVE

THE BOOK *of* WHO

Sophie should have been furious at Peter for leaving the book behind. How he had managed to put it on the workbench without her noticing was beyond her. Then again, astonishing feats seemed to be stock-in-trade for Peter Nimble. She picked up the book, still wrapped in oilskin and old twine, and felt her heart beat faster. Two strangers had trekked across the world, braved untold dangers, all to deliver a book to *her*. "What book could possibly be worth such trouble?" she whispered.

She cleared a stack of partially bound *Danse Celeste* pages from the workbench to give herself room. She turned up the flame on her lamp and settled back onto her stool. "All right," she said, laying the book on her table. "Let's have a look at you." She unwrapped the string and pulled back the folds of oilskin to find an ancient, dusty book.

"Hello," Sophie said, and for a moment, she almost thought she could feel the book vibrating beneath her fingers. As if it wanted to say "Hello" back to her.

That the book needed repair was obvious. The outside was encased in a variety of substances that suggested any number of previous adventures—barnacles, roots, mildew, seaweed, sap, moss, rust, mud, pitch, and what appeared to be chewing gum. "You've been through quite a bit, haven't you?" she said.

Despite the outer damage, the book itself appeared to be intact. The spine was reinforced with metal hinges, and iron flags protected the corners from wear. She thought she could see some sort of mark on the spine. She took a rag from the table and wiped off the grime. Pressed into the leather were four curved lines that met at a dot in the middle, creating a strange shape:

Sophie stared at the mark, which sent a tremor through her whole body. It looked oddly familiar, though she could not quite say why. She ran her fingers over the indentation, wondering if it was a sort of flower or star . . . or perhaps an arcane alchemical sign.

The book had a heavy iron latch clasp, which was encased in rust. Sophie knew better than to try to open the clasp in its present condition. "We'll have to clean you off one layer at a time," she said. She opened the leftmost drawer of her workbench and removed a small vial and a clean rag. The vial was a solvent she had purchased some years before from a traveling apothecary from the Grimmwald—back when such folk dared to visit Bustleburgh. She uncorked the vial, and instantly the air was filled with a bitter smell that stung the inside of her nose. The solvent was dangerous—for, indeed, it dissolved most things it touched, including skin. Sophie poured a few drops of the hissing spirits onto a scrap of roach sponge, which could withstand most anything.

Using the sponge, she gingerly applied the spirits to the barnacles and calcium plaque on the cover, careful not to touch the book itself. When she had finished with that, she took up a series of ever-finer blades and started cutting away the roots and moss and seaweed and all the layers underneath that encased the latch. After more than an hour, the book was finally free of its carapace.

Sophie sat back, exhausted but elated. She clasped her bell

necklace and hoped that her mother would have approved of the work. The book, she could now see, was bound in some sort of animal hide that had been dyed blue—but what animal, she could not say. It was smoother than calf and more supple than horse. She thought of the creatures named in *The Seas Beyond the Sea* and wondered if this cover wasn't made from something more exotic altogether. What would a book bound in centaur hide or dragon skin feel like?

She ran her fingers over the cover, wondering how long it had been since someone had last read its contents. Years? Centuries? The thought of being the first person to read a *centuries-old* book made her pulse quicken.

Sophie carefully lifted the latch and opened the cover. She closed her eyes briefly, breathing in the musty air that wafted from the endpaper, which seemed to swirl and shift like mother-of-pearl. She turned to the first page and was surprised to find it completely undamaged. The book was not made of printed paper but rather vellum, in the ancient custom. Written by hand in elegant script were the following words:

Sophie stared at the title. The ink, which was blue, just like the cover, seemed to shimmer in the light of her lamp. "*The Book of Who*," she whispered, and the words sent a shiver through her body—as though it were not the first time she had read this book. There was no author's name or explanatory subtitle, only the strange symbols repeated from the cover.

Sophie turned to the next page, expecting a table of contents or dedication, but instead she found a curious inscription:

> *We four books—Who, What, Where, and When—*
> *Hold all the world's magic bound within.*
> *And when assembled throughout the ages,*
> *Two words, when spoken, unlock our pages.*
> *Impossible things of all shape and kind*
> *Flow from the will of a curious mind.*

Beneath the inscription was the same mark from the cover: four curved lines converging on a dot in the middle.

Sophie traced her fingers over the blue ink and suddenly realized why the lines looked so familiar. "They're question marks!" she said, a smile breaking across her face. Indeed they were: four distinct question marks arranged around a single dot.

She turned ahead to examine the book's contents. *The Book of Who* seemed to be some sort of enormous compendium of people throughout history, complete with meticulous illustrations and cross-referenced footnotes. The entries, however, were not what one might expect from a traditional encyclopedia. They described mice in shining armor, fishermen as tall as mountains, and white-bearded children who could talk to the rain. "It's like every story in the world, all bound into one volume."

She paused at a picture of two stone wolves at the foot of a bridge. "The Wolves of Dawn," she whispered, feeling that special thrill that comes when one recognizes something of her own experience reflected in the pages of a book. Beside the drawing, the following entry appeared:

> *THE WOLVES OF DAWN: Stone guardians of the ancient city of Bustleburgh. They defended the land from goblin hordes during the Long Solstice. Some say their mighty jaws cracked open the Splint Mountains, from which the Wassail River flows.*
>
> ~For more information, see: *Book of Where*, "Splint Mountains," "Bustleburgh," "Wassail River"; *Book of When*, "Long Solstice"; *Book of What*, "Goblins"

Sophie read and reread the words, desperately wishing that

she had the other volumes so she might read further. She knew the story about the wolves, but seeing it written so plainly on the page made her feel as though it might actually be true. She wondered if the wolves really were somehow alive, and, if they were, what they made of the Pyre of nonsense being amassed right under their noses.

Sophie continued reading, and minutes turned to hours. Her lamp ran out of oil, and she was left with only the light from the crackling woodstove, which bathed the pages in an eerie orange glow. The longer she read, the more she got the impression that the book itself was somehow *alive*. The pages, if turned quickly, appeared blank. But when she lingered on a specific page, fresh entries appeared—the blue ink seeping to the surface like blood through gauze.

Every so often, she would notice the words in a certain entry blur and then rewrite themselves as if to accommodate new information, which she could only assume was changing at that very moment. She closed the book, studying the strange mark on its spine. "Who could have created such a book?" she muttered.

The moment the words escaped her mouth, the book pulled itself from her grip and dropped to the table with a heavy *thud* that made her shriek.

The book's pages riffled past in a blur, as if controlled by some unseen phantom. Flecks of ancient dust spewed up into the air, making Sophie cough. The pages reached an entry somewhere near the middle of the volume and abruptly stopped turning. *The Book of Who* lay open, its spine lightly moving up and down in the manner of a person trying to catch his or her breath after an invigorating sprint.

Sophie inched closer to the table, approaching the volume as she might a wild animal. She peered at the selected page. In the leftmost column was an entry whose words shone blue in the dim light:

> *THE STORYGUARD: Keepers of stories since time immemorial. Generally comprising four distinct guardians, each one possessing a different volume of the Four Questions.*
>
> ~For more information, see: *Book of What,* "Four Questions"; *Book of Who,* "Storyguard"

Sophie read the entry and then read it again. The word *storyguard* sent a chill through her. But more chilling still was the manner in which she had discovered the word: She had asked the book a question, and the book had answered.

She reasoned that the "Four Questions" must refer to the four separate volumes—*Who, What, Where,* and *When.* This volume cataloged magical people, and she suspected that the other books provided information on magical objects, places, and events. As to why the book had flipped to an entry all on its own, she had a hunch. She had asked it a question beginning with the word *who*.

Sophie sat back, chewing the inside of her cheek. What should she ask the book next? A hundred questions swirled around in her head, but very few of them began with the word *who*. There was, of course, one person she definitely wanted to know more about. She held the book out in front of her and spoke in a clear voice. "*Who* is Peter Nimble?"

The book obliged at once, flipping to a new entry:

> *PETER NIMBLE: Heir to the house of HazelPort and the Greatest Thief Who Ever Lived. Wielder of the Fantastic Eyes. Known aliases: Worm, Blind Pete, Justice Trousers, No-Name, the Silver-Handed Terror, the Vagabond King, an Ostrich in Mourning, Ugly Pest, You Trespassing Oaf.*
>
> ~For more information, see: *Book of Where*, "HazelPort"; *Book of What*, "Fantastic Eyes"

Sophie read the entry with fascination and a touch of disbelief. The last few aliases she recognized as things she had called him herself only a few hours earlier. Reading them now, she wondered if she had been a bit hard on him. More puzzling were the references to HazelPort (a place she had never heard of) and the business about Peter having "fantastic eyes."

Now that Sophie understood how to communicate with the book, she thought she might be able to discover a bit more about who had sent it to her. She placed her hands on the open pages. "*Who* sent Peter Nimble to my shop?"

The pages came alive again, but this time they seemed somewhat confused. First they flipped in one direction; then they flipped the opposite way. Finally they settled—a bit tentatively, it seemed to Sophie—on an entry very near the front:

THE PROFESSOR:
~For more information, see: *Book of Who*,
"Professor Cake"

Sophie shrugged, assuming that might be the man's full title. "All right, *who* is Professor Cake?"

The pages flipped to an entry very near the back:

PROFESSOR CAKE:
~For more information, see: *Book of Who*,
"The Professor"

Sophie rolled her eyes. The Professor, it seemed, was a topic the book was either unable or unwilling to discuss.

She thought back to the earlier entry about the Storyguard and wondered if that might prove a better line of questioning. "*Who* does *The Book of Who* belong to?" she said.

Pages flipped past her and slowed and stopped, landing almost gently on an entry directly in the middle. Sophie leaned close, reading the words in the flickering stovelight.

What she saw took the breath right out of her.

"It can't be," she whispered.

Written across the page was a short entry with no footnotes and no explanation. An entry that could not possibly be right. And yet there it was, staring up at her from the page:

SOPHIE QUIRE: Daughter of Coriander Quire. The Bookmender of Bustleburgh. The Last Storyguard.

CHAPTER SIX

"NEVER AGAIN!"

There are moments in life—rare for most people—when you suddenly realize that the tapestry of the world is grander and more intricately woven than you had ever imagined. This was such a moment for Sophie Quire as she sat at the open book, staring at the words before her:

The Last Storyguard

She swallowed and leaned toward the book until her nose very nearly touched the page. Her hands were always steady when she worked, but now they were shaking. She ran her fingertips over the shimmering blue ink. *Storyguard.* That was the name for the book's creators. But to be *the last* of them . . . surely that could not be good.

Sophie tucked back a strand of hair that had fallen from behind her ear. She desperately wished that Peter or Sir Tode or even the mysterious Professor Cake was with her now. She needed someone who could tell her what all this meant.

Sophie stood and took a slow breath as she tried to sort through the myriad questions swirling through her mind to find one that began with the right word. Perhaps the best person to help her was someone who had done the job already? "All right," she said, sitting and swallowing down a lump in her throat. "*Who* were the Storyguard before me?"

The pages riffled past her and then stopped on an entry of a person called Pliny the Pale. As soon as Sophie had finished reading the entry, the pages continued to Adder Col, then Boraz the Wize, then Serif Tut, then Dame Chao, then Tom Golux, and then Lady-of-the-Kirtle, and so on through history, listing what seemed like hundreds of names until it reached a final entry that included a picture of a woman with dark skin and darker hair hunched over a table surrounded by books:

CORIANDER QUIRE: *Storyguard and skilled bookmender from the Topaz Isles. Former pro-prietor of Quire & Quire Booksellers. Mother to Sophie Quire, the Last Storyguard. Her body rests in the crypts beneath Bustleburgh.*

~For more information, see: *Book of Who*, "Sophie Quire," "Storyguard"; *Book of Where*, "Bustleburgh," "Quire & Quire"; *Book of What*, "Four Questions"

"Mama," Sophie said, her voice barely a whisper. She stared at the words, one hand clasping the bell around her neck. However much she had been astonished to see her own name in the book, she was doubly so now.

She touched the picture gently, almost afraid it would disappear. It was like looking at herself, only a little bit older. She stared at the illustration: a young woman sitting at her workbench—the very same bench Sophie sat at now—mending a book. Warm tears filled Sophie's eyes and blurred her vision. She had spent a lifetime wondering what her mother had looked like, and now, for the first time, she knew.

"Sophie?" said a voice behind her.

The Book of Who jumped with a start and snapped its cover shut. Sophie turned around to see her father at the foot of the stairs. He was not wearing his dressing gown, as she might have expected, but a fresh shirt and trousers. Sophie looked out the front window and saw that the sky had turned a light purple.

"Your bed was untouched." He opened the stove door and prodded the smoldering logs with a poker. "You have been down here all night?"

Sophie wiped her eyes and offered a feeble smile. "Forgive me, Papa. I was caught up reading."

"It is not healthy for a girl to stay up all hours, even with books." He gave a soft chuckle. "Though it is perhaps even less healthy for a father to tell his growing daughter how she must behave."

Sophie kept a protective hand on top of *The Book of Who*, which had closed itself upon his arrival. The book, apparently, did not want to be shared. A part of Sophie felt the same. A part of her wanted to keep the book a secret—at least until she understood what it was. But another part of her knew that saying nothing to her father would be a sort of betrayal. She had never before lied to him, and she did not want to start now. "Papa," she said, sliding off her stool. She picked up *The Book of Who* and carried it to him. "The book I was reading, it wasn't an ordinary book."

"I should think not," he said, "if it kept you up all night."

"You don't understand." She didn't know why, but her voice was shaking. "Last night, some strangers came to the shop—well, not exactly strangers—but they were extremely strange. They came from someplace very far away. They were looking for someone to repair a very old, very special book."

Her father saw *The Book of Who* in her arms and raised an eyebrow. "Is that the special book of which you speak?"

"It's like nothing I've ever seen. It contains all the stories in the world, bound up in a single volume. And it's *alive*, Papa! All you have to do is ask it a question, and it will show you the answer. It's called *The Book of Who*."

Her father stepped back from the stove. "*The Book of* . . . ?"

Sophie had not known what her father's reaction to *The Book of Who* might be, but she was not prepared for what he did next. The moment the book came near him, he recoiled, as if in fear. "Impossible . . ." The poker, which had been clasped in his hand, fell to the floor with a heavy *clunk*.

"Papa, what is it?"

All the blood had gone from his face. "Not again . . ." he whispered, and he started pacing the floor, drawing a hand through his hair. "Not again . . ."

"Papa, what's wrong?" Sophie said. "You recognize it?"

He turned toward her, his eyes sharp. "Who gave that book to you?"

Sophie inched back. "I told you, two strangers—"

"*Where are they?*" She was nearly knocked over as he rushed past her to the front of the shop. He checked that the door was still locked and peered through the window, his eyes narrow. "Are they watching us now?"

"Papa, you're frightening me." She had never seen him like this before.

"My foolish child," he muttered, rubbing his unshaved face. "What new mischief have you brought into our lives?"

"It's obvious you recognize the book," she said, holding *The Book of Who* tightly to her chest. "Tell me what it is."

He marched back toward her and placed his hands on her shoulders. "My child, you must listen to me." His voice began to shake. "That book will destroy all our happiness. Return it to the people who gave it to you. Sell it. Throw it away. I do not care which. Only do not keep it."

Sophie stared up at him. His eyes were glistening; he was on the verge of tears. She felt her own eyes welling. "Papa, I . . ." She had no idea how to answer his pleas. "It's plain you're alarmed. But if you knew what was inside this book, you would understand why I cannot just throw it away."

His mouth twisted, as if he were swallowing a bitter herb. "So I am too late." He rose to his full height, and Sophie was reminded of just how tall he was. "Give it to me," he said, his voice cold.

Sophie stepped back toward the wall. "What are you going to do with it?"

He stepped closer, his hand extended. "Give it to me."

She swallowed. "I can't do that."

"Very well." He gave a heavy sigh. "If you cannot give it to me . . . I must take it." With surprising speed, he snatched the book from her grasp.

"What are you doing?" she cried.

"What I should have done a dozen years ago." He held the book high over his head and rushed toward the stove. "This book is a menace, and it will not darken my home!" He kicked the grate open. Red embers spilled out in front of him, charring the wooden floor.

"Wait, Papa!" Sophie ran after him, clutching his arm. "Inside that book there's a passage about—"

"Never again!" he cried, and threw *The Book of Who* into the stove.

"NO!" Sophie dove to grab it, but her father held her fast. Sparks burst into the air as orange flames rose up and swallowed the book whole.

CHAPTER SEVEN

TROUBLING *the* DEAD

Sophie lay on her bed, head in her arms, sobbing. Every particle in her body felt wrenched and exhausted. And still she kept crying.

The apartment above Quire & Quire Booksellers was a single drafty room with sloped ceilings and exposed beams. Early-morning light crept in through a cracked window above the stairs, bathing the attic in a serene purple glow that belied the turmoil of her own sorrow. A metal stovepipe ran up alongside her bed, and through it she could still hear the flames from the oven—crackling and spitting as they devoured the final pages of *The Book of Who*.

Sophie clasped the bell hanging around her neck. It was wet

from her tears. For one glorious moment, she had looked upon her mother's face. And now that moment, like her mother, was lost forever. She thought of Peter Nimble, who had entrusted her with *The Book of Who*. She wondered what would happen when he came to collect his book and found it was no more—perhaps then she would see what his silver hand was truly capable of.

Sophie tensed as she heard footsteps on the landing.

"Sophie?" Her father's voice sounded small.

"Go away," she said, pulling her knees all the way to her chin. The back of her throat hurt from crying, and it stung every time she swallowed. "I don't want to talk to you."

Her father shuffled into the room. "It would seem this day is full of tasks we wish we did not have to do."

Sophie's bed was in a far corner, concealed behind a curtain her father had hung from the rafters some years before in an effort to guard her privacy. He drew back the curtain and settled himself on the far end of her bed. He was silent for a long moment, and when he finally spoke, his voice was cracked—as though he, too, had been crying. "There is something that I think you should hear. Something that might explain why I have done what I have done."

"What is there to explain?" Sophie glared at him, her back pressed against the wall. "You burn a thing because it frightens you. You're no better than Prigg."

He winced slightly but then nodded. "I have never told you about how your mother died," he said softly.

Sophie, despite her anger, was caught off guard by this. Her entire life, he had refused to speak a word on the subject. Until now. It felt as if he were taunting her. "Haven't you forgotten?" she said. "It's troublesome luck to trouble the dead."

"Troublesome, perhaps," he said, nodding. "But necessary." He sighed, kneading the skin on the back of his hand. His fingers were so thin and so pale—so unlike Sophie's. "When I first met your mother . . . it was like meeting one who had stepped from the very pages of a story. She had roamed the world, mending books for kings and titans. And me?" He shrugged. "I was a law clerk, and not a very good one—too busy daydreaming to think of my career. Your mother was as far from me as yes is to no. And yet, when I saw her for the first time, when I looked into her eyes . . . I was hopelessly captivated." He glanced up at Sophie, meeting her gaze only for a moment.

Sophie bit the inside of her cheek, savoring the pain. "If you were so very unremarkable, why did she marry you?"

"I asked her that very question a hundred times." He shook his head. "Perhaps she was tired of roaming the world? Perhaps she saw in me a chance at a different sort of life? The only answer she ever gave was that she liked the look on my face when I read a story. Which was a lucky thing for me, because I read quite a bit back then." He smiled, as if recalling some private joke.

"Your mother and I built this shop together—me selling books, your mother mending them. We read constantly, trading stories back and forth, arguing, quoting, exploring, falling ever deeper under the spell of books." Sophie knew the spell he spoke of. She felt it every morning when she stepped into the shop. "Your mother and I lived to share books with each other. But there was one book she did not share. She would not let me or anyone else handle the book, and she kept it with her at all times. It was a blue book with iron furnishings and a curious mark on the spine."

"*The Book of Who*," Sophie said.

He nodded. "The book was a constant preoccupation—she read it compulsively. She once made me promise that if anything happened to her, I would care for the book. At the time, I thought she was overreacting . . ." He swallowed, and Sophie could read the bitterness on his face. "We were married less than a year before you were born. Around that same time, she became even more consumed with the book. She spent long hours poring over its pages— reading and rereading. She lost interest in everything around her. Lost interest in her work. Lost interest in the shop. Lost interest in her . . . responsibilities."

"You mean me," Sophie said, looking down.

Her father let out another sigh, which was no answer at all. "And then one evening, just before sunset, she told me she had to take a trip—she could not say what she might do or where she would be going. You were still a suckling babe at the time, and I asked her to reconsider, but she said the choice was not hers to make. She said the *book* compelled her to go. She gave you that necklace and left, promising that she would return the following day. And, in a sense, she was true to her word. But . . ."

"But what?" Sophie said, inching closer.

He blinked, staring out the cracked window. "It was early morning when I came upon her body. She was lying facedown at the foot of her workbench. She was cold, breathless, without a pulse." His words were stilted, as though even now, twelve years later, it was too much for him to truly fathom. "There was a jagged tear in her tunic, and beneath that, her flesh was pierced through. She had been stabbed in the heart."

"She was *murdered*?" Sophie shifted her feet, which were numb beneath her. In fact, a numbness seemed to have crept over her entire body. Her whole life, she had thought her mother must have died of consumption or fever or some other normal disease. Never, not even for a moment, had she considered *murder*. "But why would someone kill her?"

Her father shook his head again. "That was but one of many

mysteries. Despite the deep wound, there was no blood on her clothes or on the floor. I reasoned that her body must have been carried to the shop after she was killed. The entire shop had been torn apart—books knocked from every shelf, drawers pulled out, shelves overturned. Someone had been searching for something. In the days that followed, I reviewed my inventory obsessively. I knew my stock like I knew my own name, and I kept careful records. Every book was present and accounted for." He looked up at her. "Every book but one."

He did not need to say which book. "You think someone killed her to get . . . *The Book of Who*?" Sophie felt a throbbing in her head, and she thought she might be sick. "Who would do such a thing?"

Her father reached out one white hand and touched her face. "All I know is that when I saw that book in your arms this morning, I knew I could never let such a thing happen again. If someone was willing to kill to get the book from her, who is to say they would not do the same to get it from you?"

"No," she said. "The people who brought it to me—they weren't like that." But even as she said this, she realized that she didn't actually know either of them. Peter had even admitted to killing someone before. Sophie slid her legs off the bed, touching her feet to the floor. Up until this moment, everything she knew—or thought she knew—about her mother had been turned on its head. All she could think of now was her mother's lifeless body, and her father, terrified, clutching his young wife in his arms. The fact that in twelve years no neighbor or friend had ever hinted at this tragedy seemed too much to fathom. "Did you tell the authorities what happened?" she said. "Did you try to find who did it?"

"I reported the crime, of course, but no clues could be found, and the investigation was closed shortly after. In the meantime, I had a child to care for and a shattered heart to mend. The last thing I wanted was to invite more trouble to our door, and so I simply told anyone who asked that your mother had very suddenly died. I did not know her kinfolk, and so I could not contact them. Her body was laid to rest in my own family's crypt." He put his hands out to her. "It tortured me to know that her killer roamed free, but what would you have had me do?"

"You could have told me the truth." Sophie felt a coldness taking over her body, as if she had used up every ounce of sorrow until only anger remained—anger at her mother for dying, at her father for lying about it, at herself for not somehow being able to stop it. "That book was called *The Book of Who*, and it contained descriptions of remarkable people all throughout history. The reason I wanted to show it to you was because it had an entry about Mama."

She was somewhat satisfied to see that these words made an impact on her father. His eyebrows twisted upward in confusion.

"You are mistaken," he said. "That book was hundreds of years old. How could your mother be in it?"

"Because it was *alive*. I tried to tell you that, but you wouldn't listen." She paced in front of him, drawing strength from her indignation. "The words in the book could shift and change—I saw it for myself. Any question you asked beginning with the word *who*, it would answer." She stopped, staring her father coldly in the eye. "That book might have been our one chance of learning who killed Mama. But that chance has turned to ash. Because of you."

Sophie's father blinked, his expression shifting into something resembling fear. "I—I—I do not understand," he stammered. "How can a book *know* such things?"

She folded her arms across her chest. "Even if I could answer that, you wouldn't hear me." And then, "Maybe that's why Mama didn't tell you where she was going that night. Maybe she knew that you wouldn't listen." Sophie had not meant to say this, but as soon as the words came out, she knew they were true.

Sophie's father stared at the floor for a long moment, his eyes shimmering in the early light. "It is almost time to open the shop. I should go downstairs, and you should go to sleep. Before we say more things we will both regret." He pulled himself to his feet and shuffled across the attic. He paused at the doorway. "Someday I hope you will forgive me for the things you think I have done," he said, and he disappeared down the steps.

Sophie set her jaw and repeated a word she had said so many times to her father. "Never." She collapsed into bed and pulled her blanket tightly to her chin.

∞ Chapter Eight ∞
THE INQUISITOR CALLS

Sophie awoke hours later to the sound of activity downstairs. She peered out the window and saw that it was late afternoon; she had slept through most of the day. A bowl of porridge and a mug of tea waited for her on the little table in the middle of the apartment—a peace offering from her father. She could hear conversation echoing up from downstairs: Her father was giving instructions to someone whose voice sounded familiar. Sophie pulled herself out of bed and dressed. She tasted the porridge, but it had long since gone cold.

She walked downstairs to find the bookshop utterly trans-formed. Guards were marching between the shelves, carrying stacks of books in their arms. A wagon was parked immediately outside the open front door. Inside were hundreds more.

"What's happening?" she said, her mouth open in horror. She ran to her father, who stood behind the counter, talking to a man who was reading a large parchment. "Papa, what are they doing?"

The official looked up from his parchment, his golden spectacles perched at the end of his nose. "If it isn't our little book thief." It was Inquisitor Prigg. He offered the satisfied smile of someone who has bested a rival.

Sophie stepped back. "What is *he* doing here?" she asked in a cold voice.

"Sophie." Her father spoke in a soothing tone. "The Inquisitor is making preparations for Pyre Day."

"But Pyre Day isn't for another two weeks." Sophie was knocked to one side by a guard carrying a stack of illustrated limericks. He tossed the books into the wagon and returned to the poetry section, which was already half empty. Sophie turned to her father. "Papa! Tell them they can't just barge in here and take our books without permission!"

"They have permission," he said quietly, avoiding her eyes.

It took Sophie a moment to understand what he was saying. "You called them here early?" She felt a sting in her throat. "Is this to punish me?"

The Inquisitor smiled again. "It is to liberate you, and all of Bustleburgh, from the scourge of nonsense. A palsy that has gripped our city for far too long." He made a notation on his parchment. "To have a respected bookseller so willingly discard his nonsense sets a nice example for the community. In exchange for your father's cooperation, I have agreed to lift all charges relating to the rather unfortunate incident on the bridge."

Sophie glared at him. The only thing "unfortunate" about that incident was that Prigg hadn't drowned in the Wassail. "Do not fret for your livelihood," Prigg said lightly. "Think of how much room there will be for more improving literature. Soon your humble shop will be brimming with scientific treatises, law journals, spelling primers, newspapers, and textbooks—a veritable playground of erudition!" He spoke these words with what could only be described as giddy anticipation.

"*Textbooks?*" Sophie exclaimed.

"Sophie, please." Her father placed a hand on her shoulder. "I am doing this to protect you."

"Like you did with *The Book of Who*?" she said. "Perhaps they'll let you set the torch on Pyre Day, too!"

"Don't be ridiculous," said Prigg, who had stopped his writing to listen. "That privilege falls to me."

"Coward," Sophie muttered—she was looking at Prigg but speaking to her father. She watched a guard carry out an armload of half-repaired books from her workshop. She had known that the books were all going to be burned on Pyre Day—but to lose them early, and before she could properly say good-bye, was more than she could bear. "Why are you doing this?" she asked Prigg. "They're just harmless stories."

"Harmless?" Prigg rolled up his parchment and notched it under his arm. "I assure you, there is nothing harmless about filling people's heads with nonsense. Children deserve better than to be lied to about magic buttons and talking wolves. They deserve a proper, scientific education. They deserve the truth."

Sophie rolled her eyes. She had met a number of people like Prigg: They believed that telling a child made-up things was a sort of deception—as though children were gullible half-wits who believed everything they heard.

Before she could formulate a rebuttal, a guard approached. "All done here, sir," he said to Prigg. "The books are loaded up and ready for the Pyre." Sophie stared at the wagon of books in the street. Furious though she was to lose these books, a part of her did not care if they burned. She had, for one brief moment, held an *actual* magic book. How could made-up stories compare with the real thing?

"I've done what you asked," her father said. "You will now drop the charges?"

"One moment," Prigg said. He walked between the bookcases, his ebony cane tapping the floor. "In my line of work, you find that a certain type of nonsense can push people toward corruption. Even those who understand the dangers of nonsense will often try to retain one or two volumes that hold sentimental value." His eyes flashed to Sophie. "Children, especially, are susceptible to such weakness." His cane stopped at the stove in the back of the shop, which was now cold. He peered at the black burn marks on the wooden floor—scars from when Sophie's father had kicked open the door. "Fortunately, I am not so easily deterred."

He stepped back and gestured for a guard to search the stove. Sophie watched as the burly guard knelt down and put a tentative hand into the ashes. He grunted and emerged a moment later clutching a charred book in his hands. It had a blue cover and a heavy metal clasp.

"*The Book of Who* . . ." Sophie said.

Its cover was slightly burned, but it looked otherwise unharmed.

"I—I—I destroyed it," her father said. "This is impossible."

Prigg took *The Book of Who* between his thumb and forefinger. "Nonsense is what it is. And I will not stand for it!" There was a glint of hungry triumph in his eye. His hand shook slightly as he unlatched the clasp and opened the cover.

"Give it back!" Sophie cried, rushing toward him.

The guard behind her reached out and grabbed her by an arm. "Mind your tongue, lass," he growled, twisting her arm until she cried out. "Or you'll be singin' that song from the inside of a prison cell."

"You can't just take the book!" she yelled, ignoring the pain in her arm. "It doesn't belong to you!"

Prigg peered down at her. "And who, exactly, is going to stop me?" The man was doubtless posing a rhetorical question. However, he had asked *who*, and the book was compelled to reply. No sooner had he uttered his question than the book came alive. Its pages flipped with blinding speed—spraying bits of ash into the air. Inquisitor Prigg coughed, caught off guard by the sudden cloud of soot.

The book slipped from his grip and hit the floor with a heavy *whump*, its pages still turning. Sophie and her father and the guards crowded around the open book, which had come to rest on an entry in the middle of the volume. The spine breathed up and down, panting from the effort. Shining in blue ink was an entry Sophie had seen the night before:

SOPHIE QUIRE: Daughter of Coriander Quire.
The Bookmender of Bustleburgh. The Last
Storyguard.

The guard had released her arm, and Sophie stepped away from him, her eyes fixed on the words. *She* was the Storyguard, and it was her job to protect this book. She had failed before, but the book, it seemed, was offering her another chance.

"Sophie?" her father whispered. "Why is your name in this book?"

Sophie looked from her father to the Inquisitor to the guards— they were all staring at her, awaiting an explanation. "Because . . ." She swallowed. "Because I am the last Storyguard, daughter of Coriander Quire, keeper of stories, protector of the Four Questions." She did not fully understand the words she was saying, but some part of her knew they were true. The book did not belong to Prigg or to her mother or to Peter Nimble or even to the Professor. The book belonged to *her*. The book *needed* her.

Inquisitor Prigg had by this time regained his composure. His look of surprise had been replaced by a satisfied sneer. "Very well, *Storyguard*." The word was dripping with contempt. "In light of this deception, I see no choice but to reinstate the previous charges— along with an additional charge of conspiracy." He nodded to the guards. "Arrest her."

The two guards lowered their muskets and approached Sophie. Their weapons were nearly as long as she was tall.

"No . . ." She backed up, clutching her father's side. "No, you can't do this."

Sophie's father was staring at the open book, which still lay on the floor. He looked up toward the approaching guards, his fists balled. "Sophie," he said. His voice sounded tight. "Run."

The guards rushed to seize her, but Augustus Quire, bookseller, leapt in front of them—pushing them both back against the wall. "Run!" he cried as the guards attacked him with the butt ends of their muskets.

Before she could question him, before she could question herself, she snatched the book from the ground. She scrambled to her feet and raced toward the open front door, *The Book of Who* clasped tightly against her chest.

"Ignore the man!" Prigg cried. "Get the girl!"

The guards let go of her father and ran after her.

The front door was blocked by the wagon, which was loaded high with books. Sophie clambered into the wagon and scrambled up and over the bed, books spilling out behind her.

"Stop her!"

The wagon shuddered beneath her as the guards crashed into the side. Sophie dropped to the street on the far side of the wagon and disappeared down the alley—the Inquisitor's cries echoing behind her.

Chapter Nine
THE RUNAWAY *and the* ROGUE

S ophie had little trouble evading Prigg's guards as they pursued her through the streets. Even when more guards joined the chase—all waving muskets and shouting, "Halt!"—they were no match for a girl who had spent her entire life in the twisting alleys of Olde Town. She ran down forgotten staircases and across crumbling walkways, *The Book of Who* weighing heavily in her arms. By the time she slipped into the entrance to the city crypts, the shouts had receded completely, and she knew she was safe.

Sophie snuck through the underground catacombs, her path lit only by the occasional mounted torch. She soon found herself before a modest crypt with an iron door. A single word was etched into the stone above the lintel: *Quire.*

This was Sophie's family crypt, and it was the place she always went when she most missed her mother. Sophie had never been inside the crypt, which was sealed tight. Still, just being this close to her mother's body gave her a feeling of not being alone.

She huddled against the iron door, her heart aching with equal parts exhaustion and exhilaration. She had done it. She had saved *The Book of Who*—the very book her mother had died to protect.

Sophie looked closely at the book, whose pages seemed completely undamaged from the stove. She ran her thumb over the worn leather cover. "I hope you were worth it," she said. She closed her eyes, recalling the image of her father fighting two armed guards with his bare hands. The sight made her at once terrified and proud. As soon as it was safe, she would go back to him, and then they could escape from Bustleburgh together.

In the meantime, she had other concerns. She had read many exciting stories about fugitives and runaways, and something that had always annoyed her was how little attention was paid to sensible preparations. How many times had she read about—and scorned—heroines who fled their persecutors in bare feet? And yet here she was, huddled against a crypt door in the freezing cold, wearing only a light dress and no stockings. Already the sun had begun to set. She did not relish how much colder it would be down here once night came. She needed a safe place to hide.

But first she needed to ask the one question that had been

haunting her ever since her father spoke to her in the attic. She held out the book. "Who stabbed my mother?" she asked.

The cover opened, and pages flipped quickly. When the book stopped, however, it was on a place in the back of the volume where the paper had been torn from the spine. Sophie ran her fingers along the jagged edge of paper that remained. "The entry," she said. "It's been ripped out."

She wondered whether it was her mother who had done this or perhaps someone else. But why? The book clearly had known the answer to her question, but it had been rendered silent. She needed to know more about this book and what it could do. Maybe that would lead her to her mother's killer. "Who in Bustleburgh knows what to do with *The Book of Who*?"

The book's pages turned quickly. They settled on an entry with an unfamiliar name:

> *EZMERZELDA la POMME: Potion maker and*
> *shopkeeper, currently operating an oubliette on*
> *the eastern edge of Bustleburgh. Mistress of Taro,*
> *the Mandrake. Known aliases: Lady Korrigan,*
> *Miss Gossamer, Madame Eldritch.*
>
> ~For more information, see *Book of Where*,
> "Oubliette"; *Book of What*, "Mandrake"; *Book of*
> *Who*, "Taro"

Sophie smiled, staring at the list of aliases. She knew Madame Eldritch. More important, she knew where to find her. She tucked the book under one arm and stood. With a final glance at her mother's resting place, she set out toward the streets.

✦　✦　✦

At the same moment Sophie was traveling away from the bookshop, someone else was traveling toward it. Peter Nimble and his friend Sir Tode had spent an anxious day hiding among the rooftops of Bustleburgh, doing their best to stay clear of notice.

In a moment of impulsiveness, Peter had decided to trust Sophie with repairing the Professor's very valuable (and undoubtedly fragile) book. That he and Sir Tode had mistakenly tracked down the wrong person was clear enough from their conversation with Sophie the night before. In the sober light of day, he realized that perhaps it would have been wiser to accept the girl's refusal and continue their search for the *real* bookmender, which was what Professor Cake had charged them to do. But something inside Peter—what he used to refer to as his thief's instinct—had told him that this girl possessed more than she presented to the world, and that the book, in some strange way, belonged in her hands. (Sir Tode had his own opinions about why Peter had trusted the girl, and it had less to do with any "thieving" instinct than it did with his "twelve-year-old boy" instinct.)

Whatever the reason, it was now completely apparent to Peter as he and Sir Tode returned to Quire & Quire Booksellers that he had made a horrible mistake. The door was wide open. The shelves were completely empty. A breeze stirred a pile of ashes across the wooden floor.

"Good heavens," Sir Tode said, his ears twitching. "They appear to have been robbed."

Peter ran his fingers along one of the empty shelves. "Not robbed—it's too orderly." He could smell cold ashes near the stove in the back of the shop. He knelt down to study the floor with his hand. He could feel bare footprints in the ashes. "Look at these tracks— this is her, running toward the door."

"Without her shoes?" Sir Tode turned to look outside. "Why would she do that?"

"Who cares why?" Peter said, standing. "Hello? Is anyone here?" He rushed to the small room in the back. He pulled open the drawers of Sophie's workbench, letting tools spill out at his feet. "It *has* to be here." He stormed through the rest of the shop, checking every shelf, every corner, every nook and cranny.

"The girl's not here," Sir Tode said. "And neither is the book."

Peter punched his blade into the countertop—cutting deeply into the wood. His whole body felt shaky, as if he were going to faint. The Professor had trusted Peter, and Peter had failed him. "How could I be so stupid?"

At that moment, Peter heard a creaking floorboard behind him.

Instinct took over, and he spun around, his weapon poised. "Don't move!"

A man stood at the bottom of the stairs. "The shop is closed, sir," he said in a flat tone. "We are restocking our inventory. Could you please lower your weapon?"

Peter kept his blade where it was. "There was a girl working here last night," he said. "Medium height, a bit of a know-it-all. I brought her a book to repair."

"You brought her . . . ?" The man's voice faltered.

Before Peter could react, the man charged at him and grabbed him by the lapels. "YOU!" He lifted Peter clear off the floor and slammed him against an empty shelf. "It was YOU!"

"W-w-what are you doing?" Peter sputtered.

"Now see here!" Sir Tode shouted. "Unhand him!" He head-butted the man's shin, but the man did not let go.

The man leaned close to Peter—so close that Peter could hear the blood pulsing through the vein in the man's forehead. He spoke through clenched teeth. "You stole my daughter."

"We didn't steal anyone," Peter said, trying to breathe. "We're just trying to get our book back. If you can just tell us where she went or what—"

"Don't ever talk to me of that book again." The man dragged a flailing Peter across the shop and to the door, which he flung open with one hand. "GET OUT!" He shoved Peter through the open door and then took a kick at Sir Tode, who only barely avoided getting struck. "Leave my family alone."

Peter pulled himself up and ran toward the man. "Please, sir! We're only trying to—!"

Slam.

A moment later, he heard the lock click shut. Locks, of course, were no obstacle to Peter Nimble, but he understood well enough that this man would be of no future help.

"Oh, well," Sir Tode said, clopping to his side. "The good news is we know who has the book. The bad news is that it seems she's run off. What do you suppose we do now?"

Peter raised his head and smelled the air. He detected the faint odor of cold ash on cobblestone weaving a hurried path through the city. "Now we find her."

_~ CHAPTER TEN _~
MADAME ELDRITCH'S OUBLIETTE

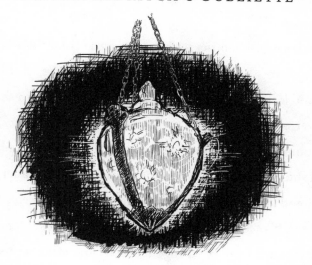

It was nearly dark by the time Sophie reached the pier that ran along the bank of the Wassail. The light from the moon reflected off the river as it flowed into the Grimmwald. When Sophie was young, this pier had been used by an endless parade of colorful ships from various foreign lands. Now it was empty.

Two sentries were pacing along the edge of the river, long muskets propped against their shoulders. Sophie waited until they had turned away from her and then snuck onto the pier, *The Book of Who* tucked snugly under one arm. She climbed down a creaking wooden ladder that led to the lower docks. A few derelict ships and rowboats were moored to the posts, bobbing on the surface of the water. In the moonlight, she could just make out a series of platforms and rope-bridges that led to a stone tower hidden beneath the pier. Sophie followed the path, careful not to let her bare feet slip on the slick wood.

She soon reached the tower, which rose from the water like a decaying tusk—the last remaining pillar of a fortress that had been destroyed long ago. There was a round wooden door in the face of the tower with a single word etched above it: OUBLIETTE.

Sophie pushed the door open and stepped inside. She found herself standing in a circular room lit with flickering amber candles, their glow diffused by a cloud of sweet-smelling smoke.

The oubliette was a forgetting room, where men and women with difficult lives took strange tobaccos and stranger teas in the hope that they might forget their pain, if only for a few hours. Forgetting rooms were dangerous places, and it was a wonder to her that Inquisitor Prigg had not shut this one down. It was said that many customers awoke to discover that they had been robbed of their possessions, and that others did not wake at all.

The air was thick with smoke, and Sophie had to cover her mouth with a sleeve of her dress to keep from coughing. She peered around the room, her eyes adjusting to the diffuse light. Men and a few women lay on soft pillows clutching hookahs and bottles, their eyes half-open but glazed over.

An old woman stirred beside Sophie, making her jump. "Child!" she said, her eyes dull, her hand grasping. "Are you from the fairy court? Has my changeling boy been released? His name is Anton. He was so small . . ." Her lids grew heavy, and she slumped to one side.

Sophie picked her way past the woman and approached the back of the room. Through the haze, she noticed a small man, only slightly larger than herself, wearing a hooded cloak that completely covered his head. Sophie recognized him as Madame Eldritch's manservant, Mister Taro. Taro had occasionally joined his mistress on her errands to the bookshop. In all her years, Sophie had never once seen his face or heard him speak. He was now seated on the floor, his legs crossed, playing some sort of sitar. It was a hollow, almost aimless tune, like a lullaby gone wrong.

Sophie cleared her throat. "I . . . I'm here to see Madame Eldritch," she whispered.

Mister Taro did not stop playing but nodded to a trapdoor in the floor beside him. Sophie knelt down and opened the door herself. She half expected to find some sort of shadowy dungeon below, but instead greenish light flooded up from a curving staircase made of intricately laced wrought iron.

Sophie clutched *The Book of Who* to her chest and crept down the stairs. She found herself standing in a room hung with tapestries. The air was warm and delicious. The smoke, which had been so oppressive upstairs, mixed here with the scent of wet stone to create a delicate perfume. Cabinets and shelves lined the walls, each one filled with a variety of bizarre objects whose only unifying element was their unusualness. Vials of shimmering liquid. Plants made of stone. A chess set made from animal bones. A sword with three blades. A toad on a chain. And a few old books that Sophie recognized all too well. There was a sign hanging from the wall that read ALL CHARMS GUARANTEED.

This was the *real* oubliette: a secret shop that specialized in artifacts both rare and dangerous—nonsense of the highest order. She could only imagine what sort of customers usually found themselves down here—surely not twelve-year-old girls.

Madame Eldritch stood behind the counter. "If it isn't the little bookmender. What an unexpected surprise." She said this in a tone that implied anything but surprise.

Sophie offered a half curtsy. "Madame Eldritch."

The woman beckoned with a graceful hand. "Come closer, child." She flashed a ruby smile. "I will not bite."

The room was lit by a series of flickering jars that hung from the ceiling, each one filled with what Sophie assumed were fireflies. Looking more closely, however, she saw that they were not fireflies but tiny human-shaped creatures with no clothes and silver-green wings. "Are those . . . *fairies*?" she said, her eyes creased with awe.

"Sprites, actually," Madame Eldritch replied. "One would need a *much* bigger jar to catch a fairy. And a death wish." She gave a weary chuckle, as if to imply some hard-won knowledge on the subject.

Sophie knew that sprites had once lived in Bustleburgh before the No Nonsense movement was born. Sometimes older neighbors would talk about how the sprites used to dance above the Wassail at twilight. Seeing them now filled her with wonder. She tapped at the base of a jar, and the little creatures fluttered toward her, clawing and knocking at the glass. "They look angry," she said.

"I'm sure they are. And if ever they escaped, it would be bad news for she who keeps them." Madame Eldritch raised her eyebrows in an exaggerated manner. "But you have not come to talk of sprites, I think."

Sophie pulled herself away from the jar. "No, I haven't." She clasped *The Book of Who* to her chest. A part of her did not want to say anything about the book. The last person she had shown it to had tried to destroy it. "I need your help with something." She walked to the counter. "It's difficult to explain."

"Not too difficult for Madame Eldritch, I think." The woman walked her long fingers along the countertop, which looked to be made of polished ivory. "I have here everything a girl your age could ever want." Her hand paused on various wares as she spoke. "A limpid glass for wisdom? A hat for luck? A love potion?" She met Sophie's eye. "For a special boy, perhaps?"

Sophie flinched. "I haven't come to buy trinkets." She felt annoyed that this woman would think she might want any of those things—especially the potion. "I only wanted to ask you a question."

"An answer to a question?" Madame Eldritch leaned back, releasing a slow breath. "But that is the rarest prize of all. There are emperors and sultans who cannot afford such a thing."

"I don't have any money, so if you're going to charge me, then I'd best not say anything at all." Sophie turned back toward the stairs, but a hand caught her wrist. The grip was gentle but surprisingly firm.

She looked back to Madame Eldritch, who was smiling. "Do not go, little bookmender." She released Sophie's arm. "You have been good to me in the past. I will answer your question. If I am able."

Sophie eyed the woman, and a shiver snuck through her body. She wondered briefly what her father would say if he knew she was in this unsavory place. Sophie pushed these thoughts from her mind, reminding herself that the book had told her to come here. "It's about this," she said, setting *The Book of Who* on the counter. "Someone brought it to the shop last night. It reminded me somehow of the books you've brought me for mending. So I thought you might know something."

If Sophie had been expecting a big reaction, she was disappointed. The woman glanced at the worn cover with an expression of something less than boredom. "You bring me a book in need of mending . . . Is it not meant to be the other way around?"

"Perhaps, but I've never seen a book like this. The ink is strange. The paper shows no age. I don't even know what it's bound in."

Madame's hands twitched slightly, but she did not touch the

book. Sophie noticed that her long fingernails were coated in red paint that matched her lips. The sharp tips shone in the sprite-light. "I can solve one mystery, I think. The binding is some sort of animal hide."

"I could tell that much," Sophie said. "But *what kind* of animal? I don't recognize the texture at all."

"Don't you?" The woman reached out, tracing a red fingernail along Sophie's jaw. "Perhaps it is not so strange as you think?"

Dread washed over Sophie as she apprehended the woman's meaning. "Y-y-you think it's bound in *human* skin?" She had, of course, read about such things in very old histories but had always suspected that this was a sort of poetic embellishment. "That's horrifying."

The woman widened her eyes. "It is not so horrifying as you say. A body can be burned or buried or fed to birds . . . Are those fates more desirable than this?" She leaned close to the book, whispering, "Hello, my long-dead friend. Whoever you were."

Sophie's mouth was by now wide open. She straightened up. "You're making fun of me," she said.

A pitying smile broke across the woman's face. "Forgive me, bookmender. It was a harmless jest. Everyone knows that human flesh isn't thick enough for binding books. And the oils would damage the paper." She said this in a way that implied that there were other things human flesh was perfect for—though what those might be, Sophie did not want to know. "We shall learn what we can of this book." The woman reached behind her counter and produced a pair of green silk gloves that went all the way to the elbow. "May I?" she asked, fitting them over her hands.

Sophie nodded. "It's very old. Just be careful."

"I always am." Madame Eldritch picked up the book, holding it at a distance as one might a coiled snake. The gloves were clearly some sort of safety precaution—though from what, Sophie could not guess. The woman touched the symbol on the spine. "That mark. It is unusual."

Sophie agreed. "At first I thought it was a flower or star. But I think it's four question marks. I'm not sure what that means, though. When my father saw the book, he threw it into the open stove. But it wouldn't burn."

"That sounds like a shadrach charm. Very powerful—impervious to common flame." She examined the spine. "Someone has gone to great lengths to protect this volume. Perhaps we can learn what makes it worth protecting." She lifted the latch and opened to the title page. Sophie heard a catch in her breath. "*The Book of Who* . . ." Her voice was almost a whisper. Sophie watched her face, which was carved into an expression of perfect wonder.

"You've heard of it," Sophie said. It was not a question.

"If you were not so smart a girl, I would lie to you and say that I did not know of it." She traced her finger along the edge of the page in an almost sensual way. "And then I would offer a trinket in exchange."

"I told you I didn't want trinkets."

"Which is why I offer none." Madame Eldritch stepped out from behind the counter, carefully removing her gloves as she spoke. "You said someone brought this book to you. Who was this person?"

Sophie stepped back. "It was a boy and his . . . friend. I think they were sent by a man called the Professor."

"The Professor?" The woman examined a jar of sprites hanging just above her head. She tapped lightly on the glass, watching the creatures blink and buzz. "I have heard rumors of a man who calls himself by that name." She looked at Sophie. "If the rumors are true, then he is not one to be trifled with."

"I'm not afraid of him," Sophie said with more conviction than she felt.

"Oh, but you should be. And of any other person who knows what you hold." Madame Eldritch cocked her head, as if the thought were just occurring to her. "Myself, for example."

Sophie stared at the woman, who suddenly reminded her less of a shopkeeper than a spider. She glanced toward the trapdoor at the top of the stairs, which was now closed. Had she shut it on her way down? She held out her open hand. "May I have my book back, please?"

"*Your* book?" Madame Eldritch opened a portable *maquillage* and began applying a fresh coat of red paint to her lips with a small brush. "It does not belong to you. You admitted as much a moment ago."

"It's getting late," Sophie said. "Papa knows I'm here and will summon the guard if I'm not back shortly."

"Summon guards to my shop?" The woman laughed, and for the first time, the laugh sounded genuine. She pursed her red lips, peering at herself in a mirror. "Tell me, little bookmender, do you know why this place is called the oubliette?"

"*Oubliette* means *forgetting place*." Sophie peered past her at the book, still lying on the counter. "The people upstairs, they come here so they don't have to remember things."

The woman stepped toward Sophie, who stumbled back. "True. But that is not all. Down here, it is called the oubliette for a different reason. When a person enters with something valuable, something I desire, that something is soon forgotten."

"And if the person doesn't want to part with it?"

The woman smiled, her red lips glistening in the sprite-light. "Then that person is also forgotten."

THE MANDRAKE

Sophie tried to step back but bumped into a harpsichord made of animal bones. "If you touch me, I'll scream," she said, knowing even as she said it that screaming would be useless. Her eyes darted from the book to the staircase at the opposite end of the room.

Madame Eldritch insinuated herself closer. "Such a talented girl," she said, reaching out and holding Sophie's chin in her thumb and forefinger. "It is truly a waste."

Sophie tried to pull away, but the woman held her fast. She detected a sweet aroma on the woman's breath—like the tobacco upstairs, only stronger. She craned her neck to escape the nauseating smell. Her eyes fell on the glowing jar hanging just above her head.

The jar full of angry sprites.

Sophie lunged upward and grabbed the jar, swinging it as hard as she could toward the wall—

Kssshshh!

The glass shattered, releasing twelve furious sprites into the air, hissing and snarling.

Madame Eldritch stepped back. *"What have you done?"*

The creatures swept through the room like a cyclone, shattering the other jars and anything else they could find. Glass rained down, and soon the chamber was filled with hundreds of shrieking little furies. Sophie crouched and covered her head as the creatures whizzed past her and descended upon Madame Eldritch, clawing and biting her face and hands.

"Get away!" she shrieked, tumbling to the ground.

Sophie did not try to help the woman. She sprang to her feet and took *The Book of Who* from the counter. Shielding her face with it, she ran up the curving staircase. She winced as her bare feet came down on shards of broken glass. She reached the trapdoor, only to find it shut tight. Through it she could hear the lilting sounds of the sitar. "Help!" she cried, pounding on the door. "Open the door!"

Sophie braced herself and rammed a shoulder against the door, which suddenly flew open. She was knocked to one side as a swarm of sprites whizzed right past her and into the room. Sophie pulled herself up after them. Delirious men and women cried out in confusion as sprites tore through the chamber, smashing pipes and tea trays and anything else they could reach. She tried to make sense of the commotion, but it was difficult in the sprite–filled haze. She clasped the book to her chest, feeling her heart pounding in her ears. Cold night air streamed in from the open front door across the chamber. She picked her way over shredded pillows and broken teapots, wincing with each step.

"Taro!" Sophie heard Madame Eldritch's voice ring out from the chamber below. "The girl!"

A small figure stepped from the shifting haze.

It was Mister Taro. His hood had fallen back to reveal his face. His smooth skin appeared almost green in the flickering light. He stared at her with unblinking black eyes.

"W–w–what are you?" Sophie said.

Taro did not answer, and a moment later Sophie understood why. A stray sprite landed on his shoulder, illuminating the rest of his face—his mouth was *stitched shut* with silver thread.

Sophie stared at his expressionless face, fighting revulsion. Keeping her back to the wall, she inched toward the doorway.

Mister Taro followed her with his unblinking eyes but otherwise did not move.

"Taro!" The voice was so loud it made Sophie jump. She glanced back to see Madame Eldritch pulling herself up through the trapdoor. Her beautiful face was marred by a hundred bites and scratches where the sprites had assaulted her. She wiped blood from her cheek and pointed straight at Sophie. "Bring me the book!"

The silent figure instantly obeyed, dashing toward Sophie, who ducked to one side, narrowly missing his outstretched hands. Then she sprang forward, racing through the open doorway and out of the oubliette.

Sophie stumbled up the narrow gangplank that led to the dock, very nearly falling into the black river below. She could feel Taro behind her, grasping for her skirt with his small hands. She crouched down and grabbed the base of the plank she had just crossed. She shoved it with all her strength. The plank slid off the edge of the dock and splashed into the dark water—the creature falling with it.

Sophie did not linger to see whether he could swim. She staggered along the path that would take her to the pier. She didn't know where she would go after that—she only knew she had to get away from that creature.

"You there!" a voice cried in the shadows ahead. "Halt!"

Sophie looked up to see the two sentries on the lower docks, standing between her and the ladder that led to the shore.

"Help me," Sophie said, gasping. "Madame Eldritch—she's after me. Her servant, he's—"

"Hold up," said one of the men, stepping closer. "I know you. You're the book thief who attacked us on the bridge. There's a warrant out for you."

That Inquisitor Prigg would have issued a warrant for her arrest was troubling, but not half so troubling as the prospect of seeing Mister Taro again. "Please," Sophie said. "You can arrest me, escort me to Inquisitor Prigg, only—"

The deck beneath her abruptly heaved to one side with a loud *slosh*. Sophie fell to her knees, dropping *The Book of Who*.

"What was that?" the first sentry cried, peering into the darkness. The deck shuddered again. He pointed. "Something's in the water!" He and the other man unshouldered their muskets.

The deck shook, and this time a hand burst right through the wood planks at Sophie's feet. Sophie and the men all leapt back in alarm.

The wet hand glistened green in the moonlight.

It had more than five fingers.

Sophie watched as Taro pulled himself up through the hole. He stood in front of her, dripping on the deck. His robe had come off in the water, and she could now see that his legs and arms were twisted and misshapen. The threads binding his mouth shimmered slightly in the darkness.

The first sentry aimed his musket, which was shaking in his grip. "W–w–what is that thing?"

Two cracks split the air as he and his compatriot discharged their weapons straight at Taro. The smoke cleared to reveal Taro, still standing. Sophie could see two dark spots where the musket shots had plunged into his green flesh. If the wounds pained him, it did not show. He tilted his head slightly, like one working a crick from his neck, and the musket balls seemed to push themselves out of his body. They landed on the dock with two dull *thumps*.

The sentries stared at him, eyes wide. The first man lowered his musket. "R–r–run!" He dropped his weapon and ran toward the water, diving headlong into the black river. The other sentry ran in the opposite direction before doing the same.

Now Sophie was alone with Taro, who was facing her, perhaps waiting for her to run as well. She stood and looked him straight in the eye. She was frightened, of course, but a part of her was simply awed. What sort of creature could survive two musket shots to the chest? And why would such a powerful creature so blindly obey a woman like Eldritch?

"Mister Taro," she said, shivering. "That's your name?"

He nodded and then stepped closer.

Sophie remembered how Taro had not moved to stop her from escaping the oubliette until Madame Eldritch had told him to do so—it reminded her of a djinni or golem, bound to the commands of its master. Sophie wondered if that might be the key to her survival. "You have to do what she says, don't you?"

He nodded again. And stepped closer still.

Sophie glanced down at *The Book of Who*, clasped once more in her arms. "'Bring me the book.' Those were her exact words. And you will not stop until the task is done?"

Another nod.

Sophie felt her heart beating hard against the book's cover. She knew that in a story the hero should do anything to protect her magic book. But this was not a story anymore. She remembered Madame Eldritch's bloody face, mangled by vengeful sprites. These things were real. And they could kill her. No book—not even a magical one—was worth losing her life.

Sophie knelt down, holding Taro's gaze as one might do with a rabid dog. "Here," she said, setting the book at his feet. "You have the thing she asked for. Now will you let me go? Please?" She hoped in this case that what people said about *please* being a "magic word" was true.

Taro looked from the book to her. He nodded yet again.

"Thank you," Sophie whispered. She turned and ran to the ladder. She climbed up it to the main pier that led into town. When she reached the street, she looked back toward the docks, but the creature and the book were gone.

Soaking and exhausted, Sophie limped through the cobblestone streets. Her feet throbbed from where she had cut herself on the glass, and her lungs felt as if they might burst in her chest. She knew that if she stopped moving, she would collapse. Her only thought was of seeing her father again, of throwing her arms around him and apologizing for not listening to his warnings, of begging for his forgiveness. At long last, she reached the small, familiar alley that led to her home.

"Papa!" she called, staggering up the front steps of the shop. The door swung open, and she was relieved to think he might still be awake. She saw the warm glow of the stove in the back of the shop. "Papa!" she called, racing between bookshelves. "It's me!"

But as she approached his old chair in front of the stove, something felt wrong. Instead of his slippered feet, she saw a pair of heeled boots and sharp black crinoline. She gripped the empty bookcase beside her. "You . . ."

Madame Eldritch sat in the chair, holding *The Book of Who*. The woman did not look angry. In fact, she appeared almost amused. Her face was smooth, bearing only the tiniest traces of the cuts Sophie had seen not half an hour before.

The woman stood and approached Sophie. "Hello, my little bookmender." Her smile flickered dark red in the firelight. "You left without saying good-bye." She leaned down and pressed her lips to Sophie's forehead.

Sophie blinked, stumbling to one side. She touched her head, and when she pulled her hand away, her fingers were covered in sticky red paint—a mark from Madame Eldritch's lips.

Sophie stared up at the woman, whose face seemed to be moving in and out of focus. "What . . . ?" she began through shallow breaths. "What did you do to me?"

The woman raised a shoulder. "What the occasion called for."

Sophie swayed backward, trying to keep herself upright. The room around her was moving now, expanding and shrinking with every breath. Her vision blurred, and she felt her whole being slipping into darkness. She let go of the bookcase and collapsed to the floor.

CHAPTER TWELVE

A GIFT

Sophie stirred in the darkness. She opened her eyes to find her-self curled up on a leather bench, her body rocking back and forth in a lurching rhythm. She thought for a moment she was back in the oubliette but then realized that she could hear hoofbeats. She was in a moving carriage. A single lamp hung from the ceiling. It swung from side to side, drawing odd shadows across the floor. Madame Eldritch sat across the carriage, with Taro at her side.

Between them lay *The Book of Who*.

"You finally wake," the woman said, looking away from the moonlit window. "I trust you dreamt well."

Sophie sat up, feeling a crimp in her neck. She massaged her throbbing forehead. *What had happened to her?* She remembered running to the bookshop, calling for her father, and finding Madame Eldritch waiting for her, and then . . .

"You drugged me," she said.

Madame Eldritch did not bother trying to deny it. "I thought it would make you easier to transport."

"You mean *abduct*," Sophie said. She grabbed the door handle and pulled with all her might, but it was locked. "Stop the carriage!" she called, pounding her fist against the driver's window. "I'm being kidnapped!"

Madame Eldritch made no move to stop her. She waited until Sophie had exhausted herself before speaking. "Your efforts are wasted. The man driving this carriage has been paid too well to be moved by the pleas of a little girl . . . however comely she may be." Her eyes flicked down to Sophie's clothes.

Sophie looked at herself and noticed that her plain dress had been replaced with a fine gown that pinched at the waist. Her neck and shoulders were bare, and she felt exposed, even in the dim light. Mercifully, she saw that she also had been equipped with a hooded cloak and a pair of leather boots. That, at least, was something. "Why am I dressed like this?" she said.

"Forgive the liberty. Your frock was torn. And it was . . ." Madame Eldritch paused to consider the word. "Disadvantageous."

Sophie understood the implication, and it might have been true for someone like Madame Eldritch, but not so for Sophie. "A gown's not very practical for travel," she said, pulling her cloak tightly over her shoulders.

"I think in time you will disagree." Madame Eldritch leaned closer, in the manner of a person wanting to share a secret. "Here is a lesson for you, little bookmender: A walled garden must have a lattice gate. Before a woman can be desired, she must reveal a bit of what makes her desirable." She reached across the cabin and drew a curl of dark hair from behind Sophie's ear, laying it artfully down her bare neck.

Sophie pulled away and retucked the hair behind her ear. "I'm not a garden. And I have no interest in being *desired*."

Madame Eldritch did not laugh outright but looked as if she wanted to. "Everyone wants to be desired—it is only a question of for what and by whom."

Sophie had no energy to debate the point. She sat up and peered out the round window in the carriage door. A half moon shone above the receding trees. It was a different moon from her night in the oubliette, and she realized that they had been traveling for at least two days. "Where are we?" she said.

"Can you not tell by the stars? We are taking the eastern road through the Grimmwald."

"The Grimmwald?" The name was enough to make Sophie shudder. She peered again through the window, looking for signs of danger in the moonlit forest. "You're not afraid of wild beasts? Or highwaymen?" There were, of course, rumors of much more dangerous things lurking in the Grimmwald, but Sophie preferred not to consider them.

"I do not fear the darkness, nor should you. Our door is securely locked—as you already know. And our driver carries a musket at the ready. And if that is not enough, we have Mister Taro." She looked fondly at the creature sitting silently beside her.

Sophie studied the manservant who had spared her on the docks. He was now wearing a black velvet suit that looked appropriate for a footman or valet. She tried to read some expression on his face, but it was impossible to see anything beyond the silver thread that held his lips together. The very sight of it made her ill.

Sophie sighed, flopping back down in her seat. Even if she could escape, there would be little hope of making it back to Bustleburgh before Taro intervened. "Where are you taking me?" she asked, her body rocking with the motion of the carriage.

"We are going to visit someone who will take a great interest in this book of yours." Madame Eldritch's hand rested casually atop *The Book of Who*, one red fingernail playing at the latch. "Someone who will pay handsomely for it, I think."

Sophie stared at the book. *Her* book. Perhaps the only hope she had of learning about her mother. "Did you read it?"

Madame Eldritch smiled. "I am a simple shopkeeper. The contents of this book are irrelevant to me. I am only concerned with its value."

"So you're just going to sell it off for money?"

"Money is vulgar but useful. It hired this carriage, for example. Still, you are right—I hope to exchange this book for something that cannot otherwise be bought. Something no bank or coffer can hold." She said this, as she said many things, in a way that implied some illicit secret. "But where we are going is not your real question, I think. What you want to know is why, if I already have the book, did I also bring you?"

Sophie shrugged. "I assume you're planning to sell me, too?"

The woman shook her head. "It is a weakness of sentiment, perhaps." She drew her finger along the curve of Sophie's chin. "I am liberating you. A girl like you does not belong in that dusty little bookshop."

"Of course I belong in that dusty little bookshop," Sophie said, pulling back. "I'm a bookmender."

"I have it on good authority that your position in the city was not exactly what one could call *secure.*" Sophie thought that Madame Eldritch must have learned about her flight from Inquisitor Prigg. "Besides, you are no common bookmender. You are the daughter of Coriander Quire. Among discerning populations, your mother was the *only* bookmender. The one person who could repair a book without letting its magic slip away."

Sophie sat up, suddenly listening much more closely. The woman must have read the wonder on her face, for she went on. "People traveled great distances to commission Coriander Quire, and many of us were disappointed to lose her services. You, like your mother, possess a rare and valuable talent—one that might serve me well."

Sophie recalled the look on Madame Eldritch's face whenever she returned a repaired book to the woman. Awe. And a touch of envy. "So I'm to be your servant," she said.

"I already have a servant." Madame Eldritch leaned back. "What I seek in you is . . . a protégé. There is much I can teach you about the world. There are places and things beyond your well-fed imagination. Things too fantastic even for books. Well, *most* books." She glanced meaningfully at *The Book of Who.*

Sophie folded her arms and stared out the window. "I suppose I should have just sold the book to you when you gave me the chance."

"You do me injury, little bookmender. I am no thief. Reach into your pocket."

Sophie looked down to find that her dress—ridiculous though it was—indeed had pockets. She reached into the left pocket and removed a leather bundle rolled up and secured with a ratty cord. "What is it?" she asked.

"A gift."

Sophie untied the cord and opened the bundle. Inside lay a row of tools: hand clamps, pincers, an awl, a leather-punch, paste spoons, and brushes. "They're . . . bookmending tools," she said. Such tools were not expensive, but something about these nonetheless filled her with hushed awe.

"They belonged to your mother," Madame Eldritch said.

Sophie looked up at the woman, unsure whether she was being mocked. But when she turned back to the tools and placed her fingers over them, she *knew*. There are legends beyond counting of enchanted objects that hold a sort of memory: swords that still ring with the screams of their victims, boots that still creak with roads long since trod, and, apparently, in this case, bookmending tools that bore the imprint of Sophie's mother's hand. "How did you get them?"

"She gave them to me." Madame Eldritch made a small shrug, as if mirroring Sophie's own surprise. "It must have been a dozen years ago. She came to my shop and asked me to prepare for her a great number of very powerful charms. She did not have money to offer, so instead she gave me those tools."

Sophie shifted in her seat. "What were the charms for?"

"They were protective charms. Guarding against all manner of harm: fire, ice, wind, earth, steel, spark, poison, disease—the ghastly gamut. I did not ask her intentions, but it seemed to me that she was planning to do something dangerous that very night, something from which she feared she might not return."

Sophie recalled what her father had told her about the night her mother left. "The charms didn't work," she said, looking down. "My father found her in the shop, dead."

Madame Eldritch raised an eyebrow. "Then she must have encountered something very powerful indeed. And all the more fitting that I return these tools to you now. Consider it a refund." She smiled not unkindly. "All charms guaranteed."

Sophie ran her fingers over the tools. "I . . . thank you." But as soon as she said these words, she regretted it. This was the same woman who had tried to trap her in the oubliette. The same woman who had drugged her in the bookshop. She massaged the spot on her forehead where Madame Eldritch's lips had touched her. "Papa would never let you take me from him. Did you kiss him, too?"

The woman made a noncommittal gesture with her hand. "For him I employed a more subtle attack." She turned to her manservant, who had remained so still that Sophie had very nearly forgotten he was in the carriage with them. "Mister Taro, *maquillage*."

Taro nodded and produced a black box with a silver handle on top. He opened the case to reveal a collection of oils and powders and implements that one might find on the counter of a fine lady's dressing room. The bottles clinked as the carriage rattled beneath them.

Madame Eldritch reached into the case and removed a round bottle of what looked like perfume. "This vial contains a wallflower charm—it lets me pass unobserved, and if someone does manage to notice me, they forget the moment they look away. Your father is doubtless sleeping soundly in his bed."

Sophie eyed the array of powders and potions, feeling a twist of confusion that was as much about her ignorance of the feminine arts as of the magical arts. "How did you learn to make all of those?" She had tried making spells when she was younger. A few of the older books from the shop hinted at recipes—newt eyes and dandelion stems and such. The results, however, were nothing but foul-smelling cups of tea.

"It only takes a little bit of practice. I could teach you, if you would like." The woman dug through her case and removed a small tin of what looked like talcum powder. "Taro," she said. "Your arm."

The creature rolled up the sleeve of his coat to reveal his bare arm. Sophie stared at his skin and felt a wave of repulsion. Taro's arm was like a stick that had been whittled to the bone. Jagged scars covered every inch of it. "I . . . I don't understand," Sophie said. "Who did this to him?"

"I did, of course." Madame Eldritch drew from her case a shining silver scalpel. "You have read many things, little bookmender. What have you read of the mandrake?"

"The mandrake is a root," Sophie said. "The proper name is *Mandragora*. It's said to be useful for making potions and spells." The woman nodded approvingly, and Sophie went on. "They say if you pluck a mandrake from the ground, its roots cry out like a newborn baby . . . and anyone who hears the cry will be instantly killed. But I don't see what this has to do with . . . him." She glanced at the manservant.

"Don't you? Perhaps you should look more closely."

Sophie studied Taro's greenish skin, ribbed with horizontal lines, his small, unblinking eyes—he reminded her of nothing so much as the texture of a gingerroot. "You're saying he's an actual *plant*?" She had to stop herself from touching his face. "But that's not possible."

"You yourself observed that the mandrake root could move and speak. I ask you, what would happen if someone could prevent a mandrake babe from uttering his deadly cry?"

Sophie suddenly realized why Taro's mouth had been stitched shut with silver thread. "You stitched his mouth to stop him from speaking."

"Clever, no?" Madame Eldritch smiled. "And now I have an endless source of this most rare and versatile ingredient. This is another lesson: To control the spring is to control the sea." She sliced off one of the tuberous knots growing from Taro's elbow. Sophie tried to imagine what it must feel like to have someone simply take a part of you. Taro was staring forward, his face devoid of emotion. It was clear he was aware of what Madame Eldritch had done, but it was not clear how he felt about it.

Madame Eldritch took the tiny bit of root and dropped it into the tin of powder. Sophie watched the woman grind the root with a miniature pestle. A heavy, sweet aroma filled the cabin. Her work completed, Madame Eldritch dabbed the powder on her face with a flat brush.

Sophie recalled the ghastly vision of Eldritch being swarmed by sprites. "When I ran from the oubliette, your face was covered with cuts . . ."

"And now it is not."

This was true. Her skin was clear and smooth and bore no traces of the attack. Madame Eldritch replaced her tools and closed the lid of her case. "Rejuvenation is but one of many useful charms. I shall teach them all to you in time." She reached out a pale hand and drew back the edge of Sophie's cloak to expose her throat. "This bell. Where did you get it?"

She was talking about the necklace that Sophie always wore. "My mother left it for me," she said. Sophie took the bell between her fingers and shook it. "It doesn't work, though. There's no sound."

"Of course there's no sound," Madame Eldritch said. "It's a dispell bell."

Sophie stared at the little silver bell. "What does that mean?"

"Charms can be tricky things. And sometimes there is need to *unwork* them. A dispell bell is used to break certain charms."

"So I can undo charms, just by ringing it?" Sophie looked at the bell, which shone white in the lamplight. "How do you know all this?"

"Because it was purchased from my shop." Madame Eldritch sat back in her seat, looking more than a little smug. "If your mother left that bell with you, then she must have feared that whatever evil she faced might soon come for you. Perhaps it is a luckier thing than I realized that I have taken you from Bustleburgh."

Sophie let go of the necklace. "Or perhaps *you* were the thing she was afraid of?"

Madame Eldritch said, "I would think a girl so well-read as yourself would know that there are more frightening things in the world than shopkeepers and mandrakes."

Sophie's body was thrown forward as the carriage suddenly slowed. She heard the driver's voice outside the cabin. "Whoa!" he called to the horses, stopping them in the road.

"I have instructed our man to deliver us to a comfortable inn," Madame Eldritch said. "It seems we have reached our destination."

The carriage remained still, but the driver did not dismount to open the door. Sophie peered through the window, glimpsing the unlit, narrow road ahead of them. "I don't think we're at the inn," she said. Her reading had taught her that roads near inns were usually wider to accommodate riders passing in both directions.

"Who goes there?" the driver called. "Show yourself."

Another voice rang out from somewhere ahead: "*Stand and deliver!*"

"Stand and deliver" was a common cry of bandits who assailed hapless travelers. "Highwaymen," Sophie whispered.

Madame Eldritch nodded to Sophie. "It seems you are correct." She sat back, displaying absolutely no signs of distress. "There is a reason our driver is armed."

Sophie gripped the edge of the bench, trying to picture the deadly encounter about to transpire just outside their carriage.

"Let us pass!" the driver called. "We have no quarrel with you!"

The horses neighed loudly, and the carriage jolted to one side. There came shouts and then a loud *crack* as a musket ball split the air.

Sophie shrieked and gripped the wall beside her. She suddenly felt very grateful for the locked door.

The driver shouted again. There was another shot fired, which sounded different from the first. If Sophie had known more about warfare, she would have known that this second shot was from a pistol. She also would have known that one musket and one pistol was the most any hired driver would carry. She sat upright, tense, straining to hear what was happening outside. "Did it work? Did he scare them off?"

There was another shout, and the carriage rocked again. Sophie heard what sounded like blades clashing against each other and then a bloody scream. A slight grin tugged at the corners of Madame Eldritch's mouth. "It would appear he did not."

Sophie leapt back as the door handle beside her started to shake. "They're trying to get inside!"

"So it would seem," Madame Eldritch said, examining her red fingernails in the lamplight. "Unfortunately for them, I possess the only key. And the lock is one from my own inventory—an iron hasp-knot from the Luck Dynasty."

The handle shook once more, and then—

Click.

"So much for your hasp-knot," Sophie muttered.

Madame Eldritch's demeanor changed at once, and she pulled away from the door. "That lock has remained unbroken for three centuries. No mortal could pick it so quickly . . ."

The door swung open.

Outside was darkness but for a silver blade shining in the moonlight. A figure stepped from the shadows. He was wearing a black hat and a black riding cloak and a bandage over his eyes.

Sophie caught her breath. "Peter!"

The boy turned toward her. He was breathing heavily, and blood was running from a cut along his cheek. He pointed the blade at Sophie. "I believe you have something that belongs to me?"

CHAPTER THIRTEEN

HIGHWAY ROBBERY

Peter Nimble stood at the open door of the carriage, blade poised. His ears were still ringing from when the driver had nearly discharged a pistol into his skull. He tried to slow his breathing and focus on the people in the carriage. "Stand and deliver," he said. This was something Sir Tode had shouted before attacking the driver, and Peter had liked the sound of it.

"How did you find me?" The question came from Sophie. It was clear that she was surprised by Peter's sudden arrival, and he half wished he could see the look on her face.

"I'll do the talking," Peter said, wiping the blood from his cheek. "Any sudden movement and it'll be your last." He held out his hand. "Turn over the book."

The ringing in his ears had subsided, and he could now hear one other heartbeat in the carriage. It was the potion maker who had a shop off the docks—her every pore reeked of drugged perfume, and Peter had to focus not to let the smell distract him.

"The book is mine," the woman said. "And I would not part with it so easily."

The boy almost had to laugh at her bravado. "I'm not afraid to fight a girl," said Peter, whose upbringing left much to be desired in the way of manners.

"Nor am I afraid to fight a boy," Madame Eldritch retorted. Peter heard her turn away from him, as though addressing another person. "Mister Taro," she said, "please get rid of this pest."

Peter listened as a third passenger—someone he had not noticed before—rose from the bench and approached him. "Who—?"

He did not manage to finish the rest of his question, because the very next moment, a rough hand snatched him by the throat and lifted him clear off his feet. Peter gasped, feeling the fingers tightening around his windpipe. He kicked and flailed, but his attacker held him fast.

"Let him go!" he heard Sophie shout.

"Taro. Release him." The moment Madame Eldritch spoke those words, the hand around Peter's neck let go.

Peter collapsed to the ground outside the carriage, gasping for air. "What . . . what is that thing?"

He heard Sophie rush to his side. "That's Mister Taro," she said, as if that explained anything. "We're safe, for the moment. He only does what Madame Eldritch tells him to do. She said to let you go, and so he let you go."

This seemed to be true. Taro was still standing in front of Peter but had made no further movement to hurt him. Peter inched back. "Then let's get out of here before she notices that I—"

He was cut off by a furious scream. "Taro!" Madame Eldritch's voice rang out from within the carriage. He heard the door swing open, and the woman rushed down the steps. She raised a hand, presumably pointing in Peter's direction. *"Kill him!"*

Peter did not need to be able to see to know what "him" she was referring to—and he had a pretty good idea why she wanted him dead. "Untether the horse!" he cried to Sophie, and he charged to meet his foe. He swiped his silver blade toward Taro's head but missed completely and plunged his weapon deep into the side of the carriage.

Taro's own movements were nearly as fast as Peter's, and the next moment Peter felt two hands grab him by the arm, dislodge his blade from the wood, and swing him up through the air. He flew clear across the road and crashed headfirst into a lamentably sturdy oak tree.

Peter fell to the ground and rolled over, groaning. "How's that horse coming?" His head was throbbing, and he could taste blood in his mouth. He heard footsteps rushing toward him, and he sprang to one side just as Taro smashed clean through the tree.

"Done!" Sophie's voice rang out.

Peter climbed to his feet, impressed with how quickly she had managed to loosen the horse. He ran across the road and leapt onto the horse, landing neatly on its back. A moment later, he felt Sophie clamber up behind him.

"Where's Sir Tode?" Peter asked, grabbing the reins. The last he had checked, Sir Tode had been busy chasing off the carriage driver.

"I'm right here!" the knight shouted. "Just go!"

Peter snapped the reins again, and the horse charged forward. Sophie screamed, grabbing Peter's waist and clinging for dear life. It was fairly clear that the girl had never been on a horse before, and she held so tightly to him that it hurt his bruised side.

Peter heard a thrashing in the woods beside them. "It's that creature," Sir Tode said. "He's trying to cut us off at the bend."

Peter snapped the reins again, pushing the horse faster. He could feel Sophie's breath on his neck, and for some reason it was distracting him from the road. Luckily, the horse seemed to have enough sense to know that it should be running away from Taro.

"Reach into my coat pocket!" Peter called to Sophie. "You'll find a little bottle with a bug inside."

Sophie apparently knew enough not to question him. He felt her loosen her death grip ever so slightly and slide a hand into his coat pocket. "Got it," she said a moment later. "Should I open it?"

"No!" both Peter and Sir Tode shouted at the same time.

"That's a silkwyrm," Peter said, forcing himself to keep his voice calm. "Give the bottle a shake—that should wake it up. And when you've got a clear shot, throw it straight at Taro as hard as you can." He very much hoped that what he had heard about girls and throwing was not true. (As it happens, it is not.)

He heard Sophie call out, "I'm sorry!" and throw the vial. There was a shattering sound as the glass hit the road, and quickly after that came a high-pitched shriek.

"Nice shot!" Peter said over the piercing shrieks of the silkwyrm. Peter had never actually seen a silkwyrm go off, but he had a pretty good idea of what it might look like. No sooner does the wyrm escape its bottle than it spins a thousand tiny, unbreakable threads around its prey—encasing it in a giant fluffy white cocoon of death.

Sir Tode, who had been watching the road behind them, turned back to Peter. "Good show, all around. I think we've lost them."

"That's not the only thing we lost," Sophie said, her arms tight around Peter's waist. "Madame Eldritch still has the book."

Peter perked up. "You mean *this* book?" He reached into his bag and removed *The Book of Who*.

He could practically hear Sophie's jaw drop. "How did you get that?" she said.

"Nicked it when I opened the door." He stuffed it back into his burgle-sack. "All in a day's work for the great Peter Nimble!"

✦ ✦ ✦

Sophie had been riding with Peter and Sir Tode for what felt like an hour. By this point, the excitement of the highway robbery had worn off, and now she was simply exhausted. Her body was stiff from riding horseback, and her dress was chafing her sides terribly. She wondered how long it had been since she had eaten. She shifted, adjusting her grip around Peter's waist. "Can we stop and rest?" she said.

"Get off if you want, but we're not stopping here," Peter said, one ear cocked to the woods. "That root creature is still after us. What is that thing, anyway?"

"He's a full-grown mandrake root," Sophie said. "His name is Taro."

The boy turned away. "Whatever he is, he's getting closer. I can smell him about a quarter league off."

Sophie stared at Peter, unsure whether he was teasing her. He had made a few similar offhand references earlier in the night—alluding to distant smells and sounds that should have been impossible to detect.

Sir Tode, for his part, seemed to believe him. "Well, then, we'd better keep moving. At these crossroads, take a left . . . and there should be a village at the top of the hill."

Sophie, who by this point had gotten her bearings a bit, shook her head. "A village? In the Grimmwald?"

"That's what he said," Peter said, turning down a small over-grown path.

"I've read dozens of histories of the Grimmwald," Sophie said. "And I'm telling you, there are no villages out this far."

"Tell that to them," Peter said, slowing the horse.

Sophie looked down to see a cluster of squat huts, most of them only a little taller than she was. There were lights on in some of the windows and smoke trailing from the chimneys. She could hear music and voices inside what appeared to be a tavern, outside of which stood a row of miniature ponies along a miniature hitching post. The doors of the tavern were only about as high as her chin. "What is this place?" she asked in amazement.

Sir Tode pointed a hoof toward a sign that was posted on the side of the road:

WELCOME TO

LITTLE WHENCE

POP. MORE OR LESS

EST. ONCE UPON A TIME

Sophie stared at the name. "Little Whence?" The name sounded vaguely familiar, and she wondered if she had, in fact, read of it in a story. "What kind of people live here? And in such tiny houses?"

Peter shrugged. "Knomes, probably." It is worth noting that he didn't say this in a sarcastic manner. The boy flicked the reins, and the horse ambled slowly through the tiny village.

Sophie dismounted and walked between the little huts with their little chimneys and little picket fences. It did not make her feel like a giant, exactly, but it did make her feel like a full-grown adult. "What are you looking for?" she asked Peter.

The boy led the horse to a small hut just off the road. "Here it is," he answered.

The building was some kind of abandoned shop. A sign over the door read:

NAT PEBBLE'S

CURIO EMPORIUM

"It's a curiosity shop," Sophie said. She grabbed the door handle and tried to turn it. "It's locked." But then the knob suddenly shook of its own accord, and she leapt back, startled.

The door swung inward to reveal Peter Nimble crouched on the other side, looking rather pleased with himself. "The window was open," he said. "Come on in."

Sophie ducked down and stepped into the shop. She had to stoop to prevent herself from hitting the rafters. Sir Tode clopped in after her. The shelves were crammed with all manner of strange windup toys and sparkling trinkets and bubbling bottles and shimmering plants. It reminded her of a much less frightening version of Madame Eldritch's shop. Peter shut the door behind them, locking it. He took a chair and propped it under the doorknob for reinforcement. "We don't have much time," he said to Sir Tode.

Sophie watched as the boy began feeling his way along the walls, touching all the shelves. He stopped at a small bookcase with claw feet. The case might once have been elegant but now only looked sad. A few lonely books lay scattered across its shelves. It seemed that even this far outside of Bustleburgh, good books were in short supply. "This is it," Peter said.

Sophie heard a sharp neigh from the horse outside. "That would be our friend Taro," Sir Tode said. "Hurry, Peter."

There was the sound of a scuffle and then galloping hoofbeats receding into the distance. "He's chased off our horse," Sophie said. "We're trapped."

"Not for long." Peter knelt down and opened his bag. "I'd stand back from the front door if I were you."

Crack!

The shop door shuddered as Taro beat against it from the other side.

Sophie rushed across the shop and huddled beside Sir Tode,

who was watching his friend with keen interest. Peter removed a hefty object from his bag that Sophie recognized as a popular style of bookend. Mounted to the front was a round brass doorknob. "What on earth are you going to do with that?" she said.

Crack!

The door shuddered again, this time taking one of the hinges off the frame. Sophie leapt back, reflexively grabbing Peter's arm. He ignored her, setting the bookend on the shelf. He turned the knob and pulled it toward himself—

Sophie gasped.

As Peter pulled the knob, the entire bookcase swung out like a door. Behind it lay a swirling gray fog.

Sophie stepped back, her eyes fixed on the endless passage behind the bookcase. "How did you . . . ?"

CRACK!

There was an explosion of splinters and twisted iron as the door behind them was ripped clean off its hinges. It crashed against the opposite wall—shattering a shelf full of glass jars. Brightly colored foam hissed and sputtered from one of the jars, spilling out over the floor. Another jar shot sparks into the air. A third one began playing music.

Taro stepped into the shop, white fibers from the silkwyrm still clinging to his torn clothes. He flexed his long, tuberous fingers.

Peter removed the bookend from the shelf and stuffed it into his bag. "We should go." He grabbed Sophie's arm and dragged her toward the bookcase.

Taro's eyes fixed on the swirling passage behind them. He sprang across the room, racing toward them, hands outstretched.

Peter shoved Sophie through the opening and jumped through after her with Sir Tode under one arm. The case clicked shut behind them, and Sophie screamed as she tumbled backward into the darkness . . .

PART TWO

WHAT

THE LOOKING-GLASS LIBRARY

I f Sophie had been expecting a nice, lazy plummet through some formless void, she was sorely disappointed. No sooner had she tumbled backward through the bookcase than her head struck a hard stone floor. Sir Tode and Peter landed on top of her a moment after, pummeling her with elbows and hooves.

Sophie looked back to the bookcase, which had shut itself behind them. "That bookcase won't hold for long," she said, crawling out from underneath the others. "We have to keep running!"

Peter and Sir Tode did not run. Instead, they stood and dusted themselves off, calm as could be. "Looks like we lost him," Sir Tode said. He sniffed at a shriveled bit of root on the floor that looked

suspiciously like one of Taro's fingers. "Or most of him, anyhow."
He kicked the severed digit into the flames of a hearth that crackled
serenely nearby.

Peter retrieved his hat, which had landed atop a threadbare
oriental rug. "We're safe now," he said to Sophie. "Even if that
creature rips the bookcase apart, he'll find nothing but an empty
wall." He flopped down into an old wingback chair, propping his
feet on a footstool.

Sophie peered around the room. She had assumed that they
had escaped into some sort of secret passageway inside the wall of
the curiosity shop, but now she could tell that that was impossible.
Secret passages did not have glowing hearths and old rugs and
comfy wingback chairs. Sophie climbed to her feet, rubbing her
eyes. "Where are we?" she said.

"We are on a secret island," Sir Tode explained. "Or, rather,
under it. It's the home of a man named Professor Cake. This is his
library."

Before her stood an enormous wall made entirely of bookcases.
Shelves of every size imaginable were crammed together—side
by side, top to bottom, wedged against one another like pieces of
a giant puzzle. For some reason, the books on the shelves had all
been arranged *backward*, with their spines facing in. There were
more bookcases above and below her. Twisting staircases led to

shelves arranged at all angles—just looking at it all made her dizzy. There were no windows, and the air was filled with a musty odor that she associated with root cellars. Somewhere in the distance, she thought she could hear the muffled roar of falling water, and above that, the faint music of glass bottles clinking against one another. "It's enormous," she said.

Enormous was an understatement. It was the biggest room she had ever seen. Sophie walked among the stacks, marveling at the endless rows of books. She tried to calculate how many lifetimes it would take to read all these stories. Most of the books looked very old. She reached to pick up one of the volumes—

"Don't touch the books," Peter called. "If anything goes missing, Professor Cake will know."

Sophie decided they must be referring to the same professor she had read about in *The Book of Who.* "This Professor of yours—is he the one who sent you to Bustleburgh?"

"Obviously," Peter said, cleaning his fingernails with his blade. "And I wouldn't get too comfortable. As soon as he shows up, I'm sure he'll send you back to where you came from."

Sophie folded her arms. "I'd like to have a word with him before he does. I want to find out how he came to be in possession of *The Book of Who.*"

Peter wrinkled his nose. "The book of *what*?"

"Not 'what,'" Sophie said. "*Who.*" She marched over to Peter and dug a hand into his bag. She pulled out the book in question. "Your Professor didn't even tell you what it was called?"

Sir Tode, who had made himself comfortable by the fire, perked up. "Indeed, he did not—he only told us it was in need of repair."

Peter snatched the book from her grasp with surprising speed. "It's just a book," he muttered, stuffing it back into his burgle-sack.

"Just a book?" Sophie rolled her eyes. "Madame Eldritch was ready to kill you for it. And I'd wager she's not the only person." She had both hands on her hips now. "Maybe that's why your Professor didn't tell you the book's name—he was afraid you'd open your big mouth and let the wrong people find out about it."

"Like you did much better?" Peter said. "If I recall, we just rescued you for the *second time* in a week."

Sophie stomped her foot. "The first time didn't count!"

"Don't be embarrassed." The boy stretched back in his chair. "You're not the first damsel in need of the great Peter—"

Peter's final words were cut off by a primal scream as Sophie lunged for the boy with open hands in an attempt to strangle him dead. Peter dodged the attack but not before tipping his chair backward. Soon the two of them were rolling across the floor, shouting insults and threats.

Now, I would like to report that Sophie proved Peter's perfect equal in terms of physical strength and fighting prowess, but this would be a lie. Sophie had never fought with anyone in her life, whereas Peter Nimble was a seasoned expert. Indeed, his biggest challenge was finding a way to restrain Sophie without accidentally running her through with his silver blade—a task he finally managed by tying her legs and hands with a bit of spare rope from his bag.

"You untie me this instant!" Sophie cried, pulling uselessly against her restraints. How the boy had managed to tie the knots with only one hand and while wearing a blindfold was beyond her.

Peter gave an exaggerated yawn. "I'm sure someone as brilliant as you can figure out how to untie a few little—" He stopped short and leapt to his feet. "Professor!" he said, his voice suddenly timid. "We were only playing."

Sophie craned her neck to see that he was now speaking to an old man with a white beard and spectacles. The man was wearing a patchwork robe and entirely too many scarves. In one hand he held a cane made from the skull and spine of what looked to be a very large bird, in his other, a steaming pot of cinnamon tea. "Gracious, Peter," he said in a tone somewhere between shock and amusement. "I see you've made our guest feel at home."

✦   ✦   ✦

Ten minutes later, Sophie, Sir Tode, and Peter were seated in comfy chairs, holding mugs of hot tea and eating candied scones.

The teapot, which seemed entirely too small to serve three people, somehow never went empty, even as Professor Cake—for, indeed, it *was* Professor Cake—refilled their cups. For his part, the Professor seemed contented to smoke his churchwarden pipe, which he refilled from time to time with chipped tobacco from his vest pocket.

Perhaps sensing that Peter and Sophie would be biased in their accounts, Professor Cake had asked Sir Tode to kindly relate their adventures thus far. Sir Tode gave a faithful—if somewhat embellished—account of the skirmish in front of the Pyre, Sophie's disappearance from the bookshop, and the rescue on the highway. Sir Tode had a dramatic flair for stories, and he was soon standing atop the table, reenacting the final battle against Taro. "... and just as the hideous monster was charging toward us," he concluded, "we dove through the bookcase and landed here, right as you found us!"

Professor Cake clapped, puffing on his pipe. "An excellent tale—and well worth the wait." Sophie noted that the smoke did not have the sweet, sticky aroma of the pipes in the oubliette. Instead, it had a warm, earthy smell, like the first day of autumn, or the ground after a summer rain. "I must confess that I had become worried. You two were a bit slower with the task than I had hoped."

"That's her fault," Peter said through a mouthful of scone. "She tried to run off with your book."

Sophie gritted her teeth. "I was *kidnapped*. And it's not *his* book." She put a protective hand on *The Book of Who*. "It belonged to my mother."

The Professor raised an eyebrow. "Your mother was an exceptionally gifted woman."

Sophie stared at him. "You knew her?"

The Professor made a noncommittal shrug. "I knew *of* her. Her work as a bookmender was unparalleled. I daresay more than a few volumes in this library were saved by her hand."

Sophie stared at the endless rows of bookcases. "So all these books belong to you?"

"Not exactly." Professor Cake released a helix of smoke. "The library is mine, but the books belong to others. Have you noticed that every one of these bookcases is unique—as if it were built by someone different?"

Sophie peered along the far wall and saw that he was right. No two cases were alike in size or construction. "It's as though they were all taken from different places."

"Indeed," the Professor said. "It's less that these shelves were *taken from* different places . . . and more that they are *still in* those places." He winked in a conspiratorial manner. "This library is something of a browsing collection, if you catch my meaning."

Sophie shook her head. "I really don't."

Peter snorted from his chair. "That must be hard for you."

"I would thank you to mind your tongue," Professor Cake said flatly. "If I recall, it was not so very long ago that I found you in a very similar state of ignorance on all manner of subjects—including this library." He shot the boy a penetrating look, which, even though Peter still wore his blindfold, seemed to hit its mark.

The boy dropped his head. "Sorry, sir." His voice was very small, and Sophie felt an unexpected pang of sympathy.

She cleared her throat, hoping to return to the subject at hand. "So you're saying that these bookcases are somehow in two places at once?"

"Take the bookcase you entered through." The Professor gestured with his pipe to the bookcase that had led them from the curiosity shop. "When you look through that case, what do you see?"

Sophie got up, keeping *The Book of Who* tucked under one arm. She approached the case and peered past cobwebs and dusty books to see the shadowy form of the abandoned curiosity shop—the strewn wares, the toppled cabinets, the shattered front door. She was relieved to see that Taro was no longer there.

"The bookcase is like a doorway between two places," she said. She looked at the books scattered along the shelf before her, all of them facing the wrong direction. "And that's why the books are turned around—because we're seeing the shelf from the backside!" She laughed, delighted at her own discovery.

Sir Tode rapped a hoof on the table. "By Jove, I think she's got it!"

Professor Cake took up his cane and rose from his chair. "Books from every corner of the map, all in one room. I call it my Looking-Glass Library."

Sophie walked along the rows, her eyes aglow with wonder. "So every one of these cases leads to a different place?" She caught glimpses of stern academies and shining palaces and dusty studies and quaint bookshops from all over the world—some seemed abandoned, while others were teeming with people. She ran her hands along one of the shelves. "You could go anywhere from here."

The Professor leaned on his cane. "In theory, yes, but that's not exactly the purpose. Most of these people have no idea that my library exists."

Sophie reached a new bookcase and stopped. The case was a little taller than she was and had no books on it. It looked into a cramped shop with an old workbench. Seated at the bench was a man with his head in his hands. He looked very old. Sophie stared at the man, a pain stinging her chest. "Papa?" she said, her voice barely a whisper.

It was the middle of the night. The shop was closed. He should have been in bed. But, instead, he was sitting there at the workbench . . .

Alone.

Professor Cake joined her side. "He can neither hear nor see you, I'm afraid. From where your father sits, this is only an empty bookcase against a solid wall."

Sophie had spent a lifetime at that workbench and never once suspected what lay just beyond those shelves. "Sometimes when I was working," she said softly, "I would get gooseflesh all up my neck and arms—and it felt as though someone were watching me. And other times I would lose books. I'd set them on that shelf and have them go missing . . . only to reappear mysteriously hours later. Papa would accuse me of being careless." She turned toward the Professor. "That was you, wasn't it?"

The Professor gave a sheepish chuckle. "I apologize for any inconvenience I may have caused you. It seems I cannot pass an unfamiliar book without giving it a quick read." This was a gross understatement: Professor Cake, like all true readers, was an incurable book filch.

Sophie was unable to look away from her father. "But why do you have a bookcase from *our* shop? The books we sell aren't magical or special . . . They're just stories."

The man peered at her over the rim of his spectacles. "My child, you of all people should know that there is no such thing as *just* a story. Though, admittedly, some stories are more valuable than others." He glanced meaningfully at *The Book of Who* tucked under her arm. "For many years now, your little shop has been the only thing standing between Bustleburgh and complete ruination. It is for that very reason that I sent Peter and Sir Tode to give you *The Book of Who*."

"You sent us to do *what*?" Peter called from the table.

"Far be it from me to contradict you, Professor," Sir Tode said, approaching. "But our mission, so far as I understood it, was to get the book repaired and bring it back to *you*."

"Yeah." Peter folded his arms. "She just tagged along. Like a pest."

"As well she should have!" Professor Cake said. "It would have been unconscionable for her to simply surrender *The Book of Who* to a pair of bandits. She is, after all, the Storyguard."

Sophie stepped back, clutching *The Book of Who*. She had not told Peter and Sir Tode what she had read about herself in the book. And she had certainly not told the Professor.

"What is he talking about?" Peter said. "Why did he call you that?"

Sophie kept her eyes on the Professor. "How . . . how did you know?"

The man made the satisfied face of someone proved correct in a deduction. "One develops a sense for such things." He drew deeply on his pipe and released a long curl of smoke. "The truth is, I have assembled you all here for a very specific, very important purpose. A purpose that has everything to do with that book and the troubles plaguing your city."

Sophie held *The Book of Who* tighter. She could feel her heart pounding against the cover. She thought of the thousands of books amassed in the Pyre, all waiting to be burned. "You want me to save Bustleburgh," she said.

The Professor shook his head. "No, my child. I want you to save the *world*."

Perhaps you've heard the riddle of the dreaming king? It goes something like this: Two brothers happen upon a king asleep beneath a tree in the forest. The brothers suspect that the king is dreaming about the forest, and that they themselves are merely characters in his dream. The first brother insists that they wake the king to discover if this is true. The second brother insists that they let the king keep sleeping, for fear that when the dream ends, they will die. And thus we have our dilemma: Should one concede a mad notion for fear that it might be true?

Sophie Quire found herself facing a similar dilemma. Professor Cake had just told her that *she* was somehow meant to save the world—a notion that was absurd beyond words. But some part of her feared that if she dissuaded him of this delusion, he might take back *The Book of Who* and send her home. And so she found herself in the unfortunate position of having to play along. "You want me to save the whole world?" she said.

Professor Cake chuckled. "Not the *whole* world—if such a thing even exists! I merely want you to save the world *in which you reside*. All of the hinterland empire, from the lofty Splint Mountains to the Grimmwald wilds to the marshes beyond. Every place you know of or have heard of is a part of your world. And it is this that you must save."

Sophie noticed Peter's confused expression, and she assumed that he was just as confounded by this prospect as she was. But she was wrong. "That's ridiculous," he blurted out, raising his blade. "If anyone is saving anything, it should be me and Sir Tode. We don't need some know-it-all tagging along."

Sophie glared at him. "I'd rather be a know-it-all than a blindfolded baboon."

"Children," Sir Tode said. "There's no need for name-calling."

"Tactless though he may be, Peter does make a valid point," Professor Cake said. "That's why he and Sir Tode will be there to help you. There is no telling what dangers you may encounter on your quest. While not lacking in spirit, you are, I hazard to say, not much of a fighter."

Sophie thought of the way Peter had bested her in combat and felt her cheeks go warm. "But, Professor," she said, "you still haven't told us what we must do. Or what danger threatens the—" She corrected herself. "Threatens *my* world."

"I should think you of all people would know," Professor Cake said, refilling his pipe with fresh tobacco. He struck a small tinderbox and lit the bowl. "Could you please tell me what your father is reading so intently at his stool?"

Sophie looked through her own bookcase, and the sight of her father again filled her with a pang. He was hunched over the work-bench, staring at a large poster covered with small black print. The individual words were hard to make out in the shadows, but she could see the header at the top: NO NONSENSE! "It's a notice for Pyre Day," she said. "They've been posting them all over the city."

"Precisely," Professor Cake said. "In two weeks' time, your city will set fire to an enormous stockpile of storybooks—tales gathered from every corner of the hinterland empire. And when that happens, your world as you know it will be lost forever."

"I don't understand," Peter said. "How can burning a bunch of books hurt things in the real world?"

"The *real* world," Professor Cake repeated with a tone of notable contempt. "The very notion is absurd. Worlds and everything in them are made real by the stories that inhabit them." He turned and paced along the shelves, his cane tapping the wooden floor. Sophie and the others followed him. "Stories are not mere diversions to occupy us on rainy days," he said. "They are a type of magic spell—perhaps the most powerful in existence—and their effect is to summon possibilities." As he walked, he gestured at the rows of different shelves, each one looking into a different place. "Every time the spell is cast, the impossible becomes a little more possible."

Sophie was trying her best to follow his meaning. "So every time someone reads a story," she said slowly, "they're actually casting some sort of . . . magic spell?"

"Precisely. Suffice it to say, if one hopes to live in a world of wonders, he had better locate himself in a place where wondrous stories abound. And if those stories were to suddenly disappear—well, that would be bad for everyone involved."

"How bad?" said Sir Tode, who was right behind Sophie.

The Professor drew on his pipe and pointed to a bookcase across the way. "You can see the results for yourself." Sophie peered at the case, which seemed to be a very large, ornately carved barrister's bookcase. Only now it was completely empty. On the other side of the case was a roomful of children, all of them seated at little tables, furiously working sums on slates.

"It's a school," Sophie said. She studied the faces of the children, all stony and scowling. "They look miserable."

"You are looking at what was once the finest school of alchemy in the world. That was before the authorities did away with all the stories. Now they're concerned with something called *economics*. A much less efficient way to make gold, if you ask me."

He pointed his cane to another empty bookcase a bit farther down. "This bookshelf used to inhabit a chapel. Now it's a factory." Sophie approached it and saw men and women working in some sort of enormous building. Instead of a river wheel, which she had seen in Bustleburgh, this factory had a blazing furnace in the middle. Men ceaselessly shoveled black coal into the fire beneath the furnace. White steam hissed out the top of the machine, which rattled and shook. "What is that thing?" she asked.

"That is a steam engine," Professor Cake said. "I daresay Bustleburgh will learn of them soon enough."

Sophie stared at the workers—their faces were black from the soot. As with the schoolchildren, their expressions were grim and lifeless. "Their eyes . . ." she said. "It's like the spark has gone completely out of them."

"And it has. These poor souls are the Dead Certain—mindless cogs in the ever-grinding wheels of progress." He turned away from the sight, as if looking upon it pained him.

"So you're saying that when Pyre Day comes, it will somehow make Bustleburgh like these other places?" She didn't really need to ask the question; already she had seen that same lifeless look on the faces of some of her customers and neighbors.

"When a population loses its stories, it loses its capacity for wonder—what remains is a life of drudgery and toil. Every day, it seems, I come upon another bookcase that looks into a world devoid of wonder. I fear Bustleburgh is next." He fixed his gaze upon her. "Unless you stop it."

Sophie stepped back from him. "But how?"

He tapped *The Book of Who* with his cane. "That book you carry with you is part of a set called the Four Questions. They contain information about every piece of magic that has ever existed— people, objects, places, and events. They were created a very long time ago as a way to help protect stories from harm."

"But how can books protect things?" Peter asked.

"These are no ordinary books, Peter. For when they are brought together, they possess the power to summon those same entries *into* the world."

Sophie recalled the words from the inscription. "'Impossible things of all shape and kind,'" she said, "'flow from the will of a curious mind.'" Sophie stared at the book in her arms. Her mother's name was inside of it. What would happen if she summoned that entry?

Professor Cake cleared his throat in a way that sounded very much like a rebuke. "The Four Questions are not to be used lightly. They are an ancient weapon in a battle that has been raging since the beginning of time—a fight over the very nature of the universe. A battle between questions and answers, between *What if* and *What is*, between imagination and information, wonder and doubt. Or, as your Inquisitor Prigg puts it: between nonsense and common sense."

"Which side are you on, Professor?"

The old man gave a tight smile. "The losing side, I'm afraid." He peered out at the rows of shelves, so many of them empty. "When *The Book of Who* appeared in my library, I recognized it for what it was, and I hoped that—if a new Storyguard could be found and the Four Questions assembled—there might be a chance to reverse the tide."

"So you knew that the book would pick me to be its Storyguard?"

He shook his head. "I have known a number of Storyguard in my years, and they are all of them unique but for one trait: They understand that stories are more than the sum of their words. Indeed, many of them love stories beyond their own lives. Which probably explains why most Storyguard are killed in the line of duty."

Sophie lowered her head. These words triggered a swill of dread that she had been keeping at bay. "The line of duty," she said. "Is that how my mother died?"

The Professor placed a wrinkled hand atop hers. "I do not know for certain. But I suspect that finding these books will reveal the truth. Historically there are four Storyguard at any given time, one protecting each book. They often live in secret, occupying the farthest corners of the map—from the deserts to the tundra to the ocean and everywhere in between. Even I do not know who or where they all are. What I do know is that when the world lost your mother twelve years ago, the others seemed to disappear with her. The world hasn't seen the other Storyguard or their books since."

Sophie held *The Book of Who* close. "If this was my mother's book, how did you get it?"

"She gave it to me . . . more or less." He tapped the bookcase that looked into Sophie's shop. "I found it on the floor of my library the same night she died, lying in front of this very bookcase. Your mother had somehow pushed it *through* her shelf and into my library—I've never seen anything like it." He looked at Sophie. "I've been keeping it safe ever since."

"That doesn't make sense." Sophie clutched the book even closer to her chest. "When Peter gave the book to me, it was covered with roots and grime and all manner of decay—it looked like it had been buried for a hundred years."

Professor Cake nodded, leaning on his cane. "Ah, yes, well, I knew this book was very precious, and I couldn't risk it falling into the wrong hands. And so I made sure the only person who could open it was someone who *deserved* it."

Sophie wrinkled her nose. "You put those things on it to test me?"

Peter gave a chuckle. "It wouldn't be the first time." He had himself endured a very similar "test" at the hands of the Professor two years earlier.

"I'm pleased to see that you have your mother's touch," Professor Cake said. "Apparently *The Book of Who* was similarly impressed."

Sophie thought of what her father had told her about how he had found her mother's body—facedown on the floor not five feet from where Sophie was standing now. "If you found *The Book of Who* inside your library—that means giving it to you was the last thing my mother did before she died."

He nodded. "It would seem so."

Sophie looked own at *The Book of Who*, which she could almost feel breathing in her arms. "And if I can find the other books . . . they might even lead me to her killer."

CHAPTER SIXTEEN

STUFF *and* NONSENSE

Inquisitor Prigg stepped over the splintered wreckage that had once been the front door of the small curiosity shop. And by *small*, he meant actually *tiny*. His taller soldiers had been forced to crawl on their hands and knees just to get through the door. "Stuff and nonsense," he muttered, his voice thick with disgust.

Bright puddles of liquid fizzled and sputtered on the ground, releasing all manner of noxious odors. Manikin dragons and windup toys rapped against their glass cages, trying to get out. Prigg stopped before a singing orchid that had fallen onto the ground, its clay pot shattered. The flower emitted a faint, lovely song that was known the world over as a perfect cure for melancholy. Prigg listened for a moment, then lowered his heel onto the blossom, crushing it flat.

He turned around to address the man who had led him to this place, a salty carriage driver from Olde Town. "And when, exactly," Prigg said, "did this altercation occur?"

"*Exactly* is a bit tricky, sir," the driver said. "I own no watch, but it was well past midnight, if the moon be any judge. I was driving a fare down the road when we were attacked by highwaymen. Well, more of a highway*boy*, really. He had a pet with him, the ugliest cat I ever did see—and it could talk, too." He opened his eyes wide. "Terrible nonsense, they was. There was a scuffle, and they stole my horse and rode her to this place. I'd have never found her again if it weren't for all the lights and explosions." He scratched his head. "Tell you honest, I been taking fares up and down these roads for years and never even knew this village existed."

"That's because this village was hiding," Prigg said. Little Whence was a knomish village, if the diminutive buildings were any indication. The owner of the shop had surely fled by now. As had the rest of the town's inhabitants. Doors had been left open, fires still smoldering in the kitchens, stables and larders half-filled. He smiled at the thought of their undoubtedly hasty flight. The very sight of Bustleburgh guards on the march had been enough to scatter these disgusting creatures to the farthest corners of the Grimmwald.

Prigg looked at the man. "May I ask who you were transporting through such treacherous roads at such a late hour?"

The driver blushed. "A fine lady, sir. As lovely as a hot meal on a cold day. Skin like fresh cream from the pail, and eyes so bright they'd have shamed the moon." He sighed, his own eyes looking glassy with stupidity. "One word from her lips was like—"

"Spare me," Prigg said. The driver was apparently an aspiring poet. "Did this enchanting lady happen to travel with a mute servant? A fellow named Taro?"

The driver gasped. "How did you know?"

Prigg gave a tight smile. "An educated guess." It had to be Madame Eldritch, the tea–seller who worked near the port. Wherever she went, a trail of stupefied men followed. Just that morning, in fact, Prigg had visited Augustus Quire the bookseller and found him similarly befuddled. He did not know Eldritch's connection to Quire, but it was clear that a connection existed. "Did this woman have anyone else in her company?"

The driver nodded. "A young girl with dark skin—she didn't appear to be from Bustleburgh. She was asleep when we left the city but lively enough when I was assaulted. She ran off with the highwaymen."

"The Quire girl," Prigg said. "It has to be." He clenched his fists, furious at how she had slipped through his grasp once again. He turned to his chief deputy, a useful (if ruthless) mercenary named Torvald Knucklemeat. "What do you see?"

Knucklemeat stepped over the rubble and splinters, his pistols clattering against his body with each step. He wore a patch over one eye like a storybook buccaneer. He rubbed his stubbly chin. "The man ain't lying about one thing: Your fugitives were here—there's clear cuts on the walls from the boy's blade. And those are hoofprints in the mud, sure enough." He knelt down, studying the floor. "Now, that's interesting."

Prigg went to join him. "What is it?"

Knucklemeat pointed to a bookcase that looked like it had seen better days. "This case here."

"What about it?" Prigg said.

"The wood ain't normal, sir." Knucklemeat spat a wad of tobacco on the floor, a disgusting habit that made Prigg's stomach turn. "There's a bit o' *shine* about it, if you follow my meaning."

Prigg did follow. Knucklemeat, whatever his shortcomings, had a rare ability to spot nonsense. The really dangerous kind. The kind that otherwise managed to stay hidden in plain sight. How the man did it, Prigg preferred not to ask. "An enchanted bookcase," Prigg said.

"Wouldn't surprise me!" Knucklemeat stood up, scratching under his eye patch. "Not for nothing, but I think I seen another bookcase like this once before in the 'wald. Found it abandoned in the woods a few years back. Probably a pile of splinters by now. You want me to pay it a visit?"

"Bring the bookcase back to me," Prigg said. It was probably a false lead, but he could not afford to miss anything.

Knucklemeat tipped his hat and stepped out into the darkness. Prigg remained where he stood, turning over clues. The bandit, the book, and now Eldritch. It seemed that nonsense was drawn to Sophie Quire like maggots to cheese.

"Inquisitor?" It was one of the guards he had brought from the city. "We've searched the entire village, sir. All the inhabitants are gone." It was clear from his demeanor that he, like all the other guards, was frightened of these woods and what they might hold. Up until today, he had lived in the certainty that nonsense didn't exist—and now that beautiful, efficient certainty was under attack.

Prigg wiped his hands and stepped outside to his waiting horse, which was hitched to an iron carriage that traveled with him always. "They are not gone. They're hiding in the shadows. Like vermin." He surveyed the cluster of little thatch-roofed huts, with their little doors and little rooms and little windows and little beds and little tables and chairs. "They may even be watching us now."

He walked to an open fire pit, where a plucked borogrove was roasting on a spit. He knelt down and removed a smoldering log from the fire. "Let us show them that they cannot hide from the light of progress!" He spoke loud enough that any person or creature lurking in the shadows would hear him. "Not anymore."

He touched the end of the log to one of the thatched rooftops. The roof instantly caught fire and smoke billowed from it. Within seconds, the entire house was ablaze. Prigg watched approvingly as the fire moved from one hut to another, until he was encircled in flame. Within seconds, Little Whence was reduced to a ring of smoldering timber.

"Stuff and nonsense," he said, the flickering firelight reflecting in his pale eyes.

CHAPTER SEVENTEEN

THE CASE *of the* RATTLING BOOKCASE

Sophie watched Professor Cake tend to his crackling hearth, her mind reeling with all the things he had just told her—not the least of which was that she was somehow meant to save her world. She had read enough stories in her life to be familiar with the trope in which heroes make a great show of being reluctant when told they must embark on a dangerous quest. They often refuse the call to adventure, only to change their minds at the very last moment. This had always bothered Sophie, who thought that such dithering was both unrealistic and unheroic. But now that *she* was the hero and *she* was being told she must embark on a dangerous quest, she suddenly understood just how difficult it was to take that first step. "So you need me to find these books and stop Pyre Day from happening," she said. "Why not just send Peter and Sir Tode?"

"Let me be clear on one thing," the old man replied. "It is not I who asks you to do this—it is the book that asks you." He placed a hand on her shoulder. "When *The Book of Who* named you as its Storyguard, it did so because it knew that you were the only one who could help it. Not Peter. Not Sir Tode. Not even myself."

"Yes, but look at me . . ." She stared up at him, clasping the book in her arms. Sophie knew she was smart. But she also knew that the knowledge found in books was not what it took to survive in the real world. Being smart had not helped her escape from Madame Eldritch. Being smart had not saved her from Inquisitor Prigg on the bridge. "I'm a bookmender. I'm not meant for adventure."

"For once I agree with her," Peter muttered.

Professor Cake asked that Sir Tode and Peter allow Sophie a bit of time to consider what was being asked of her. "The task may have chosen Sophie," he said to them, "but now Sophie must choose the task." Peter seemed a little put out by this request, but he did not argue, and he and Sir Tode wandered off to some unseen location.

Sophie soon found herself pacing the library with the Professor at her side. Professor Cake said nothing more of *The Book of Who* or her task, but only puffed on his pipe, a long trail of smoke curling up from the bowl. The two of them walked through the maze of stacks in relative silence. She stared at the thousands of books on thousands of shelves, all facing spine-in.

"Here's a shelf you might find interesting," Professor Cake said, stopping at the end of a row. "It's from HazelPort."

As Sophie followed him to a wide bookcase that looked to be made of sandstone, she caught the distinct smell of the ocean. "HazelPort," she said, recalling the name from *The Book of Who*. "That's Peter's home."

"HazelPort is where he was born, though I'm not sure he'd call it home." With the stem of his pipe, he pointed to a book on the middle shelf. "Have a look at that one, with the gold edging."

Sophie reached up and took the book from the shelf. It was a newly printed volume with gilded pages. She opened the cover—

An Oral History
of the Kingdom of HazelPort
as Faithfully Recorded by Sir Tode, Royal Storyteller
(with decorations by the traitorous and unworthy ape
Jawbone, whose life was mercifully spared by
the Good Queen Peg—long may she live!)

Just then, Sophie heard the light clopping of hooves on the floor. "I see you've found something truly inspiring!" It was Sir Tode approaching.

Sophie's eyes went wide, and she turned toward the knight. "You're a *royal* storyteller?" Before this moment, she had not known such a thing existed, but she was nonetheless impressed. She had, in fact, never met an author in person before. As you can imagine, it was a singularly thrilling experience. Should you ever be so lucky as to encounter an author in your life, you should shower her or him with gifts and praise.

Sir Tode preened with visible pride. "It's more of an honorary title, really. But I take the work seriously. That's the first of what I hope will be many volumes."

"Sir Tode is many impressive things," Professor Cake said. "But when he began his career, he was a hapless shepherd without a penny to his name. And Peter was less, even, than that."

"Quite right!" Sir Tode added. "As I say in my introduction: 'From the bitterest roots grow the sweetest fruits.'"

Sophie turned back to the book, flipping through the chapters, all of which had lovely, storylike names. She reached a chapter near the end called "The Vagabond King." It was marked with an illustration of a baby floating in a basket. Perched on the edge of the basket was a large black raven.

She began to read the chapter aloud: "'Now, for those of you who know anything about blind children, you are aware that they make the very best thieves—'"

"That's enough reading," said a voice right behind her. Peter had somehow reached her without making a sound. He pulled the book from Sophie's grasp and replaced it on the shelf.

Sophie stared at the boy, who seemed at once disdainful and afraid. However much Peter Nimble might have presented himself as a heartless mercenary, it was clear to Sophie that there was more to his story than that. And for reasons she could not quite explain, it was a story she very much wanted to learn. She turned to Professor Cake. "When do we leave?"

+ + +

Sophie, Peter, and Sir Tode made preparations to embark—preparations that chiefly involved eating a plate of honey biscuits and drying their muddy clothes by the fire. "Savor every bite," Sir Tode said, licking his mustache. "If there's anything my adventuring has taught me, it's that food is too often in short supply."

"Professor," Peter said through a mouthful of biscuit, "how do you think we should start? Do you know where the other books are?"

"If I knew that, I would have gotten the books myself." Professor Cake turned toward Sophie. "Perhaps you should ask the Storyguard."

Sophie shifted, uncomfortable. "Madame Eldritch was going to sell the book to some sort of collector," she said, wiping her hands on her skirt. "Maybe we should try to talk to him and learn more about the books." She held *The Book of Who* in her open hands. "Who was

Madame Eldritch going to find?" she asked. The book unlatched it-self and opened to an entry. She read it aloud for Peter's benefit:

> BARON MAGPIE: *Collector at the outermost*
> *edge of the Grimmwald. Currently resides in the*
> *Ivory Tower, lost library of the hinterland em-*
> *pire, whose shelves house* The Book of What.
>   ~For more information, see: *Book of Where*,
> "Ivory Tower," "Grimmwald"; *Book of Who*,
> "Storyguard"; *Book of What*, "Book of What"

Peter tilted his head. "So this baron has one of the other books?"

"That must be why Eldritch knew he would be interested in *The Book of Who*—she was planning to sell it to him." Sophie was becoming increasingly convinced that Madame Eldritch did not fully understand what *The Book of Who* was. If she did, she might not have been so eager to sell it to some rich baron.

"So we've got to get to this Magpie fellow," Sir Tode said. "But how do we find him?"

"The Ivory Tower is famous in hinterland lore," Sophie said. "It's an ancient library with thousands of books. But no one knows where it's located." She looked at the library. "Surely one of these bookcases could lead us there, couldn't it?"

Professor Cake shook his head. "Alas, I did once have a bookcase that led to the Ivory Tower. But a few years back, some fool bricked it up. Perhaps that's the work of our mysterious baron?"

"That would have been too easy anyway," said Sir Tode, never one to be daunted. "I'd imagine that one of these other cases could at least get us into the right neighborhood."

"Yes, but *which* bookcase?" Peter pointed out. "It could take years to find the right one."

Sophie held out *The Book of Who* and thought carefully before speaking. "Who owns the bookcase within this library that is closest to the Ivory Tower?"

The Book of Who opened up and turned to a new entry:

> SCRIVENER BEHN: *Nomad scribe from the Scarabian Peninsula. Storyguard of* The Book of Where. *History unknown. Location unknown. Fate unknown.*
>
> ~For more information, see: *Book of Where*, "Scarabian Peninsula"; *Book of Who*, "Storyguard"

"Well, that's not much help," Sir Tode said. "Practically everything about him is unknown."

Peter turned toward Professor Cake. "Professor, I thought these books were supposed to know everything."

"No, not everything," Sophie said, recalling how the books

had been able to tell her precious little about Professor Cake himself. "But it does tell us something—that his last known location was somewhere close to the baron's home."

"It is a curious omission, I'll admit," Professor Cake said, stroking his beard. "And I'm sure the reason for Scrivener Behn's being unknown is rather worth knowing. In the meantime, there is some good news, and that is that even if I do not know where Scrivener Behn is, I do know where his bookshelf is located in my library!" He turned, indicating for them to follow him up a winding staircase that led to a platform very near the ceiling.

Sophie soon found herself standing beneath a small bookcase that was crammed full of all manner of things—tarnished oil lamps, relish jars, hand mirrors, decks of foreign playing cards, a cage stuffed with painted birds' eggs, a pair of chain-mail gauntlets, and what looked like a goat's horn filled with rotting food. Pretty much anything you might imagine *except* actual books. Stranger still, the case itself seemed to be alive, rattling and shuddering in the wall. The junk on the shelves clinked and clanked loudly.

"I knew a bit of Scrivener Behn and his work," said Professor Cake, peering up at the case. "He used to carry this bookcase on his back, if you can believe it. He spent his life roaming the map, collecting stories from the different people and creatures he encountered. This bookshelf contained many rare treasures. Though, as you can see, it's no longer in use . . ." He reached up and prodded some of the rattling junk with his cane. "I haven't seen or heard from Behn in many years. As I said, he disappeared around the same time that your mother died." He scratched his bearded chin. "If nothing else, this case can get you closer to Baron Magpie and *The Book of What*, but I'm afraid you'll be on your own after that."

Sophie turned toward him. "You're not coming with us?" The thought of leaving the Professor—of leaving this place—suddenly filled her with a profound sadness.

The old man smiled. "I'm afraid you might find me a bit creaky for adventure." He rocked back on his heels, peering at the endless rows of books. "Besides, my work here keeps me quite busy. Yours is not the only world I hope to save today. Which reminds me . . ." He drew a golden pocket watch from his vest and consulted the face. Sophie noticed that the watch had a great many more hands than a traditional clock, and they turned in both directions. "I have a pressing appointment with a delegate from the Parliament of Rooks. Seems they're having a spot of trouble with something called an indifferencing engine . . ."

He returned the watch to his pocket and turned to Sophie. His face was missing its usual hint of a smile and instead looked quite serious. "Sophie Quire," he said, "you are a Storyguard. Just as your mother was before you. Remember your nature above all. If ever you doubt who you are or why you have been chosen for this task, you need only consult that book in your arms. The Four

Questions may reveal many answers, but they are not the *solution* to what plagues your world." He put his wrinkled hands on her shoulders. "*You* are the solution, Sophie."

Sophie had no way of knowing this, but these words were very similar to the words Professor Cake had spoken to Peter Nimble on the shores of his island two years before. They were words the man had spoken many times in his life, and words he would speak many more times in his future.

Perhaps Peter made the connection, for he gestured to himself and Sir Tode. "What about us?" he said. "Are we just tagalongs?"

"Gracious, no!" The man smiled at Peter. "You are the supplemental solution to whatever unexpected problems might hinder the primary solution in her journey!" He said this in the tone of someone hoping to elicit a laugh, but no laugh was forthcoming— probably because everyone else was still struggling to parse his logic. One thing was clear enough: This was not the answer Peter had hoped for.

"Yes, well . . ." Sir Tode chuckled. "I suppose it beats *sidekick* . . . or *pet.*"

"I should say so!" the Professor said, stepping back. He took his ostrich-spine cane, which he had hung from a nearby banister. "And now, if you'll excuse me, I must be off." He gave a slight bow and shuffled around a corner between two bookcases that Sophie had not noticed before. She listened for the sound of his cane tapping against the floor but heard only the crackling hearth several floors below.

"Did he just . . . disappear?" Sophie said. "How?"

Peter shrugged. "I find *how* is not a very useful question to ask when it comes to Professor Cake."

Sophie and the others turned back to Scrivener Behn's abandoned bookcase, which they hoped might lead them close to *The Book of What*. The bottom of the case was just slightly above eye level, making it quite difficult to see what might be on the other side. It shook and groaned above them, its contents rattling on the shelves. "I've seen a lot of bookcases in my life," Sophie said, "but never one that could move."

"The Professor indicated that it was portable," Sir Tode said. "Perhaps there's someone shaking it on the other side?"

Peter removed the enchanted bookend from his bag. "We'll find out soon enough." He reached up and felt along the bottom shelf for a place to fit the bookend.

Sophie studied the rattling junk. "I think maybe you should step back."

Peter snorted. "I think I can handle a big bad bookcase." He wedged the bookend onto the bottom shelf and turned the knob—

Crash!

The case swung open, and an avalanche of junk spilled out on top of him, knocking him to the ground. He cried out as he was pummeled by a seemingly endless stream of pots and pans and chairs and rugs and spindles and lamps and mirrors and baubles and hats. "Get back!" he sputtered, hacking his way free of a pair of ladies' stockings. "We're under attack!"

Sophie watched the encounter with no small amount of delight. She was reassured to see that Sir Tode was similarly enjoying the performance. "Righto, Peter," the knight said. "You show that laundry what-for!"

The tide of junk eventually tapered off, and Peter became more aware of his situation. He pulled himself free, his ears flushed red. "You could have warned me," he said, kicking a wooden goblet across the floor.

"I *did* try to warn you," Sophie said. "Or perhaps you're deaf as well as blind?"

Peter turned toward her, replacing his hat. "Who said I was blind?"

Sophie stared at the boy, who, despite his blindfold, seemed completely serious. She recalled what she had read in *The Book of Who* about Peter having "fantastic eyes." Perhaps that was more than a figure of speech? Before she could ask him why a boy who could see would wear a blindfold, Peter marched past her and hoisted himself up to the open case.

"Are you coming?" he said, reaching his hand down toward her.

Sophie gripped *The Book of Who* in one hand and took Peter's hand in the other. With some small struggle, she managed to climb up through the case with her dignity still intact. She found herself sitting in the back of an open wagon. Mounds of random junk lay scattered across the bed.

"Tally-ho!" called a voice behind her. The next moment, Sir Tode flew up through the hole and landed beside Sophie with surprising agility.

Peter retrieved his bookend and pulled the bookcase closed. "Well, that was a new one," he said, adjusting the bag around his shoulder. "You'll have to put that into your next chapter, Sir Tode."

"Indeed, I will!" Sir Tode exclaimed. "I shall call it 'The Case of the Rattling Bookcase.'"

"Speaking of rattling," Sophie said, raising her head. "Has anyone noticed that the wagon has stopped moving?"

"I did," said a quiet voice nearby.

Sophie leaned to one side, looking past the back of the wagon. A man stood behind them on the road, leaning casually against a tree. He wore a tattered red coat and had a patch over one eye. Slung across his shoulders were no fewer than three flintlock pistols.

A fourth pistol was in his right hand.

And it was pointed at Sophie.

TORVALD KNUCKLEMEAT

It is one thing to see a gun in the wild; it is another thing altogether to have a gun pointed directly at you. Sophie stared at the
man before her, who was watching her with his one good eye—the
other was hidden behind a black silk eye patch. The man smiled at
Sophie. "Down from the wagon, if you don't mind."

"Who are you?" she asked, pressing herself against the bookcase,
which was now firmly shut.

"My friends call me Torvald Knucklemeat . . . not that I have
any friends." He spat out a gob of tobacco juice through the gap in
his front teeth. "I'm the one who owns this wagon, which up until
recently was loaded to the brim with all manner of valuable goods—
goods belonging to me. One moment I'm hauling this old, empty

bookcase back to the city when I hear this big loud crash behind me. Imagine my surprise when I pull over to find two little stowaways—three, counting the pet."

Sir Tode growled. "I am no one's pet."

"Easy, kitty. I'll blow them whiskers right off your face." If the man had been startled to hear Sir Tode speak, he did not show it. He propped his elbow on the back of the wagon in a philosophical pose. "Now, I don't know why you lot thought to board this here wagon, but I do know that it was a hefty mistake."

Peter stepped right to the edge of the wagon. "The mistake was threatening my friends."

Sophie was just as worried about Peter as she was about the gun. She could tell he wanted to fight the man—but no blade, no matter how fast, could parry a bullet.

The man smiled up at Peter. "You must be the hero of the bunch. I've met my share of heroes. Not too fond of them, if I'm being honest. Heroes tend not to think things through. For example, they pick fights with men who've got pistols pointed at their girlfriends."

Sophie's eyes went big. "I'm not his girlfriend!" She knew it was ridiculous to be concerned about that in a moment like this, but some things cannot be helped.

He flashed a rakish grin. "Well, you ain't his sister—I can see that plain enough." He squinted, peering at her—it almost felt as if he were looking at her *through* his eye patch. "Where is it you're from, exactly?"

Sophie pulled her cloak tightly around herself. Something about his gaze made her flesh creep. "My father's from Bustleburgh. My mother's from . . . the Topaz Isles." This, at least, had been what *The Book of Who* had told her.

The man's eye widened. "The Topaz Isles, you say?" He worked the wad of tobacco under his bottom lip in a manner that suggested deep contemplation. "Aren't you the mysterious one."

Sophie stared right back at him, refusing to give him the pleasure of making her squirm. Torvald Knucklemeat was a tall man with a face that seemed to epitomize the word *rugged*. His skin was weather-beaten and tan. He had clearly not shaved for several days. The patch he wore over his eye felt almost excessive. The only clean part of him was a golden star that hung from the lapel of his threadbare coat. "That badge on your coat," she said. "You work for Bustleburgh."

"I'm a deputy officer," the man said, adjusting his badge. "The Inquisitor charges me to sniff out dangerous nonsense."

"Doesn't he have guards for that?" Sophie said.

"The easy stuff he leaves to the guards, but sometimes nonsense can be a bit shy to show itself. Lucky for me, I have an eye for such things." So saying, he lifted up the flap of his eye patch. Sophie, despite her discomfort, was too compelled to look away. She saw that his eye had been replaced with a cloudy glass ball that shimmered in the early-afternoon light. The skin around the eye was crisscrossed with angry red scars.

"What is that?" Sophie asked.

"It's a scrying jewel," he said, replacing the patch. "Swiped it from an old fortune-teller in the marshlands. I put it in myself— not pretty, but extremely useful in my line of work. Helps me spot unusual things."

"You put a jewel in your eye socket?" Sophie broke away from his gaze. "That's revolting."

"It's not *that* bad," Peter muttered.

Sophie looked at the remaining junk scattered across the wagon bed. Nearly everything in the wagon, she could now see, would qualify as nonsense. She turned over an old flowerpot with her toe— inside was a writhing crop of little bean sprouts. Beside it was a little mouse nestled inside a fur slipper. Beyond that, a Scarabian oil lamp that was unlit but still radiating heat. "The Grimmwald is supposed to be free," she said. "The No Nonsense laws don't apply this far."

"They don't, strictly speaking. Technically, I'm only supposed to gather things within city limits, but I find it's slim pickings nowadays—most nonsense types have pulled up and fled by the time I come knocking. So I cast my net a little wider." He gestured to the forest around him. "There's more bounty to be had out in these parts—and they don't know you're coming."

"You can't just seize people's things without a warrant," she said. "You're nothing more than a common *thief*." Sophie noticed Peter out of the corner of her eye. The boy lowered his head, his face turning red.

Knucklemeat laughed. "If the Inquisitor has a problem with my methods, I'm not hearing about it. It's all fuel for his Pyre."

"That sounds like Prigg, all right," Sophie muttered.

Knucklemeat's face lit up. "So you've met him?" He rubbed his chin in mock rumination. "Interesting. Very interesting . . ."

Sophie felt a tremor of alarm. There was something queer about this man. It was as if he knew far more than he was letting on. The sooner they got away from him, the better she would feel. "My dear deputy," she said in her most polite voice, "we came to your wagon by accident. The truth is . . ." She took a breath, deciding that honesty, perhaps, might be the best policy. "The truth is, my companions and I have come here in search of a man named Magpie."

Knucklemeat grinned. "You're looking for the baron?" He laughed, as if this were the funniest thing he had heard in a long time.

"So you know him?" Sir Tode said.

"I've done business with the man once or twice." Knucklemeat spat another glob of tobacco juice onto the ground. "He's a connoisseur—a collector. When I find something too pretty to let burn in the Pyre, I bring it by his castle. The baron likes one-of-a-kind things.

And he pays well." He nodded toward Sir Tode. "I'd wager he'd pay quite handsomely for that friend of yours."

"We're not selling Sir Tode," Peter said.

Sophie smiled as sweetly as she could, half wishing she had some of Madame Eldritch's befuddling perfume. "Do you think you could find it in your heart to point us in the direction of this baron's estate?"

"It's not half a day's ride from here, straight down the river," Knucklemeat said. "Not that it'll do you much good without an invitation. The baron's not one for unexpected visitors."

"We'll take our chances," Peter replied. He turned to Sophie. "Let's go."

"Not so fast," Knucklemeat said, raising his gun. "As we've already established, I'm a deputy officer. While I'd love nothing more than to let you go, that would be neglecting my sworn duty." He stepped lazily around the back of the wagon. "You see, I can't help but recall something the Inquisitor mentioned last time I saw him. Seems there's a fugitive who's given him a bit of a headache. A swart-skinned girl, right about your age, who assaulted him and his men. She made off with a very unusual book." His eye moved down to *The Book of Who*, clasped tightly in Sophie's arms. "Not unlike the one you're holding right now."

Sophie stepped back. "I'm sure you're mistaken." The idea that Prigg cared so much about finding her was distressing, to say the least.

Knucklemeat stepped closer. "More important, there's a bounty on your head. And that's not something I turn my nose up at."

"Don't you touch her," Peter said, charging toward the man.

Without missing a beat, Knucklemeat fired one of his guns—knocking Peter's hat clean off his crown. "Easy, hero. I'd much rather tie you up than bury you, but if you keep on like that, bury you I will." He slid the emptied pistol into the bandolier around his waist and drew a fresh one. "Howsabout you stow that blade?"

"I can't stow it," Peter said. He pulled up his sleeve to reveal the iron cap at the end of his arm. Sophie found herself again awed by the sight, and she wondered what might have caused such horrible scars.

Knucklemeat whistled, peering at the blade. "Is that giant-forged? I never seen the stuff up close. Definitely valuable. Wonder if it'll hurt when I cut it off." He grabbed a pile of shackles that lay in the bed and slung it over his shoulder. "Onto the ground, all three of you—we're taking a little trip." He stepped back from the gate. "Hands nice and high."

Sophie approached the edge of the wagon, but Peter did not move. He was facing the man, his jaw clenched, his breathing shallow. Sophie put a hand on his sleeve. "Peter, don't . . ."

The boy did not seem to hear her at first but then lowered his blade. "You really think thieves are that horrible?" he asked.

"I think dying is horrible," she whispered. "So let's listen to the man and get down from the wagon. Please? For me?"

"That's right, loverboy," called Knucklemeat. "Listen to your girlfriend and get down here."

"I told you, I'm not his girlfriend!" Sophie snapped. She picked up her skirts and climbed off the back of the wagon. Between the book and her dress, it was hardly graceful, but at least she made it without falling into the mud.

Sir Tode hopped down with little trouble and joined her side. "Stay back, Sophie," he said under his breath, so quiet that Knucklemeat could not hear. "And whatever you do, don't make any sudden sounds." The knight was watching Peter with a look of intense concentration.

Sophie looked up at Peter, who was still on the wagon.

"Fine," Peter said with a note of resignation. He raised his hands in surrender and jumped down from the bed. His feet hit the mud, and he slipped forward. "Whoa!" he cried, colliding straight into Knucklemeat.

"Watch it!" the man shouted. He grabbed Peter by the coat and shoved him hard against the wagon gate. He pressed his arm into Peter's neck, choking him. "You think it's smart to test a man with a gun?"

"Guns are a coward's weapon," Peter said coldly. "They're for people too afraid to get their hands dirty."

Knucklemeat struck Peter across the face with the handle of his gun and then pressed the muzzle against his cheek. "Do I seem afraid to you?"

"Peter!" Sophie tried to run toward him, but Sir Tode held her back.

"He knows what he's doing," the knight warned.

Sophie, however, was unconvinced. Knucklemeat had Peter pinned against the wagon, a loaded pistol aimed at his face. The boy, for his part, looked utterly unafraid. She heard a soft *click* as Knucklemeat drew back the flint hammer with his thumb. "Any last words, hero?"

"More of a question." Peter cleared his throat. "How do you plan to shoot me with an unloaded gun?" He held out his open hand—

A small lead bullet lay nestled in his palm.

"How . . . ?" Knucklemeat pulled the trigger on his weapon, but it responded with a dull *clack*. "That's impossible!" He pulled the trigger again and again, refusing to believe. "How . . . ?"

Sophie could not have said it better herself. She stared at the boy, her mouth open. "You . . . you stole a bullet out of a loaded gun?" She had seen Peter do incredible things, but this was entirely too much.

Peter grinned at her. "Maybe thieves aren't all bad?"

Knucklemeat stepped back from Peter, his face bloodless. "A

neat trick, but there's a reason I keep spares at the ready." He threw his useless weapon aside and reached for another pistol.

What happened next was very hard for Sophie to understand. In a heartbeat, Peter had somehow leapt onto the wagon gate and then flipped over Knucklemeat's head. In a single, singing motion, he whipped his blade down the man's back—cutting clean through his gun belt, which fell to the ground, leaving the man unarmed. He kicked Knucklemeat square in the rump, and the man tumbled down to his knees and into the mud with a tremendous *squish*.

"Bravo!" Sir Tode cried, then turned to Sophie. "Told you he knew what he was doing."

Knucklemeat lay on the ground, helpless, Peter's silver blade pointed at his throat. "What now, boy?" he growled. "You going to gut me?"

Peter stepped back and picked up the shackles that Knucklemeat had dropped when he fell. "No, now we're going to the baron's castle." He threw the chains into the man's lap. "And you're going to take us there."

✦   ✦   ✦

The journey through the Grimmwald took longer than Sophie anticipated. The forest seemed to grow wilder with every passing mile. The paths through the forest were muddy and narrow, many of them choked with ivy and weeds.

Knucklemeat sat beside Sophie on the driver's bench, clutching the reins, shackles jangling from his hands. He was singing a disgusting tavern song called "The Maggot and the Corpse"—a song whose length seemed to be limited only by the number of body parts the singer could call to mind. Sophie, meanwhile, passed her time browsing through *The Book of Who*, reading various entries about fantastical people long forgotten. Despite what Professor Cake had told her, she found it difficult to reconcile the notion that these were not merely storybook characters but actual people who had lived and walked upon the earth.

She happened—by chance, really—to turn to the entry on Peter Nimble, which she had first read in the shop. One line in particular leapt out at her:

. . . Wielder of the Fantastic Eyes . . .

She looked back at Peter, who was crouched in the bed of the wagon, keeping a careful watch over Knucklemeat—*watch*, in this instance, being a term of art. Or was it? She stared at the blindfold wrapped tightly around his eyes. "Peter?" she said, closing the book. "Can I talk to you about something . . . personal?"

Peter shifted slightly. "If it's about how much you despise thieves, I'd rather you didn't."

Sophie ignored this comment and continued. "When I first opened

The Book of Who, I found an entry about you in it. The book said you had 'fantastic eyes.' And then later, in the Professor's library, you made it sound as though you weren't blind at all . . ." This was not exactly a question, but her meaning was clear.

"That's because I'm not blind," Peter said, still facing forward. "Not anymore, at least."

Sophie noticed that Sir Tode had turned around to listen to the conversation. Perhaps he, too, was curious about Peter's answer.

"My eyes were pecked out by ravens when I was a baby," he said after a moment, and Sophie could tell that the memory still pained him. "I grew up completely blind, and that was all I knew. But then I met Professor Cake."

"The fantastic eyes," she said. "The Professor restored your sight?"

"It was a bit more complicated than that," he said, scratching Sir Tode between the ears. "Maybe Sir Tode can tell you about it when you've got the time. And knowing the way he goes on, you'd need *a lot* of time."

Peter had said this as if he were hoping to change the subject, but Sophie was not ready for that. "I don't understand," she said. "If you can see, why do you still wear a blindfold?"

Peter shrugged. He looked to be considering his words very carefully. "I'm not ungrateful for what the Professor did. I just feel more comfortable this way. I feel more like myself."

"Fantastic eyes," Knucklemeat muttered next to Sophie.

"Shoulda known it wasn't no ordinary blind boy who swiped my bullet." This was meant as a gripe, but Sophie thought he looked considerably comforted by the thought that he had been bested by some magical force.

CHAPTER NINETEEN
THE BOOK of WHAT

While Sophie and her friends were venturing ever closer to Baron Magpie's castle, they could hardly have imagined that Madame Eldritch was already there, comfortably installed in the man's parlor.

"You can imagine my surprise, Madame," said the baron as he poured two glasses of a glowing amber liqueur, "when I found your valet at my door holding your calling card." He handed a glass to Madame Eldritch, who sat on the edge of an eft–hide divan. "I am not accustomed to visitors, even less those who can navigate my quickbramble."

"Perhaps you forget that it was I who sold you the saplings?" Madame Eldritch brought the glass to her lips in a manner that thoroughly suggested drinking. She, however, knew better than to drink things offered to her by men like the baron.

Baron Magpie laughed, downing his own drink with hasty relish. He was a tall, fleshy man with a thin mustache, silver wig, and surprisingly small eyes. Though he claimed not to have been expecting company, he was smartly dressed in a violet waistcoat. "Yes, well, I'm a man who values his privacy. This tower was a lost ruin when I found it—parchments and books strewn everywhere. As you can see, I've put quite a bit of work into the place. I'm sure you recognize more than a few artifacts on the walls."

"Indeed, I do," Madame Eldritch said. The baron was one of her richest and most loyal customers. But he was also reclusive, and until this moment, she had never actually met him in person. "As for why I have ventured so far to meet you, call it a weakness of curiosity." She slowly traced one silk-gloved finger around the rim of her glass. "After so many years of doing business with the famous Baron Magpie, I found myself wanting to see him in the flesh." She did not so much speak this final word as carve it up on a platter.

"Famous?" The man wrinkled his nose. "I'm not sure I like the idea of being known in Bustleburgh. It's a bad business up that way—what with all that No Nonsense nonsense."

"Perhaps my private fascination has clouded my perception." Madame Eldritch rose from her chair but not before making the calculated move of unclasping her cloak, which fell from her neck to reveal her bare, perfectly smooth shoulders. "And now that I have seen your magnificent home, I can understand your desire to keep it a secret."

The baron's eyes widened ever so slightly, as if he were appraising a piece of art. "More ambrosia?" He took her glass, which had somehow emptied itself, and turned to refill it.

Madame Eldritch walked the length of the room, examining the vast assortment of rare and valuable objects: moon clocks and ebony urns and miniature fig trees and an entire cabinet dedicated to teaspoons. She wondered if this man even knew the power of the things he had purchased. She suspected he did not. Men like the baron were all about the pursuit. Give them a thing they desire, and all they can think to do is preserve it under glass.

"How *are* things in Bustleburgh?" the baron called, fresh drinks in hand. "Rumor has it, the whole city's been taken over by some pyromaniac zealot—Pigg, or some such—who's obsessed with burning magical artifacts." He offered her a glass. "A terrible waste."

Madame Eldritch did not share her own thoughts on the matter, which were complicated. She did not approve of Inquisitor Prigg or his ilk, but she very much liked watching things burn. "It is, at least, good for business," she said. Her gaze landed on something mounted high on the wall. "Is that what I think it is?" she asked, her lips slightly open.

"The jewel of my collection," the baron said with no small amount of pride. "A gelding—perhaps the last of its kind."

Before them hung the head of a unicorn. Its horn was narrow and slightly twisted. Its eyes were wide and glassy. Its skin was pulled tightly around its jaw to reveal a row of small teeth. A cluster of brittle white hairs clung to the chin.

"Cost me more than I'd like to admit," he said. "I tried to keep him alive, but he was quite old, as you can imagine. Couldn't bring myself to dispose of the carcass, so I had him stuffed."

Madame Eldritch stepped closer to the creature. "He is magnificent . . ." This woman who made a practice of letting nothing surprise her was genuinely awestruck. She wet her lips. "And the horn?"

"There's no magic in the horn, if that's what you're wondering. Apparently all that stuff about eternal life was just a rumor. Still, it's a remarkable specimen."

Madame Eldritch raised an eyebrow. "Indeed." The word *specimen* in regard to such a noble creature disgusted her. For all his wealth, Baron Magpie was still a fool. Of *course* unicorn horns could extend life, if prepared correctly. She herself was proof.

The baron smoothed the curl of his mustache. "Speaking of specimens, that's one I'd like to add to my collection." He regarded Taro, who was patiently sitting on the divan. "What is it, exactly?"

"*His* name is Taro," Eldritch said. "He is *Mandragora*."

"A mandrake! I've never seen one so large." The baron removed a monocle from his waistcoat and notched it under one eye. "Is it true what they say about the scream?"

"He is not for sale," Madame Eldritch said.

The baron laughed, clapping his hands. "You know me too well!" He leaned closer to her, lowering his voice so that Taro could not hear. "But perhaps I could change your mind . . ."

"I don't change my mind," she said coldly. "Ever."

At these words, Taro bowed his head and closed his eyes.

The baron laughed again, though this had not been a joke. "Don't sound so sure, Madame. In my experience, everyone has his price . . ."

Madame Eldritch noted his hungry expression and wondered if it had been a mistake to come to this place. She had learned some years before to always demand payment upfront from the baron, for every time she sent him a delivery, the courier always mysteriously disappeared. Perhaps the disappearances were not such a mystery after all?

"It is time we put aside pleasantries," she said, stepping back from him. "You asked before why I had ventured so far from Bustleburgh to visit you."

He nodded. "And you changed the subject."

She smiled, as though pleased with his observation. "As you know, I make it my business to find things that people desire." She walked past him, her fingers absently playing on the edge of a pedestal bearing a coin-encrusted skull. "I have recently encountered a certain book—a book that I believe might be of great interest to you."

The man arched an eyebrow. "I'm listening."

"It is an old book and looks very much to be out of use. The cover is animal hide of indeterminate origin, though I suspect salamander. On the spine is a curious mark." She stopped at a small window, which was foggy from the cold autumn air outside. Slowly, she drew four converging question marks on the glass.

The man stared at the mark, his eyes now very wide indeed. "And the title?"

Again, Madame Eldritch raised an eyebrow. "Judging from the look on your face, I think you already know the answer."

He set down his glass. "Come with me, please."

✦   ✦   ✦

Madame Eldritch and Taro followed the baron down a series of corridors, each one secured by doors that opened by lever. "You may have noticed that I keep few servants," he said, mounting a curved marble staircase. "Truthfully, I prefer my own company. I had an engineer from Bustleburgh run cables and clockwork through the walls of the entire castle—that way I can open doors and get about quite effortlessly. More important, it assures that none of my collection goes running off." He pulled a golden lever at the top of the stairs, and the door before him swung open.

He led Madame Eldritch along a narrow balcony that overlooked a ballroom with polished marble floors. The air was filled with a pungent, musky odor. A hundred different creatures growled and cooed and hissed and chattered below. "This," he said over his shoulder, "is my private zoo." From end to end, the hall was lined with tall golden cages arranged very much like pillars. Within each cage was a different type of animal, each one unique. There was a weeping rhino-saurus, a squawking dodo, a singing mouse, a slithering basilisk, a brooding ape, a silver goose, a shivering mooncalf, a three-headed dog, and even a small, emaciated griphon. The cage doors had no locks and instead seemed to be controlled by long chains connected to levers along the balcony—no doubt allowing the baron to open the cages without endangering himself.

Madame Eldritch walked the length of the balcony, peering at the hungry creatures beneath her. "Taro, stay close," she whispered as they followed their host down a narrow stairway.

The baron led them down several more hallways until they reached a pair of heavy wooden doors. "Here we are," he said, teasing the ends of his mustache. "The library." The doors swung wide to reveal a dimly lit room with floor-to-ceiling bookcases on every wall.

Madame Eldritch had, of course, heard of the lost library of the Ivory Tower, and, seeing it now, she was not disappointed. A casual inspection revealed thousands of ancient volumes, many thought to be lost forever, any one of which would have commanded a handsome price in her shop. The most unusual touch was an enormous silver tigress that lay curled up in a back corner. The moment Madame Eldritch passed through the doorway, the beast sprang to her feet and lunged toward her. A golden chain around her neck stopped the creature mere inches from Madame Eldritch's face.

Taro grabbed the tigress by the leash and threw her backward across the floor. The cat was on her feet in an instant. She roared and charged toward him.

"Down, Akrasia!" the baron said sternly. "Madame Eldritch is our guest."

The tigress stopped at his command. She growled and licked her teeth, pacing back and forth, her yellow eyes narrowed to slits. Madame Eldritch, who had very nearly been devoured, trembled at the not-unpleasant tickle of actual fear that had briefly seized her. "She is a magnificent pet. How long have you had her?"

"She came with the library," he said, laughing. "I've tried to get rid of her, but there's no getting past that chain."

The baron peered at his bookcases. "Ah! Here it is." He slid a book from his shelf and brought it to Madame Eldritch. It was an old volume with a dark green cover, iron furnishings, and a familiar mark on the spine. "The book is terribly damaged but priceless nonetheless."

Madame Eldritch took the book in her gloved hands. She opened the clasp and turned to the title page:

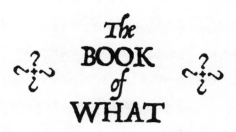

The BOOK *of* WHAT

Baron Magpie peered a little too closely over her shoulder. "It's one of four volumes, apparently. Each one named after a different question." He said this with the pedantic enthusiasm of a collector. "They're older than dust, and I'm quite keen to have the whole set."

Madame Eldritch turned to the next page and saw an unusual inscription. She read it aloud:

We four books—Who, What, Where, and When—
Hold all the world's magic bound within.
And when assembled throughout the ages,
Two words, when spoken, unlock our pages.
Impossible things of all shape and kind
Flow from the will of a curious mind.

"Some sort of riddle or silly joke," the baron said. "I can't quite make it out."

Madame Eldritch stared at the words, which to her were far from silly. She knew spells when she saw them, and this was a spell. "Impossible things . . ." she whispered. She wondered what the two words might be that could unlock the power within these books. She wondered what a person could do with such power.

"Yes, well," the baron said, "if you think you can find the others, I'd be willing to pay a great deal. There's nothing that plagues me more than an incomplete set."

"Indeed." Madame Eldritch knew that the wise course would be to return the book to the baron, but somehow, she could not bring herself to give it back to him. And in that moment, Madame Eldritch, who made a point of never changing her mind, changed her mind. She locked eyes with Taro, who gave no visible response. "The book is a fine specimen," she said, closing the cover. "Unfortunately, I was mistaken about finding its match. The book I encountered was not part of this set. I am sorry to have wasted your time."

"Are you quite certain? Perhaps I'd like to have it anyway."

Madame Eldritch slowly removed her gloves to reveal shining fingernails—freshly painted for just such an occasion. "Alas, I did not bring it with me. But perhaps there is still an opportunity for us to do business." She walked behind him. "What if I were willing to part with the mandrake?"

The baron turned toward her, his eyes wide. "Do you mean it, Madame?"

"Please," she said, stepping closer. "Call me Ezmerzelda."

The baron swallowed. "And you may call me Klaus."

Madame Eldritch smiled. "Klaus . . ." She ran a red fingernail along his flushed cheek. "Perhaps we could discuss the details someplace more private?"

Baron Magpie did not answer but for a dumbstruck nod. Madame Eldritch led the man from the library into the darkness of the hall, the heavy doors closing behind them.

Chapter Twenty

QUICKBRAMBLE

Afternoon passed into early evening, and the forest closed further around Sophie and her companions. They soon rounded a bend to find that the path was blocked with thickets. "We're getting close now," Knucklemeat said, and slowed the wagon. "This here's his garden."

Thorny black branches twisted and twined to create an impenetrable barrier. Sophie craned her neck, trying to see some sign of an entrance or path. "Those bushes are blocking the path," she said. "Why would he plant them like that?"

Knucklemeat sniffed. "Oh, you'll see." He continued driving until they were only a few paces from the brush. He pulled the reins and slowed the wagon to a stop. The horse nickered nervously.

"Everyone keep still, and try not to make any sudden noises." He urged his horse forward. There was a rustling sound as the bushes suddenly came to life, growing thicker and longer.

"Well, that's a neat trick," Sir Tode said, climbing onto Sophie's lap for a better view. "I don't suppose you've got some hedge shears in the back of the wagon?"

Tendril-like branches slithered and twisted, forming themselves into a sort of thorny gate. The branches shuddered as bright roses of varying colors appeared all over the gate.

Peter leaned close to her. "What is it?"

"What is it?" Knucklemeat repeated, amused. "Are you telling me you've never seen quickbramble before?"

Sophie looked at the man beside her, who appeared to be completely sincere in his assertion. "Quickbramble is extinct," she said firmly.

"Extinct?" The man rolled his eyes. "Spoken like a true Bustle-burgher. You don't believe a thing until it's coiled round your neck."

"It's obviously real," Peter said. He cocked his head as if trying to hear a way through. "How does it work? Is there a lock?"

"I'm not sure," Sophie said. "There's an old nursery rhyme about it:

"Quickbramble, quickbramble, ramblers take heed.
Pick right, you pass. Pick wrong, you bleed."

Like all children in Bustleburgh, she had grown up singing that verse, but she had never really paused to consider its meaning.

"That's pretty accurate," Knucklemeat said. "So far as nursery rhymes go." He gestured toward the flower-covered gate. "You see those roses?" Sophie looked at them, each one slightly different. There were normal rose colors, such as red and yellow and white, but mixed in with them were stranger hues—gold and cobalt and black and emerald and even one that looked translucent. "The brambles won't let you pass unless you pick the right color," Knucklemeat explained, "and the only person who knows that color is him who planted it. Unless, of course, you know what to look for." He tapped his eye patch.

"So which color is it?" Sophie said.

Knucklemeat peered at the flowers. "Ah, I think I see it—that pearly one near the top. It's a bit high up for you lot; you'll have to uncuff me so I can grab it." He held up his shackled hands.

"Not a chance," Peter said. He hopped down from the back of the wagon. "I'll do it."

Knucklemeat slumped back. "Can't blame me for trying."

Peter walked to the middle of the gate and raised his head, smelling the air. He pointed his blade directly at the rose that Knucklemeat had described. Its white petals shimmered like oil on water. "This one?"

"That's the one," the man said. "Watch out for thorns."

Sophie noticed a slight twitch at the edge of the man's mouth, as if he were suppressing a grin. She thought back on the nursery rhyme, recalling its final words: *Pick wrong, you bleed.*

She sprang up. "Peter, wait!"

But it was too late.

The boy had reached up and plucked the flower from the gate. The quickbramble sprang to life like a nest of snakes. Thorny tendrils grabbed hold of his arm and pulled him into the thicket. He flailed, slashing his blade, but more branches came and bound him tightly, lifting him clear off the ground. He uttered a stifled scream as branches snaked around his entire body and pulled him deeper into the shadows.

"Whoops!" Knucklemeat said, laughing. "Must have been wrong about that color. Clumsy me."

"Peter!" Sir Tode leapt to his feet.

But the boy either could not hear him or could not speak.

Sophie whirled around and grabbed Knucklemeat's arm. "Help him!" she cried.

Knucklemeat pulled his arm away. "Allow me a counteroffer: Uncuff me, and I'll tell you the right color."

Sophie looked back to Peter, who was now upside down—a rope of branches tight around his throat.

"We're losing time," Sir Tode said, his voice panicked. "Just give him the key!"

"Not yet." She turned back to Knucklemeat. "How do I know you won't just lie to me like you did to him?"

"You don't," he said. "But you'd better be quick in deciding—your boyfriend's looking a little blue in the face." He held up his shackled hands. "Tick, tock."

"Sophie!" Sir Tode hissed. "I appreciate your determination, but we don't have time for this. Peter's dying in there!"

Sophie lunged forward and snatched the reins from Knucklemeat's hand. "Hey!" the man bellowed. "What are you doing?"

"Keeping you honest." She snapped the reins, and the horse galloped straight into the quickbramble. The moment the wagon touched the gate, branches lashed out. The horse gave a piercing neigh as tendrils snaked around its legs and neck. The entire wagon lurched to one side; its wheels lifted clear off the ground.

Knucklemeat screamed as quickbramble grabbed hold of his body. "You stupid brat!" he snarled. "If I die, the rest of you die with me!" He kicked and thrashed as quickbramble wrapped around his feet and legs, holding him fast.

"That's the idea," Sophie said as thorny tendrils wrapped around her own body. "Which flower?"

By now the entire thicket had worked itself into a roiling mass of thorns. Peter was nowhere to be seen. Knucklemeat's horse uttered a chilling cry as it was dragged to the ground. There was a loud crack as one of the wagon wheels snapped to splinters.

Knucklemeat roared as black thorns dug into his neck. "Fine!" The man pointed a finger into the twisting branches. "It's over there! The green one!"

Sophie looked at a green blossom that was just above her head. She tried to reach for it, but a branch caught her hand short. "I can't reach it!" she said.

"TRY HARDER!" Sir Tode shouted from somewhere inside the thicket.

More branches were twining around her body, squeezing the breath from her lungs. Sophie lunged forward and grabbed hold of the flower with her mouth. She bit down on it and ripped it from the stem.

There was a crash as Sophie, Sir Tode, and the wagon fell back to the ground. The quickbramble quietly retreated to the edges of the path.

Sophie spat the flower from her mouth and scrambled to her feet. "Peter!"

The boy lay on the ground, his clothes torn to ribbons. Dark blood ran down his arms and face. "Are you alive?" She knelt beside him and took his head in her hands.

Peter lolled his head toward her. "That was . . . smart thinking with the carriage . . ." He gave a faint smile. "Though you could have been a little faster."

CHAPTER TWENTY-ONE

A COLD RECEPTION

O nce tamed, the quickbramble had been eerily accommo-
dating for Sophie and her companions. The branches pulled
away in front of the wagon to create a broad path that followed the
river to a rocky ledge at the farthest edge of the Grimmwald. No
sooner had they passed than Sophie heard a rustling sound as the
quickbramble crept back over the path behind them, sealing them
within the grounds.

They soon found themselves before a small castle at the edge of
a sheer cliff. Knucklemeat pulled the reins to slow his horse. "That's
the baron's home," he said. "He calls it the menagerie."

"The menagerie?" Sophie stared at the castle. "Why does he call
it that?"

"You'll find out soon enough." The man chuckled, as though this was a particularly funny joke.

Sophie stared at the structure, which glowed orange in the dusky light. It was a small keep with one tall tower, the color of polished bone. The castle was built directly over the mouth of a thunderous waterfall that spilled into the hinterland marshes a hundred feet below. Sophie thought of the countless stories she had read about the Ivory Tower's ancient, magical library—and here she was, actually about to step inside. She noticed a trail of smoke wafting from one of the many chimneys. "We're in luck," she said. "It looks like he's home."

"Not sure I'd call that luck." Knucklemeat shifted his weight. "You really think your little ruse will work?"

"It'll work," Peter said. So far as plans go, theirs was a fairly simple one. It had been decided that Sophie would pretend to be a merchant hoping to sell Sir Tode to the baron's one-of-a-kind collection. If what Knucklemeat had indicated about the baron was true, Sir Tode would be a more-than-appealing prospect. Meanwhile, Peter would sneak inside and procure *The Book of What*.

"All right," Sophie said to Peter as she climbed down from the wagon. "Wait till we're inside, and then sneak through one of those slotted windows. When you find the book, give a cry, and we'll all run for it." She helped Sir Tode wriggle himself into a birdcage they had found in the back of the wagon.

"Just make sure to take me with you when you run," Sir Tode said as she closed the cage door on him. "I don't like the thought of ending my days on display in some cage."

"What about him?" Peter asked, nodding toward Knucklemeat. "If I leave the wagon, he'll drive off the first chance he gets."

Knucklemeat made a mocking face. "You wound me."

Sophie put *The Book of Who* under one arm and then picked up the cage. "Chain his hands to the wagon wheel. If he can't reach the quickbramble blossoms, he's as trapped as the rest of us." She turned toward the castle steps and took a deep breath. "Wish us luck."

"I've got something better than luck," Peter said, rummaging through his bag. He pulled out Knucklemeat's gun belt. "I . . . um . . . I thought you might want this." He thrust his arm out, offering the gift.

Sophie set down the cage and took the belt. The four holster straps had been cut apart and retied to make wide, crisscrossed loops. "It's a book strap," Peter explained. "So you can carry the books but keep your hands free. The belt part might still be a little big. I . . . um . . . couldn't quite tell your waist size." He stepped back, adjusting his burgle-sack. "It was probably a dumb idea."

"No, it's perfect." Sophie slung the strap over one shoulder like a bandolier and cinched the buckle. She slipped *The Book of Who* into one of the four straps—it fit perfectly. She ran her fingers over the three remaining slots, each waiting for its own book. Soon another would be filled, and she would be that much closer to finding out the truth about her mother. She looked up at Peter, who was facing the ground, shifting his feet from side to side. "Thank you," she said softly.

"Adorable." Knucklemeat made a *tsk* sound. "If he's not your boyfriend, it's not for want of trying."

Peter straightened up. "You should get moving," he said to Sophie a bit brusquely. He grabbed Knucklemeat's chains and dragged him off the bench. "And you should keep your mouth shut." He wrenched the man's arms backward as he secured the shackles around one of the wheel spokes.

"Just keep him distracted," Peter called. "I'll give you to the count of two hundred before I go in."

Sophie turned back toward the castle. She picked up Sir Tode's cage and started up the long stone stairway. Sir Tode had been uncharacteristically quiet since escaping the quickbramble. She thought she knew why. "I should have just listened to you about unchaining Knucklemeat earlier," she said quietly. "Peter's life wasn't worth the gamble."

Sir Tode nodded, blinking. "Brave though he is, Peter's just a boy. It's easy to forget that sometimes."

"It won't happen again."

Sir Tode chuckled kindly. "I don't believe that for a second, Sophie Quire. You can no more stop being clever than he can stop being brash—it's almost like each of you was handpicked to antagonize the other."

They reached the top of the stairs, which ended at an impressive pair of wooden doors with an enormous golden knocker in the shape of a bird's claw.

"Wait," Sir Tode said. "First lock my cage."

Sophie looked at the cage door, which was shut but not latched. "That's not necessary."

"Of course it is," Sir Tode said. "You are a merchant, and you've come to sell the baron something very valuable, something that he'll desperately want. You must act the part—if you don't believe it, neither will he, and then we'll all be in trouble."

Sophie nodded and latched the cage. She smoothed out her skirts, hoping very much that this dress made her appear older than twelve. She thought of the way Madame Eldritch had spoken back in the oubliette when she was trying to sell her trinkets and potions: The woman had made each one sound lovely and just a little dangerous. Sophie brushed her hair from her face and took a deep breath. She took the knocker and struck it against the door three times.

For a moment, the castle was silent, but then she heard a ratcheting sound. The giant doors unlatched, slowly pulling apart as if of their own accord.

"Phantom doors," Sir Tode said, peering through his cage. "Is the baron a magician, as well?"

Sophie shook her head. "I heard gears shifting inside the walls." Some of the newer buildings and factories in Bustleburgh had automated clockwork running through them. But she had never before heard of someone rich enough to afford such a thing in his home.

"*Clockwork.*" Sir Tode uttered the word like a curse. "Terrible, sneaky stuff. Keep your wits about you."

Sophie carried Sir Tode over the threshold into the entryway of the castle. As soon as she was inside, the doors shut behind them. She walked into the foyer, her boot heels echoing with each step. She had never before been in so fine a space. Torches flickered along the walls, reflecting brightly off the polished marble floor. Before her stood a high rotunda flanked by two curved staircases and a series of doors covered in gold filigree. She stared at the shadows, searching for some sign of servants or valets.

"Which way are we meant to go?" Sir Tode said.

Sophie shrugged. A prickling at the back of her neck made her feel she was being watched. She cleared her throat and spoke to the empty room. "I seek an audience with the baron."

She heard a clicking sound, and the doors directly in front of her swung apart. The entryway filled with a pungent, musky aroma, and she could hear the sounds of animals growling and cooing beyond the open doors.

"I suppose that's as much a welcome as we're going to get," Sir Tode said. "Remember: confidence."

Sophie carried Sir Tode into an enormous open hall lined with tall cages that stretched up to the ceiling like pillars. Inside each cage was a different creature. Even in the dim light, Sophie could tell that these were not normal animals. Rather, they were beasts she had only read about in books. Beasts she never imagined to actually exist. And they all looked hungry.

Sophie clasped her mother's bell around her neck. The appearance of a little girl and a caged cat-man-horse in their midst had excited the creatures to distraction. They snarled and barked and slavered, rattling the bars of their cages. Sophie leapt back as a hinter-boar rammed its tusks against its cage, trying to bite her.

"I guess we know why he calls it the menagerie," Sir Tode said.

Sophie peered down the hall, which was dark but for the light of a crackling hearth at the far end. A rather rotund man was seated before the fire in a large chair. "Baron Magpie?" she called.

The man, who was facing away from them, did not answer.

Sophie adjusted her grip on Sir Tode's cage and approached. "Baron, we thank you for graciously allowing us to enter your fine menagerie. I have come with a business proposition that I think might intrigue you." She reached the baron, who had still made no move to greet or even acknowledge them. "I trust we have not offended you by calling . . . ?"

Still the man made no response.

Sophie felt a prickle of dread in her breast. She swallowed. "Baron Magpie?" She stepped around in front of the chair, and her voice failed her. Sir Tode's cage slipped from her hand and crashed to the floor.

Baron Magpie sat before the hearth, his eyes wide with fear. His face was deathly pale but for a sickening purple around his nose and mouth. A dribble of white foam ran from his dark lips.

"He's dead!" Sir Tode exclaimed from his cage, which had toppled to one side.

Sophie righted the cage and studied the man. "I . . . I think he's still breathing." She stepped closer, observing the baron's rattling breath. Tears welled in his unblinking eyes. "He can hear us!" She could sense his whole body quivering just beneath the skin, as if his every muscle was tensed. "He's been paralyzed by some kind of poison."

"Paralyzed?" Sir Tode said. "By whom?"

Sophie reached out and touched the man's cheek, which was cold in spite of the fire. Four thin red cuts ran all the way from his temple to his jugular—trickling blood. Sophie pulled her hand back. "Someone with very sharp fingernails."

Animals snarled and screamed all along the hall, beating against their cages, desperate to get free. Sophie took a step back. "We have to get out of here." She picked up Sir Tode's cage.

She heard a grinding sound in the floor and turned around just as the tall doors leading to the foyer clicked shut.

"We're trapped," she said.

Sophie felt Sir Tode shift his weight. "I'm curious," he said. "If the baron's right here, then who just closed the doors?"

"An excellent question," said a voice in the darkness.

There was a cascading rush of light as torches all along the hall came alive, illuminating the space. Sophie blinked and peered up to a long balcony. "Eldritch!" she cried.

Indeed, it was Madame Eldritch, looking as pleased as a poacher. Clasped in her slender, red-tipped hand was a green book that looked sickeningly familiar.

"Hello, little bookmender," she said warmly. "I was hoping you might stop by."

CHAPTER TWENTY-TWO

TRAPPED *in the* MENAGERIE

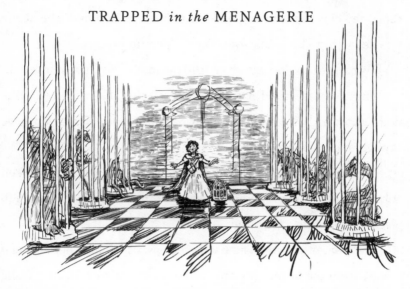

Sophie stared up at Madame Eldritch. The woman's face showed no hint of surprise or consternation. Taro stood beside her, looking placid as always. "I suspected you might not be so easily deterred in your search for the books," the woman called down. "As you can see, neither am I."

Sir Tode growled within his cage. "We have no quarrel with you, sorceress."

"Sorceress?" Madame Eldritch gave a delighted laugh. "You do me honor. I am a simple shopkeeper, nothing more."

Sophie fixed her eyes on the book in the woman's hand. "You murdered him for the book," she said.

"It was only a scratch." Madame Eldritch walked the length of the balcony, her red-tipped fingers running along the rail. Taro remained close behind her, his eyes trained on Sophie. "The baron was becoming a bit"—she eyed Taro—"presumptuous."

"Whatever could have given him the idea?" Sir Tode muttered.

The woman waved a hand dismissively. "He will live." She nodded toward *The Book of Who* at Sophie's side. "I see you have brought me my book."

"It's not *your* book." Sophie narrowed her eyes at the green volume in the woman's hand. "Neither is that one. I'll thank you to give it to me." She swallowed. "Please."

The woman raised an amused eyebrow. "You came here to steal a book from the baron. My only crime was in stealing it first." She lifted *The Book of What* and opened its pages. "I will admit, little bookmender, that I did not fully understand what you had brought me when you came to my shop. But now that I see what these books truly are"—she snapped the volume shut—"you will appreciate that I cannot part with it quite so easily as before."

Sir Tode stood in his cage, growling. "Madame, I demand that you release that book to us this instant, or we shall be required to take it from you by force. We have bested you and your manservant once already."

The woman's face darkened. "You will find it a bad mistake to threaten a woman such as myself. That is a lesson most only have to learn once." She walked her fingers to a polished golden lever that protruded from the balcony rail. Sophie saw more levers running along the length of the rail and deduced that these must have been what Madame Eldritch had used to operate the castle doors. "A frivolous man, the baron," she said. "He possessed so many great wonders but knew so little of how best to employ them. Take this clockwork, for example. An intricate web of mechanical cunning. But, like any web, it is only as dangerous as the spider who controls it." She wrapped her hand around the lever and pulled it.

Sophie heard a ratcheting sound from one of the cages beside her. Three of the polished golden bars were being lifted by a chain—releasing the creature inside. The beast, which looked like a small fur-covered octopus, spilled out onto the floor of the room. It righted itself, giving a horrible, birdlike squawk that echoed through the great hall.

"W-w-what is that thing?" Sophie said.

"I thought one so well-read as yourself would be familiar with the bush-squid," Madame Eldritch answered. "In my youth, the Wassail was teeming with them." Sophie had not heard of any such beast, and she wondered how long ago Madame Eldritch had been born to know such creatures. "We called them the Nine-Armed Death. They have a habit of snatching unsuspecting travelers from boats. After they blind you with their ink, they use their beaks to rip the spine from your body—quite painful, I'm told. This is a pup—newly born, at that," she said, sounding a tad disappointed. "I wonder if its mother is about."

Pup or not, the creature was terrifying. Sophie leapt backward to keep herself free of the squid's grasping tentacles. She held Sir Tode's cage tightly in her arms.

The bush-squid squawked at Sophie and started moving toward her. Black ink oozed from its furry appendages and spread across the slick marble floor. The beast was clearly unaccustomed to moving on polished stone and had to resort to a series of rolling lunges to reach its prey.

Sophie turned and ran as fast as she could toward the main doors. When she reached them, she pulled the handles, but they refused to move. "Peter!" she cried, pounding at the doors. "Help!"

"It seems your highwayman is nowhere to be found." Up on the balcony, Madame Eldritch walked to another lever. "As you can see, I have no shortage of animals that would be more than happy to make a meal of you and your friend. However, I would prefer not to let such a skilled bookmender die at the hands of senseless beasts. The exchange is simple: Give me the book, and I will release you."

"Never!" Sir Tode shouted from his cage.

"We need to find some other way out of here," Sophie said, scrambling free of the approaching squid. "Or at least get off this floor. The baron wouldn't make an enormous hall like this with only one door. There must be *some* other passage . . ."

"What about those?" Sir Tode pointed a hoof toward a row of gleaming golden levers directly beneath the balcony.

"It's worth a try," Sophie said. She had no idea what the levers might control, but it was their best chance. She clutched Sir Tode's cage and ran toward them.

Animals growled and snarled as she passed. Claws and talons and tusks rammed against the bars, trying to grab hold of her tender limbs. Sophie reached the row of levers and pulled the one nearest to her. She heard a ratcheting sound beneath her as a tile from the floor slid away to reveal a trapdoor. A rank odor of rotting flesh wafted up from the dark hole.

"I'm not sure I want to go down there," Sir Tode said.

"Me, neither." Sophie tried another lever farther down the line. This one controlled a small dumbwaiter beside the hearth where the baron still sat, paralyzed. The dumbwaiter slid open to reveal light from a room on the other side—a way out!

Madame Eldritch apparently saw the dumbwaiter as well, because her next action was to hastily pull her own lever. "I warned you, bookmender!" she called.

There was a ratcheting sound, and another cage opened before her. Inside the cage was an enormous creature that looked like a tusked ape. It had matted red fur and three-inch claws. The beast leapt from the cage, landing squarely on top of the approaching bush-squid. With a snarling roar, it ripped the bush-squid clean in half, then flung its twitching remains to the floor. The ape creature turned toward Sophie, a hungry look in its beady eyes.

"*That* one, I recognize," Sir Tode said, his voice quavering. "RUN!"

Sophie grabbed Sir Tode and sprinted toward the dumbwaiter. She heard a bloodthirsty howl as the ape charged after them on all fours, its fists cracking the marble as it thundered across the room.

She pushed Sir Tode through the opening, then clambered after him. The entire wall shuddered as the ape creature tried to tear its way through.

Sophie touched down on the other side to find a long, twisting hallway. She raced down the hall and up a narrow staircase, which led to two heavy wooden doors. The doors looked as if they might be able to lock from the other side. She heard an earth-shaking roar, which she assumed was the ape breaching the menagerie wall. She pulled one of the doors open and closed it behind her, latching it with a heavy metal bolt that she hoped would at least slow the ape.

Sophie dropped Sir Tode's cage. She was gasping for breath, her knees were weak, and she was having trouble focusing her eyes. Her hope of getting *The Book of What* had completely given way to the hope of mere survival. She knelt and tried to loosen the latch on Sir Tode's cage door, but her hands were shaking too much to be of any use. "The lock is jammed," she said. "It must have bent when I dropped the cage."

"Don't waste your time," Sir Tode said. "That ape's coming after us—not to mention Eldritch. We have to find a way out of here."

Sophie gave up on the cage door and forced herself to take a slow breath. She could still hear animals screaming and shrieking in the menagerie. She thought of Peter. He would certainly have heard the ruckus inside the great hall, but she had no way of letting him know where she had run to. She looked around the room. Rows and rows of books lined the walls, all of them in carved wooden cases that went right to the ceiling. "It's a library," she said.

There was a roar in the hallway and then a thunderous crash as the heavy wooden doors heaved and burst apart in an explosion of splinters. "So much for knocking," Sir Tode said. The ape stomped into the room, its nostrils flared. It grinned at Sophie, drool running down its matted beard. It licked its lips, revealing a row of jagged yellow fangs.

Sophie inched back from the creature, which towered over her. "Peter! Help!" she cried.

What occurred next was hard at first for Sophie to process— the events happened so fast that they came to her in a flash of disconnected sensations. She felt something soft brush against her arm and then heard a piercing snarl. The ape, which had moments before been bearing down on her, tumbled backward and crashed into the wall. There was a flurry of roars and grunts. Tufts of fur and what was very possibly blood filled the air. At last, the ape released a horrible, gargling howl and then slumped to the floor, dead.

Sophie stared at the wreckage, breathless. Standing atop the ape was a magnificent silver tigress, her white mouth ringed with blood. The creature regarded Sophie with narrow yellow eyes.

Sophie swallowed, unsure whether the animal was sizing her up for dessert or awaiting some other response. "Thank you . . ." she gasped. "We owe you our lives." She wondered if such an animal could understand her words.

The tigress slinked down from the corpse of the ape and bowed her silver head. "You are most welcome, my cub," she said. Her voice was creaky, as if she had not spoken for a very long time. "And now that I have secured your gratitude, perhaps you would be so kind as to answer the following questions. Who are you? And what are you doing in my library?"

CHAPTER TWENTY-THREE
THIEVING WAYS

Peter had counted only to ninety-six when he heard Sophie's first scream from inside the menagerie. The sound had been faint; he had barely heard it through the windows along the north-facing turrets. He spun around, his weapon raised. "Did you hear that?"

"What's the matter?" said Knucklemeat, who was lying in the mud, his hands shackled to the front wheel of his wagon. "Afraid your little ruse didn't quite go off as planned?"

Peter ignored the man, focusing his senses on the castle. He heard gears grinding deep within the walls and what sounded like doors swinging shut. "She's fine," he said, though he feared the opposite. "And if things get bad, she's got Sir Tode to protect her."

Knucklemeat gave a hearty laugh. "That little kitty—protect her? Why, he can't even scratch with those clumsy old hooves."

"Sir Tode's saved my life more times than I can count. And he's incredibly durable." This was true: More than once during their travels, Peter had seen his friend shake off what would have been killing blows to almost any other creature. Small though he might be, the knight had a talent for not dying.

Peter paced in front of the castle steps, his ears and nose alert for any signs of trouble within. He detected a foul bouquet of musk and dung wafting from the windows—the smell of wild animals. And below that—rising up from the ground, it seemed—was the rancid tang of rotting flesh. He turned back to Knucklemeat, who was humming to himself. There was something the man wasn't telling them about this place. "Just how much do you know about the baron?"

A high-pitched squawk rang out from the castle—it sounded to Peter like some sort of very large bird.

"That one I heard," Knucklemeat said. "I'd say either a pygmy roc or a bush-squid. If memory serves, the baron's got both in his collection."

Peter did not bother asking the man what either of those creatures was. Nor did he bother finishing his count to two hundred. In an instant, he had bounded up the castle steps and was standing at the front doors. But they were tightly secured, and he could find neither handle nor lock. He suspected rightly that the doors must be controlled by some mechanical system within the walls. With no lock to pick, he would have to find another way inside. He felt along the edges of the doorway until his hand took hold of some thick ivy that had grown up the wall. He grabbed it and started working his way up to a window on the second floor.

From inside the castle, he could hear new noises—animals roaring and screaming. He didn't know what was happening, but it didn't sound good. "Hurry up, you clod," he muttered as he pulled himself slowly upward. In his younger thieving days, he would have been able to scale the wall at twice the speed—but, having no right hand, the work was now considerably slower. By the time he reached the windowsill, his whole body ached terribly from the strain.

The window was secured with golden bars, which Peter was able to pry apart and slip through easily. He dropped to the floor and tried to gain his bearings. He was standing in a torchlit corridor. The noises he heard were all coming from beyond a door just across the way—a cacophony of angry animals all screaming for blood. He sniffed the air, trying to pick out the individual odors of different creatures. One familiar stench rose above the others. "Ape," he said.

Peter hesitated, unsure what to do: He had promised Sophie that he would find *The Book of What*, but what good was the book if she was dead by the time he brought it to her? The thought of

Sophie and Sir Tode encountering a wild ape made his stomach clench up—he himself had very nearly died at the hands of such creatures many times. And then he heard it, one small voice ringing out over the chaos—

"Peter! Help!"

Peter's hesitation vanished. If Sophie was calling for him, then any hope of tricking the baron was lost.

Peter sprinted down the hallway in the direction of her voice. He soon found a narrow door. Like the front doors of the castle, it had no lock, but Peter was able to run his hand along the seam and find the small spring mechanism that released the latch. The moment the door opened, his ears were assaulted with the sound of dozens of wild animals. The cacophony was very nearly more than he could stand.

Amidst the chaos, he heard one shrill cry: "Taro! Stay with the book!"

It was Madame Eldritch. Peter ducked behind a polished suit of armor and hoped she had not seen him. He had been lucky enough to survive one encounter with the woman's mandrake servant, but he didn't relish the idea of a second round. He heard what he thought might be Taro leaping over a railing to the floor below. By now, Peter had deduced that he and Madame Eldritch were standing at opposite ends of a long balcony that overlooked some sort of cavernous hall. From the sound of it, the chamber below was filled to capacity with dozens of animals, all of them beating against the bars of cages. He tried to listen for Sophie or Sir Tode but could no longer hear them.

"The bookmender begins to vex me . . ." Madame Eldritch's voice grew louder as she walked in Peter's direction.

Peter pressed himself against the wall, hoping very much that the armor beside him was keeping him hidden from view. He took a breath and slowed his heartbeat, trying to concentrate on the approaching footsteps. Madame Eldritch marched past him, and as she did, Peter caught a new odor that he had not detected before— the faint smell of very old pages.

Peter grinned and slipped out from his hiding place. He followed the woman to the end of the balcony, and when she stopped to open the door, he placed the tip of his blade against her nape. "Stand and deliver," he said.

Eldritch, who was already standing, slowly turned around to behold her assailant. "If it isn't our dashing young highwayman," she said in a tone that led Peter to believe she might be smiling. "I wondered where you had gotten to."

"This makes twice I've robbed you," Peter said. "I should think you'd be used to the feeling by now."

CHAPTER TWENTY-FOUR

AKRASIA

At the very moment that Peter was stealing *The Book of What* from Madame Eldritch, Sophie was standing in Baron Magpie's library, staring openmouthed at the silver beast that had just saved her life.

"That's a first for me," Sir Tode said from his cage. "A library with its own tiger."

"Not a tiger," Sophie whispered. "A *tigress*." She could tell from the narrow shape of the head that the beast was female. Female tigers were supposed to be smaller than males. But this creature was enormous—her eyes were nearly level with Sophie's own.

"You may call me Akrasia." The tigress eyed Sir Tode, still locked within his cage. Something resembling a smile crept across her face. "You have packed a lunch, I see."

Sir Tode stood in his cage. "If your aim is to intimidate, it will not work. You're not the only one here who has bested an ape in combat."

Recalling her manners, Sophie cleared her throat. "This is my companion, Sir Tode. My name is Sophie Quire." She tried to curtsy but found that her shaking knees were not quite up to the challenge.

"Hello, Sophie Quire." Akrasia licked her teeth, which were wet with blood. "The old witch spoke of you to the baron—the Bustle-burgh girl who had found *The Book of Who*." She walked a slow circle around Sophie, studying her like a loaded trap. "It is a remarkable volume you carry. May I ask how you came to be in its possession?"

Sophie placed an instinctive hand on the book. It was obvious that the tigress's question was far from innocent—obvious that she knew that the book was special. "It belonged to my mother."

The tigress stopped pacing. "Indeed?" She licked a front paw.

"Baron Magpie," Sophie said, "is he your master?"

Akrasia gave a contemptuous growl. "I have no master. I have a jailer." She stretched her neck to reveal a thick golden collar. Attached to the collar was a long thin chain that snaked across the floor to a bolt on the far wall—long enough to give her free rein of the library. "As you can see, mine is no common bond."

Sophie reached out and felt the collar. It was warm to the touch, half-buried in thick silver fur. She noted that it had no lock or clasp and wondered how it had come to be around the tigress's neck in the first place. The links of the chain were thin, no larger than what you might find on a necklace. "Surely you can break such a small chain." It seemed absurd that such a mighty creature could be held captive by such a slender tether.

Akrasia turned back to her. "The chain is small but powerful—it is an enchanted trap, commonly known as a widow's might. Once set, its bond is inviolable."

Sophie let go of the chain. "What does that mean?"

The creature lowered her head. "It means I will never taste the rain or feel the sun on my back. It means I will never feel the earth beneath my paws or swim in the river. It means I will live out the rest of my days tethered to this wall, guarding this library."

Sophie felt a pang of recognition and shame. How many times had she felt trapped in Bustleburgh? But seeing this majestic creature chained to a wall, never to see the world outside, she suddenly understood what being trapped really meant. "I'm sorry," she said.

"A bad business, enchantments," Sir Tode said, warming up to a favorite subject. "I am the victim of a pretty nasty hex myself. The hag who placed it on me ran off centuries ago, leaving me stuck in this absurd form for . . . well, forever." If his intention had been to cheer up the tigress, it did not seem to be working.

"It seems we are both abandoned creatures," Akrasia said. "You by your hag, me by my mistress."

"Your mistress," Sophie said. "Who was she?"

The beast's eyes flicked to *The Book of Who* at Sophie's side. "What does your book tell you, Storyguard?"

That the creature knew she was a Storyguard alarmed Sophie. But this did not seem like the time to ask her about it. Instead, she removed *The Book of Who* and held it in her hands. "Who was Akrasia's mistress?" she asked. At once, the book opened and flipped to an entry:

VEENA BLUESTOCKING: Storyguard and scholar from the Lower Antipodes. Notable works include The Seas Beyond the Sea *and* March of the Kobolds. *Former mistress to Akrasia, the tigress. Deceased.*

~For more information, see: *Book of Who*, "Akrasia," "Storyguard"; *Book of Where*, "Antipodes"; *Book of What*, "Four Questions"

"Veena Bluestocking . . ." Sophie stared at the name. "We have books written by her at the shop—I've read them all." She closed the book, looking up at the tigress. "Your mistress was a Storyguard. Just like my mother."

"And she was murdered," Akrasia said. "Just like your mother."

Sophie inched back, clasping the necklace at her throat. "You knew her?"

"Not only her, my cub." Akrasia stepped closer. "You and I have met before. Many years ago. My mistress brought me to your mother's bookshop. I was newly born then, as were you, and we played together at the foot of your mother's workbench. I'm sure you've been told that you bear a striking resemblance to her."

Sophie felt that shivering thrill that accompanies coincidences so extraordinary they can only be called fate. She certainly had no memory of playing with a tiger cub. Then again, she remembered very little from her infancy. But now, when she pictured herself at her mother's feet, she could almost see a small silver cat licking her face, its tongue coarse against her newborn skin. "Why were you at the shop?"

"Your mother had requested that my mistress come to her shop in secret. Your mother needed to consult *The Book of What*, which my mistress guarded. She confided to my mistress that she had read something troubling in her own *Book of Who* about one of the other Storyguard, something that frightened her a great deal."

Sophie stared at the creature's narrow yellow eyes. It was impossible to know whether she was telling the truth. "What was she afraid of? What happened to my mother?"

"There is only one person who can answer that question. His

name is Scrivener Behn." The tigress's voice had a dangerous edge. "It is but one of many things he must answer for."

"Scrivener Behn . . ." Sophie said. "He's another Storyguard, the keeper of *Where*. *The Book of Who* told us that his location and fate were unknown. Do you know where he is?"

Instead of answering, the beast snapped her head up, looking past Sophie. "Someone approaches," she said, growling.

Sophie turned around to see Peter racing down the corridor, something green tucked under one arm. "Peter!" Sophie cried. "We're in here!"

"Mind the dead ape in the doorway!" Sir Tode called.

Peter leapt over the carcass and landed beside Sophie, gasping for breath. "I . . . thought you . . . might want . . . this . . ." He held out a green book.

Sophie stared at the book—it had a green cover marked with four question marks.

"You found it!" If she hadn't been otherwise occupied, she might have very nearly hugged him. Instead, she ran her fingers over the pages, which were ripped along the spine. Holding a book in such need of repair made her regret being so far from her workbench. "How did you manage to get it from Madame Eldritch without her noticing?"

"Oh, I think she noticed," Peter said, sounding a bit too pleased with himself.

Sophie strapped the book to her belt and peered back at the hall. "What about Taro—did you defeat him?"

"Not exactly." He lifted his head, searching the air. "Where are we?"

"You are in my library," Akrasia said behind him.

Peter, who was not accustomed to people sneaking up on him, spun around. *"Who's that?"* His blade was right in the tigress's face.

"This is Akrasia," Sir Tode said. "She's a tigress who guards the library. She knew Sophie's mother."

Peter did not waste time on further introductions. Instead, he ran to the barred windows. "We'll have to see if we can pry these bars loose." He reached into his bag for a long metal file.

"Er, Peter," Sir Tode said, "before you get too far along, it seems we've managed to jam the lock on my cage—terribly embarrassing. Perhaps you might be willing to apply your lock-picking talents and set me free?"

"No time." Peter started filing the base of one of the bars. "We've got bigger problems."

"Bigger how?" Sophie asked.

"You know how the baron had all those wild animals locked in cages?" Peter said. "Well, they're not in cages anymore."

At that moment, a great crashing sound rang out from somewhere deep within the castle. The air shook with the howls and snarls and screeches of a dozen vicious monsters.

"Peter," Sir Tode said in a chiding tone, "what did you do?"

"I couldn't help myself," he replied. "Besides, I thought it would create a nice diversion."

"What's he talking about?" Sophie said.

The library shuddered as unseen creatures stampeded pell-mell through the castle.

Sir Tode gave an exasperated sigh. "Peter has a thing about cages—he can't pass one without releasing whatever's inside. Even if that something *wants to eat us!*"

"Let's talk about this later." Peter stepped back from the window, which remained barred. "We need to find another way out of here before—" He stopped in midsentence.

"Before what?" Sophie asked.

Akrasia pulled away from her and growled. "Before *he* finds us."

Sophie turned around to see Taro standing in the doorway of the library. His clothes were soiled and torn—she presumed that he had been forced to battle his way through many a hungry beast to find them. He cocked his head, his dark eyes fixed on the books strapped to Sophie's body.

Sophie inched toward Peter. "So when I asked you if you stopped Taro, and you told me 'not exactly' . . ."

"I meant *not exactly.*" Peter raised his blade and rolled back his shoulders. "En garde!" He leapt toward Taro, slashing his blade through the air.

Taro did not respond except to reach up and catch the blade before it struck his head. He wrapped his gray fingers around the tip of Peter's weapon, his eyes still on the books at Sophie's side. With a sharp movement, he flung Peter clear across the library. The boy sailed past Sophie, his body smashing into the far wall.

"Peter!" Sophie cried, rushing to him.

Peter rolled over, brushing splinters from his coat. "Keep behind me!" he said, squaring off in front of Taro.

The commotion in the library had been loud enough to attract other beasts. Already, a trio of razor-billed vultures had found the room and begun fighting over the body of the dead ape. Sophie heard a hissing as a feathered python slithered past Taro and into the room.

"I fear we are very quickly becoming outnumbered," Sir Tode said, cowering in his cage.

Sophie inched backward, reaching out for Akrasia. But the tigress was not there. Akrasia had retreated to a spot by the wall that housed a series of golden levers. Rising onto her hind legs, the beast took hold of a lever with her jaws and, with surprising alacrity, pulled it down.

Sophie felt a rumbling directly beneath her. A panel of the checkered floor pulled away to reveal a small trapdoor. As in the menagerie, the room filled with a foul stench that put her stomach into her throat. "What's down there?" Sophie asked, peering into the darkness.

"There is a sewer channel that leads out of the tower," Akrasia said, rushing past her. "Follow the river—it will take you where you need to go." With a snarl, she pounced on Taro. The tigress and the mandrake tumbled across the library and crashed into one of the wooden columns supporting the ceiling. Rubble rained down from above.

"What about you?" Sophie called. "We can't just leave you chained up here."

Akrasia sprang to her feet. "I will survive." She spat out a chunk of grayish flesh that might or might not have once been Taro's elbow.

Sophie felt Peter at her arm. "She's giving us a chance to get out of here," the boy said. "We'd be fools not to take it." He pulled her toward the open trapdoor.

Sophie grabbed Sir Tode's cage and, with a final backward glance at the tigress, leapt into the darkness.

CHAPTER TWENTY-FIVE

THE NINE-ARMED DEATH

Sophie tried to scream as she plummeted down the long, narrow shaft, but the rush of air took the breath from her lungs. She fell for what must have been at least thirty feet before crashing to the floor, Sir Tode's cage landing on top of her. To her relief—and then, immediately, dread—her fall was broken by something soft and slimy beneath her.

Sophie struggled to her knees. "What's down here?"

Peter, who had jumped after her and was already on his feet, helped her up. "I'd rather not say."

"Good heavens," Sir Tode exclaimed in the nasal tones of a person trying very hard not to breathe. "It smells like a sewer crossed with an abattoir."

"Follow the river, my cub!" A voice rang out high above them. "But whatever you do, don't raise the floodgate."

"Akrasia!" Sophie cried.

But Akrasia could no longer attend her. Taro had appeared at the opening and was trying to climb down after them. The tigress pounced on him and dragged him away. The two of them disappeared from view, battling their way across the floor of the library.

Sophie heard a giant crash, and the next moment, the opening was sealed shut by a fallen bookcase, leaving them in complete darkness.

"We have to help Akrasia!" she cried as rubble and books rained down on them.

She felt Peter's hand grab her own. "No—we have to keep moving."

Sophie picked up Sir Tode's cage and then took Peter's arm and followed him through the darkness.

For those of you who have never had the pleasure of visiting a dungeon, it will suffice to say that such places are as dreadful and damp as every romance and revenge-ballad has ever described. Most romances and ballads, however, leave out one crucial fact: Dungeons are generally built underground and, thus, have no windows. Without a torch to light the path, Sophie was forced to stumble blindly through complete darkness, clinging for dear life to Peter's arm.

"Just stay with Peter," Sir Tode said in a reassuring tone. "He's in his element down here."

"I wouldn't go *that* far," Peter said. "It would be nice to use my nose without gagging."

They soon came upon what Sophie assumed was the channel that Akrasia had spoken of. She could hear water moving beside her. She tripped, her dress catching on something brittle and sharp—something that clattered across the slick floor. "Please tell me that wasn't a skeleton," she said.

On this subject, Peter remained troublingly silent.

They soon came to a larger area that was dimly lit by two rows of open trapdoors in the ceiling. An enormous iron gate separated the chamber from the rest of the dungeon. "I think that's the menagerie up there," Sophie said. She could hear the distant roars of animals. The foul odor was stronger here, and, as her eyes adjusted, she began to realize why.

Huge deposits of dung and molted fur rose up from the ground like rotting mountains. Thousands of skeletons and animal corpses lay scattered across the stones, many of them with viscera still attached. She stumbled backward, her eyes fixed on a skull that looked disturbingly human. "I think I'm going to be sick . . ."

"They cannot hurt you," Sir Tode said. "Just close your eyes, and breathe through your mouth." Sophie slid her trembling fingers through the slats of Sir Tode's cage so that she might feel the warmth of his mane. She could not tell for certain, but she thought that the knight might be trembling as badly as she.

"Over here," Peter said, ahead of her. He was standing at the edge of the channel, where a few steps had been cut into the stone. Floating on the black water was a small shallow boat that put Sophie in mind of a psychopomp's ferry. "The tigress said we needed to follow the river, so we'll probably want a boat. You untether it, I'll work on a way out of here."

Sophie watched as Peter ran to the floodgate that separated the dungeon from the river outside. The gate was made of thick iron bars and, like all doorways in the castle, looked to be controlled by some sort of gear-based mechanism. Peter climbed up the metal bars to better examine the gears. "Once we're past this gate," he called, "it shouldn't be hard to row ourselves to shore."

"Just make sure we get to shore *before* that waterfall," Sir Tode said. "I've had plummets enough for one day."

"Wait!" Sophie called. "Akrasia warned us not to raise the floodgate."

"We don't need to raise the whole thing. I'm just trying to open this service hatch so we can slip through." He climbed up the side of the gears and started working on the release. "Just worry about that boat."

Sophie rolled her eyes and set Sir Tode's cage in the boat. She knelt down and started working on the thick rope tethering it to the walkway. The boat had clearly not been used in ages, and the knot was encased in a thick layer of slime, which she had no choice but to remove with her hands. She listened to the animal cries echoing upstairs and thought of Akrasia, fighting for her life in the library. "We should go back for Akrasia," she said. "She knows something about what happened to my mother—something she's not telling me."

"Perhaps so," Sir Tode said. "But currently, our goal is to keep you—and the books—safe. And that means getting out of this place before we're eaten alive."

A sharp clicking sound echoed from the darkness behind them. Sophie turned to see an enormous shadow slide between two mounds of carrion behind the dungeon gate. Its movements had a familiar, lurching pattern, and she thought she could see long ten-tacles moving across the floor. It rotated its body toward them, raw meat dangling from its beak. The creature raised its barbed limbs, which undulated in the darkness in a sort of hypnotic dance. Its red eyes glinted in the dim light.

Sophie stared at the swaying tentacles, a prickling nausea taking over her body. "I think it's another bush-squid."

Sir Tode peered through the slats of his cage. "This one's *a bit* bigger." He swallowed.

This was an understatement. The squid's head nearly touched the vaulted ceiling. Its long arms were thicker than tree trunks, its eyes the size of dinner plates. Sophie recalled what Madame Eldritch had said about the first squid being just a pup. "That must be the mother," she said, stepping back.

The enormous bush-squid wrapped its furry tentacles around the thick iron bars that separated it from fresh prey. It squawked and pulled violently on the bars, sending chunks of rubble falling from the ceiling.

"Peter, forget about the service hatch!" Sir Tode called. "Just get us out of here before that squid brings the whole place down right on top of us."

Sophie pulled out the last loop of the tangled knot. She gathered up her skirts and climbed into the boat. Once free from its mooring, it drifted along the current toward the gate. "We're on our way to you, Peter!" she called, trying her best to steer with a paddle she found in the bottom of the boat. "How's that floodgate coming?"

"Done." Peter pulled his hand back from a gear, which began ratcheting the gate up into the ceiling with a heavy *clink, clink, clink.* He dropped down from the archway into the boat, which sloshed perilously to one side.

The three of them drifted out of the dungeon and into the main river. Sophie took a deep breath of fresh night air. Since they had entered the castle, the sun had sunk below the horizon, leaving the sky a lightless purple. She stared over the cliff's edge at the endless marshland that stretched into the horizon—the farthest reaches of the hinterland empire.

There was a loud splashing sound from inside the dungeon. Sophie looked over her shoulder toward the place where the bush-squid had been. The iron gate that had separated it from the rest of the dungeon was no longer visible. She turned back around and began paddling more quickly.

"Easy," Peter said, gripping the side of the boat. "It's not a race."

"The bush-squid," Sophie said, still paddling. "I think raising the floodgate set it free."

She looked down at the water, which had suddenly taken on a hue as black as ink. She plunged her paddle into the water again, but this time something grabbed hold of it. The entire boat jolted to one side as the oar was ripped from her grip. The paddle disappeared beneath the surface and then burst up again, broken in two. "Forget about rowing to shore—we have to get out of here," she said. *"Now."*

Already the boat had drifted to the center of the river and was moving quickly with the current toward the edge of the waterfall. Sophie leaned over the front of the boat and began paddling with her hands.

"Um . . ." Sir Tode said. "Are we really sure that over the waterfall is our best option? Not all of us are strong swimmers—especially when locked in cages."

There was a loud splash directly behind them. Sophie's eyes went wide as a thick, furry tentacle rose from the water. "Peter, get back!" She grabbed his coat and pulled him toward her just as the tentacle lashed down, attaching itself to the side of the boat. There was a splash as three more tentacles appeared and latched themselves similarly, holding the boat fast against the current. Sophie kicked at one of them with the heel of her boot until it slithered back.

The water sloshed over them as the head of the creature, as large as a haystack, broke the surface. The beast opened its enormous beak and released a deafening squawk that made Sophie's ears ring.

Soon all nine tentacles were out of the water, grasping for the boat. "Back, foul beast!" Sir Tode cried, trying with little success to strike an attacking tentacle with his hooves. The tentacle coiled itself around his cage and lifted Sir Tode over the water.

"Get down!" Peter spun around, very nearly taking Sophie's head off. His blade sliced through the tip of the squid's tentacle—cutting it in half. Sir Tode's cage flew through the air and landed on the bank of the river with a violent clatter.

The squid's remaining arms flailed in pain, releasing the boat once more to the current. Sophie and Peter spun around as they slid ever farther away from Sir Tode, who was kicking at his cage door with all his might.

"Stay there, Sir Tode!" Peter called. "We're coming!"

"No!" Sophie caught his arm. "We can't go after him."

"Let go!" Peter shouted, pulling himself free. "What are you doing?"

But Sophie never got the chance to explain this to Peter—for it was at that very moment that the boat slid over the crest of the waterfall and plummeted into the depths below.

PART THREE
WHERE

CHAPTER TWENTY-SIX

INTO *the* HINTERLANDS

Sophie blinked her eyes and found herself staring up at a swirling gray sky that was at once blinding and dim. She was lying in the boat from Baron Magpie's dungeon, the stench of death still clinging to the rotting planks. Her clothes and hair were soaked through, and her cloak had been placed upon her like a blanket.

"You're awake," Peter said, standing over her. He offered her a strange gourd that was filled with water. "Drink this."

Sophie pulled herself up and sipped from the gourd. Her stomach ached terribly, and it was all she could do to keep herself from bringing the water back up. "What happened?" she asked, gripping the sides of the boat, which sloshed to one side as she moved.

"We went over the waterfall," Peter said, taking a seat on the bow. "The current swept us down a few miles before letting up. Now we're just floating." He busied himself with carving some letters into the side of the boat with the end of his hook: *The Scop.*

"We're in the outer hinterlands?" Sophie wondered aloud. She peered up at the swirling fog that blotted out the sun. They were traveling through a flat, marshy land covered in ancient, twisting trees. Glittering moss clung to every surface. Beams of golden light shone down through the fog overhead, illuminating the river, which snaked back and forth among the trees and vines. The entire place was alive with the tics and chitters of frogs and insects. Though it was still autumn in Bustleburgh, down here the air was warm and wet, like summer after a storm. "How . . ." She sat up. "How long have we been here?"

"All night. When we fell down the waterfall, you were flung from the boat and carried off by the current. Your head struck a rock, and you went under."

Sophie touched her head and found a painful cut on the crown. "And you saved me."

Peter shook his head. "Not me. Him." He nodded toward a spot behind Sophie's shoulder. She turned around and saw Taro sitting directly behind her on the stern, his hands folded calmly in his lap.

"How did you . . . ?" She inched back from him. "What are you . . . ?" Try as she might, Sophie couldn't formulate the proper question. Finally she settled for a simple "Why?"

Taro did not answer.

"He's been sitting there like that all night," Peter said. "Just watching you sleep. Pretty creepy, if you ask me."

Sophie decided that if Taro had meant to hurt her, he would have done so already. They were—for now, at least—safe. "I don't know why you did it," she said. "But . . . thank you nonetheless."

Taro, as usual, said nothing in reply.

Sophie sat up on the bench and examined the rest of the boat. A hole in the floor had been plugged by Peter's burgle-sack. Someone had fashioned a makeshift oar out of fronds. "Where's Sir Tode?" she asked, suddenly remembering what had happened with the giant bush-squid outside the castle.

Peter lowered his head, stopping his carving. "He's still up there somewhere—the water was too fast. By the time the current let up, we were miles away."

Sophie reached out and clasped his shoulder. "Peter, I'm so sorry."

The boy pulled away and began rowing. "It's my fault," he said, his voice tight with anger. "He asked me to unlock his cage, but I couldn't be bothered—I was so focused on escaping. If it weren't for that, he could have gotten away from that creature. He'd still be with us."

"You can't blame yourself like that," Sophie said. "Sir Tode knew exactly what he was doing—he lived for adventure. And we still have one way to check on him." She drew *The Book of Who* from its slot in her harness. The pages were wet but otherwise unharmed. "Who is Sir Tode?" she said. The cover opened and flipped to an entry, which she read aloud for Peter:

> *SIR TODE: Formerly Shepherd Tode, knight errant from the Valley of Nod, royal storyteller of HazelPort. Hexed by a hag during the Tournament of Boots to roam the earth in the combined body of a horse, cat, and man. Known accomplice of Peter Nimble.*
>
> ~For more information, see: *Book of Who*, "Peter Nimble"; *Book of What*, "Hags"; *Book of Where*, "Valley of Nod," "HazelPort"; *Book of When*, "Tournament of Boots"

"See?" she said, closing the book. "If he were deceased, the book would say it." She was not certain about this point but desperately hoped that it was true. "And something tells me it would take more than some old squid to do him in."

Peter nodded, as if willing himself to believe it. "Did I ever tell you about the time he slayed a fire-breathing dragon back in his shepherding days?" He gave a slight smile. "Well, he didn't slay it, exactly . . . It choked on one of the sheep in his flock."

Sophie laughed despite her horror. "I'm sorry I brought you to that tower," she said, more serious. She found herself wondering about these adventures he and Sir Tode spoke of. Could they really all be true? Then again, she reminded herself, she was living an adventure—one as perilous as in any book she had ever read—and it was all because of them. Perhaps Peter and Sir Tode drew catastrophe toward them as a lamp draws moths?

"The way I see it," Peter said, "the sooner we find your books, the sooner we can go back for him. Besides, Sir Tode would never approve of us quitting midquest. So where do we find the next book?"

"Akrasia said we're looking for Scrivener Behn—that's the Storyguard Professor Cake told us about. She told us to follow the river, so at least we're going in the right direction."

"And you trust her?" Peter said, sitting beside her.

"I don't know. I think she's hiding something, but I also think she wants us to find the books. She saved my life from that ape—she didn't have to do that." Sophie drew *The Book of What* from her harness and opened the cover. The book had a deep cut running up from the bottom of the spine. "It looks like someone tried to rip it in half."

"Maybe your tigress friend got hungry?" Peter ventured.

"Or maybe someone tried to take *The Book of What* and she didn't like that?" Sophie said, recalling how Akrasia had referred to it as *her* library. "Someone like Madame Eldritch," she said, looking at Taro.

Taro's face betrayed nothing.

"Either way, we need to keep moving." Peter leaned over the book. "What should you ask first?"

Sophie knew the answer to that—it was the very question she had tried to ask Akrasia before they were interrupted. "My mother used *The Book of What* shortly before she died. She found something in it that frightened her." She held the book out in her hands. "What was my mother looking for?"

She closed her eyes, bracing herself for the cover to swing open, but it did nothing. "What was my mother looking for?" she asked again, but the book remained silent. "What's the point of having a magic book if it doesn't work?" Sophie threw the book down.

"Maybe Akrasia was lying to you?" Peter said.

"Or maybe it's something else," she said, lifting the book back up to examine its damaged pages. "This tear in the spine . . . Maybe that prevents it from working."

"Well, that stinks." Peter gave a theatrical sigh. "If only we knew someone who was able to repair damaged books."

"Knowing how is one thing," Sophie said, "but without the right tools, I can't—" She stopped short.

"What is it?" Peter said.

Sophie did not answer but reached into her pocket and retrieved the parcel that Madame Eldritch had given her in the carriage. "My mother's bookmending tools." She removed the leather cord and unrolled the bundle across her knees. She ran her fingers over the worn tools. They filled her entire body with an electric energy. It was as if she had reached back through time and felt her mother's warm touch. She studied the tear in *The Book of What*, inspecting the frayed edge of the spine. "Eel skin," she said.

"What?" Peter asked.

Sophie set the book on the bench and started arranging her work space. "These pages are vellum—they need to be patched with something that can bend without cracking. I need you to dive into the water and get an eel or some other sort of fishy creature—the larger, the better."

Peter hesitated, poking his paddle into the murky water. "Can't you just—I don't know—stitch them back together with thread?"

"Not if I want them to stay in one piece," Sophie replied. "The first law of restoring books is that you never damage the original materials—stitching with thread would mean making holes in the pages. We need to patch them."

Peter sighed. "Fine." He set down the paddle and began to remove his soiled shirt. "No peeking," he said.

Sophie averted her eyes but then remembered that Peter could not see her. She watched him as he unlaced his shirt and pulled it up over his head. Sophie gasped slightly to behold Peter's bare back. He was pale and thin, almost emaciated. Scars and bruises and cuts covered his entire body. Some of the wounds looked very old, but some looked recent. She wondered if this was the price he paid for moving blindfolded through the world—and if so, why would he *choose* such a life?

Sophie heard a sound behind her and turned to see that Taro was also staring at the boy, his dark eyes unblinking. Sophie remembered how Taro's own figure looked similar to Peter's—worked over with cuts and scratches. But Taro's pains were the result of his servitude to Madame Eldritch, whereas Peter served neither mistress nor master.

"I'll have to swim clear of the river's current," Peter said. "Keep the boat moving—I'll catch up with you." He removed his boots and then dove into the water. He made almost no sound as his body disappeared beneath the surface. Sophie peered over the edge, trying to watch him as he swam around a bend to a small cove along the bank. She turned back to Taro, who was fixedly watching *The Book of What* on the bench.

She scooted toward him. "Taro, why did you save me from drowning?"

Taro blinked but did not reply.

Sophie reminded herself that Taro had to be treated a bit like the books—only capable of answering questions phrased in the proper way. In Taro's case, the question needed to be something he could answer without speaking—something that could be answered with a yes or a no. "Did Madame Eldritch tell you to protect me?" she said.

Taro shook his head.

"Did she tell you to protect Peter?"

Again, he shook his head.

Sophie watched his gaze, which had not left *The Book of What*. "Madame Eldritch told you to stay with the books, didn't she?"

Taro nodded.

Sophie sat back. "Which means you didn't really rescue me. You were just trying to save the books from getting carried off by the river. Isn't that right?"

At this question, Taro finally looked up from the books. And instead of nodding or shaking his head, he did something Sophie had not expected—

He *shrugged*.

Sophie folded her arms, feeling that peculiar irritation that comes from conversing with the taciturn. "Well, if you think that makes me any less grateful, you've got another thing coming. Books or not, you saved my life. And yet you obey Madame Eldritch like a slave. What hold does she have over you to inspire such blind loyalty?"

Sophie did not expect an answer, but here again she was surprised. At the mention of Madame Eldritch, he looked away from her, his thin mouth tugged upward in a slight smile.

✦ ✦ ✦

Peter returned half an hour later with three wriggling eels skewered on the end of his blade. The creatures had silver skin that shone iridescent in the hazy light. "You'll need to cure them first," Peter said, putting on his shirt and boots. "And we could use the food." He set to work making a small fire, using flints from his bag.

"Are you sure it's wise to start a fire on a boat?" Sophie asked as he made sparks over a pile of dry moss he had scraped from a low-hanging vine.

"I wouldn't call it wise," Peter said, "but you need eel skins, and there's only one way to get those—unless you prefer to just rub bloody gobs of raw fish meat on the pages. Plus, I'm hungry."

Sophie watched him, a little confounded. In Bustleburgh, getting dried and stretched eel skins was as simple as going to the market. Here, however, she would have to make them herself. She and Peter spent the next several hours stretching and pounding strips of eel skin until they were so thin they could see through them.

After that, there was a matter of making paste to affix the pages to the newly constructed spine. For that, Peter went out and brought back some tree sap, a handful of mushrooms, and a little bit of moss, which Sophie thought might make a serviceable epoxy. She set to mixing the ingredients in a mortar made from a half gourd.

Taro had by now taken an interest in Sophie's work and was watching over her shoulder as she ground the ingredients with the pestle that had once belonged to her mother. "It's not bonding,"

Sophie said, wishing very much she had some way to boil the ingredients down—or at the very least some mineral spirits.

Taro tapped her shoulder and then reached to his neck, where a small tendril had begun to grow. He winced as he tore the fiber from his neck and offered it to her.

"Are you sure?" Sophie asked.

Taro nodded.

She dropped the root into the gourd and mixed it in with the other ingredients. Taro's tendril worked like a charm (for, indeed, it was a charm), and the mixture instantly turned into a perfect epoxy—as clear and smooth as honey.

"Thank you," she said, adding, "I can see why Madame Eldritch values you so highly."

Taro did not answer but looked away and closed his eyes.

Within the hour, Sophie had managed to affix long eel-skin patches to the damaged pages of *The Book of What*. She ran her fingers over the work, which—despite the less-than-ideal conditions—was as fine as any she had ever done. She hoped her mother would have approved.

"First things first," she said, putting her tools aside. "What did my mother search for in *The Book of What*?" At once, the book's cover swung open on her lap and flipped through pages. It came to an entry near the back:

ZEITGEIST: Elemental creature summoned and controlled by force of will. It is thought that these creatures were responsible for the creation of the Fourth Age of Magic, as well as for bringing about a peaceful resolution to the War of the Bees.

~For more information, see *Book of When*, "Seven Ages of Magic," "War of the Bees"

Sophie read and reread the words. "I don't understand," she said. "Why would she need to find this entry?" Unfortunately, there was no such thing as a *Book of Why*, and so her question remained unanswered.

"Akrasia said that your mother was concerned about one of the other Storyguard," Peter said. "Maybe you should ask the books about that?"

Sophie looked up at him. "You weren't even in the room when she said that."

"Don't forget who you're talking to." Peter smiled. "I can hear a lot more than I let on. For example, I'm fairly certain that roasted eel doesn't agree with your stomach."

Sophie squirmed, feeling suddenly very uncomfortable. "Moving on," she said, and she took out *The Book of Who*. "Who was the Storyguard my mother was afraid of?"

The cover swung open, and the pages flipped past until they settled. Sophie stared at the open book, a jagged edge where the page had been torn out. "No . . ." she said, staring at the page that wasn't there.

"Who is it?" Peter said. "Who was the Storyguard?"

"I don't know." Sophie looked up from the book. "But they also murdered my mother."

CHAPTER TWENTY-SEVEN

TWO SURVIVORS

Inquisitor Prigg stood over the wreckage of the Ivory Tower, a lost library that had once been the jewel of the hinterland empire. He knew of the place, of course—everyone did. But he never considered that he might actually find himself standing at its doors.

With Pyre Day so close, Prigg had not intended to venture this far from town. But when his deputy Knucklemeat had staggered into his office, bloody and tattered, with a story of his escape from the hands of the Quire girl and her as-yet-unnamed rescuer, he knew a personal trip was necessary. Prigg had ordered two dozen of his best men to accompany them to the scene of the crime. He had ridden out on his steed, which had been followed by a windowless carriage with sides of solid iron—the contents of which he dared not leave unsupervised, not even for a day.

"This here's the spot," Knucklemeat said as Prigg dismounted his horse at the foot of the castle. "I'll be expecting the city to reimburse me for my troubles—and that includes a new holster for my guns."

"If you bring me that girl," Prigg said, "you will have all the holsters your avaricious heart desires." He looked out over the smoldering field of quickbramble that had until that afternoon blocked the road. It had taken six of his men half the day to burn a path through the writhing thicket. He consoled himself with the thought that he had perhaps just eradicated the last known quick-bramble plant in the world—one could hope, at least.

Prigg and his men entered the castle, which they found in complete shambles. Wild beasts ran freely about the hallways, eating and defecating wherever they saw fit. Pillars and doors and windows throughout the entire structure had been damaged beyond repair. The entire eastern wing—including two bedrooms and a library— appeared to have collapsed altogether, leaving little more than a few animal corpses and a pile of rubble. Strewn throughout the rooms and hallways was a vast assortment of strange goods and artifacts— things that had long ago been outlawed in Bustleburgh.

"It seems our baron had a penchant for nonsense," Prigg muttered as he picked his way through the wreckage. He gave orders for his men to collect and inventory whatever illegal goods they found—including the beasts, which were to be dosed with ether and corralled in the foyer.

The full scope of Baron Magpie's turpitude became apparent when they reached the ballroom. The man had apparently been using the space to house a sort of private zoo. Enormous cages were spread throughout the hall—all of them now empty. It seemed that the Quire girl and her accomplice had elected to release these abominations from their confines before fleeing the grounds.

Prigg found the baron in that same room—or what remained of him, at least. His body had been fairly picked over by the escaped animals, leaving scarcely more than his bones and a pair of velvet slippers. "A man who trades in nonsense digs his own grave," Prigg said as his guards carried the remains past him.

"Well put!" Knucklemeat said, sounding a bit too familiar. "Let's hope there's a similar end for those damnable brats who done it—a hearty meal for a pack of wild beasts."

"Language, Deputy," Prigg said. "The man who utters vulgarities incriminates only himself." He continued his tour of the castle, ending in the main foyer, which his soldiers had converted into a base of operations. An enormous pile of illicit goods lay at one end of the room, beside it, a cluster of wild animals, all sedated and chained. "What's the final count?" he asked the guard who had saluted upon his entrance.

The guard consulted a list. "Two vultures, a rhino-saurus, a glob of singing pudding, some sort of winged donkey, a very large frog, and this." The man held up a battered birdcage. Inside sat a small creature resembling a cat with hooves. The creature shivered, its wet fur clinging to its tiny body. "We found it in the mouth of that great, ugly octopus thing on the rocks—looks like the monster choked while trying to swallow the little fellow whole." He rattled the cage. "How's that for lucky?"

"I wouldn't call it lucky," said a small voice within the cage.

The guard cried out in alarm and dropped the cage. "It s-s-speaks!" he stammered.

"Indeed." Prigg knelt and stared at the wretched little creature, still huddled behind the mangled bars. He narrowed his eyes, noting the way the hair around its snout rather resembled a mustache. "I do believe we've met before."

"*Indeed,*" the creature said in a mocking tone. "I do believe I had the pleasure of head-butting you in the rump." He bared his teeth in a grimace.

The guard, who had apparently recovered from his shock, picked up the cage. "You want me to put him with the rest of the beasts, sir?"

Prigg stood. "Not just yet. He is an accomplice of the fugitives. We will keep him for questioning."

Another guard approached from the hall. "Sir, we found

something in the big room. It's a . . ." He appeared to blush. "You may just want to see for yourself."

The guard led Prigg and Knucklemeat to a corner of the ballroom that had been buried under a collapsed balcony. The wreckage had since been removed to reveal a large golden cage. Huddled on the floor of the cage was a woman with auburn hair and pale skin. Her dress had been torn up one side to reveal a scandalous glimpse of milky thigh.

"Now, that's a fine specimen," Knucklemeat said with a revolting leer.

The woman lifted her head and met Prigg's gaze. "At last, I am rescued." She burst into tears.

"That's quite enough of that." Prigg removed a handkerchief and tossed it to the floor of the cage. "What are you doing in there?" he asked the woman.

"I am a simple shopkeeper from Bustleburgh." The woman stood, dabbing her dark eyes with the handkerchief. "The baron kidnapped me and kept me prisoner in this cage. He tortured me, used me as his slave. I am only grateful that you came before I could starve." Prigg observed that the woman looked far from starvation. She turned her head, letting her auburn hair fall provocatively upon her bare shoulder. "You may call me Ezmerzelda."

Prigg stepped back. "I know well who you are, Madame Eldritch. You sell drugged tea in Bustleburgh." He had, in fact, heard that she sold much more in her shop. "I am surprised to find you so far from the safety of the city."

"No more surprised than myself," the woman said. "I had given up hope of being rescued, but now you are here."

Prigg put his hands behind his back and paced the length of the cage. "Forgive me if your story fails to excite my sympathies. That tear in your skirt was not made by tusk or tooth; it was done by your own hand. Your hair is disheveled but not dirty. As for those tears? Well, you would not be the first woman to employ such a tactic on an unsuspecting man." He allowed himself a small chuckle. "Madame Eldritch, I believe the more likely scenario is that you played a part in all this wickedness, and when the beasts got loose, you realized this cage was your safest bet for survival." The woman's face hardened slightly as he said this, which was all the confirmation he needed. "A sound plan but for one unfortunate complication: The collapsed balcony appears to have broken the release mechanism on your cage door, leaving you trapped in earnest."

The woman gave a smile that looked rather forced. "An impressive deduction."

"It is common sense, nothing more." Prigg took back his handkerchief. "If your own actions have led you to this place, I see no need to intervene." He turned toward his guard. "Leave her." Prigg and his men started for the door.

"Wait!" the woman cried. "The girl you search for—the girl who did all this—I know who she is."

"As do I," Prigg shouted back. "She is a bookseller's daughter."

The woman clutched the bars of her cage. "But I know *where* she is going—my loyal servant Taro is with her now."

Prigg, despite himself, turned toward her. "Go on."

The woman raised her eyes to meet his. All traces of the demure victim had vanished—replaced with the spark of a huntress. "Take me with you. And I will lead you straight to her."

Prigg considered this for a moment. "Very well," he said, and continued through the foyer toward his horse and carriage. "Lock her up with the cat," he said to one of his guards. "We leave immediately."

The guard saluted. "Yes, sir. And the nonsense? There are several very valuable items—jewelry and paintings and such. What shall you have us do with those?"

"We have no need for such things," Prigg said. "Burn them."

The man faltered. "What of the animals, sir?"

Prigg eyed the creatures, all huddled together in a corner. "Burn them," he said. "Burn them all."

CHAPTER TWENTY-EIGHT

THE NIXIES *of* KETTLE BOG

Sophie, Peter, and Taro had traveled nearly two days on the winding river. With every mile, the land became more and more wild and overgrown. The ceiling of fog, which had seemed almost warm at first, had since turned cold and suffocating. What had once been a rushing river was now an ambling slough.

Sophie spent her hours studying the books of *Who* and *What*. It was thrilling, finally, to have the ability to compare footnotes between entries of people and objects—of course, she still didn't know the *where* and *when,* but these two were enough, at least, to piece some things together. She soon found herself slipping into the comfortable space of a reader. It was almost as though she had never left her father's bookshop.

Sophie noticed that Peter had taken to facing toward the Grimmwald as they sailed—the direction of Sir Tode. "Yesterday I could hear the animals from the menagerie crying out above the marshes," he said, adjusting his grip on the paddle. "Now the sounds are gone."

Sophie wondered if he had heard Sir Tode's voice among those cries. "It's not your fault," she said, looking up from her books. "Sir Tode knew what he was doing."

Peter turned toward her, his expression difficult to read behind the blindfold. "If he hadn't been in that cage . . ."

"The door was jammed," Sophie said, putting her books aside. "You couldn't have helped him out even if you wanted to. Not with Eldritch chasing us."

"It's not that," Peter said. "He shouldn't have been in that cage in the first place."

"Well, the cage was my idea," Sophie said. "So if you want to blame anyone, blame me."

"You're not listening!" Peter snapped.

Sophie shifted her weight. It was clear that the boy was speaking of something that went beyond what had transpired at the menagerie. "Explain it to me," she said.

Peter sighed, shaking his head. "Sir Tode wasn't meant to be like that—cursed in that body. Professor Cake gave us a bottle with a message in it—a message from a hag begging for someone to help her. If we rescued her, she would have surely helped Sir Tode. We had a cure, right in front of us. All we had to do was sail out and find her."

Sophie recalled what they had told her that night in the bookshop. "Sir Tode said the hag was gone."

"She was, by the time we got there," Peter said. "But we didn't go right away. I wouldn't let Tode leave." He sighed again. "I begged him to go on *one more* adventure instead. And then another after that, and another after that."

"I don't understand," Sophie said. "Why wouldn't you go find the hag right away?"

Peter shrugged. "Sir Tode is the only friend I've ever had. I think I was afraid that if he changed, if he was turned back into a man . . . maybe he wouldn't need me anymore." He swallowed. "If we had gone to the island right away, then the hag might still have been there. And Sir Tode would have been cured, and he wouldn't have been inside that cage."

Sophie did not know what to say to this. "When we get *The Book of Where*, we'll use it to find him." She placed her hand on his, only for a moment, and then resumed her reading.

✦   ✦   ✦

The river continued to bleed into the land, becoming ever more shallow. By midafternoon, Sophie could hear rocks and sticks scraping their little boat's hull, as if trying to run it aground or pull it under.

"We're stuck," Peter said after their boat finally stopped in a flat, swampy area that reeked of sulfur and decay. The water was stagnant but for the places where bubbles burst from the steaming surface.

Sophie stared at the bubbling marsh. "Kettle Bog," she said.

"You've heard of this place?" Peter said.

"In old hinterland fables. It's said those who set foot in the bog never return. Only, I can't remember why . . ."

"In my experience, those sorts of reports are usually a bit exaggerated," Peter said. "One thing's clear, though: These waters are no good for boat travel. We're going to have to continue on foot." He slung his burgle-sack over his shoulder and gingerly hopped to a felled tree nearby. "Come on," he said, extending his hand for her to grasp. "We should get to firmer ground before we're sucked under." He was right; the bog had already begun to pull the boat beneath its greedy surface.

Sophie cinched the harness around her shoulders and secured the books of *Who* and *What* into their slots. She took Peter's hand and followed him onto the tree, which was slick with iridescent orange moss. Taro, as ever, remained close behind her.

The three of them inched along the slick trunk, which began to sink under their weight. Sophie grabbed hold of Peter with both arms as the trunk rolled to one side and they sank into the warm muck. She shrieked as something slithered past her ankle. "Did you feel that?" she said, gripping Peter's arm. "I think there's something down there."

"I suspect there are lots of somethings," Peter said. "Stay close." Carefully, they waded through the bubbling bog, but with every step, they sank even deeper. Sophie noticed that the water was unseasonably warm for this time of year. "I think we're standing on top of a sulfur deposit," she said, now up to her waist. "That would explain the bubbles—not to mention the smell."

"Good to know," Peter said, trying with little success to wade through the mire. He opened his bag and started digging inside.

"No, it's not good," Sophie insisted. "A gaseous pocket beneath wet earth creates a silt-trap. We can easily be sucked under." She tried to pull her foot up but found it firmly caught in the mud.

"Calm down," Peter said. "You act as if you haven't seen quicksand before." He pulled a coil of rope from his bag. "All I have to do is loop this around one of those trees, and we can pull ourselves free." Using one hand and his teeth, he quickly knotted the end of the rope into a large noose.

"Oh!" Sophie fell to one side as she felt something cold slide past her skirts. Taro, who was still behind her, grabbed her shoulders and helped her right herself.

Sophie turned back to Peter, who had yet to throw his rope. "Do you think you could hurry a little?"

Peter, however, did not answer. He was facing the far end of the swamp, his face set with alarm. "We're not alone," he whispered. "There's someone else in the—"

"WORM!" A bellowing voice split the air.

Sophie turned around to see a large man in the bog behind them. The man was hardly dressed for the conditions, wearing only a vest and an open shirt, both of which were marred with mud and swamp weed. His face was a shifting blur of features that never quite settled into place.

"You miserable little worm." The man took a step closer. "I warned you, if I ever saw you again, it'd be your head."

Sophie at first did not understand what the man was referring to, but then she realized that he was speaking not to her but to Peter.

"Mister Seamus . . ." Peter said, almost in a whisper. "How could . . . How did you find me?" All the blood had drained from his face, and Sophie could see that he was trembling.

"Thought you could escape me, worm?" the man said with a snarl. "Thought you could leave me to rot in that stinkin' fish heap?" The man sloshed through the bog toward him. "GET BACK HERE!"

"Don't touch me!" Peter staggered backward, slashing his blade through the air.

"Peter, no!" Sophie cried. But it was too late. Peter had fallen into the bog.

Sophie grabbed his arm and tried to pull him free, but she succeeded only in dragging herself deeper under. Meanwhile, the man, who seemed to have grown even taller, was wading toward them, still screaming, "WORM!"

Peter huddled against Sophie, cowering. "Don't let him take me," he said, whimpering. "Don't let him . . ."

"Taro, help!" she cried. "Stop him!"

Taro lunged for the man, but the second he touched his arm, the man disappeared into a wisp of pollenous smoke. Taro was left holding a creature that looked like a knot of seaweed with one large yellow frog's eye. The creature croaked and slipped from Taro's grip, wriggling back beneath the water.

"Peter," Sophie whispered, "you're safe. He's not real. He's not real."

Real or not, the damage had already been done—Peter was up to his neck in the bog and struggling to keep afloat. Sophie and Taro tried to pull him free, but they succeeded only in getting themselves stuck, as well.

"Stay calm," Sophie said. "If you struggle, you'll only make it worse." She felt another creature swim past her waist. Whatever it was, there were more than one of them. The bog was now alive with croaking sounds. She let go of Peter with one hand and drew *The Book of What* from her belt. She unclasped it and opened the cover. The pages were wet, but she knew that wouldn't matter.

"What creatures live in Kettle Bog?" she cried. The answer came quickly:

> *NIXIES: Freshwater sirens known to populate a marshy region of the hinterlands called Kettle Bog. Nixies possess a unique sensitivity to the fears and desires of those near them, which they often mimic to lure prey to its death. Famous victims include: Gunter the Large, King Hansel, and Peter Nimble (imminent).*
>
> ~For more information, see: *Book of Who*, "Gunter the Large," "King Hansel," "Peter Nimble"; *Book of Where*, "Hinterlands," "Kettle Bog"

"Nixies," Sophie said, snapping the book shut. "Of course!"

Perhaps you have heard of nixies in your own reading? If you have, then you know them to be a breed of shape-shifting predators that appear to gullible fishermen in the form of scandalously shaped maidens or buckets of treasure in the hope of luring said fishermen to rocky shores. It is widely believed that nixies can change their appearance to reflect the innermost desires of their prey. These particular nixies, however, seemed to be doing the opposite— inciting panic so that their victims might be sucked into the bog. So far, it was working.

Sophie, Peter, and Taro were now up to their necks in the simmering mire. "Stay calm," Sophie called. "They're trying to drown us. If we don't move, they can't hurt us."

She heard splashes as two more copies of the brutish man Peter had called Mister Seamus rose from the water. "*Worm!*" they both shouted, and they lunged for the boy.

"They're not real, Peter!" she called. "They can't touch you." But the boy had already disappeared into the bog.

Sophie spat out a mouthful of acrid sludge, struggling to keep her head above the surface. She could feel more nixies around her, swimming past her legs and waist. "Help!" she cried, her eyes blurring with tears as she slipped beneath the mire.

However bad drowning in water may be, drowning in mud is unquestionably worse. The feeling of thick sludge as it fills one's nostrils, ears, and mouth is like a squishier version of being buried alive. A slow, muffling terror overtook Sophie as she felt her body slip deeper into the slough. Her heart throbbed in her head, and her limbs ached from the pressure of the mud, which was slowly crushing her. Her last thought was of the books of *Who* and *What*, which would also be lost to the bog. And with them would go all hope of finding the truth about her mother.

A loud splash jolted Sophie from her stupor. Something heavy— something *real*—had plunged into the mud next to her head. "Grab hold!" a voice cried from somewhere above.

Sophie felt something near her fingers and grabbed hold of it. It seemed to be a chain connected to a large slab of stone. She felt the tether go taut as it pulled the stone—and her—up through the suctioning mire.

Sophie's head broke the surface of the bog. She gasped, tasting air again. She clung to the chain as it dragged her out of the water and onto shore. She collapsed on the peaty ground, coughing up muck and water and bile. She opened her eyes to see the line that had saved her life. The thin gold chain was bolted to a heavy stone that lay behind her. The other end of the chain snaked across the ground and out of view. Sophie's eyes followed the chain until she found herself staring into the eyes of her rescuer. "You!" she said, still gasping.

Akrasia stepped out of the shadows. "Hello, Sophie Quire," the creature said. "It seems our paths cross once more."

CHAPTER TWENTY-NINE

BLOOD FOLLOWS

Sophie and Akrasia worked quickly to rescue Taro and then Peter from the bog. Taro seemed relatively unharmed, but Peter had swallowed quite a bit of mud and was not breathing when they first pulled him out. When he suddenly started coughing and sat up, it was all Sophie could do not to throw her arms around him.

All three of them had dozens of nixies clinging to their bodies like leeches, and it was delicate work to remove the creatures. The books of *Who* and *What* were both wet but otherwise undamaged. Sophie cleaned them off as best she could with the hem of her cloak, which was itself muddy. Also muddy were her boots and hair and dress, and even the inside of her mother's bell necklace.

"It is lucky I came when I did," Akrasia said as Sophie wrung out her hair. "If I had found you a moment later, it might have been corpses I fished from the bog instead."

"I don't know why you keep saving me," Sophie said. "But I'm grateful nonetheless."

"It is I who should thank you." The beast lowered her head. "I was condemned to spend my life chained to that library wall. As you can see, that wall is no more." She pawed the block of rubble at the end of her chain. "I have your masked friend to thank for that. If he had not started that stampede in the menagerie, I would be chained there still, burned alive."

"Burned?" Peter said, sitting up. "Did the animals start a fire?"

"They did not. A Bustleburgh officer and his men came after you escaped—he was looking for a girl who had assaulted one of his deputies. He had his men set fire to everything they found—books, artifacts, even the animals. They called it all *nonsense*."

"Inquisitor Prigg," Sophie said. "He must be following us. But why?"

"Perhaps the answer is closer than you realize." Akrasia glanced down at the books of *Who* and *What*, which lay beside Sophie. "Where those books go, blood seems quick to follow." Again, Sophie had the feeling that the creature knew more than she had chosen to reveal.

"What about Sir Tode?" Peter said. "Our friend who was stuck in the birdcage?"

"The hoofed cat. I remember him." Akrasia bobbed her head as if considering whether to answer. "He was captured by the men. There was talk of forcing him to reveal your location."

Peter chuckled. "Good luck with that." The news that Sir Tode had been captured alarmed Sophie, but it seemed to put Peter at ease. Perhaps getting captured was something Sir Tode had experience with?

"They also found the potion seller," Akrasia continued. "She promised to lead them to you in exchange for her life." Upon hearing that Madame Eldritch was alive, Taro looked up. Sophie thought she caught the hint of a smile behind his stitched mouth, as though he was gladdened to hear of her survival.

"How would Madame Eldritch even know where we were going?" Sophie asked.

Akrasia turned toward Taro and growled. "How, indeed?" she said, stepping near. "Perhaps this one is leaving a trail of breadcrumbs?"

Sophie rushed between them. "Taro's with us," she said firmly. "Don't hurt him."

The tigress bared her teeth. "I am not accustomed to being ordered about by children."

Sophie felt herself pulled backward as Peter stepped in front of her. "If you touch Sophie, I will skin you alive," he said to Akrasia. Sophie was surprised to see Taro standing beside Peter, hands raised—they were both protecting her.

Akrasia, for her part, looked completely unmoved by the display. "Spare me your posturing," she said, licking a paw. "If I wanted the girl dead, it would be as simple as letting you lead her down another waterfall or through another bog."

Sophie touched Peter's arm. "Akrasia saved our lives," she whispered. "She won't hurt us."

Peter remained where he was for a moment, clearly torn. He stepped back. "If she makes one false move, I'm going after her."

"You are welcome to try," Akrasia said. The tigress turned from him, sniffing the air. "We should keep moving if we value our freedom." She pushed into the brush, the chain and stone dragging behind her. "The Bustleburgh soldiers have horses and wagons and fresh supplies. I venture to say they will overtake us by sundown tomorrow."

"Us?" Sophie called.

Akrasia stopped at the bend, looking coyly over her shoulder. "Of course, little bookmender. You and your companions have liberated me from my cell, and I must repay the debt." She flicked an ear. "If your swim with the nixies has proven anything, it is that you three would not survive the hinterland marshes without a guide. I can take you to the one who wields the next book."

"Scrivener Behn," Sophie said. "You know where he is?"

"I know where he *was*, and that is enough." Akrasia raked her claws against a tree trunk. "I excel at finding things that wish to remain hidden."

Sophie put her books away and climbed onto the rock next to her. "How will you find him? Did he tell you where he was going?"

"He did not have to. I am a hunter. I can follow his path."

Peter, who was some distance behind them, made a scoffing sound. "You're telling me you can still tell where he went. *Twelve years* later?"

"Perhaps not his exact footsteps, but the direction he traveled, yes."

"She's lying," Peter said, catching up to them. "Even I couldn't smell a trail that old."

"I am a tigress. We do not hunt by smells or sounds or footprints in the grass. We hunt *fear.* We are drawn to fear as a bee is drawn to nectar, as a child is drawn to her mother's breast, as deep is drawn to deep." She turned to Sophie, her eyes wide. "And Scrivener Behn was *very* afraid."

"Why was he so afraid?" Sophie said.

"I do not know," Akrasia said, peering into the haze. "He came to me on the night of the last Evensong."

"The what?" Peter said.

"Evensong is the sacred ritual of the Storyguard," Akrasia said. "Storyguard are meant to live solitary lives. Their duty is to keep the Four Questions safe and separate—even going so far as to keep their locations unknown from one another. Every so often, however, the Storyguard gather for a sacred ritual during which they summon an entry from the books. It is a way of restoring magic that has been lost."

"Do you remember it?" Sophie said. "The last Evensong?"

"It was twelve years ago," she said. "I was but a cub then, but I could still perceive that there was something dangerous on the horizon. I could smell it on the wind, like so much blood. And then there was your mother's warning."

"About the fourth Storyguard," Sophie said. She could suddenly feel her mother's necklace heavy on her throat.

"Your mother feared the Storyguard was plotting something foul, something that involved the Four Questions. She warned my mistress to protect herself, to take precautions against betrayal."

"And did your mistress listen?" Peter asked.

"Alas, she did. The ceremony was set to be held in Bustleburgh, beneath a pregnant moon. My mistress left me behind in her carriage, fearing for my safety. It was the last I ever saw of her. If your mother had not intervened, my mistress would have taken me with her to the ceremony, and I could have protected her from harm."

"Or," Peter said, "you would have died with her."

"What happened at Evensong?" Sophie asked.

Akrasia shook her head. "I do not know, for I was not there. Some hours after my mistress left me, a man appeared at the door of my carriage. The man was another Storyguard, a Scarabian named Scrivener Behn. He had with him the books of *What* and *Where*.

His face was drawn and trembling, and he was very frightened. When I asked him what had happened, he only told me that my mistress had died—that they had all been betrayed by one of their own. He took the carriage and fled the city, riding straight to an abandoned tower at the edge of the Grimmwald—a place he had seen described in *The Book of Where*. He placed *The Book of What* under my care, and, to ensure that I did not abandon my post, secured around my neck the widow's might." The beast lowered her broad head. "I never saw my mistress again."

"But who was the Storyguard who betrayed them?" Sophie said.

"Eldritch," Peter said. "It has to be."

Sophie looked at Taro, but his face betrayed nothing. "I don't think so," she said. "Madame Eldritch has an entry in *The Book of Who*. But when I asked it who killed my mother, the book turned to an entry that had been torn from the spine."

"The final Storyguard's identity is the least of our troubles," Akrasia said. "It would be very bad for all of us if he or she found the remaining books before you did. For that reason, we should keep moving."

"Maybe it doesn't matter to you," Sophie said, "but to me it's everything. I need to know what happened to my mother—*why* it happened. And these books can do that." She hoped that these books could do much more than that, but she did not dare speak that hope aloud.

Akrasia studied Sophie, as though she might be able to read the things within her heart. "It seems we all have our reasons," she said, turning away.

Sophie watched the beast. Something about her story wasn't quite right. It wasn't that she was lying, but it definitely felt as if she weren't telling them everything. "Akrasia," Sophie called after her.

The tigress looked back at her. "Yes, my cub?"

Sophie clasped the leather strap of her book harness. "Why are you really helping lead us to Scrivener Behn?"

The tigress almost showed a hint of a smile, as though she was grateful for Sophie's directness. "Scrivener Behn imprisoned me against my will for twelve long years. Had you not intervened, I would be there still. In exchange for this, I am going to lead you to him so you might find *The Book of Where*. And then I am going to kill him."

✦   ✦   ✦

Sophie and the others trudged through the marshes on foot, following whatever trail Akrasia claimed to sense. The matter of Akrasia killing Scrivener Behn plagued Sophie, but she knew well enough that there wasn't much she could do about it until they found the man. After the bog, the river had managed to reconstitute itself into an actual river—albeit a broad and swampy one—and they followed its course as best they could. Sophie's legs ached from walking, and the harness carrying the books cut into her shoulder. It did not help that her clothes were still muddy from the bog, and all she had eaten for two days was eel and part of a snail the size of Sophie's head that Akrasia had brought back from goodness knows where. (*The Book of What* identified it as a "hermit tongue.")

The group ventured deeper into the marshes, which seemed to grow ever more dense. Strange animals chirped and gurgled and howled just out of sight, probably kept at bay by Akrasia. Sophie considered using *The Book of What* to identify the animals but thought she might prefer ignorance. The haze that permeated the land seemed to grow denser by the hour. Soon Sophie could barely see twenty feet in front of her, and she started holding the middle of Akrasia's chain for fear of being left behind.

Evening came and with it fog so dark even Akrasia could not see a way forward. The group decided to set up camp on a knoll near the river.

Akrasia went off to hunt some food for supper, and Taro waded into the reeds to catch some of the sprites that had appeared in the cool of night. Sophie watched him trying to catch the little flickering lights that whizzed and blinked above the rippling water.

Peter had taken it upon himself to build a fire, which he was currently doing with little luck. Sophie found him crouched over a pile of soggy thistles. He held a small flint in his hand, which he was trying unsuccessfully to spark against the rocks. "It's too humid for a flint," Sophie said. "You'll never get a fire that way."

Peter threw the rock down. "Then I guess we'll be eating our supper raw," he said. "Again."

"There's another method." She took a fallen branch from the ground and began stripping off the twigs and leaves.

"That wood is too green," Peter said. "It won't light."

"I'm not going to light it." Sophie pulled up her skirts and knelt down beside him. She rummaged through Peter's open bag until she found a long piece of leather cord, which she tied on either end of the stick to make a curved bow. She found a piece of dry stick, this one about the size of her finger, and looped it into the middle of the cord. Then she placed the small stick against a flat piece of bark covered with thistledown.

"Just watch," she said, and she began working the bow back and forth. The stick in the middle of the cord spun against the bark, and soon the friction had created enough heat to ignite the thistledown. Sophie blew on the embers, which crackled and smoked and spread across the rest of the kindling. Soon they had a roaring fire. "See?"

Peter held his hand out over the flames. "Where did you learn to do that?" It was clear she had impressed him.

Sophie shrugged. "There's a whole three-chapter section about fire-starting in the *Merrie History of Robinson Crusader*. I must have read the book a dozen times."

Peter smiled. "Maybe it's not so bad being a know-it-all."

Sophie folded her arms. "Maybe if you read a few more books, you'd learn there are other ways to accomplish things than brute force."

Peter sat back. "We all didn't grow up in a perfect home like yours." He threw a rock into the fire, which created a small burst of sparks. "Some of us were too busy trying to survive to waste our time with dumb books."

Sophie had not expected to touch a nerve, but it seemed she had. Moreover, she didn't know exactly what to do with the notion that she had enjoyed a "perfect home"—her life in Bustleburgh had often felt dreary to the point of suffocation. She wondered what things he must have endured in his own life to make him see her life as perfect.

"May I ask you something?" she said. Peter did not answer, and she decided to take his silence as permission. "When we were in the bog, and the nixies first appeared, they took the form of a man with great big hands and no face. The man knew you. He kept calling you something . . ."

"*Worm*," Peter said, lowering his head. "He called me *worm*." He pronounced the word like the vilest curse.

Sophie moved closer to him. "Who was he?"

Peter sighed, scratching the back of his neck. "The man was named Mister Seamus. He was my . . ." He shook his head, searching for a word. "He took me in when I was young. He used to keep me locked in his basement, fed me scraps and gruel. He was the one who taught me how to steal, how to survive." Sophie remembered the scars she had seen on Peter's body and wondered what else the man had taught him. "When I was ten, I ran away from Seamus—the Professor helped me."

"I don't understand," Sophie said. "I've seen you brave real danger a dozen times, never once showing even an ounce of fear. What is it about this man that so frightens you?"

Peter shrugged, poking the fire with the end of his blade. "I guess some part of me is still afraid he might find me and drag me back to that basement."

Sophie shifted and stared into the fire. Something about the way the flames moved was almost hypnotic. "If he was so terrible, why didn't you just leave sooner?"

"I've wondered the same thing," he said. "I used to tell myself I was afraid he would turn me over to the constable, but that wasn't it . . ." He shrugged again. "I think, deep down, some part of me believed him when he told me I was worthless. Like I didn't *deserve* better."

Sophie stared at his face, still flickering orange in the firelight. She recalled what he had said to her that first night in the bookshop. "Wanting more out of life isn't something to apologize for," she said. "It's that wanting that makes you who you are." Before she knew what she was doing, Sophie leaned toward him and pecked him, ever so softly, on the cheek. "You deserve more than you realize, Peter Nimble."

Peter turned toward her, his mouth open, his cheeks turning red. Even with his blindfold in place she could read the alarm on his face. She got up from the ground and ran into the trees before he could say a word.

CHAPTER THIRTY

OLD SOULS

Adventures can be funny things—one moment you might be fending off monsters and the next fending off mosquitoes. In Sir Tode's case, he had traded just such an exciting battle for a long slog through damp, humid swamp in the confines of a rolling prison cell. It did not help that his cell mate happened to be Madame El-dritch—a less-than-stimulating conversationalist. Skirmishes and chases were one thing, but boredom was another thing altogether. Boredom is anathema to the adventurous spirit, and when mixed with hunger (as it very much was in this moment), the effect could be downright toxic. Presently, Sir Tode was curled up in a corner of a rattling wagon—the same wagon, in fact, that had brought him to the baron's castle. After being rescued (if such a word could be used) by Inquisitor Prigg, Sir Tode found himself transferred into the bed of Knucklemeat's junk cart, which had been refitted with bars from one of the baron's animal cages so that he and Madame Eldritch could be jailed together.

The menagerie had been burned per Prigg's instructions. The screams of the trapped animals had rung through the forest for what felt like hours. Sir Tode, who had been able to see the flames glowing long into the night, shuddered to imagine what pains those unfortunate creatures had suffered.

That had been two days ago, and now Sir Tode was cold, hungry, and (as we have established) crushingly bored. Knucklemeat's wagon had not been thoroughly cleaned, and a few stray bits of junk lay scattered near the front of the wagon, along with the bookcase that connected to the Professor's library, now sealed tightly shut. Sir Tode stared at the empty bookcase, trying not to think of the crackling fire and cozy chairs on the other side.

"You seem to have an unnatural interest in furniture," said Madame Eldritch, who sat against the cell door in the back of the wagon. She was weaving a shallow basket out of sticks that she had pulled from passing branches.

Sir Tode glared at her. "You seem to have an unnatural interest in things that are none of your business."

Madame Eldritch smiled in a way that made Sir Tode fear he had revealed more than he had intended. "My Taro informed me that you previously eluded capture by slipping through a bookcase—perhaps you plan to do so again? If so, I should hope you would let me accompany you."

Sir Tode was not sure how Taro—whose lips were stitched tighter than a corset—could have "told" Eldritch anything. "Even if that were true, and I'm not saying it is, the bookcase wouldn't open without some way to unlock the passage. I don't suppose you have a magic bookend tucked away in that wig of yours?"

"I'll have you know that this hair is quite real," Madame Eldritch said, teasing a strand of auburn hair. "I cut it from the head of a wood nymph myself."

Sir Tode rolled his eyes and flopped rather dramatically onto his belly. He stared out at the hazy jungle, wondering where Peter and Sophie were at that very moment. He tapped a hoof against the bars of the cell. "What's come of your little turnip friend? I daresay he could make short work of these bars."

"And your friend could make short work of this lock," she said, resuming her weaving. "But it seems, for the moment, that we are left to our own devices." She held up the completed basket, inspecting its shape. "Taro is occupied on other business."

Sir Tode raised an eyebrow. "Might that business have anything to do with the Four Questions?"

The woman smiled. "It might."

Sir Tode rose and walked toward her, stumbling slightly in the rocking wagon. "What do you want them for, anyway? You told Sophie that you only wanted to sell *The Book of Who*."

"This is true." Eldritch reached through the bars and took a branch from a quagberry bush as they rattled past it. "That was before I realized what the books truly were—and what they could do for me." She inspected the berries and then put them into her basket.

Sir Tode wrinkled his nose. "You're not telling me you hope to become a Storyguard?"

Eldritch gave a laugh of genuine amusement. "I am not interested in *guarding* anything. What interests me is the power sealed within those books." She caught a golden butterfly that had been foolish enough to land on the edge of the wagon. "There are methods—very old methods—of extracting the magic from enchanted things. Of course, the process can be a bit *traumatic*." As she spoke, she tore the butterfly's wings into small bits and sprinkled them over the contents of her basket.

Sir Tode thought he understood her meaning. "You want to destroy the books," he said. "For what?"

"You and I are not so different as you assume." She spat into her basket and mixed the contents into a paste. "We are both old souls, born into worlds that have since fallen away. We are relics, remnants from a forgotten age." She glanced at him and seemed to read the question forming in his mind. "Your eyes carry the restless weight of one who no longer has a true home."

Sir Tode inched backward. "How old are you, exactly?"

"Older than I appear, to be sure." She pulled a strand of nymph-hair from her head and added it to the basket. "Do not let my youthful bloom deceive you."

Sir Tode rolled his eyes again. "I'm in no danger of that." He stepped closer and sniffed the contents of her basket, which now resembled a lump of black dough. "I hate to tell you, but you're a terrible cook."

"This is not food," she replied as she pulled back her skirts. Lashed to one thigh was something long and sharp.

"Is that what I think it is?" Sir Tode asked, stepping back.

Eldritch smiled, holding out what was unmistakably a unicorn horn. "I liberated it from the baron's collection before entering the cage." The horn looked as if it had been broken, rather than cut, from the skull. "Perhaps the last one in existence."

"I haven't seen a unicorn in . . . centuries . . ." Sir Tode said. All at once his mind flashed to an ancient memory of lush hillsides and thatch-roofed huts and maypoles and the sounds of dancing and music of the people in his village—a harvest celebration. He saw himself, a child of nine, seated on a rock at the top of the hill, watching his father's flock, unable to join the other children. He heard rustling in the trees behind him. Hoofbeats on the soil. He approached the woods, his staff clasped in both hands. And there, under the orange moon, he saw her: a unicorn, watching him. The creature was magnificent, with a shining silver mane and proud black eyes. Steam rose from her nostrils in the cool air. The beast stared at Tode for one perfect moment and then retreated into the forest. Even in those days, unicorns were rare, and a sure sign of a good harvest. Young Tode had been so excited that he ran down the hill to tell the whole village what he had seen. But no one in the village believed him.

Sir Tode broke from his reverie. He watched as Madame Eldritch dipped the tip of the horn into the black dough, which sizzled on contact. "Is it true that unicorn horns can extend life?" he asked.

"It is. And that had been my hope for it at one time," she said, examining the point of the horn, which shone black in the diffuse light. "But that was before I found myself locked in a cage and in need of a sharp point. I will sacrifice this treasure in order to gain a greater prize."

Sir Tode flopped back down. "So you think those books will somehow grant you longer life?"

"I do not think it," she said, dipping the horn again into the paste. "I know."

"Have you considered for a moment that those books are *important*? That keeping those books safe is the only thing standing between Bustleburgh and complete ruin?"

"Bustleburgh is a den of fools," she said without looking up. "What do I care if it lives or dies?"

"I've met my share of monsters. I've survived wild apes and sea dragons and even sleep-deprived hags. But I have never seen a creature as heartless and depraved as you."

"Heartless?" she said. "I am only practical. Also, you seem to forget that, were it not for my intervention, you would be in that little cage still, starving."

"If it weren't for *your* intervention, we wouldn't have this mess at all! Don't think I've forgotten who it was who tried to kidnap the girl or who ambushed us in that hall. And, for the record, staying in the baron's castle would have suited me just fine. It takes a lot more than a little starvation to put Sir Tode down, thank you very much." Sir Tode immediately regretted this last disclosure. It was not something he usually spoke of—and certainly not to someone like Eldritch, who had a way of using even small bits of information to her advantage.

Eldritch's eyes lit up. "But the picture becomes more clear." She set aside her basket and moved closer. She held the unicorn horn in front of him. "If I were to grind up this horn and prepare a potion of life for you, what would happen?"

"You'd have wasted a perfectly good potion." Sir Tode sighed, deciding that it could not hurt to tell the woman what she had already guessed. "It would seem that I can be rather, er, *immortalish*."

Perhaps it would be helpful in this moment to explain some of the particulars of Sir Tode's affliction. We have already established that he had been cursed to live out his days in the combined bodies of a cat, man, and horse, but the exact terms of this curse were a bit more complicated. To put it plainly: Sir Tode did not age. While everyone Sir Tode knew and loved died, he remained as he ever was, doomed to wander the earth until he either undid the curse or was killed. In some darker hours, he had considered finding a way to end his own life. It was in this very state of despair, in fact, that Sir Tode first met Peter Nimble—an encounter that had all but erased his desire to leave this world.

Madame Eldritch gave a laugh—one more genuine than she usually allowed. "This is irony. While I toil and murder to keep myself alive, you live forever against your own will."

Sir Tode lurched to one side as the wagon came to a stop. The journey, it seemed, had come to a hitch. Eldritch quickly concealed the horn behind her back. A moment later, Prigg appeared at the wagon with Knucklemeat at his side. The two men had been riding horses at the front of the caravan beside a locked wagon whose car looked to be made of solid metal. What the wagon housed was unknown to Sir Tode, but he knew it couldn't be good.

"Our party has reached a fork in the river," Prigg said to Eldritch. "Which way do we go?"

Eldritch closed her eyes and made a show of feeling the air. Of course, her actual method for learning the direction was far simpler. Sir Tode had observed that, every time she was asked to give directions, she consulted a small scrap of root that was wrapped around her wrist. Sir Tode suspected that this bit of root was able to work like a compass—pointing her in the direction of its source.

Eldritch opened her eyes, pointing firmly to some marshland that looked to Sir Tode as if it were boiling. "This way, sir. Quickly—the trail grows fainter every moment that we linger here."

"Don't believe her, sir," Knucklemeat said. "There's not a word this one says that isn't calculating."

Madame Eldritch glared at the man as though she were presently calculating how she might best remove his head from his body.

Knucklemeat snorted and spat. "Sir, Kettle Bog is a well-known death trap to the hinterfolk—we march in there, and not one of us gets out. I'd advise we continue down the river and cross where the water's calmer. It might take an extra few hours, but at least we'll be in one piece."

Prigg nodded. "Very well." He turned to Knucklemeat. "See if you can't encourage our guest to be a bit more honest in the future, hmm?" He marched off to the front of the caravan.

Knucklemeat chuckled. "It'll be my pleasure." He turned toward Eldritch. "Seems like someone needs a lesson in manners."

The woman stared at Knucklemeat, her expression softer. "Why are you even taking orders from that idiot bureaucrat?" She clutched the cell door with one hand, pressing herself against the bars. "When it's clearly *you* who should be leading the caravan." She shifted her legs, letting one of them reveal itself through the tear in her skirts.

Sir Tode, who was sitting behind her, could see that she was still holding the unicorn horn behind her back, clutched like a knife. He watched the exchange, uncertain whether he should intervene.

"I can help you," Madame Eldritch continued. "Together we can find the books—and keep them for ourselves."

Knucklemeat looked pleased at the prospect, and he stepped closer. "Is that so?" His face suddenly flashed to rage as he snatched a fistful of her auburn hair. "Is that so?" he repeated more loudly, and he wrenched his hand down, pulling at her mane through the bars of the cell.

Madame Eldritch screamed, collapsing to her knees. "Let go of me!" she cried, swinging the unicorn horn at Knucklemeat.

He caught her wrist in midswing. "Careful now." He twisted her hand backward, and she screamed again.

Sir Tode watched this with a sense of building horror. "I say!" he said, galloping to the edge of the cell. "She may be a witch, but she's still a lady!"

Knucklemeat ignored him, twisting her arm farther. "Drop the weapon, or I'll make sure to break your hand so it don't heal right."

Madame Eldritch's hand opened, and the unicorn horn clattered to the bed of the wagon.

Knucklemeat picked it up—its sharp point dripping with poison.

"Genuine unicorn horn." He sniffed it. "A bit stale." He peered at the tip with his patched eye. "Some kinda rictus charm. And I'm guessing your *plan* involved plunging it through my heart."

Eldritch glared at him, clutching her wrist, her face rigid with fury. "Your throat, actually."

For some reason, this made Knucklemeat laugh. "Just goes to show you: There's no keeping secrets from a man who sees all." He tapped his eye patch with the tip of the horn. "Now, if you'll excuse me, I've a march to lead." He tossed the horn into the air and caught it as he returned to the front of the caravan.

Madame Eldritch clasped the bars, staring at the man who had just stripped away her chance at escape.

"Tell me, Madame," Sir Tode said as their wagon lurched forward, resuming its journey. "What's the point of living forever if it's in a world controlled by men like that?"

CHAPTER THIRTY-ONE

THE LIGHTHOUSE *at the* END *of the* WORLD

The following morning, Sophie awoke to find their camp enveloped in a shroud of gray mist. "What's happened?" she said. "Where are we?"

"It's the fog," Peter said. She had not noticed him standing right beside her. "It should burn off in the afternoon sun."

Sophie wasn't so sure. The fog was so thick that it was difficult to see more than ten feet in front of her. "Can you still find your way?" She rubbed the back of her neck, which was sore from sleeping on *The Book of Who*, which she had tried unsuccessfully to use as a pillow.

Peter nodded. "I can still hear and smell things. But it's harder to tell where they're coming from." Sophie looked at his hand. She wondered if she should take it in hers and help guide him. Wasn't that what you were supposed to do to help a blind person? She reached toward him . . .

"You are awake," Akrasia said, sliding out from the fog.

Sophie pulled her hand back from Peter. "I—I—I just woke up," she stammered. She wondered how long Akrasia had been watching them. The tigress had blood on her mouth, and Sophie knew she must have been off hunting. Sophie stood and slung her book harness over her shoulder. She picked up her cloak, which had been her blanket, and shook out the twigs.

"We need to keep moving," Akrasia said. "The Inquisitor's caravan is but half a day's ride from us."

"Then let's get moving." Sophie turned around, searching the bushes. "Where's Taro?"

There was a sound of movement in the trees above her. A moment later, Taro dropped to the ground. He was holding a sort of globe-shaped cage woven from reeds and vines. Inside the cage were at least twenty sprites, all spinning and fluttering and blinking inside. "It's a sprite-lantern," Sophie said. She recalled with a brief flash of dread how similar lamps had adorned the walls of Madame Eldritch's oubliette.

Taro offered the lantern to Sophie. She took it and noticed that the fog around her seemed to lessen. "The sprites keep the fog at bay," she said. "Did you learn this from Madame Eldritch?"

Taro nodded.

She peered more closely at the lamp and saw that the sprites inside were not trapped, as they had been in Eldritch's lamps; rather, they were able to move in and out of the cage at will. The thing that kept them together was a single white mushroom that Taro had placed in the middle of the cage, which the creatures were eating with a great deal of zeal. "It's brilliant," she said. "Everyone, stay close to me. If we get separated, just look for the light."

Akrasia crouched down and studied the ground where the fog had cleared. Unlike the previous day, she seemed a little less sure of herself. "This way," she said after a moment.

Sophie raised the lantern and led the group into the fog.

✦   ✦   ✦

As the hours wore on, the fog grew even thicker. The group continued moving slowly over the lush terrain, stopping every few minutes for Akrasia to study the trail. The sounds of chittering wildlife, which had filled the forest the day before, were now completely gone. There remained only the sound of their own footsteps and the ripple of the river in the distance.

Though she would never admit it, Sophie was in a great deal of pain. A life of reading prepares one for many trials—but none of them physical. Her shoulders had been rubbed raw from where the harness chafed against the skin. Her feet were wet and blistered. Her hands and legs had cuts all along them from the nixies. She had not slept in an actual bed for over a week. Even the task of holding a small lantern out in front of the group was taxing her strength.

"Oh!" she cried out as she tripped on a root.

Peter caught her. "Careful now," he said as he helped right her. "I've got you."

At last, they reached a flat bed of moss-covered rock where the fog was so thick that Sophie could barely see the end of her own arm. She slipped on the moss and, in an effort to break her fall, dropped the lantern to the ground. "No!" she cried as she watched the lantern tumble into the fog and splash into what she assumed was the river. The sprites scattered into the air, their tiny lights getting smaller and smaller until they had disappeared altogether.

Now they were completely unable to see.

Sophie felt Akrasia move beside her. "You should all take hold of my chain," the tigress said.

Sophie knelt down and grabbed the links, which felt so small in her hand. She could feel Peter's hand next to hers. "Akrasia, do you know where Scrivener Behn went from here?"

"I do not," Akrasia said after a moment. "The fog makes it difficult to focus."

Sophie thought she knew what the tigress meant. The air felt heavy against her skin, her hair, her eyes. It was difficult to breathe, and she felt shaky all over. "I don't think it's good for us to be here," she said. "We have to find shelter. Or maybe more sprites." She wondered if *The Book of What* could somehow guide them to safety, but that presumed she could actually read the book through all this haze.

She felt a nudging against her shoulder and turned to see the vague outline of Taro's arm. He was pointing into the distance.

"What is it?" Sophie said, looking in the direction of his finger. She squinted into the swirling fog. A gentle breeze swept across the ground, and for a brief moment, she could see a light shining above the trees. "There's something out there," she said. "Let's go."

Slowly, Sophie and the others moved toward the light, all of them holding tightly to Akrasia's chain. The going was slow, as even Peter tripped over roots and rocks. Sophie could hear rushing water, and she realized that they were moving downstream. Above that, she could hear a creaking sound that seemed to be coming from just ahead. It reminded her of the ships that docked along the canal in Bustleburgh. The fog thinned out as they neared the light, and soon Sophie was able to let go of Akrasia's chain. "We're almost there," Sophie said, climbing toward the glowing beacon just beyond the trees.

She stepped over the ridge and stopped. The fog had cleared enough for her to see that she was on a bank overlooking the farthest reaches of the Wassail. The river was broad and flat and moving very quickly toward the edge of a steep ridge. Beyond the ridge was not more land but a swath of darkness that seemed to stretch out into infinity. "What is that?" she whispered, inching back from the black abyss.

"Congratulations, my cub," Akrasia said. "I believe we have reached the end of the world."

Sophie stared at the vast, dark expanse. Just looking at it filled her with a dread she could not quite describe. She didn't know if she wanted to run screaming from it or plunge headlong into it. Unlike a waterfall, whose roar could be heard for miles, this water was completely silent as it slipped over the edge of the chasm—as if sound itself could not even escape from such darkness.

"I don't understand," Sophie said. "Is that where Scrivener Behn went?"

"It's difficult to tell," Akrasia said. "I could sense Behn's fear— it was very strong—and then . . . nothing." She inched backward from the canyon. "Whatever he found in this place, it was enough to distract him from mortal fear."

Peter seemed unperturbed, perhaps owing to his blindfold. He raised his head. "What's that creaking sound?" He pointed off to one side. "Over there."

Sophie turned and peered through the fog. At the very end of the river, just before the water plunged into the canyon, floated a large structure with a light at the top. "I think . . . it's a lighthouse," she said.

"What's a lighthouse doing here?" Akrasia asked. There was

a quavering sound in her voice, and Sophie thought that Akrasia might be more frightened than she let on.

Sophie started down the ridge toward the river. The rickety structure groaned and creaked on the surface of the water. "It looks like some kind of floating city," she said. *City* was a generous word. The lighthouse seemed to be cobbled from a mass of wagons and schooners and rafts and galleys and docks and gangplanks that had all been lashed together with ropes—thus saving it from falling over the edge. The top of the structure was a sort of ramshackle lighthouse, which shone with a steady greenish light.

Sophie and the others approached the edge of the river. Enormous moorings had been looped around rocks along the riverbank to prevent the structure from being swept over the edge and into the darkness beyond. A rope-bridge stretched from the bank to the structure on the other side.

Sophie slowly walked along the bridge, which swayed perilously from side to side with each step. The water rushed beneath her. One slip, and she would find herself swept into the river—carried right into the abyss. She reached the dock on the other side and peered at the assortment of buildings, which creaked and swayed above the current.

"Who do you think lives there?" Peter whispered behind her. Sophie heard an uncertain quality to his voice, which was unusual.

They approached a ramshackle building; it looked like a tavern, from which music and voices could be heard. A sign above the swinging doors read:

THE LAST RESORT

"Let's find out," Sophie said, and pushed through the doorway.

CHAPTER THIRTY-TWO

VESPERS

Sophie stepped into the Last Resort, which looked very much like an ordinary tavern and not at all like an ordinary tavern. The entire structure bobbed and tipped with the motion of the river, creaking loudly. A thick cloud of smoke filled the air, making the already dim atmosphere even dimmer. The people here apparently knew the effects of sprite-light, because the creatures were visible in the rafters, eating from little feeders filled with what looked like silver moss; their spectral light shone down through the haze to illuminate tables of men and women hunched together, talking in low voices and laughing. Some people were eating, others were playing games of cards or draughts, and still more were reading books. In one corner, two women with dark blue skin played a single instrument that looked and sounded like a hurdy-gurdy. It took a moment for Sophie to realize that the women were joined together at the spine.

"Who's making that music?" said Peter, who had come in behind her. "I can hear four hands but only one heartbeat."

"It's a cyanese twin," Sophie whispered. Most people in Bustleburgh had heard tales of cyanese twins, but they had been taught to believe that they were a sham, that their bodies were not actually joined together. But watching those four indigo hands darting along the fretboard, it was clear that these women could think and move as one.

The twin was not the only magical being in this place. As Sophie's eyes adjusted to the light, she could make out more strange figures. There was a pack of she-boars sipping tea, a sleeping kobold, a centaur talking with three winged old men she suspected were *wampires*, a fat man covered with feathers clutching a silver egg, a bespectacled worm smoking a gourd hookah, two trolls eating dandelion stems, and what appeared to be a child playing a game of mumblety-peg with a corpse. Several people in the room had stopped talking and were now watching the new arrivals with expressions somewhere between amusement and alarm. Sophie stared back at them, her heart racing.

"What do you see?" asked Peter, who must have been able to sense Sophie's discomfort.

Sophie swallowed, her eyes darting from face to face. "It's like every magical creature I've ever read about—come alive." With each face, she could recall stories that went with them: "The Sombre Child," "Little Tomkin," "Heinrich and the Silver Egg."

"Tread lightly, my child." Akrasia pressed her soft head against Sophie's hand. "Stories are not so tame when encountered outside the page."

"Welcome to the Last Resort, missy," said a brawny woman at the bar. She wore an old turban and had yellow scales along her neck and arms. "You're free to hitch your ship or wagon to whatever post you can find along the docks—just make sure you tie it tight, 'less you wanna lose it to the Uncannyon."

"We haven't any ship or wagon." Sophie eyed the steaming bowls of stew on the counter behind the woman. "But we are very hungry. What would it cost for a meal and a place to stay?"

"We don't take dulcets or any other coin at the Last Resort. Everyone here pays the same way." She pointed a webbed finger at a sign on the wall. Sophie knew that Peter could not see the sign, and so she read it aloud:

LAST RESORT
FOOD & SLIP
One Story / Day
Payable at Vespers

"I don't understand," Peter said. "We pay her in stories?"

The woman snorted. "Not me, dearie. I wouldn't know what to do with 'em. You pay Scrivener Behn. He'll be by within the hour to collect his fee."

Sophie smiled, turning to her companions. "Scrivener Behn!" She saw that Akrasia was also smiling, but in an altogether more tigerly way. Sophie felt a wave of worry about what would happen when Akrasia saw the man who had imprisoned her for twelve long years. She turned back to the bartender. "So the scrivener is really here?"

"Not at the moment," the woman said. "He'll be around shortly for Vespers."

Sophie wasn't sure what that meant, exactly, but it didn't matter. They had found Scrivener Behn, which meant they were that much closer to finding *The Book of Where* and learning the truth about her mother. "There's four of us," she said. "Do we each have to tell a story?"

"That depends on how many of you hope to eat." The woman scratched some marks on her neck that looked very much like gills. "It's one story per plate—no splitting."

"If only Sir Tode were here," Peter muttered. "He could feed the whole room."

The barmaid stacked some empty mugs and bowls on a tray. "Pick a table, and I'll bring some stew," she called. "You'll want to fill up before the scrivener gets here. Vespers can take a while—especially when there's newcomers."

Sophie and the others found a table in a dimly lit corner where the sprite-feeder must have been empty. Sophie looked at the other patrons, who she sensed were trying very hard not to look like they were looking at her. She found herself very grateful to be seated next to a mandrake, a tigress, and a legendary thief.

The dimness turned out not to be a problem, for as soon as Taro was seated, several dozen sprites settled on his head and shoulders, apparently drawn to him as they might be to a tree.

True to her word, the barmaid (whose name was Liesel) returned a few minutes later with mugs of hot wassail and bowls of stew. "Fresh wolpertinger," she said. "Our own Saint Marty caught it this morning on the shore. Watch out for antler bits—they'll cut your tongue up real good."

"Now, this is food," Peter said, slurping up a spoonful. "You can actually taste where it came from."

Akrasia sniffed at her bowl before taking a tentative lap. "I prefer my meat uncooked," she said, and pushed the bowl away with her snout. Taro did not eat. But he did dip his finger into the mug of wassail and kept it there for the duration of the meal.

Sophie had to agree with Peter that the stew did taste different from what they had been subsisting on, but she wasn't sure it was better. There were tentacle-shaped vegetables and bitter spices and what, indeed, looked to be chunks of antler. The wolpertinger—a sort of horned rabbit that Sophie had been forced to look up in *The Book of What*—had a gamy flavor and took a long time to chew. At any moment it felt as if the contents of the bowl might spring to life and start trying to eat her. Still, as it has often been said, hunger is the best seasoning, and she soon found herself finishing her bowl and asking for another.

It was some time later when the barkeep rang a small bell for Vespers. All the people in the tavern stopped their business and pulled their stools away from their respective tables to form a large circle. Sophie and the others did the same.

The room grew quiet as a tall man walked into the room. He wore a long monk's robe and carried a sheaf of blank paper. His skin was dark—darker than Sophie's. He had a bald head, and his face was salted with white stubble that formed a long goat's beard at the end of his chin. A pair of thick magnifying spectacles hung around his neck, the sort used by people who had ruined their eyesight from years of reading or writing in poor light. Tucked behind his ear was a feather quill, though plucked from what strange bird she could not say. The long feather shone silver in the glow of the sprites around him.

"It is he," said Akrasia. She was emitting a low growl, and her entire body had gone tense.

Sophie put a hand on Akrasia's collar, trying to soothe her.

"Promise you won't do anything rash," she whispered. "Not until we've talked to him."

The tigress did not answer, but she did stop growling. Sophie turned back to Scrivener Behn. The man was not old, but he carried a weightiness about him that felt somehow timeless. He took a seat at a table and set out his inkwell and paper. He put on his spectacles and dipped his pen. "Who will begin?" His voice was deep but very gentle.

The first volunteer was the cyanese twin, who spoke with two voices in a tongue that Sophie did not recognize. From the uncomfortable expressions of some of the others in the room, it was clear that they did not understand, either. Judging from the gestures made, Sophie thought the twin's story might be about some kind of very large worm—or perhaps a snake—that bore a hole through the sun. The scrivener, for his part, listened attentively, copying down every word as quickly as it was spoken. "Thank you," he said softly when the twin had concluded her story. "The world may have forgotten your tale, but we shall not." He took a new sheet of paper and asked for another volunteer.

"I got one," said an enormous man with a great big beard. It was warm in the tavern, but the man insisted on wearing a giant bearskin cloak—complete with head and claws—that went all the way to the floor. The man's beard was so long and tangled that it was difficult to tell where the cloak ended and his face began.

"It's a tale from my younger days as a farmer," he said. "About a poacher I caught trying to nick a nest of dragon eggs. It all started on a summer morn . . ."

Sophie stared at the man—his grizzled face, his matted hair, his feral eyes, and, most of all, that bearskin cloak. Something about him was maddeningly familiar. "I know you!" she blurted out, snapping her fingers. "You're Saint Martin!"

The man, who did not look like the type accustomed to being interrupted, emitted a peevish growl. "Obviously." He turned back to the scrivener. "As I was saying, this poacher came down the dragon roost—"

Sophie, however, was undeterred. "You're the *real* Saint Martin," she said. "From the Bruin's Bath."

This drew an unexpected burst of laughter from the other patrons, and Saint Martin's already ruddy face darkened to a deep red. "The Bruin's Bath!" he muttered, disgust thick in his voice. "I've defended nations with my bear hands, killed trolls, and hunted witches—but you slip in *one* little dung heap, and that's all they remember about you for the next hundred years . . ." He jabbed a thick finger at Sophie. "You keep on like that, lass, and maybe my next story'll be about how I gobbled up a little girl."

"Hey!" Peter got up from his stool. "I don't appreciate you threatening my friend."

The man stood up. His head very nearly grazed the roof. "What are you gonna do about it? Stick me with that toothpick?"

Peter stood his ground. "Faster than you can blink."

Sophie had read many stories about Saint Martin, and if even half of them were true, then this was not a man they wanted to anger. "Peter," she whispered, "I appreciate the gesture, but I'd rather take the insult and keep you in one piece."

It is lamentably common among chivalrous sorts that they are more intent on defending a woman's honor than listening to the actual wishes of said woman. In this spirit, Peter ignored Sophie's request and raised his weapon. "Apologize," he said. "I won't ask again."

There was a palpable tensing in the room as everyone watching seemed to hold their breath. Saint Martin growled at the boy. "Haven't you ever heard what they say about poking a bear?" He reached for the cowl of his bearskin cloak—

"Martin," said a calm but commanding voice. It was Scrivener Behn. Everyone in the room—even Saint Martin—turned to look at the man. "The children meant no harm," the scrivener continued, still writing. "You should be flattered that your legacy remains in any form. That is more than most of us get. Even if it's less than we deserve."

Saint Martin stared at Peter, his teeth set in an ugly grimace.

"You're lucky it's Vespers . . ." He let go of his cloak and lumbered back to his stool.

"Thank you, Martin," said the scrivener. He turned to a new page. "Perhaps it is time we hear a story from the girl and her companions, who have brought with them so much trouble."

Every person in the circle turned to face Sophie, who suddenly felt very uncomfortable. "W-w-what kind of story?" Her voice shook slightly, and her hands were wet with perspiration. Sophie, who had read thousands of stories in her life, found herself unprepared when faced with the task of telling one herself.

The man dipped his quill in the inkwell. "You will tell the first story every person tells when they arrive at the Last Resort," he said. "The story of how you came to find yourself here, at the edge of the world."

Sophie nodded, clasping the bell hanging from her neck. The scrivener would not look at her, and so she wasn't sure whom she should address. She settled on staring at a cluster of sprites at the far end of the room. "My name is Sophie Quire. I'm a bookmender from Bustleburgh. I'm here because . . . well, because we're looking for you, Scrivener Behn."

There was a murmur in the room. The scrivener's pen had stopped moving.

"Sophie Quire?" he said, almost in a whisper. He looked up

from his work for the first time since appearing at the Last Resort. When his eyes met Sophie's, his face shifted into a portrait of perfect wonder. He tilted his head, and his mouth moved as if he were trying and failing to find something appropriate to say. "You are the very picture of your mother."

Sophie tried to keep the shiver from her voice. "So I'm told."

❧ CHAPTER THIRTY-THREE ❧
THE BOOK of WHERE

Sophie met the scrivener's dark gaze. The room creaked as the Last Resort swayed slightly in the current. Looking directly at the man now, she could see that his skin was not quite so dark as she had thought; rather, he had marked himself with tattooed letters that covered every inch of his face and hands—a living book. "I am the last Storyguard," she said to the room. "Daughter of Coriander Quire. Keeper of the books of *Who* and *What*. And I've come for *The Book of Where*."

"You have come for more than that, I think." Scrivener Behn's voice was unexpectedly soft. He rose from his stool, speaking to the room. "Vespers is adjourned." If anyone in the tavern object- ed, they kept these objections to themselves. Behn collected his paper and ink and motioned at Sophie. "What I have to say is for you alone."

Akrasia growled beside Sophie. "The girl is not the only one owed explanations."

The man looked at the tigress. His eyes moved the length of her golden chain, and his expression softened. "Forgive me, Akrasia. It has been many years since we last met, and I did not recognize you. You may come, as well. But the others must remain here."

He walked toward a small room behind the bar. Sophie started to follow him, but Taro rose and blocked her path. She tried to step around him, but he grabbed her arm. "You have to stay here, Taro," Sophie said. "I'll be all right."

The room swayed perilously to one side. "He's not worried about you," Peter said. "He's worried about the books. He won't let them out of his sight."

Sophie took a breath and nodded. "Then you'll have to keep them," she said to Peter. She removed the harness from her shoulder and placed it in Peter's open hand. She was surprised at how much it pained her to voluntarily give up the books.

"If you're in trouble, just cry out," Peter said, putting the books over his shoulder. "I'll come get you."

Scrivener Behn watched from the doorway with some measure of confusion. "You trust this boy?" he asked her.

Sophie nodded. "With my life." As soon as she said the words, she knew they were true. She looked down, blushing, grateful that Peter couldn't see her face.

"Worry not, Behn," Saint Martin chimed in, folding his arms across his brawny chest. "If the brat tries to make a run for it, I'll squash him flat."

Sophie parted from Peter and Taro, following the scrivener through a narrow door in the back of the galley. Akrasia was at her side, her chain trailing behind her like a second tail. Sophie was grateful to have the tigress with her but fearful of what it might mean for Scrivener Behn.

The door led directly to the base of the lighthouse that shone over the entire structure—the same light that had guided them through the fog. Though the buildings had been lashed together with ropes, between their doorways was a shifting gap at her feet through which Sophie could see the river rushing beneath her. The sight made her stomach turn in on itself. "Courage, my cub," Akrasia said, moving beside her. "We are too close to our goal to be slowed by such a thing as fear."

Sophie stepped over the threshold and into the lighthouse. The narrow, circular stairs creaked under her feet as the tower bobbed and tilted on the river's current. Stacks of unbound papers covered the steps, leaving very little room to walk. Akrasia followed closely behind, her gold chain rattling against the risers as she climbed.

"I suspected someone might be coming to this lighthouse,"

Scrivener Behn called back to them as he mounted the stairs. "For many years, I have watched closely the location of the remaining Questions using *The Book of Where*. Your *Book of Who* had been missing for some years, to only very recently appear in Bustleburgh."

"It was hidden in the library of a man named Professor Cake," Sophie called. She wondered if she was breaking some sort of rule by speaking of the Professor to another person. "He's the one who charged me to collect the Four Questions."

Scrivener Behn paused, swaying slightly with the rocking motion of the lighthouse. "Professor Cake?" He shook his head. "I should have known that the Professor might be involved in this somehow."

"So you know him?" Sophie said, resuming her ascent.

Scrivener Behn waved a hand in a vague manner, as though trying to grasp the ungraspable. "I have not had the honor. But a man in my trade cannot help but hear rumors of he who moves behind the stories. If you are all here at the Professor's urging, then we can be assured that this quest is not in vain—nor is it simply about collecting lost books. There are dark things on the horizon."

"Pyre Day," Sophie said. "Bustleburgh is collecting every storybook in the hinterlands and is planning to burn them all in a big ceremony."

"That may be true," he said. "But they will not burn *all* the stories."

Sophie looked at the stacks of papers lining the stairs—some nearly as high as her knees—all covered with cramped handwriting. She picked up one of the fallen pages, which contained a handwritten account of a fable called "The Old Man and the Tree." "Did you write this?" she asked.

"Only in the most literal sense," Behn called back. "I am merely a scrivener, transcribing the stories others tell me. Though I have been forced to take on other roles in recent years—binding, mending, and then there's the lighthouse."

Sophie reached the top of the stairs, which opened onto the deck of the lighthouse. The space had been converted into a sort of bookbindery. Pots of ink and discarded quills and loose pages perched on every surface. Stacks of books and paper covered the floor in haphazard piles. Sagging bookshelves were filled with crudely stitched volumes whose spines bore their titles. Some titles she could read; others were in languages unknown to her. Sophie had never lived near the ocean and was largely unfamiliar with lighthouses. She had read enough to know that they usually employed oil or wood to keep a flame lit. This lighthouse, however, did not use oil or wood—instead, it contained a flickering cloud of little pale lights that darted in all directions.

"They're sprites," Sophie said. "There must be hundreds of them." In fact, there were thousands. The creatures were so thick in the air that Sophie nearly had to cover her eyes. The lighthouse walls were encircled with tall, open windows, and the rafters were coated in a dark, glittering moss with tiny white mushrooms sprouting up. "This was the light that guided us here," she said.

"You and many others," Behn said, putting away his pen and sheaf of paper. "I had not meant for this lighthouse to become a refuge. I had, in fact, wanted to keep it hidden. But *The Book of Where* had another plan for me, it would seem." He smiled and Sophie recognized on his face a sort of fondess similar to what she felt for *The Book of Who.* "Over the years, the lighthouse has drawn many wayward pilgrims, all of them driven from their homelands. It is a tolerable arrangement." He held out one hand, and a sprite landed on the edge of his thumb, the pale glow reflecting brightly in his eyes. "I once roamed the map in search of stories, and now the stories come to me."

Sophie looked at the tiny letters covering Scrivener Behn's long fingers—so dense they made his skin appear black in the dim light. "Those words on your hands and face," she said. "What are they?"

"Not just my hands and face." Scrivener Behn pulled up his sleeve to reveal that the marks covered his entire arm and presumably the rest of his torso. "These are not words, but letters from different alphabets—a thousand scattered tongues writ upon my flesh. They are a spell. Any person who speaks one of these tongues will understand and be understood. It is a helpful thing in my trade."

"That's how you could talk to the cyanese twin," Sophie said.

"And yourself," he added. "My own native language is not

spoken in the hinterlands. I grew up speaking the sand tongue from the Scarabian Peninsula. It is the language of an ancient country, many thousands of miles from this place."

The lighthouse rocked to one side, sending Sophie and Akrasia into a wall. "What fool chooses to build a village on the water?" Akrasia said, growling. It was clear she did not approve of the decision, for she had been pacing nervously ever since setting foot on the docks.

"I did not choose to live at the mouth of the Uncannyon," Behn said, his face bathed in the sprite-light. "It is *The Book of Where* that told me to settle here. And so I obeyed."

"The Uncannyon." Sophie recalled that Liesel had also used that word. "Is that what you call the abyss beyond the ridge?"

"It is rather more than an abyss," he said. "An abyss is simply a large pit, which is something we can all imagine, but the Uncannyon is something beyond imagination. The Uncannyon is the unknown frontier that lurks beyond the edge of perception. Its depths cannot be plumbed or even comprehended. The Uncannyon swallows anything or anyone that enters it—nothing escapes from its grasp."

Sophie had read her share of stories in which heroes ventured into what was fondly referred to as "the unknown." In those stories, "the unknown" usually ended up being a land or country that was in fact very well known by its previous or current inhabitants. But this thing that Behn spoke of—this infinite darkness—seemed altogether different. "When I asked *The Book of Who* about you, it couldn't give your location. Was that because of the Uncannyon?"

He nodded. "I needed to hide *The Book of Where* someplace where even the other books could not find it." He opened a drawer in his workbench and removed a book with an orange cover. "It seems my time of hiding is at an end."

He gave the book to Sophie, who took it in her open hands. The book was damaged from years of neglect. It was clear that Scrivener Behn was many things, but a bookmender he was not. She unlatched the clasp and opened the cover to the title page, which was written in orange ink. For a moment, she was confused, for the title was in a language she could not read, but then the letters shifted into more familiar words:

"The title just changed into my language," she said. "What does that mean?"

"It means that you are the book's new guardian," he said, drawing his inscribed fingers over his inscribed scalp. "It means that my long work is finally done." His face bore an expression of both sadness and relief.

Sophie held the open book in her hands. At last, she had the one book that could point her to the location of the final volume. "Where is *The Book of When*?" she asked. The pages came alive, flipping first in one direction and then the other. At last, the book closed itself.

"It didn't answer my question," she said, looking up at Behn.

The scrivener moved closer. "I will admit that this puzzles me. Until very recently, I knew *The Book of When* to be in Bustleburgh. It must have changed location—gone someplace even this book cannot find." He stroked his long beard. "Curious indeed."

"Enough with these riddles." Akrasia moved in front of Sophie. "You have given the girl her book, and now it is time to give me what I deserve." She bared her teeth. "Vengeance for the life you stole."

Scrivener Behn did not seem to quaver but met her yellow gaze. "We have both been prisoners, Akrasia. You in your library, I in my lighthouse." If he was frightened by the prospect of being killed, it did not show. "My blood will not give you back your mistress or your lost years. All I can offer is my story, and perhaps it will allow you to see that the things I have done, I have done for a greater purpose."

"Please," Sophie whispered to the beast. "I didn't just come here for a book. I came here to learn the truth about my mother. Don't rob me of that. Not when I'm so close."

Akrasia remained where she was, her entire body tensed like a coil. "Tell your story, Scrivener," she said, growling. "And know that you are speaking for your very life."

Scrivener Behn would not be the first person in history whose life depended on his ability to tell a story. If you ever find yourself in such an unfortunate position, know that the truth of your words matters much more than the tone of your voice. Behn seemed to understand this, and when he began speaking, it was not with oratory flair but with stilted, cautious words. "I can tell you well what I recall from the night your mistress died, for I was with her when it happened. Not a day goes by when I do not recall her death with sorrow."

Scrivener Behn took a deep breath, releasing a trembling sigh. "It happened during what would turn out to be our last Evensong. Do you know this word?"

Sophie recalled what Akrasia had told her. "It is the ceremony where the four Storyguard meet and summon magic into the world."

"The details for the next Evensong were always decided by consulting the Four Questions. *The Book of Where* would tell us the location. The date was given by *The Book of When*, the subject of the recitation decided by *The Book of What*. And *The Book of Who* dictated who should perform the recitation.

"Per the books' instruction, this upcoming Evensong was set to be held in Bustleburgh—a place we already knew, for the hinterlands was home to one of our members. As the foretold date approached, the Storyguard all made their way to the city. Your mother arrived early so that she might offer her mending services to the local population. It was during that time that she met and married your father. You were born soon after.

"I was the next to arrive, having taken a more scenic route through the Grimmwald, collecting stories as I traveled. When I met your mother in the city, she was agitated. She tried to warn me of something troubling about the keeper of *When* and advised that I take precautions to protect myself and *The Book of Where*." He lowered his head. "I did not listen.

"The hour finally came, and we four assembled along the shores of Bustleburgh, at the feet of the Wolves of Dawn. It was the middle of the night, and the stars were luminous and fiery. It was there that tragedy struck. At the very moment when we were meant to begin the summoning, the fourth Storyguard—the traitor—produced a fascinator." He looked at Sophie. "You are familiar with these?"

"I think it's some kind of trap," Sophie said.

He nodded. "It is a candle whose effect is to petrify all who look upon it for as long as it burns. Instantly, the three of us were fixed in place—unable to move or even blink. The traitor took the books from us and spoke the Two Words that unlocked the power of the Four Questions. The books brought forth a beast unlike any I had ever seen—a swirling vortex of unbridled power and rage."

"The Zeitgeist," Sophie said, recalling what *The Book of What* had told her back in the bog.

"Perhaps that is the creature's name. I only know that, before it could fully manifest, it was ripped in two and disappeared into the night air—dead before it had ever lived . . ."

"Why did it die?" Sophie said.

The man looked at her. "Your mother killed it." He shook his head. "Somehow. I still do not understand. All I know is that, unlike myself and poor Veena, Coriander managed to break free from the fascinator's charm and stop the summoning. She wrestled *The Book of Who* from the traitor's hands and fled into the streets, the traitor following her." He closed his eyes, as though still remembering that night twelve years before. "That was the last I ever saw of either of them."

"She was murdered in the bookshop," Sophie said. "Stabbed through the heart."

"Your mother's sacrifice was not in vain," Scrivener Behn said. "Not long after she fled, the fascinator's wick burned away, and the flame died. I soon found myself able to move again."

"And my mistress?" Akrasia said. "What of her?"

Scrivener Behn looked at the creature, whose face bore an expression more of fear than anger. "She was an old woman, and frail. It seemed the effects of the fascinator had not only stopped her hands and feet, but also her heart. I'm sorry.

"All was not lost, however. The traitor had fled in pursuit of Coriander, leaving behind the books of *What* and *Where*, which I collected. I found myself alone in a foreign city with two books that needed protection—that needed to be hidden someplace where the traitor could never find them. And so I did what I had been trained to do."

"You asked the books?"

"*The Book of Where* told me where to go. I took Veena's carriage and sped to the woods, her companion tigress at my side. I soon found myself before an abandoned castle with a library unlike any I had seen before or since." He looked at the tigress. "I knew you would protect the book, Akrasia, but I had to ensure you didn't despair and abandon your post, and so I asked *The Book of What* if there were some way I could keep you from straying. It told me to use a widow's might."

Akrasia growled. "And you obeyed without question."

"I did," he said. "Just as I obeyed *The Book of Where* when it told me to hide myself at the mouth of the Uncannyon—the only place where I could escape the eye of the traitorous Storyguard. Our lives did not matter, but the books had to be protected."

Sophie watched Akrasia, whose yellow eyes were narrow. The floor beneath her was vibrating from the tigress's growls. "And my mistress?" Akrasia said. "You left her dead in the street?"

Scrivener Behn shook his head. "Veena Bluestocking was from

the Antipodes. I knew something of the customs of her people, so I carried her to the river and laid her to rest on a small boat." He stared out the open window at the vast darkness stretching beyond. "I like to think that the waters might have carried her body into the Uncannyon. And that she is there still." He lowered his head, his story complete.

If this answer mollified the beast, Sophie could not tell. It was, perhaps, enough that it had prevented Akrasia from attacking the man.

Sophie reached down and placed a hand on the tigress's thick mane. "Scrivener Behn, you said that the Four Questions can summon any entry into the world." She swallowed, almost unable to speak the words. "Does that mean they could bring back my mother?"

The man searched her eyes, his expression laden with compassion. "Even if you had all four books, I fear you could not raise the dead. To speak your mother's name would likely summon only her bones. I'm sorry."

"It is as I have foretold, my cub," Akrasia said, her voice gentler than it had been before. "Where these books go, blood follows."

Sophie clutched *The Book of Where*. It felt as if her chest had been hollowed out and might cave in if she squeezed too hard. During this entire journey, she had held out a hope that these books would somehow draw her closer to her mother—and maybe even provide a way to see her once more. Instead, they had done the opposite—

bringing her absolute understanding that she would never see her mother again. "It's like Papa always told me," she said, sniffing. "It's troublesome luck to trouble the dead." She thought of how far she had traveled, all the dangers she had faced, all for these books that only brought destruction.

"Scrivener Behn," she said after a moment. "I need to know something. What was the traitor's name?"

"Haven't you guessed it?" said a voice behind her.

Sophie turned around to see a man standing at the top of the stairs. He was tall, rail–thin, wearing gold spectacles and an immaculately tailored blue coat. In one hand he held an ebony cane. "Inquisitor Prigg?" Sophie said.

The man gave a warm smile. "I do hope I'm not interrupting."

CHAPTER THIRTY-FOUR

PLIGHT *of the* COMMON MAN

S ophie stared at the man standing before her. He was watch–ing her with an expression rather like a cat that had found a particularly delicious mouse. "*You're* the Storyguard?" she said.

"Storyguard?" Prigg gave an almost winsome laugh. "Now, there's a name I haven't heard in a very long time." He shook his head, moving away from the steps. "I am but a humble civil servant, wholly devoted to the common man."

His eyes crept over the stacks of books lining the floor. "It seems you've kept yourself busy, Behn." He picked up a book entitled *The Hall of Many Voices* and flipped through its pages. "I wondered how fresh nonsense kept finding its way into Bustleburgh. I should have suspected you were behind it." He tossed the book out the open window into the darkness. There was a faint splashing sound as the book struck the river somewhere far below.

"What have you done to the pilgrims?" Scrivener Behn demanded.

Prigg made a noncommittal gesture with one hand. "I presume you are speaking of that rather crude assemblage of relics and freaks downstairs." He drummed his fingers on the stair rail. "I have this encampment surrounded by six dozen troops, all with muskets at the ready. They have been instructed to fire if I do not return in the next five minutes. To put it more plainly: If you touch me, everyone downstairs will die."

Akrasia growled. "You think I care for the lives of those pilgrims?"

"No. But I do think you care for the life of the girl," he said. "And if something happens to me, she, too, will die."

This seemed to restrain Akrasia's wrath, for which Sophie was grateful. "How did you find us?" she said.

Prigg raised an eyebrow. "For that, you have Madame Eldritch to thank. She led us straight to you. I suspect she thought she might be able to turn the odds in her favor . . ." He reached out the window and caught a sprite as it wove through the fog. "Though that seems unlikely now." Prigg closed his fist, crushing the sprite. There was a small shriek, and then the light from the creature was gone.

"Where's Sir Tode?" Sophie said, recalling what Akrasia had told her about his being captured.

"I presume you're referring to that hideous pet of yours?" Prigg said. "He is unharmed for the moment. Whether he remains unharmed is entirely up to you." He held out his hand. "I shall have that book now."

Sophie clasped *The Book of Where* to her chest, inching back. "So, this whole time, you weren't chasing me for breaking laws," she said. "You just wanted the book."

"Perceptive as always. But *want* is not a strong enough word. For twelve years, I have toiled at the foot of the Pyre, inspecting every bit of nonsense that passed through those gates and receiving not so much as a whisper of a clue about where any of the Four Questions might be hidden."

Sophie felt a quiver in the back of her spine as she realized what the man was saying. "That's the reason you let us keep the bookshop open," Sophie said. "In case it appeared there."

"Your shop was *The Book of Who*'s last known location—it seemed like a wise precaution. I allowed Madame Eldritch to continue operating for very similar reasons." He stepped closer. "Even so, you cannot imagine my surprise when I came across the book nestled safely inside your stove—and my irritation at your flight. Though I suppose I should have expected as much. You are not the first Quire I have made the mistake of underestimating."

"You're a traitor," Scrivener Behn said. "You had a sworn duty to protect magic."

"A traitor? To whom?" Prigg gave a humorless laugh. "It is true that I once thought as you did. For many years, I toiled in service of magic, valiantly working alongside my fellow Storyguard to pre-serve stories in the world. Until one day I finally sat down and read my precious *Book of When*. An infinite chronicle of magic at work in the world. And do you know what I discovered? I discovered the truth: that magic is a cruel, heartless beast." He walked the length of the room like a barrister before the court. "Do you remember the Celestial Quadrille we summoned, Behn?"

Scrivener Behn nodded. "It was an ancient dance of the con-stellations, not seen for millennia. The Storyguard summoned its return to the Icicle Mountains, whose skies now come alive every solstice. A lost wonder restored through our good work."

Prigg put a hand to his heart. "That's true—and it *is* quite beautiful to behold. Less beautiful are the floods it creates every year, wiping out villages and flocks at the foot of the mountains." His face was dead sober.

Scrivener Behn shifted slightly. "Is this true?" He sounded genuine in his shock.

"True as the ticking of a clock," Prigg said. "You and the other Storyguard were already off to someplace new, conjuring up more horrors. I, however, stayed behind to tend the wounded. And it was there I saw the salvation of these people—not by magic potion or sacred ritual, but by the studious application of medical science at the hands of trained physicians. And in that moment, I realized the truth: Magic has no care for the plight of the common man."

He walked in front of them, his cane behind his back. "For countless centuries, magic gripped the ordinary world in a vise of terror. Fairies used to steal children away and leave sickly changelings in their stead. House cats would rob their masters. A forest was just as likely to eat you as shelter you. When you offended a beggar crone, she did not sue you in a court of law—instead, she cursed you and your children and your children's children. People ate fairy fruit and went mad with hunger. Djinni granted wishes designed to trap you in your own desires. When there was an earthquake or blizzard or hurricane, you could be sure it was due to some king or queen feeling sad—the amount of destruction caused by lovesick royalty is incalculable!" His voice echoed loudly in the open room. Sprites scattered around him, as if they, too, were listening.

He wheeled around, stepping closer to Sophie. "You have spent a lifetime reading about magic. Can you deny what I say?"

Sophie stared at him, refusing to flinch. She knew he was right— at least in a sense. The stories she so loved were filled with the exact horrors he had mentioned and a hundred others besides: dragons and witches and ghouls and tyrant kings and wicked stepmothers. Things that, if Sophie had encountered them in her own life, she would have denounced as evil. And still, she knew deep within herself that this man, whatever he was, represented an evil much greater.

Prigg seemed to take her silence for assent. "When the next Evensong was determined to be held in Bustleburgh—in my homeland—I knew something had to be done before that place, too, was destroyed."

"So you decided to destroy it first," Scrivener Behn said.

"No, my foolish scribbler. I have made this world better. Safer. More dependable. There are no more fairy feasts in Bustleburgh, but neither are there starving widows. The lame man no longer experiences miraculous healing, but he now has a physician to soothe his pain. Children have no time for perilous adventures, because they are employed in productive work. We have no glass orchards or wishing wells, but we do have courthouses and factories and hospitals and schools."

"But to destroy all magic everywhere . . ." Sophie said. "There must be some other way."

"Haven't you been listening?" Prigg said. "The world is not big enough for both man and magic—perhaps it never was. In order for man to live, *magic must die.*"

"Magic cannot die," Scrivener Behn said, stepping toward him. "So long as there is wonder in the hearts of men, so, too, will there be magic."

"On that count, my old friend, you are very right. Which is why I do not intend to destroy magic, but rather destroy the thing that creates it."

It took a moment for Sophie to realize what he was implying. "Stories," she said, holding *The Book of Where* to her chest. "You want to destroy every story in the world."

Prigg smiled like an approving schoolmaster. "Precisely." He clapped his hands, and two armed guards appeared at the landing. One of them was holding a torch. Prigg took the torch from him and stepped to Scrivener Behn's bookcase. "Why don't we start here?"

+ + +

Peter was lying on the deck of the Last Resort, one arm pulled behind him, Knucklemeat's gun pressed against the back of his skull. He wrinkled his nose, smelling the sweet odor of burning paper somewhere high above. It was coming from the lighthouse. He didn't need to ask who had set the fire. Prigg had gone up there with two guards, one of whom had been holding a torch. He only hoped that Sophie was still safe.

"I'll be taking this back," Knucklemeat said, unlooping the book harness from Peter's shoulder and putting it over his own. "And no squirming. You wouldn't want my trigger finger to slip."

Taro and the other pilgrims were all corralled in the middle of the tavern, surrounded by about fifty armed guards, with more outside on the shore. The sound of their approach had been muffled by the fog and had caught everyone off guard. Peter, who should have heard them nonetheless, had been so focused on trying to listen to Sophie's conversation up in the lighthouse that he hadn't realized what was happening until it was too late.

Now they were all just waiting for Prigg and the others to return from the lighthouse, which was ablaze above them. Peter could feel the hot air radiating down through the roof as the tower burned. He could smell the flecks of ash swirling through the air. He could hear the screams of sprites as their wings burned in the flames. He gritted his teeth, desperately hoping that Sophie was unharmed. He didn't care about the mission or the books. But Sophie had to be alive.

The door in the back of the galley opened up, and Prigg stepped out. More footsteps followed—too many to count. "Sophie!" Peter cried, pulling against Knucklemeat's grip.

"I'm here," she said. She grunted as a guard shoved her to the ground beside him. Her heartbeat was muted, and Peter thought she might be holding something to her chest. Another book, perhaps?

"No funny business, you two," Knucklemeat said, and drew a second gun from his belt. "I've got bullets enough for you both." He spat an acrid glob of tobacco onto the floor beside Peter's face.

Akrasia snarled as several guards jabbed bayonets at her back and forced her to the floor.

Peter could smell fresh blood in the air. He turned his head away, unable to block out the sound of blades piercing the beast's flesh.

"Every wound you inflict upon me," the tigress snarled at her attackers, "I will pay back a hundredfold."

"We tried to stop 'em, Behn," called Liesel. Her voice was strained, thin, and Peter thought she might have a bayonet against her throat. "But there were too many of 'em."

Scrivener Behn was standing at the door. "This is how you treat innocent folk?" he said, his voice numb with shock. "What of your noble laws now?"

"Ends over means, old colleague," Prigg said.

Peter was confused by the word *colleague.* Did Prigg and Behn know each other somehow?

"But you are right," Prigg continued. "We are neither of us born fighters. I have no appetite for needless bloodshed, and I'm sure you feel the same. If you order your associates to surrender, they may just listen. I promise each of them will receive a fair trial back in Bustleburgh."

Scrivener Behn was silent for a moment and then turned away from Prigg to face the others. Peter could hear the man's heartbeat, which was slow and steady. "Friends," he called in a loud voice. "You came to me seeking asylum, but it seems there is no such thing. Not for us. You are each of you the last of your kind. These men and men like them have taken everything you have—your homes, your kinsmen, your peace. And now they want to erase even the memory of you from this world." He shook his head. "And perhaps they are within their rights to do it. The world seems determined to leave ones such as us behind. And who are we to toil against the irresistible march of progress?" He spat this last word out like a curse. "The Inquisitor has promised that if we lay down our arms, he will spare our lives. Such as they are."

He faced the creaking rafters and took a heavy breath. Every person in the tavern was watching him. Even the sprites had stopped flying in order to hear his words. "But perhaps we should have one final Vespers. Tell one last story before we are snuffed out for good." Peter could almost hear the grin playing at the edge of his mouth. "We can call it 'The Battle at the Last Resort.'"

BATTLE *at the* LAST RESORT

Sophie's heart hammered inside her chest as she stared up at Scrivener Behn. The man's speech had had an almost electric effect on the room. Guards inched back, adjusting their grips on the stocks of their muskets. The pilgrims in the middle all nodded at one another—sober and stone-faced.

"You heard Behn," Saint Martin said from the middle of the room. He adjusted his thick bearskin cloak, the lifeless bear's head draped over his enormous shoulders like a second self. "Let's give 'em a story worth remembering." He grabbed the hood of his cloak and pulled it over his head. There was a ripping sound and a flash of lightning—the sight was shocking enough to send a few of the closer guards stumbling backward. Sophie, too, covered her eyes. And when she looked up again, she saw not Saint Martin the man, but an enormous black bear with shining red eyes and long ivory teeth. The bear roared so loudly it shook the very rafters.

"It's just a trick!" Prigg called. "Stand your ground."

But it was not a trick. The bear was real, and it was furious. It lunged at the guards, sweeping its mighty claw down in a terrifying arc that smashed clear through the floor of the tavern to reveal the black river below. Guards scrambled back, trying to keep free of the beast as it loped after them. Sophie watched, breathless—Saint Martin the Bruin King was taking on half a dozen armed soldiers with only his bear hands.

The Battle at the Last Resort had begun.

A moment later, every pilgrim in the tavern had joined the fray. Scrivener Behn broke free of the guard holding him and tackled the man to the ground. The she-boars charged down the planks at some guards standing at the far wall—routing them right out the windows. Liesel, who seemed to know her way around a fight, drew a long kitchen knife from her apron and leapt at another man with an ululating cry. Others followed suit, grabbing whatever they could to fight back. Taro lifted his captor over his head and threw him clear across the room, knocking out a contingent of guards in the corner like so many candlepins. Even the sprites joined the fighting, darting at the unprotected faces of the guards.

Prigg drew his blade from his ebony cane. "Fire!"

His men wasted no time in obeying the command. The air split with a dozen cracks as the first wave of men fired their muskets into the scrum. The smoke had scarcely cleared before another round of shots rang out. While one line of solidiers fired, the other reloaded so that the assault was almost constant. The pilgrims might have enjoyed the element of surprise, but these soldiers enjoyed the element of strategy.

"Shoot them down!" Prigg called from atop a table. "Give no quarter!"

Hot brimstone filled the room. The entire structure creaked and groaned as its walls were shattered by musket balls and slashing claws. Many pilgrims, like the hobgoblins and cyanese twin, were less skilled at fighting, and their compatriots grouped around them to protect them from harm.

Sophie lay on the ground, still pinned beneath Knucklemeat's knee. She could feel her mother's bell pressing into her throat. She watched Peter, who had pulled free of Knucklemeat to join the fighting. Screams rang out all around her as creatures and men alike fell. This was not how battles looked in her mind when she read of them. This was a horror.

Knucklemeat didn't let his charge keep him from battle. Using his free hand, he unloaded one shot, then another, at various creatures, a bloodthirsty glint in his one eye. His flintlock went off right beside Sophie's head, momentarily blinding her. She heard a neighing scream and looked up just in time as the body of a centaur came crashing down in front of her—a bullet lodged right in the noble beast's throat.

"Like picking ripe plums from a heavy bough," Knucklemeat said, drawing a fresh pistol. "Haven't had this much fun in ages."

Sophie heard the sound of a rattling chain. She caught movement from the corner of her eye—a silver streak moving toward them. She ducked down as Akrasia leapt upon Knucklemeat. The man let out a scream as he fell backward, trying to fight himself free of the beast's jaws. Knucklemeat grabbed hold of Akrasia's chain, looping it around her neck and pulling with all his might—choking her.

"Akrasia!" Sophie cried, scrambling toward her.

She felt a hand snatch her arm. It was Peter. "We have to get you to safety," he said, dragging her through the chaos. Sophie pulled herself away from Akrasia and followed Peter to the back wall. Bodies were strewn everywhere. Bullets whizzed over her head. How Peter could hear anything amidst all this was beyond her, but she didn't question it. They reached the bar and scrambled behind the counter.

"Stay here," Peter said, releasing her arm. "Whatever you do, don't let go of that book." He turned back toward the fight.

Sophie felt a surge of panic. "Wait!" she cried. "Where are you going?"

Peter faced the open front doors. "Sir Tode's out there," he said. "I've got to save him."

✦　　✦　　✦

With the smoke and the screams and the musket blasts and the fire overhead, it was becoming increasingly difficult for Peter to make his way through the tavern. Years ago he had found himself caught in a battle between ravens and thieves on a structure very much like this one. Had it not been for Sir Tode's bravery, Peter surely would have died. Now it was his turn to return the favor.

Peter crouched down, trying to slow his racing heartbeat and concentrate on the sounds around him, listening for Sir Tode's small voice amidst the chaos. He placed his hand on the creaking floorboards, which were slick with blood—not all of it human. He could feel the river rushing beneath him, vibrating up through the rickety structure. He could feel the heat from the fire raging overhead, and already two beams had collapsed from the ceiling. He wasn't sure how much longer the moorings would remain secure. If they broke, the entire floating structure would be carried off into the abyss.

He fixated on a space across the room. Cool air was coming in through two swinging doors—that was his way out. He took a breath and then sprang into action, racing across the room. He slashed his blade, fending off guards and pilgrims alike on his way to the other side.

"Don't let the boy escape!" Prigg's voice rang out. "Fire!"

Crack! Crack! Crack! Crack!

A volley of shots rang out behind him. He dove through the doors—the wall behind him bursting apart in an explosion of splinters. He hit the open deck with a hard thud and rolled toward the edge. There was a searing pain in the back of his shoulder, and he thought one of the musket balls might have grazed him. He groaned and pulled himself to his feet.

Away from the smoke and gunfire, it was easier for him to navigate his surroundings.

"Peter!" cried a familiar voice from the fog. "There's a bridge to your right!"

"Sir Tode!" Peter turned to his right and found a narrow, swinging bridge that led to the far shore. The musket graze had not killed him, but it did sting. He had to grip the rope of the bridge to keep from tipping into the water and being swept over the edge of the abyss. Behind him, he could feel the heat from the burning lighthouse as it swayed perilously on the river's current.

"Stop right there!" cried a voice up ahead. Peter heard three sets of boots on the bridge as guards from the shore marched to intercept him.

Musket balls whizzed over him as he rolled across the rickety slats. Peter sprang to his feet and attacked the three guards all at once with his blade. He knocked the muskets from their hands and then kicked all three of them over the edge of the bridge and into the water. The men screamed and sputtered as they were carried by the river toward the edge of the abyss—then, just as suddenly, their voices vanished. Peter didn't have time to think about what fate awaited the men at the bottom of that depth. He had a friend to save.

"I'm coming, Sir Tode!" he shouted, and continued to the far shore.

✦ ✦ ✦

The fog along the river's marshy bank was so thick that Sir Tode could hear Peter's approach before he could see him. The last several minutes had been an exercise in acute anxiety as the knight strained to make sense of whatever was happening at the lighthouse, which was now half-covered in flames, rocking to and fro. Madame Eldritch had been watching with him, though she refused to admit that she, too, was nervous.

When Peter's lithe figure emerged from the fog, Sir Tode nearly did a backflip. "Over this way!" the old knight cried. "We're trapped in this blasted cell!"

Peter soon reached them at the back of the wagon. "Peter!" Sir Tode said, clopping to meet him. "You look about as bad as I feel."

"Not half so bad as you smell." The boy reached through the bars to pet the old knight's scruff. His hand paused, and he sniffed the air. "Who's that with you?"

"That would be Madame Eldritch," Sir Tode said. "My esteemed travel companion."

Peter tipped his hat. "It looks like I'll be saving you, as well." He cracked his knuckles and knelt in front of the cell's lock.

"Do not trouble yourself," Madame Eldritch said. "My Taro comes directly."

Sir Tode followed her gaze to the nearby shore. Flashes of light illuminated the fog as muskets went off, followed by a dozen splashes. The fog slid back to reveal Taro standing around a dozen fallen guards. The mandrake's clothes were ripped to rags. At least five broken bayonet ends protruded from his back and shoulders. Who knew how many bullets scarred his body? Yet he was still standing.

Madame Eldritch stood up, brushing her hair behind her shoulders. "And he has brought me a present."

Sir Tode could see that he was indeed holding something in his hand. "Good heavens!" he said. "He's got the books of *Who* and *What*."

Taro reached the cell and pushed Peter aside. He grabbed the door with his free hand. There was a terrible wrenching sound as he ripped the door clean off and threw it down. It fell into the water with a heavy splash.

"I thank you," Madame Eldritch said, holding out her hand.

Taro helped her to the ground and then offered her the harness containing the books. Madame Eldritch clasped both hands to her breast, as though receiving flowers from a suitor. "Loyal as ever."

Sir Tode noticed something moving in the fog behind Taro. Before Madame Eldritch could take her prize, the mandrake staggered forward, collapsing to his knees, a look of shocked pain on his silent face.

"Taro!" she cried, catching him in her open arms.

Standing directly behind Taro was Torvald Knucklemeat. He clutched his bleeding throat with one hand. In his other hand was the butt end of the unicorn's horn. The horn had been snapped in half—the sharp end now buried in Taro's back. A black stain of viscous sap spread out from the wound. "Told you it'd come in handy," Knucklemeat said, winking at Madame Eldritch.

Madame Eldritch, however, gave no response. She was on her knees, clutching Taro, who stared up at her with unblinking eyes. A thin trail of black sap leaked from his wordless mouth. His body convulsed sharply with each sputtering breath. The harness of books lay on the ground, the strap still clasped tightly in his hand. Madame Eldritch touched his face, her own hands trembling and wet, covered in Taro's dark blood. "My child," she said, her voice hoarse. "My child . . ."

Taro made a sort of gargling sound—something between a gasp and a cry—as if trying to speak through his stitched lips. Madame Eldritch pulled his head close to hers and whispered something. She traced her fingers over Taro's mouth, and the shimmering threads disappeared. Taro sighed, his mouth open wide.

Sir Tode inched back, knowing something of the mandrake's cry. It was said that anyone who heard it would die of madness.

"What's she doing?" whispered Peter.

"Giving him his say," Sir Tode said.

Sir Tode watched as Taro blinked up at Madame Eldritch, breathing heavily, his lips moving wordlessly. He raised a shaking hand and touched her hair with trembling, tuberous fingers. He leaned close to her and whispered something in her ear. Madame Eldritch closed her eyes as Taro spoke. The sound was almost imperceptible, though Sir Tode thought he might have heard the faintest ringing of bells in the dark air. With a final gasp, Taro's head fell back, and he was dead.

Sir Tode swallowed; his tongue felt dry in his mouth. "Congratulations," he said to Knucklemeat. "You've just murdered one of the world's last true wonders."

Knucklemeat wiped a fake tear from his eye. "Shame on me." He knelt and examined the lifeless body of his prey. "Still, it's not all bad." He grunted, trying with little success to pry the book harness from Taro's grip. "Maybe we can boil him and make a nice stew." He chuckled at his own joke.

Madame Eldritch stood, her red-rimmed eyes trained on Knucklemeat. The youthful beauty of her face had been replaced with a chiseled look of cold hatred. "Before the next moon," she said, "I will make sure you choke on that grin of yours."

Knucklemeat's face paled slightly, but he quickly recovered with a hawking snort. "It's a date."

He gave a sharp whistle, and guards came from the fog and surrounded them, weapons high. Peter, at first, made to fight them off, but Sir Tode put a hoof on his shoulder. "Don't, Peter," he whispered. "There's been enough bloodshed for one day." He looked out toward the lighthouse, burning brightly in the fog. "It's up to her now."

CHAPTER THIRTY-SIX

LOST *to the* UNCANNYON

Sophie huddled behind the tavern counter, trapped and ter-rified. Screams and gunshots clashed above her. She closed her eyes tightly, trying not to envision the violence happening just on the other side of the bar. The only good news, if anything could be considered good news, was that Sophie's hiding spot behind the counter had kept her safe from Prigg. *The Book of Where* was still with its Storyguard—for now, at least.

Muskets and bayonets weren't Sophie's only concern. The fire from the lighthouse had spread to the galley of the tavern, which was now consumed in flames. Soon the entire structure would be reduced to ashes, and everyone aboard would plunge into the river and straight over the edge of the Uncannyon.

Sophie got to her knees and braved a peek over the top of the bar. Scrivener Behn stood on the counter above her, shouting to his compatriots. He was not giving orders like a normal commander. Instead, he spoke in an almost poetic cant, shouting each pilgrim's story as they fought. "*Five men surrounded Saint Martin,*" he cried over the din, "*but still the Bruin King would not fall.*"

Indeed, Saint Martin had not fallen. He was in the middle of the Last Resort, staggering, wheezing, his body soaked with blood. His ursine cloak had been stripped from him, and he was but a man, yet he still fought with the fury of a bear. Holding no weapon but the leg of a shattered stool, he fought back half a dozen guards who surrounded him.

Inquisitor Prigg, for his part, had ordered his soldiers to build a barricade out of fallen tables behind which he was able to give commands without fear of harm. He ordered volleys of musket fire, one after another.

Sophie watched the battle, desperately wishing that Peter were with her. She had seen him flee under musket fire. She had seen Knucklemeat follow him. That Peter had not yet returned with Sir Tode surely couldn't be a good sign. Scrivener Behn let out a scream as a bullet struck his leg. He fell from the bar and landed next to Sophie with a mighty crash. "The pilgrims are losing," Sophie said. "What do we do?"

The man looked up, his teeth bared and bloody. "You must get the book to safety."

Sophie looked toward the front of the tavern—Prigg's barricade stood between her and freedom. A flaming rafter collapsed in the galley behind her, showering sparks into the air. "But how?" she said. "We can't get past those guards."

"Then maybe we should remove the guards." Scrivener Behn pulled himself up from the floor and staggered to a platform near the front of the tavern, now little more than a pile of flaming splinters.

"Behn, no!" Sophie cried. She started to run after him, but Akrasia appeared at her side, blocking her way.

"Did you not hear him?" the tigress growled. "If you lose that book to Prigg, all of this has been for nothing."

Scrivener Behn was in the middle of the room, marching straight toward the barricade—straight toward the guns. Musket shots whizzed past him. He cried out as a musket ball struck his side, knocking him to the floor. But he rose to his knees and continued to crawl.

The man grabbed hold of an enormous wooden lever in the floor that was connected to an anchor winch. Two huge ropes stretched out in either direction, each tethered to one side of the river. These ropes were what kept the lighthouse from being carried off into the current. "Brothers and sisters!" he called, pulling himself upright. "Drop your arms."

One by one, the creatures in the tavern stopped fighting. "We have spilled enough blood," Behn said, looking out at them. His body was shaking, and it was clear he was fighting for every breath.

Prigg suspended the shooting and stepped out from behind his barricade. "So, you surrender."

Behn nodded, his face bloody, his breathing labored. "I do."

There was a strange silence in the room that only moments before had resounded with screams and gunfire. Only the sound of the river rushing beneath them and the fire blazing overhead could be heard. The remaining pilgrims—no more than twenty strong—were watching Behn now. Sophie looked at their faces: Their expressions were a mixture of exhaustion and defeat and fear.

"We have fought to live in a world that no longer will have us," Behn called to them. "Our story has been told." He turned toward a shattered hole in the hull, staring out at the Uncannyon—the Great Unknown whose depths could never be plumbed. "It's time we go home." He gripped the massive lever and pulled it with all his strength. The moment he had finished, he collapsed to the floor.

The Last Resort lurched to one side as the winch released the ropes that anchored the structure to shore. Sophie stumbled forward, falling against Akrasia, who was there to catch her. There was a jolt as the one remaining bridge snapped taut—groaning to keep the entire structure from being swept away.

It only took Prigg and his guards a moment to realize what was happening. While the guards were uncertain of the meaning, Prigg, however, knew full well what would happen if they floated into the Uncannyon—a darkness from which no living thing could return. He had no intention of seeing it firsthand.

"Get to shore!" he cried, running as fast as he could toward the one remaining bridge, which was creaking under the strain of the river's current. Then, with a huge shudder, the bridge gave way, and the flaming lighthouse slid along the current toward the waiting abyss.

Scrivener Behn and the remaining pilgrims did not run with Prigg, nor did they jump overboard. Instead, they stood in a circle in the middle of the room, all of them holding hands: Liesel, the sombre child, the cyanese twin, Saint Martin. Their expressions were not peaceful, exactly, but neither were they fearful. They were ready for whatever awaited them.

Sophie took a step toward the group, but Scrivener Behn stopped her with a hard glance. "This is not your story, Sophie Quire. You will not share in our fate."

"Quickly, my cub." Sophie felt Akrasia push her toward a hole in the floor. "We must swim."

Sophie looked out toward the approaching Uncannyon. "The current's too strong. I can't make it to shore."

"I can," Akrasia said. She took the back of Sophie's cloak in her jaw and leapt into the river—

Splash!

The breath went out of Sophie as her body hit the water. The river was colder than she had expected, the current stronger. It was all she could do to keep hold of the book in one hand and Akrasia's collar in the other.

There was a great, creaking snap as the second bridge gave way and fell into the water. Guards screamed as they tumbled from the bridge and into the river. The lighthouse, freed from its mooring, lurched to one side. A wave sloshed over Sophie, carrying her and Akrasia toward the shore. Flailing guards screamed as the current swept them toward the edge of the waiting Uncannyon. Sophie clung to Akrasia, watching as the burning lighthouse sailed after the men, growing smaller and smaller . . .

And then it was gone.

"They're dead," Sophie said, gasping. Despite nearly having drowned, she found her throat hoarse and dry. "All of them. Just like that. Dead."

"There are worse deaths than oblivion, my cub," Akrasia said, paddling against the current, her eyes fixed on the shore. The beast's teeth were bared, and it looked as if the current were stronger than she had reckoned.

At last, they reached the far shore, and Sophie could feel the security of a rock beneath her foot. She let go of Akrasia and pulled herself up onto a mossy outcropping. When she had caught her breath, she looked up to see that Akrasia was still in the water, paddling to keep her head above the surface. "What are you doing?" Sophie called.

"It is this cursed chain," the beast snarled. "The stone drags in the current and pulls me with it."

"Keep fighting," Sophie cried. She grabbed hold of Akrasia's golden collar and tried to pull her ashore, but it was no use. Akrasia was too large, the current too strong.

"Run, my cub," Akrasia snorted, struggling to breathe above the water. "If I am to lose my life, I can be consoled with the thought that it was not wasted. Whatever happens, do not forget our first words—" Before she could say more, the river took hold of her massive body and swept her toward the darkness.

"No!" Sophie cried, reaching after her, nearly falling back into the water herself. She kept her eyes trained on the tigress, who snarled and splashed—fighting against her fate to the very end. She gave a final roar as she disappeared over the edge of the Uncannyon.

"Akrasia!" Sophie screamed so loudly it stung her throat. She fell to her knees, clutching *The Book of Where*. Tears came to her eyes and she let them fall. This was not how her adventure was supposed to go. People—real people whom she loved—had died. Because of her.

Sophie's sobs subsided, and she became aware of others approaching her. She looked up to see guards standing in the haze. And they were not alone. Prigg was standing with them, holding the books of *Who* and *What* in his hands, their blue and green covers stained with something black that reminded Sophie of blood. The last she had seen of those books, they had been in Taro's possession in the Last Resort. There was no way he would have turned them over to anyone but Madame Eldritch. "What happened to Taro?" she said, water dripping down her face.

Prigg sighed, peering farther upshore toward a caravan of wagons. "If you're referring to that hideous weed belonging to Eldritch, he had a rather unfortunate encounter with my deputy, Mister Knucklemeat."

Sophie stared into the haze. Lying at the foot of a nearby wagon was a shape that looked very much like a corpse. "You murdered him?" She hadn't even been sure that was possible.

"Him and anyone else who stands between me and the Four Questions." The man's gaze slipped down to *The Book of Where* in Sophie's arms.

"I'll die before I give you the book," Sophie said, standing.

"You're almost right," he said. "But it's not you who will die." He waved his ebony cane. "Bring the prisoners."

No fewer than a dozen guards emerged from the fog, holding both Peter and Sir Tode. There were three loaded muskets trained on each of them. Peter's head was bleeding where he had been struck, probably by the butt end of a musket. He had cuts all along his arms and a bloody gash in his shoulder where a musket ball had grazed him.

"Peter," Sophie whispered.

"You've doubtless read enough stories to know how this scenario plays out," Prigg said.

"In my experience," Sir Tode said through gritted teeth, "the villain dies, and the heroes prevail."

Prigg nodded. "Ah, but which of us is the villain?"

"Don't listen to him, Sophie," Peter said. "Whatever he asks."

"Oh, I'm not asking," Prigg said lightly. "Asking is what one does when he lacks sufficient power to enact his will." He turned to the guards. "Shoot them both."

Two of the guards drew back the hammers of their muskets. Neither Peter nor Sir Tode reacted.

"Wait!" Sophie cried. "I'll give you the book. Just don't shoot." She stared at Prigg. "Promise me you won't hurt them."

The man smiled. "You're hardly in a position to exact promises."

Sophie took a step backward, right to the edge of the rushing river. "Promise." She felt her heel slip on the slick, mossy bed of rock. "Or I'll dive into the water with *The Book of Where*, and you'll lose it forever."

Prigg stared at her, his sneer hardened into contempt. "Determined to the end," he said. "You are your mother's daughter."

He waved his cane at his guards. "None of these men will harm your compatriots." He gave a smile as tight as a vise. "You have my word."

It was not a very broad promise, but it was enough to keep Peter and Sir Tode alive long enough to escape. "Agreed," she said, stepping away from the water.

"Sophie, no!" Peter cried, but it was too late. Sophie had already reached Prigg and handed him *The Book of Where*.

"And you must do one more thing for me," Prigg said, taking the book under his arm. He reached into his coat pocket and removed a crumpled piece of blank paper with a torn edge. "Do you know what this is?"

Sophie stared at the paper, a torn-out book page. Even at this distance, she could recognize its weight and texture. "It's the missing page," she said. "From *The Book of Who*."

"Indeed, it is." Prigg peered at it like a curious fish. "Your mother tore it out of *The Book of Who* to ensure that, even if I obtained the Four Questions, I might never be able to use them."

Sophie swallowed a lump in her throat. She was soaked from head to toe and shivering. This was why Prigg's entry had been missing from *The Book of Who*, why Sophie had not been able to learn the name of her mother's killer. "So even if you get all four books, they're useless to you unless you can fix the page," she said.

"Precisely," Prigg said, stepping closer. "Which is why you're going to mend it for me."

PART FOUR

WHEN

CHAPTER THIRTY-SEVEN

THE BOOK of WHEN

The mending of *The Book of Who* was perhaps the greatest moment of sorrow in Sophie's entire life. She knelt on the bank of the river, dutifully reaffixing the missing page into the book. Sprites danced above her in the misty air, casting an eerie light on the vellum pages. Sophie did not once look at Peter or Sir Tode, who were both standing next to her, muskets at their temples. She could hear gunshots in the wilderness; Knucklemeat and the rest of the guards were waging battle in the marsh with the few pilgrims who had escaped from the lighthouse.

Sophie's hands were muddy and shaking, and the needlework was cruder than usual. But the moment her stitching was complete, the blank page filled with blue ink—

SIGMUND PRIGG: Former Storyguard from the hinterland empire, now acting as Bustleburgh's Grand Inquisitor. Killer of no fewer than two Storyguard. Current owner of the Four Questions.

~For more information, see: *Book of Who*, "Storyguard"; *Book of What*, "Four Questions"; *Book of Where*, "Hinterlands," "Bustleburgh"

"I'm sorry, Mama," Sophie whispered, putting away her tools, their handles wet with tears.

Prigg took the open book in his hands, reading the entry with a look of great relish. He walked to a windowless carriage at the front of his caravan and removed an iron key from his pocket. The carriage looked to Sophie like a great iron vault mounted on wheels, which is precisely what it was. "One never can be too careful," he said, unlocking and opening the door. The inside of the carriage was empty but for a single book with a blood-red cover.

"*The Book of When*," Sophie whispered.

Prigg removed the book from the carriage. "At last . . ." He was now clutching all four volumes—*Who, What, Where,* and *When*—in his thin arms. "After twelve long years, they are united for one final Evensong." He took a rapturous breath, his eyes closed.

Sophie watched him, a knot forming in her stomach. These were the books her mother had died to protect. Not just her mother. Also Veena Bluestocking, Scrivener Behn, Taro, Akrasia, and dozens more. And Sophie had just handed over the last book. More than that, she had repaired it for him. "What have I done?" she whispered, her eyes blurry and hot. She wanted to lunge for him, rip the books from his hands. But the bayonets pressed against her back were too many, too real a reminder of just how fragile she was. "What happens now?" she said to Prigg, trying to keep the tremor from her voice. "You say *I wish*, and the books do anything you tell them to?"

Prigg looked at her. *"I wish?"* He clucked his tongue. "You disappoint me, Sophie Quire. A true Storyguard would have solved the riddle long ago. It's written plainly enough on the page." And so saying, he opened *The Book of Who* and recited the inscription:

> *We four books—Who, What, Where, and When—*
> *Hold all the world's magic bound within.*
> *And when assembled throughout the ages,*
> *Two words, when spoken, unlock our pages.*
> *Impossible things of all shape and kind*
> *Flow from the will of a curious mind.*

Sophie turned over the words of the riddle, seeing the letters in her mind. "W–H–A–T–I–F . . ." She blinked. "It's an acrostic— the first letter of every line of the poem creates a phrase—a child's game!" She kicked the mud. "How could I have been so stupid?"

"Now's not really the time," Peter said, still crouched, blade poised. "We have bigger problems."

"Indeed, you do," Prigg said as he laid the four books on the ground in a circle. He stood in the middle and spread out his arms. "WHAT IF . . ." he said in a loud tone. At these words, all four of the books trembled and shuddered and then lifted clear off the ground. They hovered in a ring around him, slowly turning like satellite moons. The man smiled, savoring this moment of absolute power.

Prigg paced along the shore, the books moving with him. "A battlefield is no place for serious conversation. I suggest we relocate to somewhere more comfortable." He paused, rubbing his chin in rumination. "*Where* might that be?" As soon as he uttered this question, *The Book of Where* spun around and opened its cover. Pages riffled automatically until the book stopped on an entry. Prigg read the book floating before him. "A fitting choice!" He cleared his throat and read aloud: "'Quire and Quire Booksellers.'"

Sophie heard the rustling of pages. There was a shiver in the air, and the next thing she knew, she was standing in the middle of her father's bookshop. The cries of battle, the gunshots, the smoke, and the flames were suddenly replaced with an eerie calm. The walls she had known her entire life now surrounded her on all sides. She stared at the ceiling, the floor, the sagging bookshelves, all cast orange in the light of early dawn. Peter and Sir Tode were beside her, turning about in similar confusion.

"What just happened?" Peter said, spinning around.

"I, er, think we're back in the bookshop," Sir Tode said.

"Indeed, we are!" Prigg was beaming, looking about as pleased with himself as a man could be. "You have no idea how many times I've dreamt of this moment."

Sophie stared at the cramped shop, at once familiar and alien to her. It seemed smaller than she remembered. The cries of battle still echoed in her ears. "What happened to the guards?" she said. "And the pilgrims?" She thought of Akrasia, pulled under by the rushing current.

"They're still fighting, I suppose," Prigg said. "It's really not my concern."

"S-S-Sophie?" said a voice behind her. Sophie turned around to see her father, who was standing at the foot of the stairs, looking entirely confused. "How did you get here?" He looked at Prigg. "What is the Inquisitor doing with those books?"

"Stay back, Papa," Sophie called. "Prigg's the one who killed Mama."

It took a moment for her words to register. "He *what*?" His face was ashen.

"With this very blade, in fact," Prigg said, unsheathing his cane.

"I hunted her down and drove the steel through her heart . . . right . . . here." He tapped the foot of the workbench. "You can imagine my disappointment when I turned her body over to find no *Book of Who*—only a torn page, clasped in her hand." He offered Sophie's father a small bow. "Really, I must thank you, sir. If you hadn't summoned me to your shop two weeks ago, I might have never discovered *The Book of Who* in your stove. All my years of patient work would have been for naught."

Sophie looked at her father, who was watching Prigg with an expression of pure shock. "It was you . . . all those years . . . and it was you . . ."

"You can now understand why I was not more helpful when you approached me about finding Coriander's murderer." He shrugged. "It was a profound conflict of interest."

"Perhaps you've forgotten one thing," Peter said. "Without your guards, you're a little outnumbered." He and Sir Tode stood side by side, ready to fight.

"Quite right," Prigg said. "*What* might even the odds?" In answer, *The Book of What* moved in front of him and opened to an entry. Prigg's face lit up. "Ah, yes! *Quickbramble, quickbramble, ramblers take heed . . .*"

Sophie heard a rustling sound at her feet. She shrieked, leaping next to her father as thick cords of quickbramble sprang up seemingly from nowhere and grasped at her ankles.

"What is that?" her father cried, throwing his arms protectively around Sophie. More tendrils appeared from the walls and ceiling and wrapped tightly around them both, binding them together.

"Not again!" Sir Tode hissed and snarled as the quickbramble lifted him clear off the floor. He dangled a few feet from the ground, swinging his hooves.

"Sir Tode!" Peter shouted, slicing through the branches at his feet. He lunged for his friend, but no sooner did his feet leave the ground than the quickbramble slithered through the air and caught him by the arm. Peter screamed, swiping at the weeds as the quickbramble tightened around his body and pulled him back against a bookcase. For every branch he hacked off, two more appeared. He kicked and thrashed as the thorny branches wrapped around his neck. His face turned a deadly crimson.

"Peter, stop!" Sophie cried. "You're going to get crushed."

Enraged as he was, Peter must have heard the truth of her words. He stopped struggling against the quickbramble, which in turn stopped choking him. He gasped for breath, his face returning to normal.

"A prudent surrender," Prigg said.

"I knew a man like you once ... " Peter said, still breathing hard. "He was obsessed with wielding power. He died like a miserable worm."

"My dear boy," Prigg said. "What I desire is the *end* of power." Now that Sophie and the others had been restrained, it was clear

Prigg felt more comfortable—comfortable enough, even, to engage in the storied tradition of villainous monologue. "What I have done in Bustleburgh, I will now do the world over. From the Fennel Sea to the Ice Barrens and everyplace in between." He spread his arms wide. "I will purge magic from every corner of the map. When I am through, mankind will be rid of nonsense once and for all." As he spoke, his voice took on a commanding strength. The books of *Who*, *What*, *Where*, and *When*—still floating around him—began to spin more quickly to match his passion.

"Hold up," Sir Tode said, adjusting himself in the brambles. "You're using magic books to destroy all magic? Feels a bit like cheating."

Prigg gave an almost pitiful smile. "Cheating is what magic does best. You of all people should appreciate that."

"But the books don't work that way," Peter insisted. "They create magic, not destroy it."

"You are quite right," Prigg said, tapping his chin. "How does one fight fire with fire?"

Sophie shifted away from her father, her eyes fixed on *The Book of What* floating before Prigg. "The Zeitgeist," she said. That was what her mother had been frightened to find in *The Book of What*.

Prigg's face lit up. "Ah, so you've heard of it!"

"What in blazes is a Zeitgeist?" Sir Tode said.

"It's an elemental beast," Sophie replied, recalling what she had read in *The Book of What.* "It is thought to have ushered in one of the ages of magic. It is controlled by something . . ." She closed her eyes, trying to recall what she had read. "Feelings, or ideas, maybe?" She shook her head. "I can't remember."

"Will," Prigg said helpfully. "The Zeitgeist is controlled by force of will. Whatever you imagine, the Zeitgeist will become. When summoned, it obeys the will of the minds around it. If the minds are divided, the Zeitgeist will tear itself into nothing—as most often occurs." He raised a finger. "But if all the minds around it are unified under a single idea, the beast will grow in strength until nothing can contain it." He marched to the front window and removed a poster. "Fortunately, we have just such a single idea in Bustleburgh."

Sophie stared at the words across the top of the poster:

No Nonsense!

"The Pyre." Sophie felt a sickening dread in the pit of her stomach. "You were just manipulating them. Convincing them to hate magic . . . all for this."

"Precisely." Prigg paced in front of her, the four books floating slowly around him. "And what better day to harness this collective will than Pyre Day?" He swept a hand toward the front window, inviting her to behold the view.

Sophie looked and saw Bustleburghers rushing up and down the alley—many more than usual, given the early hour. She looked at their eager faces, their fine clothes. Many of them were clutching books in their arms. "Today is Pyre Day," she said, her voice small.

"And what a day it shall be!" Prigg said. "You see, Sophie Quire, I have not just been searching for these books. I have also been orchestrating the perfect conditions for their use. I tried to summon the Zeitgeist twelve years ago and failed. Your mother saw to that." He gave a tight smile. "But even without her meddling, I could never have accomplished my task alone. The history of magic is that of lone heroes against faceless hordes, but the history of man tells a different story: strength in numbers. When I summon the Zeitgeist from these pages, it will be fueled by thousands of minds—all of them clamoring for the death of stories."

"A world without stories is a world without magic," Sophie said, recalling what Professor Cake had told her in the library.

"That's the idea," Prigg said, walking to the door. "And now, if you'll excuse me, I have a Zeitgeist to summon."

"You're just going to leave us here?" Peter said, twisting in the brambles.

"Well, I *was* planning to kill you, but time seems to have gotten away from me." He rubbed his chin, looking at the Four Questions. "*Who* might be trusted with such a delicate task?" *The Book of Who* opened and flipped to an entry. Prigg read it and smiled. "The very man I had in mind! Torvald Knucklemeat!"

No sooner had he said these words than Knucklemeat appeared beside him on the floor of the shop. He was crouched in a fighting position, dripping wet, with one pistol drawn. Blood flowed from a long gash in his side. His other pistols were neatly slotted into his holsters, which he had since reclaimed from Taro's lifeless body, not without some apparent struggle: The mandrake's severed fist was still clasped around the buckle of the harness. Whatever confusion Knucklemeat might have felt about being summoned to a bookshop via magical book quickly gave way to delight when he saw Sophie and the others bound up in quickbramble. He stood and tipped his hat to Prigg. "Looks like you've been busy, sir."

"Busy and then some." Prigg opened the front door and took a deep, rapturous breath. "I have some pressing business that cannot wait. The girl should remain alive—I might find myself in need of a good bookmender."

Knucklemeat nodded. "And the rest?" He was staring straight at Peter.

Prigg shrugged. "The rest you can kill in whatever order pleases you." He nodded to Sophie. "Happy Pyre Day!" And so saying, he stepped lightly out the door, whistling as he went.

CHAPTER THIRTY-EIGHT

PROMISES

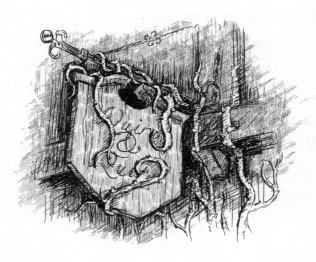

While Prigg cheerily strolled toward the impending Armageddon, Sophie and the others remained rooted to the spot, as it were, confined by endless cords of ever-tightening quickbramble. Peter, who would ordinarily have been their best hope at escape, had been so worked up into knots that his arms were twisted backward behind his legs.

Knucklemeat, their jailer, seemed quick to appreciate the difficulty of their situation. "Eenie, meenie, miney, moe . . ." he said, walking in front of them. "Kill you fast or kill you slow . . ."

Sophie knew that these were not the correct words to the rhyme, but it didn't seem like the time to quibble. She glanced over her father's shoulder toward the shop window. She would have screamed for someone to help them, but the streets were now empty—everyone had already reached the Pyre grounds and was preparing for the celebration. "You have to let us go!" she said to Knucklemeat. "Prigg is heading to the Pyre right now. If we don't stop him, every scrap of magic in the world will be destroyed—and that includes your precious scrying eye."

Knucklemeat shrugged. "So I'll get another."

"You don't understand! There will be no scryglass. No nonsense. No magic at all. The world will be nothing but a wasteland!" She thrashed against her bonds, which only clenched tighter, compressing her lungs.

"Wasteland or not, there will always be room for men in my line of work." Knucklemeat tucked his hands into the belt of his holsters. "Can't say the same for bookmenders."

Sophie was getting nowhere. And every second that passed brought Prigg closer to the Pyre. She tried a different tack. She tilted her head down, lowering her gaze, recalling the way Professor Cake had spoken to her in the library. "Bustleburgh needs you, Torvald Knucklemeat. Cut us free. Together we can stop him before it's too late."

Sophie did not think her performance was laughable, but Knucklemeat laughed nonetheless. "It's already too late," he said. "I've promised the Inquisitor that I'd kill you off. And when it comes to killing, I'm a man of my word."

That much she believed. Sophie felt her father's arms, wrapped tightly around her sides, tighter even than the quickbramble. "Papa," she whispered, turning up to see his face. "I shouldn't have run from you. I should have listened . . ." She could feel the thorns tensing against her throat, choking her words back.

"No, child." He shook his head, and she could see tears in his pale eyes. "This . . . this is my fault. Your mother made me promise that if something ever happened to her, I would keep the book safe. If I had not brought Prigg here . . . If I had not broken my promise to her . . ." He closed his eyes and pressed his mouth to the top of Sophie's head. "Forgive me, my love." It was unclear whether he was speaking to Sophie or to the wife he had lost.

"Ain't that sweet?" Knucklemeat said, wiping an invisible tear from his good eye. "Think I'll leave dear old *Papa* for last—give you two a bit more time."

"Did you show the same mercy to Taro?" Peter called from the wall. "When you murdered him?"

"Nope. Tossed his scraggy corpse over the edge of the world— boots and all." He looked admiringly at the severed hand clenched tight around his harness. "Well, not *all*."

"What kind of brute wears a hand as a trophy?" Sophie said.

Knucklemeat sniffed. "And why shouldn't I? It's not every day a man slays a mandrake. Thought I'd keep a little souvenir." The truth was a little more complicated than that. Loyal even in death, Taro had held fast to the harness containing the books of *Who* and

What. Try as he might, Knucklemeat had not been able to break the mandrake's grip. And so, rather than leave the harness behind, Knucklemeat had elected to chop off Taro's hand at the wrist and cast his body into the river. The cries of Madame Eldritch as her loyal servant's corpse floated into the shadow had rung for miles through the hinterlands.

"And what about Eldritch?" Sir Tode said. "Did you kill her, too?"

"The little minx gave us the slip before we could apprehend her." Knucklemeat spat on the floor. "Not that it'll do her much good. Alone in the hinterlands? She's probably been eaten alive a dozen times over by now." He laughed again, as if amused by the thought.

Sophie wasn't sure how she felt about Madame Eldritch escaping. She hated the woman, but she hated Knucklemeat and Prigg even more—perhaps it was worth having the former running free if it vexed the latter? In any case, none of that had any effect on their current predicament. By the time Prigg unleashed the Zeitgeist, Madame Eldritch and everyone like her would be as good as dead.

"So you're here to kill us," Peter said. "Who are you going to start with?"

"I should think that's pretty obvious." Knucklemeat drew something small from a pouch on his belt. He held it up in front of Peter. "You know what this is?"

"Obviously not," Sophie said. "He can't see it."

"Aye, but this lad, he don't need to see it." He waved it mysteriously in front of Peter's face. "Do you?"

Peter set his jaw. "It's a bullet."

"Astonishing!" Knucklemeat said. He tossed it into the air and caught it again. "And not just any bullet, is it? This here is the *very same* bullet you swiped from this very gun." While saying this, he loaded the bullet into the muzzle. He drew a paper of gunpowder from his pocket and tore off the end, spitting it onto the floor. "You left it in the back of my wagon. Thought I'd keep it just in case our paths ever crossed again." He carefully poured the gunpowder into the pan and set the lock.

"I should warn you," Peter said. "I've been shot at before. It hasn't taken."

"Oh, I'm not going to use it on you." He swung his arm away and pointed the gun at Sir Tode. "I'm going to use it on your pet."

"Sir Tode!" Peter cried, thrashing against his bonds. The quickbramble snaked around his head, pulling him back. Blood ran down his face where the thorns had cut into his brow.

"Steady, Peter," Sir Tode said. He was staring straight at the gun, his features cut with steely resolve. "That's no way for a hero to go out. And if I'm to die, then I can think of no better way than at the side of my dearest friend." There was a tremor in his voice, but beneath that was something deeper, truer. "It has been an honor to journey at your side. I wouldn't take back a second of it."

"A touching eulogy." Knucklemeat drew back the hammer, which made a sharp *click*.

"Wait!" Peter cried, pulling his head free. "I have something! Something you want. Something more valuable than any treasure you've ever seen." He was breathing heavily. Rivulets of blood ran down his pale, trembling face. "Spare his life, and I'll give it to you."

Knucklemeat kept his pistol ready, but he did not pull the trigger. "I'm listening."

"Peter . . ." Sir Tode said in a warning voice. "What are you doing?"

Sophie watched all this, horror mixed with confusion. What was Peter offering to the man? And why was Sir Tode so frightened?

"Let's see this treasure first," Knucklemeat said. "Then I'll decide."

Peter took a breath and nodded. "Take off my blindfold."

"No!" Sir Tode cried, but it was too late. Knucklemeat had already grabbed the boy's blindfold and ripped it from his head.

Peter blinked to reveal the most extraordinary pair of emerald-green eyes that Sophie had ever seen.

Droopy poets are often fond of saying that the eyes are the window to the soul, which is ridiculous on its face. But when one looked upon Peter's eyes, the statement felt almost true. Looking into Peter's eyes was like looking into a thousand different stories, each more impossible than the last. "Peter," she said, breathless.

"Your eyes. They're . . . *fantastic.*" This was truly the only word for them.

Knucklemeat, who had been similarly dumbstruck, seemed to regain himself. "The girl's right on that count," he said, his voice touched with wonder. "Prettier than a diamond mine and twice as large."

Torvald Knucklemeat, who could see more than ordinary people, understood that Peter's fantastic eyes were not just beautiful. He understood that they held a deep magic within, the likes of which the world had never seen. "They'll make a nice set of cufflinks." He holstered his pistol in favor of his machete. "Only question is: Do I kill you before or after I cut 'em out?" He traced the blade along Peter's cheek.

"A question for the ages," said a voice from the far corner. "Is life more painful than death?"

Knucklemeat spun around. "Who goes there?" He had two pistols drawn.

Sophie strained against the quickbramble, which held her fast. Out of the corner of her eye, she saw a figure step through the bookcase. It was a woman with ghostly pale skin and tangled auburn hair.

"Madame Eldritch!" Sophie exclaimed.

"Hello, little bookmender." The woman's voice had the drained quality of someone who has no more tears, no emotion left at all within. All traces of the charming enchantress had vanished. Eldritch's fine dress had been reduced to a cape of tatters—muddy and torn. Her hair was a thicket that rose up from her shoulders, coated with burrs and leaves.

Knucklemeat seemed to have regained his composure. "Thought you'd have enough sense to keep clear o' these parts, witch." He snorted and spat in her direction.

The woman released a weary sigh and stepped around the glob of spit. "How many times must I explain? I am a simple shopkeeper." This may have been true, but she could not have looked more like a witch if she had tried. "I have traveled a very long distance, at great pain, to find you, Torvald Knucklemeat."

"How flattering," he said.

Madame Eldritch's lip curled. "You have something that belongs to me." She stepped closer, her fingers playing on the edge of her tattered cloak. "Something I want back." She tried to take a step closer, but Knucklemeat stopped her with the muzzle of his pistol, which he placed right at her heart.

"That's close enough, witch," he said.

The woman closed her eyes and took a deep, luxuriant breath. "You're right. It *is* close enough." Her eyes opened again to reveal a look of cold hatred. "Taro," she said in an icy voice. "Kill."

No sooner had Madame Eldritch uttered the word *Kill* than the hand of Taro came to life. It released its grip on Knucklemeat's harness and crawled up the man's shoulder. Knucklemeat leapt back, dropping his pistols to the floor.

"Get it off!" he cried, trying to knock the crawling hand from his body, but by that point it was too late—Taro's fingers had found their mark. Knucklemeat let out a gurgling scream and fell to the floor as the thin, root-shaped fingers clenched around his windpipe.

Madame Eldritch stood over Knucklemeat, watching with an expression of bloody triumph. "The last time I saw you, I promised that you would choke on that smile. You will see now that I am a woman of my word."

Much as Sophie wanted to see Knucklemeat dead, she found herself unwilling to watch him die. She buried her face in her father's chest, closing her eyes. She could feel her father's hands tighten around her shoulders.

When the act was complete, the hand of Taro released its grip and sprang back—its fingers splayed out like little legs. Knucklemeat's body lay motionless on the floor, limp as a bag of boiled potatoes. The hand of Taro skittered over the corpse and climbed up Madame Eldritch's tattered dress. It perched itself onto her shoulder, nestling close to her cheek.

"My dear Taro," Madame Eldritch said, almost tenderly. "Loyal even in death."

Sophie released a slow, trembling breath. This killing had taken place not ten feet from where she stood. Knucklemeat's face was turned away from her—a fact for which she found herself eminently grateful. She turned to Madame Eldritch, swallowing dryly. "There should be a blossom buried in the thicket."

"I am not a child," Madame Eldritch said. "I know how quick-bramble works." She walked directly to a corner of the thicket and plucked a blossom buried deep near the base. At once, the thorny tendrils released their grip around Sophie. She and the others all collapsed to the floor.

"You got Taro," Sophie said, gasping. "Why . . . why did you release us?"

The woman paused, considering her response. "An old friend once asked me the point of living in a world ruled by petty men." Her gaze slid toward Sir Tode. "I am beginning to see the wisdom of his words. And I think it is perhaps time to change that world."

Peter stood up, and Sophie found herself again surprised by the light of his emerald eyes. "How did you get into the Professor's library?" he demanded, peering into the open bookcase behind him.

"You're not the only one to receive an invitation from Professor Cake. When I had nowhere to run in the marshes, I came upon the abandoned bookcase in my jailer's wagon. I found that what had once been a bookcase was now a doorway—opened by some unseen hand. I passed through it and found *him* waiting for me."

"And?" Peter prodded.

"And we had a conversation in which he tried to convince me of certain things." A small smirk played at the edges of her mouth. "Chiefly that I was not so wicked a person as I liked to believe."

"You're lying," Peter said. "The Professor would never help a person like you."

"The Professor contains multitudes that you can hardly fathom. And he wasn't helping me—he was helping *you*." It was unclear to Sophie whether the woman was referring directly to Peter or to all of them in the room. "I did not come here to bicker. I came here to stop Inquisitor Prigg. You, Sophie Quire, are the Last Storyguard. And if we can wrest those books from his hands, perhaps you can summon something to end this madness."

"But it's too late," Sophie said. "Prigg's halfway to the Pyre by now. We'll never reach him in time."

Madame Eldritch turned toward the open bookcase. "Perhaps there is another who can speed your path?"

Sophie saw a shadow stir in the darkness. One silver paw stretched onto the floor of the shop, followed by another. Two yellow eyes appeared above a row of sharp teeth. "Hello, my cub," said a low, growling voice.

"Akrasia!" Sophie cried, running to meet the tigress. She wrapped her arms around the beast's great neck, burying her face in matted layers of warm fur. "I thought you were lost."

"And I would have been, if my chain had not caught upon the

rocks at the mouth of the Uncannyon." The tigress glanced back at the chain and stone still trailing behind her. "I was left dangling over the precipice, trapped between this world and the next." She bowed her head. "It was Eldritch who rescued me from that dire place."

"Come, bookmender." Madame Eldritch placed a hand on Sophie's shoulder. "The hour is upon us."

Sophie looked back to her father, who had said almost nothing since his release from the quickbramble. He sat on the floor, his back against an empty shelf, watching her with pained eyes. And here she was, about to leave him once more. And this time, she might not return. "Papa . . ." she said, but she could not find the words.

Sophie's father stood and stepped toward her. "You have too much of your mother in you." He touched her face. "I was wrong to ever think you should remain inside this dusty shop."

Sophie gave him a hard embrace. She shut her eyes tight, letting tears spill down her cheeks. "I don't want to leave you again, Papa."

Her father smiled down at her. "Go, my child. You have a world to save."

❦ CHAPTER THIRTY-NINE ❧

PYRE DAY

It was a crisp, windy morning in Bustleburgh—perfect weather for burning books. Sigmund Prigg walked cheerily down the street, surveying the buzz of activity. Every man, woman, and child in the city had turned out for the celebration that would symbolize their freedom from the shackles of ignorance and superstition, their arms filled with stacks of storybooks to cast into the Pyre.

As predicted, it was the biggest Pyre Day to date. There were food venders and musicians and souvenir-hawkers wandering the streets. Fashionable women had used torn-up books to make bonnets and folding fans. Men had spiced their tobacco with shredded bits of paper, claiming it helped improve the flavor of their pipes. Mill workers and servants were given the morning off to join the festivities. A contagious excitement filled the air. For generations, this city had been consigned to a backwater garrison at the edge of the civilized world—but now (at last!) the people of Bustleburgh had outgrown their childish ways and were ready to enter a sensible new world.

Prigg walked under one of two hideous wolf statues, whose stone paw he could not help but touch for luck as he passed. "Just look at them," he said to no one in particular. "The bright faces of our future world." This crowd, this cheery mob, was his creation. He had not told the people that the Pyre itself was a fool's errand. Eradicating individual pieces of nonsense was impossible, when one got down to it: For every one thing you burned, two more cropped up. And yet he had devised a way to do what the Pyre could not. That his plan relied on the creation of one last magical thing (the Zeitgeist) rankled him slightly. It wasn't an elegant solution— but then, practical solutions rarely are. That pragmatism was what made Prigg superior to common men. He was not afraid to break a few eggs to make an omelet. The thought of omelets made Prigg hungry. Perhaps he would treat himself to one after saving the world.

"Inquisitor?" said a guard with a sallow, pudgy face. "The Pyre's all set. You can start whenever you're ready."

"Thank you," Prigg said. He looked at the books of *Who*, *What*, *Where*, and *When*, which lay in a sack at his feet. He had bound them with rope so as not to alarm the crowds. These four books, to which he had once so foolishly dedicated his life, seemed almost embarrassingly small before the massive Pyre. He wondered what he should do with the Four Questions once his plan was complete. The honorable thing to do would be to destroy them, but a part of him wondered if he might prefer to keep them. It had been tremendously thrilling to use them in the bookshop, and he rather liked the idea of having them on hand. *Just in case*, he thought.

Prigg took the bag of books and approached a wooden dais that had been erected in front of the gates. It was a sensible, plain structure, devoid of frills and ornamentation. No nonsense. The crowd became silent as Prigg assumed his place. Another guard handed him a flickering torch, which he raised above his head.

"Men and women of Bustleburgh!" he shouted, his voice ringing out across the river. "After years, our diligent work has come to an end. Today we put to death those superstitions and trivialities that have for generations held us captive. We bury fancy and erect a monument to fact. We ignore the siren song of *what if* for the stolid comfort of *what is*. Today we say, *No more nonsense!*" He lowered his torch and lit the Pyre.

The crowd burst into riotous cheering. Thousands of men, women, and children were packed shoulder to shoulder along the bridge and shore and streets. More people hung out from windows and balconies. All cheering for him.

The books were perfect fuel, and in a matter of seconds, the entire Pyre was engulfed in flames. Prigg stared up at the black plume of smoke that rose up like a column to the heavens. The heat was overpowering. He dabbed his brow with a handkerchief and breathed the ashen air.

"This Pyre is but the first spark," he called out over the roaring fire. "Here starts a flame of progress that will spread and grow and will not stop until the very world is consumed in its light." *A bit florid*, he thought, *but effective*. "Let us shed the shackles of our past and march boldly into a modern, sensible tomorrow." He spread his arms wide like a ruler of old.

People in the crowd were all cheering now, waving flags and handmade banners high over their heads. "No nonsense! No nonsense! No nonsense!"

Prigg took *The Book of What* from the bag and opened it to the page he had marked. "Citizens of Bustleburgh, I present to you the end of nonsense. I present to you . . . the Zeitgeist!"

A tremendous rumbling sound seemed to vibrate up through the earth. Prigg was very nearly knocked off the dais as a great wind swept out from the pages of the book and whirled like a cyclone around the burning Pyre, stoking the flames high—so high that their raging peak could not be seen from Prigg's vantage point. The black plume of smoke spread from horizon to horizon, blotting out the sun until only the light of the Pyre remained.

Prigg kept one hand on his wig and peered upward at the sky.

Truth be told, he did not know exactly what would appear when he summoned the Zeitgeist. His knowledge of the creature was based on accounts from ancient stories. Every description of the creature was a little bit different—a watery serpent or a hungry storm cloud or even a living avalanche. He suspected that it made use of its surroundings. He wondered what the creature would make of this place.

By now, the howling wind was so loud it hurt his ears. Prigg closed his eyes. He imagined he could actually hear the thousands of swirling thoughts that had summoned it into being, all of them saying, "No Nonsense!" in one accord.

And then, just as quickly, the wind vanished.

Flags stopped moving. People stopped chanting. They stared up at the sunless sky. The Zeitgeist was gone. There was no rushing or wind. No choir of voices. Only the crackling of the Pyre remained.

The spirit of anticipation quickly gave way to mild disappointment. Rumblings of "Is that all?" and "So what?" began to ripple through the crowd.

Prigg scanned the red horizon, a wave of dread creeping over him. Where was the creature? It had to be there somewhere. In the water, in the ground, somewhere. It *had to* have worked.

A piercing scream cut through the confusion. Prigg saw a woman in front of the crowd. Her eyes were wide with terror. "The P-P-Pyre," she said, pointing. "It's alive!"

Prigg turned around to face the pile of burning books.

Only, it wasn't a pile anymore.

There was a muffled crackling sound as the books on the Pyre drew themselves up from the ground and slowly, impossibly, came to life. Like metal filaments on a lodestone, the books clung to one another to form a single mass. Flaming columns of books spread out from the sides of the Pyre like enormous limbs as the Zeitgeist reshaped itself into a massive, hulking three-legged beast. A tail of fire waved back and forth, whiffling the air as it moved. Two glowing pits appeared at the top of the pyre—eyes like embers. The creature opened a huge, flaming maw and *ROARED*.

The crowd screamed as a wave of heat singed the air above them. Prigg stood stock-still on the dais, his mouth open, transfixed by the creature before him—a hundred feet tall and burning with rage.

It was more beautiful than he could have possibly imagined.

CHAPTER FORTY

THE ZEITGEIST

Sophie was still three blocks from the bridge when she heard the first roar of the Zeitgeist. The sound seemed to echo up through the ground and rattle her very bones. She clutched Akrasia's mane as the tigress raced through the twisting alleys. The beast's chain and stone trailed behind her, casting sparks against the cobblestone street. "Faster," Sophie whispered.

Sophie and Akrasia emerged from the alleys to find that the entire shore was packed full of people, all of them staring agape at the Pyre. Orange light shone off the river, rippling and glinting in the smoky haze. The flames moved strangely, seeming to draw themselves up from the ground.

Akrasia stopped running. Sophie let go of her neck and slid to her feet. "The Pyre," she whispered. "It's come alive." From this distance, she could not see the books within the beast's body, but she knew they were there. She could hear them, smell them, burning and crackling and dying forever. The fiery beast swayed from side to side, charred books spilling from its body like flaming detritus.

Sophie shielded her eyes from the glare and saw a figure on a wooden platform in front of the gates. "It's Prigg," she said. The man looked absurdly small before the hundred-foot Pyre.

A hush fell over the crowd as Prigg spread his arms wide. "Now!" he shouted to the beast. "Go forth and do your work! Do not stop until you have cleansed every corner of the world of nonsense!"

There was a halfhearted smattering of applause from the crowd, though it was obvious that their enthusiasm for this endeavor had dramatically decreased.

The Zeitgeist shifted itself, turning to face the one who had addressed it in such a bold manner. The beast angled down its massive, flaming head, focusing its ember eyes on the tiny man at its feet.

Inquisitor Prigg stared defiantly back at it. "No, no—you're not listening!" He pointed again, this time with both arms. "The nonsense is *that* way!"

The beast growled, then opened its jaws to reveal an enormous flaming tongue. Charred books spilled from its open mouth.

Prigg inched backward, swatting embers from his face. "What are you doing?" He tripped over the bundle of books, which he had set on the platform beside him. "Stop it this instant!" He shook his fist at the skies. "I am your creator, and I command you to—"

Sigmund Prigg's final words were likely meant to be *Stop it*, but we will never know for sure, because at that very moment the Zeitgeist leaned down and swallowed the man in one go.

The crowd watched in complete, horrified silence. It was not clear, exactly, whether the man was being eaten or burned. What was clear was that it was painful. Sophie dug her fingers into Akrasia's fur, her own heart beating wildly. Inquisitor Prigg's screams rang out for a long and uncomfortable minute, and then they were gone. The sight was sickening, but more sickening still was the fact that the Zeitgeist, having finished its snack, had now turned to face the rest of the mob. It tilted its head, mouth open and hungry. It took a tentative step toward the open gates. Toward Bustleburgh.

A panicked uproar swept through the crowd on the far side of the river as people pushed to cross back over the bridge. Sophie stared at the Zeitgeist, which took another step toward the city. "I don't understand," she said. "If that thing's meant to destroy nonsense, why did it kill Prigg?"

Akrasia backed up, her hackles raised. "And why is it looking at Bustleburgh?"

Whatever the cause, it was becoming increasingly clear that Prigg's monster had its own ideas about what—and whom—it wanted to consume. With a tremendous roar, it raised two fiery fists over its body and brought them down on the wall that separated it from the city. Huge chunks of burning stone soared through the air, plunging into the river like rogue meteorites.

Bustleburghers screamed in terror, running in every direction, climbing over one another to escape the approaching beast. The Zeitgeist worked its way toward the edge of the river, smashing through the factories and mills and docks that lined the shore. One by one, the buildings collapsed in a burst of smoldering rubble.

Peter and Sir Tode were the first to catch up with Sophie and Akrasia. Madame Eldritch and Sophie's father were soon to follow.

"Good heavens," Sir Tode said from inside Peter's burgle-sack. "I'm suddenly very glad there's a river between that thing and us."

Peter was watching with similar awe. "It's enormous," he said, inching back. Sophie glanced at the boy. His green eyes were wide and unblinking, as if he couldn't look away even if he wanted to. She wondered if that was part of the reason he preferred the blindfold: Perhaps death and destruction were not so frightening when you could not see them? Sophie reached out and held his hand in her own.

The panic had by now spread to Sophie's side of the river. She was nearly knocked over as men and women rushed to get away from the beast. "What's it going after?" she called, still watching as the Zeitgeist smashed its way along the shore. "Why is it trying to get to the water?"

"It doesn't want the water," Madame Eldritch said. She reached up and clasped Taro's hand in her own. "It wants my shop . . ."

The beast reached down over the water and grabbed hold of the round tower that housed Madame Eldritch's oubliette. With a tremendous roar, the creature ripped the entire tower clean from the water—charms and baubles and incense and a thousand treasures spilled out from the bottom. The beast raised the tower over its head and poured the nonsense into its mouth, chewing. When it was finished, it hurled the empty tower clear across the river.

"Run!" Sophie cried as the tower sailed over her head and— *crash!*—smashed into the courthouse behind her. Stone and glass rained down on the terrified crowd as the courthouse steeple cracked and slid off the roof, crashing to the ground in an explosion of rubble. Men, women, and children ran pell-mell in all directions, mad with terror. The beast roared again, its hot breath warping the very air, and lumbered toward the bridge. If anything, it looked even bigger than it had a moment before.

Peter and Sir Tode were already lost to the crowd. Akrasia and Sophie's father created a barrier in front of Sophie, fighting off people to stop her from being trampled.

"We have to stop it from crossing that bridge!" Akrasia growled, bracing her flank against the stampeding mob. "If it makes it to the city, everything will be destroyed!"

Sophie shielded her eyes from the heat and peered more closely at what remained of the city Pyre grounds. The podium where Prigg had been standing was now a skeleton of flaming lumber. Dangling from one of the shattered beams was a cloth bag. Even from this distance, the shape was unmistakable. "The Four Questions!" she cried. "They're still on the platform!"

"The books are nonsense!" Sophie's father called, dodging a group of retreating guards. "Shouldn't the beast have eaten them?"

Sophie didn't know. "There must be some reason they were spared. If I can get the books back, I may be able to summon something to stop the Zeitgeist."

This was easier said than done. The crowd was too thick to get through, and it was all they could do not to get carried off in the human current. "The Four Questions will have to wait," Sophie's father cried, pushing back a charging stevedore. "There's no way through all these people."

Sophie clung to her father, staring out over the mob. "The only way across that bridge would be to go above the crowd. But that's impossible, unless we suddenly sprouted—" She stopped short, staring at the bridge.

"What is it?" Akrasia said, rearing onto her hind legs. "What do you see?"

Sophie was watching a small figure scaling one of the lampposts along the railing, moving high above the crowd. The figure glanced back toward her for a moment, revealing the most remarkable pair of emerald-green eyes. She smiled. "I see . . . Peter Nimble."

CHAPTER FORTY-ONE

THE GREATEST THIEF
WHO EVER LIVED

Peter Nimble was a warrior who had faced death dozens of times in his career. He had fought bullies and sea serpents and kings and thieves and brigands and apes and even an entire army of rats. But none of that mattered at the moment, because right now he was scared.

When Sophie had said she needed some way to retrieve those books, he knew it was up to him. But what he had not reckoned until this very moment was that he was not his usual self. The smoke from the flaming beast and the screams from the mob had left his stronger senses effectively useless. All that remained were his emerald eyes.

It was difficult enough weaving through the crowd to get to the bridge, but once he had scaled the outer turret and begun climbing the first lamppost, he began to realize that what he was doing was impossible. One-handed boys were not meant to leap between lampposts. One-handed boys were not meant to fight their way through mobs or race headlong into the arms of flaming monsters. One-handed boys were not meant to be heroes.

"Er," Sir Tode said from his place in Peter's burgle-sack, which was dangling perilously from Peter's thin shoulder. "What's the holdup?"

"I . . . I can't do it," Peter said. His one good arm was wrapped tightly around the iron post. A cold sweat prickled across his brow. He could feel his hand slipping. The lamppost shuddered and swayed as people raced past it, fighting to reach the shore. He swallowed, trying to slow his heartbeat, which was pounding loudly in his ears. "The emerald eyes . . . I can't concentrate . . . I can't focus . . ."

"It's nothing you haven't done a hundred times before." Sir Tode screwed up his snout. "Can't you just shut your eyes and *pretend* you have the blindfold on?"

"There's too much noise and smoke," Peter said. "I can't hear or smell anything." He clenched his jaw, looking away from the crowd—a dizziness had overtaken him, and it felt as if the entire world were spinning.

He tried to focus on the next lamppost, but the gap was impossibly wide. The height from the ground was farther still. If he slipped and fell, he would be trampled by the mob. And even if he made it, he would be running right into the arms of the flaming Zeitgeist. He felt a twisting in his stomach, recalling again the sight of Prigg being eaten alive, his body consumed in flames.

The Zeitgeist roared on the opposite shore, its hot breath creating a rash of steam atop the water. "I have to get down," Peter said, loosening his grip. "I have to get down now."

"Peter," Sir Tode said. "Look at me!"

It was not a request. Peter swallowed and turned toward his friend—a friend whose face he hardly recognized in plain sight. Sir Tode stared at him, holding his gaze. His yellow eyes were wide and unblinking, and it was difficult for Peter to tell whether the knight was scared or angry or both. "Now, I've seen you escape death a hundred times," Sir Tode said. "I've seen you walk a wire across the towers of Moog. I've seen you steal the gold fillings out of a sleeping pirate's mouth. I've seen you fend off three angry bugbears with nothing but a bar of soap and your wits. I've seen you *swipe a bullet from a loaded pistol.*" His feline face crinkled. "You are Peter Nimble, Heir to the House of HazelPort, Vagabond King of the Wild Seas, the Silver-Handed Terror, and the Greatest Thief Who Ever Lived . . . and that girl back there needs you."

Peter swallowed, staring out at the long bridge, at the mob of screaming people, at the hundred-foot flaming monster waiting to greet him on the other side. "I . . . I think I can make it . . ." he said weakly.

"This is no time for *I think*," Sir Tode snapped. "If that beast crosses the bridge, this city and everyone in it will burn. It's up to us to stop that." He settled into the burgle-sack, bracing himself. "If we're to meet our end, let us meet it like heroes. With our eyes open. And our weapons held high."

Peter nodded, adjusting his feet on the post. He fixed his gaze on the next lamppost—forcing out every other thought, every other image, every other fear. He gripped the horizontal bar at the top of the lamp and swung his body around like a gymnast, turning again and again, moving faster and faster until the entire world was a blur. And then he let go . . .

They say time waits for no man, but that first leap between lampposts was without question the longest moment in Peter's life. As he soared, screaming, he could see the lamppost moving slowly toward him, growing ever larger as he approached, his arms and legs swinging wildly through empty air . . .

Peter's body struck the far lamppost with a bone-breaking *clang* that resounded through his entire body. He gripped the iron with both arms and legs, hanging upside down like a clumsy possum. "I did it!" he cried.

"Well done!" Sir Tode said. "Only a dozen more to go!"

Peter pulled himself upright and looked to the next post. This leap, while technically the same distance as the first one, seemed smaller somehow, and Peter managed to make it with little trouble.

By the fifth lamp, he was almost enjoying himself as he bounded through the air above the stampeding crowd. "Bravo!" Sir Tode cheered as Peter managed a final backflip before landing lightly at the far end of the bridge. "I think I shall have to devote an entire chapter to this little adventure! I'll call it 'A Leap of Faith.'"

Peter crouched low to the ground, bracing himself against the tremendous heat radiating from the Pyre. He stared up at the Zeitgeist, which was towering directly above him now, burning books spilling from its maw. "Hold on tight," Peter said, and he raced headlong into the flames.

"On your right!" Sir Tode shouted.

Peter dove to one side as the beast's tail smashed down upon the spot where he had been only a heartbeat before. Earth and rock exploded from the impact. He tumbled sideways across the ground and scrambled back to his feet. Not as graceful as he would have liked, but he was still alive.

Peter stared at the hazy field, searching for the place where Inquisitor Prigg had been. Piles of burning books lay scattered across the field like charred corpses. "Where are the Four Questions?"

"Up ahead!" Sir Tode shouted, pointing a hoof. Through the smoke and rubble, Peter could see a bag dangling from a piece of flaming wood.

"Hold on!" Peter cried, racing toward it.

He snatched the bag, opening it. Inside were the four books— *Who*, *What*, *Where*, and *When*—slightly singed but still intact. "Now we just have to get them back to—"

"Jump!" Sir Tode cried.

Peter dove down from the podium just as the beast's tail swished through the air directly above his head. The wooden podium shattered into flaming splinters. "Thanks for the heads-up," Peter said as he raced to the opposite shore.

The way back across the bridge was made much easier by the fact that Peter was no longer running *against* the crowd. Indeed, the mob of people very nearly carried him across as they pushed and shoved and scratched and bit to get clear of the rampaging Pyre.

"Miss me?" Peter shouted, throwing the bag toward Sophie as he met her on the street. It was not a very good throw, but she caught the bag nonetheless.

"You have no idea," she answered. He caught a spark in her eyes that he wished he could have seen more of. Sophie held the bag over her head and cried, "*What if!*" At once, the four books burst from the bag and floated around her, awaiting her command.

People screamed as the bridge shifted beneath them, one of its railings collapsing into the river. Men, women, and children slid off their feet and splashed into the dark water below. "The walls of the canal are too high," Peter said. "They'll drown before they can reach shore."

"Then we had better save them," Sophie said, drawing back her sleeves. Peter stared at the girl, her dark hair twisting in the wind, the four books floating around her, her skin orange against the glow of the Pyre. He had not actually ever met a sorcerer in his life, but he thought that she looked the part.

Sophie spoke loudly over the chaos. "What can save the people in the river?" No sooner did she say the words than *The Book of What* came to life and flipped to an entry.

Peter watched her expression as she leaned over the page to read the answer, a slight grin on her face. "What does it say?" he shouted, struggling against the mob to stand in one place. "What do we need?"

She looked up at him, her grin breaking into a smile.

EVERYTHING *but the* KITCHEN SINK

Sophie stared at the entry in *The Book of What*:

THE LAST RESORT

"The Last Resort," she said aloud, and instantly a cold shiver of wind swept through her. Her entire body was trembling, and for a brief moment she felt as though she were standing outside of herself. She searched the horizon for some sign that the summoning had worked.

"There!" Peter shouted. "By the pier!"

Sophie ran with him to the edge of the canal. Hundreds of people were splashing and sputtering, trying to keep afloat on whatever scraps of burning debris they could find. An eerie green light appeared deep beneath the surface of the water. It was a light Sophie recognized. "Sprites . . ." she said.

The light grew brighter and brighter, and then, with a tremendous splash, the top of the lighthouse burst from the surface of the river like a mortar shell from a cannon. It rose high into the air before crashing back down onto the surface of the river.

The Zeitgeist snarled as water splashed up against the bridge, which was currently buckling under its mountainous weight. It swiped at the top of the lighthouse, which bobbed just beyond its reach. Sophie drew the hair from her eyes and stared at the rickety wooden tower. It was broken and burned but still in one piece. And there, shouting orders on the deck—

"Pilgrims, hold fast!"

It was Scrivener Behn! And Saint Martin! And Liesel the barkeep! And a dozen other pilgrims, along with a handful of (very confused) guards who had been aboard when the Last Resort was cut from its moorings. They were all of them working together to keep the structure intact.

"Behn!" Sophie thought her heart might burst from the joy of seeing him alive.

"Ahoy, Storyguard!" Scrivener Behn cried out, a hand held high. "It seems our story is not yet told!"

The Zeitgeist roared again, swiping a fiery claw at the keeling lighthouse. "We have to get those people out of the water before they drown," Sophie cried.

Already, Scrivener Behn and the pilgrims had started pulling people from the water onto the vessel. That their rescuers were magical creatures aboard a sprite-fueled lighthouse did not seem to trouble those drowning in the Wassail.

Madame Eldritch, who was standing beside Sophie, opened her eyes wide. "Impossible," she whispered. "Nothing returns from the Uncannyon." Her fingers drifted up to Taro's hand, nestled closely on her shoulder.

Sophie watched the rescue on the river, her heart nearly bursting at the thrill of it. Hundreds of people saved from drowning. "I did that," she said, breathless. "I *summoned* the Last Resort from thin air!" She stared at the four books floating before her—unlimited power awaiting her command.

Akrasia moved beside her. "I do not mean to interrupt your moment of triumph, Storyguard, but the battle is far from won. The beast approaches."

Sophie looked at the bridge. The Zeitgeist was now thundering toward the opposite shore—straight for the main city.

"Peter," she said, "you and Sir Tode have to get the remaining people as far from shore as possible. Keep them away from the newer buildings. Try to steer them toward the old quarter—stone burns slower than wood."

"I'm not leaving you here to fight that thing alone," Peter said.

"But I'm not alone—I have the books." Even now, Sophie could feel the power of the Four Questions coursing through her body. There was a static crackle to the air that made the tips of her hair float like black fronds.

"I will stay with Sophie," Akrasia said. "If the creature comes too near, I can speed her away."

"Go," Sophie said, looking straight into Peter's eyes. "For once you actually have someone who *wants* to be rescued."

Peter opened his mouth as though he wanted to say something more to her. But then he simply nodded and ran toward the frantic crowd.

Sophie watched his figure retreat into the distance. She felt a tightening in her chest as she thought about what might happen if they never saw each other again. "Right," she said, turning back toward the bridge. "Time to slay a monster."

She spread her arms out and spoke to the books. "What can stop the Zeitgeist?"

At once, *The Book of What* moved in front of her and opened to an entry. Sophie stared at the words, and her excitement quickly melted into confusion—

THE FOUR QUESTIONS: The books of Who, What, Where, and When, whose ancient pages chronicle all magic—past and present—in the world. The books are kept by the Storyguard, who are charged with their protection and responsible use of their power. Presently in possession of Sophie Quire, the Last Storyguard.

~For more information, see: *Book of Who,* "Sophie Quire," "Storyguard"; *Book of When,* "Evensong"

"I don't understand." She grabbed the book, shaking it. "Why isn't it answering my question?" Obviously the books could stop the beast—but how? She shut the book and asked the question again, but again the book returned to the same entry.

She snapped the book shut, shaking it. "What do you want from me?"

The Zeitgeist roared, tearing up the last lamppost and hurling it toward the city. People screamed as the lamppost slammed and skidded across the cobblestones, taking out several rows of storefronts.

Akrasia knocked Sophie down to protect her from shattering glass. "This is no time for questions," she growled. "You must act."

Sophie stood back up, wiping the dust from her eyes. If the books would not help her, she would have to do it herself. She scanned the horizon, looking for some inspiration, some idea of how to stop the Zeitgeist from crossing into the city. Her eyes fell on what remained of the two wolf statues at the mouth of the bridge.

"Who are the Wolves of Dawn?" she said in a loud voice.

At these words, *The Book of Who* snapped open and flipped to the entry—

> *THE WOLVES OF DAWN: Stone guardians of the ancient city of Bustleburgh. They defended the land from goblin hordes during the Long Solstice. Some say their mighty jaws cracked open the Splint Mountains, from which the Wassail River flows. The wolves stand guard on the eastern edge of Bustleburgh, which is currently being destroyed by a flaming Zeitgeist.*
>
> ~For more information, see: *Book of Where*, "Splint Mountains," "Bustleburgh," "Wassail River"; *Book of When*, "Long Solstice"; *Book of What*, "Goblins," "Zeitgeist"

The blue ink on the page glowed brightly, illuminating the hazy air. There came another rush of wind. Sophie stared up at the bridge. There was a great howling sound as the wolf statues came to life—

ferocious titans made from living rock. The beasts tore themselves free from their bases and leapt in front of the Zeitgeist, hitting the ground with an earth-cracking *crash*. They growled and snapped their granite fangs at the flaming Pyre.

"It worked!" Sophie said. "It really worked!"

The crowds behind Sophie, having heard the howls, slowed their retreat and stared at the massive stone titans who had appeared to protect them. "The Wolves of Dawn" was a story every one of them had grown up hearing, but none of them had ever actually believed that it was true. The mythical beasts were now crouched before them, protecting them from invasion as they had a thousand years before.

The Zeitgeist and the wolves squared off—fire versus rock— neither making the first move. The wolves darted back and forth, snarling and snapping at the Zeitgeist. The flaming Zeitgeist shifted backward, raising its arms in self-defense. "It's working!" Sophie said, grabbing Akrasia's neck.

But Sophie spoke too soon. With a mighty howl, the wolves lunged for the Zeitgeist, but the Zeitgeist did not retreat. Instead, it simply opened its flaming maw wide and, with one, horrible, fiery gulp, consumed the wolves whole. Sophie heard pained yelps and the crunching of stone and then nothing.

There was a horrified moment of silence as everyone in Bust- leburgh considered what had just happened: a thousand-year- old pair of titans had returned from the past to defend their city—and they had been killed in less time than it took to squash a mosquito.

The Zeitgeist reared its head, which seemed to have grown even larger. "With every piece of nonsense it eats," Akrasia said, "it gets bigger."

Sophie stared up at the approaching beast, feeling a hard chill of resolve. She had spent a lifetime preparing her mind for this moment, reading hundreds upon hundreds of stories—she was ready for this. She marched straight toward the beast, the books circling her torso, her tattered cloak flapping behind her. "You want nonsense?" she cried, drawing back her sleeves. "I'll give you nonsense."

What followed was a battle unlike any seen before in history. A lone girl—a Storyguard—summoning every manner of nonsense to defeat a flaming pyre of books. "What are storm billows?" she cried. "What are lightning wasps?" Artifacts and creatures not seen for millennia suddenly leapt from her pages in a flurry of magic. She tried to bind the Pyre with silkwyrms. She tried to petrify it with a Gorgon's Mirror. She tried to smother it with a Pantagruelian Toad. She tried to freeze it with a Gelid Wind. She tried to plunge it into a Grazing Abyss. She tried to douse it in a Weeping Pot. She tried to shrink it with a Drink-Me-Not. One by one, the manxome monster scorched, smashed, shredded, and swallowed everything she threw at it. And with each piece of nonsense it consumed, the Zeitgeist only got bigger and angrier.

"This is impossible!" she shrieked in rage. The elation of possessing unlimited power had now given way to despair. Sophie had tried everything but the kitchen sink—and had there been an entry on kitchen sinks in the books, she might very well have tried that, too—with no success.

The Zeitgeist, meanwhile, seemed to have tired of this barrage of nonsense. It knocked aside a flock of Tar Geese and turned toward Sophie, its eyes narrow. With a great roar, it charged straight for her—claws over its head, its mouth wide and crackling. Sophie fell backward, staring up into the gaping maw—a swirling vortex of molten books.

Sophie felt herself pulled backward as Akrasia dragged her to safety. "We must get you out of here, my cub."

Sophie looked through the smoke ahead to the towers of old Bustleburgh. There was a chance they could escape in the crypts beneath the streets, but first they had to get there. "To the alley!" she said, pointing toward an ancient stone archway. Beyond that point lay the twisting passages of Olde Town. Sophie knew those streets better than any person in Bustleburgh. Surely she could lose the beast there.

Akrasia lowered her head and raced beneath the archway. The air whipped Sophie's face as they descended a curving stairway, and she had to close her eyes to stop from getting dizzy. "To your left!" Sophie cried, looking up just in time. Akrasia sprang off a barrel and turned a sharp left down a covered footbridge.

The Zeitgeist was still following them, but it was having trouble navigating the narrow alleys. Sophie could hear thousand-year-old stones crumbling as the beast tore at the walls of Olde Town.

They reached the entrance of the crypts to find that it had already collapsed—blocking their path. Akrasia slowed, panting. Her body was shaking, and it was clear that she had sustained injuries from their flight. Sophie let go of the tigress's collar and spilled onto the cold cobblestone. The Four Questions were still floating around her, though they, too, looked tired.

A distant roar rang out and the ground beneath Sophie shook as the Zeitgeist toppled another ancient building—the academy, perhaps? "It's impossible," she said, trying to claw through the rubble. "I've tried everything I could think of to stop it, and nothing works."

"Perhaps you are asking the wrong question," Akrasia said through labored breaths. She was limping, and Sophie could see a deep gash along her side where she had been cut by falling rock. "Perhaps it is not a matter of *what* but *who*?"

The tigress seemed to be saying more than Sophie could understand. "If you know something, just spit it out," she said.

Akrasia's striped tail wove back and forth above her. "It is the question I asked the first moment I met you. The question we all must answer." She stared hard at Sophie, her yellow eyes flashing. *"Who are you?"*

This was hardly the time for riddles, but Sophie had no better options. "Who am *I*?" she said. At once, *The Book of Who* moved in front of her and opened its cover. It flipped to an entry in the very middle—

SOPHIE QUIRE: Daughter of Coriander Quire.
The Bookmender of Bustleburgh. The Last
Storyguard.

For a brief moment Sophie had thought Akrasia's question might actually lead to a solution. But that hope was dashed as soon as she read the entry—the very same entry she had seen when she first discovered the book. "Nothing!" she said, showing Akrasia the page. "It says I'm a Storyguard. But what good is a Storyguard against *that* thing?"

Akrasia, however, did not look discouraged. She stared at Sophie, her cat eyes growing brighter. "Look closer, my cub." She placed a silver paw on the page. "You are not merely *a* Storyguard. You are *the* Storyguard—the last of your kind."

Sophie stared again at the words. "But what does that mean?"

"Even when the beast killed Prigg, it did not harm the books."

Akrasia's voice sounded more urgent—the excitement of someone discovering a new thought as they spoke. "Perhaps that was not an error?"

Sophie stared at the four books moving slowly around her. "The Four Questions," she said. "The Zeitgeist doesn't want to eat them."

Akrasia crouched beside her. "Perhaps the beast understands what we do not—that these books are the source of its power. And if it was the magic within these books that created the beast, perhaps that same magic can destroy it." She tilted her head to meet Sophie's eyes. "Do you understand what I am saying, my cub?"

Sophie remembered what the books had told her when she asked what could destroy the Pyre.

"The Four Questions," she whispered. "*They* can stop the Pyre." It felt as if her heart had ceased beating. And her mouth felt very dry. She swallowed. "If I want to destroy the monster . . . I have to destroy the books."

CHAPTER FORTY-THREE

THE LAST STORYGUARD

Sophie stared at the four books circling around her—*Who*, *What*, *Where*, and *When*. The books she had struggled so hard to find. The books her mother had died protecting. The thought of throwing them into the Pyre, of just letting them burn, made her sick. "I can't *destroy* them," she said, backing away from Akrasia. "I'm the Storyguard—"

"The *last* Storyguard," Akrasia said. "And this is your final task. The furnace is waiting. You need only to cast them into the flame."

"The books won't burn," Sophie said. "Papa tried it in the shop."

"Perhaps they will not burn in an ordinary fire. But that monster is far from ordinary. Its flames are themselves magical—their only purpose is to consume other magic. If anything can destroy the Four

Questions, it is that beast." Akrasia took a step forward. "You must try, my cub."

Sophie knew in her deepest of hearts that Akrasia was right. She knew that if she were reading her own story, she would see the truth of what must happen. She reached out and drew the Four Questions into her arms, holding them tightly to her chest. The screams, the destruction, the raging Pyre all melted away. All she could think of were the countless pages that she would never read, countless wonders that she would never summon. In a single moment, all those stories would be lost forever. Along with her own hope of summoning—or trying to summon—her mother. Of seeing her one last time. "But a world without these books . . ." she said. "It will be the very thing Prigg wanted all along."

"Prigg was correct on one count," Akrasia said. "The books are too dangerous for this world. Where Prigg has fallen, countless more like him will rise up. You have seen what the hearts of common men can yield for the world of magic." She met Sophie's eye. "The books must be destroyed, my cub."

"My mother died to protect these books," Sophie said. "I can't just destroy them." Flecks of burning embers rained down around her. She stared up at the city—a once-shining beacon reduced to ruin. All because of these books. She closed her eyes. "I'm sorry, Mama . . ."

The ground rumbled beneath her as the Zeitgeist's roar echoed close by. "We have to get to its mouth," she said. "That's the only way to reach the heart of the Pyre."

There was a deafening crash as the wall directly behind them burst into rubble. Flames spilled out, surrounding Sophie as the Zeitgeist towered over them—so tall that it blocked out the sky. Crackling books spilled from the beast's open mouth like flaming drool.

Akrasia lowered her back for Sophie to mount. "Let's draw it out into the open," she growled. "Before there's no city left to save!"

Sophie grabbed hold of Akrasia's collar. The tigress leapt between mounds of flaming rubble. But before they could slip through the passageway—*crash!*—a fresh pile of rubble blocked their path. "We're trapped," Akrasia said, snarling.

"Not for long," Sophie said, looking at *The Book of What*. As if reading her very thoughts, the book opened wide to an entry—the very entry she had wanted. "What are wings?" she cried.

Sophie had not been sure how the wings might appear, but when she spoke the word, she heard Akrasia snarl and falter in her steps. There was a ripping sound as golden feathers sprouted from the tigress's mighty shoulders, gleaming in the light of the Pyre.

"Akrasia," Sophie said, awestruck. "You look magnificent."

"I look ridiculous," she growled, racing forward. "But let us fly."

Sophie held on to Akrasia's collar with both hands. The tigress raced the length of the alley straight toward the wall of flaming rock, her wings flapping with broad strokes. The first moments were tense, and it looked as if they might not take to the air, but then a gentle breeze came beneath them, and Sophie felt both the tigress and herself lift off the ground and over the rubble.

The Zeitgeist thundered after them, swinging its long arms, trying to knock Akrasia from the air. The winged tigress swooped and ducked between the flames, climbing higher and higher into the broiling sun.

"We're flying!" Sophie cried, clinging to Akrasia for all her worth. The books were still moving with her, spinning faster now—so fast they were a blur. Wind whipped her face, whether from the Pyre or their speed, she could not tell. She clenched her eyes shut, afraid to see the ground so far below. Then she forced herself to open her eyes, seeing the burning rooftops all across the city. Bustleburgh looked like a battlefield, littered with rubble and ash. Crowds of tiny, screaming people were staring up—all of them pointing at her. And there, looking up from the front of the crowd, was one pair of emerald-green eyes.

Akrasia beat her golden wings, climbing even higher until the air became thin around them. Sophie peered at the mouth of the beast, now directly below them—a swirling cauldron of crackling storybooks. The heat was so great that she could feel the ends of her hair singeing. She couldn't help but think that this was the very same thing that Prigg had seen right before being eaten alive. She let go of Akrasia's collar with one hand and drew the Four Questions into her arm, holding them to her chest. "I'm ready," she said.

"Hold tight, my cub!" Akrasia shouted, and swooped toward the chasm.

Sophie forced herself to keep her eyes open as they hurtled into the Zeitgeist's open mouth. The heat was like nothing Sophie had ever imagined. It felt as if her insides were boiling. She screamed as Akrasia's collar seared her hand, the golden chain bursting into flame. Sophie felt a jolt as Akrasia's body keeled to one side—her golden wings burning into nothing. The books, still in Sophie's arms, were now glowing red, searing her hands, her chest, but Sophie refused to let go—not until they reached the heart of the Pyre.

She screamed as her body slipped away from Akrasia and fell deeper into the crackling depths, the Four Questions still clasped in her arms . . .

✦   ✦   ✦

When Peter Nimble saw Sophie and Akrasia fly into the air, it was unlike anything he had ever experienced. He had encountered many wonders in his life but *seen* very few. And the image of this girl riding on the back of a winged tigress, soaring up over a flaming Zeitgeist, was more majestic than anything he could have imagined. His heart was racing so fast it was as though he were up in the air with Sophie.

But the wonder of this sight quickly gave way to terror when that same girl and tigress plunged headlong into the open mouth of the beast, disappearing into the flames. "Sophie!" Peter cried.

The Zeitgeist released a terrific howl, spinning its body around. The ground beneath Peter shook as the beast stumbled forward, lurching to one side. It roared, twisting its body as if in terrible agony, books spilling from its maw. "We have to save her before she's burned alive!" Peter shouted, fighting his way past the gawking crowd.

"Wait," Sir Tode called from inside Peter's burgle-sack. "I think it's weakening." Slowly, astonishingly, the Zeitgeist began to crumple in on itself, growing smaller.

Peter stopped, his mouth open. The mighty beast howled and thrashed, and with each turn its body continued to shrink. "She's killing it," he said. The Zeitgeist kept compressing itself, and then, with a final roar, it burst like a firecracker. Peter was knocked onto his back as tens of thousands of charred books shot high into the air in a slow arc and then rained down on the streets below like so much flaming confetti. People ducked for cover, hiding beneath bridges and awnings to stay clear of the falling nonsense.

Peter scrambled to his feet and ran with Sir Tode to the place where the Zeitgeist had been. They found a huge, charred mountain of books—many of them miraculously intact, pages flickering like dying embers. "By Jove, she did it," Sir Tode said. "She really did it."

"Sophie!" Peter cried, racing toward the smoldering wreckage.

"SOPHIE?" There was a brief, agonizing stillness as he searched for any sign of life. He tore through piles of burning books—not caring about the burns on his hand and legs, only caring about her. "She's not here," he said, falling to his knees. But then he turned and saw that Sir Tode was staring out at the river, waving a hoof over his head.

"Storyguard, ho!" he cried.

Peter turned around to see Sophie and Akrasia climbing onto the deck of the lighthouse, soaking wet but very much alive.

You have doubtless read many scenes in which two young heroes race toward each other and indulge in some sort of amorous embrace. This did not happen to Peter and Sophie. In fact, by the time the two children were standing face-to-face, they had each become rather shy and somewhat tongue-tied.

Sir Tode, however, had words enough for everyone. "Huzzah! Huzzah!" the knight exclaimed, clopping between them as they met on the smoldering pier. "A death-defying plunge into the belly of the beast. I can't wait to write this one down! You simply must tell me what it was like inside that crackling inferno—*ooh!* That's a good title for a chapter, don't you think?"

Sophie and Peter did not answer. They walked together through the demolished streets, their hands not quite touching, while Sir Tode trailed behind them, already composing the first lines of what would come to be known as his greatest chapter.

ALL CHARMS GUARANTEED

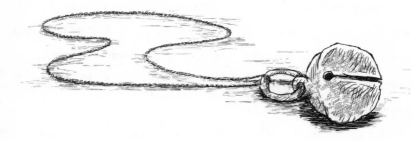

The end of the Pyre brought a calm over Bustleburgh that the city had not seen for many years. A gentle breeze came off the mountains and blew the soot from people's eyes. Overhead, the dark clouds broke, and a soft, cool rain sprinkled down on the city, washing away the ashes, quenching the last of the fires.

Sophie was proud, but not too proud to accept Peter's help as she limped through the streets. The Four Questions—which had ignited within the Zeitgeist—had left painful burns along her chest and arms, burns that would need medicine and time to heal. Akrasia, too, had been badly injured. Her silver coat was now charred and black, and there were two ugly scars where her golden wings had been burned away from her body. But for the first time in twelve years, she was free of the widow's might and her step was lighter than Sophie had ever seen.

Virtually every person in the city had seen Sophie and Akrasia's flight into the mouth of the beast. And they now crowded around her, many reaching out their hands to touch the robe of the girl who had rescued them. Even those who distrusted nonsense had to grudgingly accept that they were grateful for her sacrifice. It was from the heart of this crowd that Sophie heard a familiar voice call her name. "S–S–Sophie?"

It was her father. His clothes were tattered and charred, his face drawn. He looked like a man who had just seen his only child burned alive (which, to be fair, he was), and to behold her now left him trembling. "Is it really you?"

"Papa!" Sophie let go of Peter's arm and rushed to meet him. "Papa! I did it." She wrapped her arms around him. "The books are gone."

"My child, my sweet, stubborn child." He kissed her on the head over and over again, and Sophie could feel his warm tears on her skin.

"It's over," she said, burying her face in his frail chest. "It's all over."

"It is not *quite* over, little bookmender."

Sophie looked up to see Madame Eldritch standing apart from the crowd. The woman's face bore a familiar expression—the expression of someone who wields a secret that she knows you would like to hear. "What is it?" Sophie asked her, letting go of her father. Whatever dreadful thing the woman was preparing to reveal, it could not be worse than what Sophie had already endured.

Madame Eldritch ran one finger along Taro's hand. "As you know, I happened to be in the Professor's library when you were captured by the Inquisitor. Which means I heard what Prigg said about how he stabbed your mother."

Sophie thought of Prigg's face as he described plunging his blade into Coriander's heart. Even now that he was dead, even after hearing his final screams in the mouth of the Zeitgeist, she knew he had not suffered enough. "And?"

Madame Eldritch raised one eyebrow into a perfect arch. "And it is just as I told you that night so long ago in my carriage: If your mother used the charms she purchased from me, then she was not so easily slain."

Sophie's father placed a protective arm around his daughter. "Why would you say this to us? I found her cold body—I held it in my arms." His voice was hoarse and shaking. "Doctors examined her!"

Madame Eldritch flicked a hand. "Do not speak to me of doctors. Did doctors rescue you from the quickbramble? Did doctors save this city from ruin?" She stepped closer to him. "Where is she now?"

Sophie's father shook his head. "I laid her in the Quire crypt."

"And in all this time, did you ever visit her?"

He inched back, running a hand through his thin hair. "It's troublesome luck to trouble the dead," he said. "Besides, I had the shop and Sophie and . . ." He lowered his head. "And I was afraid of what seeing her like that would do to me."

"After what has transpired this day, I should think we are all beyond fear." Madame Eldritch turned and walked into the hazy light. "Let us visit her now."

Sophie and her father followed the woman to a canal at the far end of Olde Town. The main entrance had been destroyed, but Madame Eldritch showed them a different, older path hidden in the canal wall. They wandered together through the dark catacombs. Bodies were laid in stone tombs, which were sealed with binding cloth. Thanks to the rampaging Zeitgeist, many of the city's streets had collapsed in on themselves. For the first time in centuries, daylight shone into the tombs, which were thick with cobwebs and dust.

Sophie had walked these catacombs many times, but this time her every step was accompanied by a sense of tingling dread that she could not fully define. Why was Eldritch taking them to this place? And what could they possibly find there? They stopped at the familiar iron door, which had survived the collapse of the street. A beam of warm light shone from above onto the word overhead: *Quire.*

Sophie held her father's hand, which was shaking. She had stood at this door before, but it was clear from the look on his pale face that he was on alien soil. "I don't have the key," he said softly.

"Let me," said Peter, who had followed them there. Sophie watched as he knelt down and picked the lock with his slender fingers. It was astonishing to see how carefully he moved, how he almost seemed to be speaking to the lock as he worked. It reminded her of her own work mending books.

The lock clicked open. Peter pulled back the heavy door, which screeched on its neglected hinges. "After you," he said, stepping back.

Light flooded into the small chamber, illuminating motes of ancient dust that spun and eddied in the quiet air. Sophie stood with her father, holding his hand. Together, they stepped into the chamber, which had no smell, save the cool petrichor of damp stone. The room was filled with stone shelves, upon which lay the dusty remains of forgotten corpses—now only scraps of bone and cloth. On a shelf in the back of the room lay a woman with dark skin and darker hair, now streaked with gray. Her face was smooth and unblemished, her expression peaceful. She looked like nothing so much as a person asleep.

Sophie stared at the woman who looked so familiar to her. "It's really her," she whispered. She peered at the woman's features, for the first time truly understanding what her father meant when he said they were so alike. It was like looking into her own future. And her past.

Sophie's father clutched his daughter's arm. "Impossible . . ." Sophie could hear his breath trembling. "She's dead. She should be turned to dust."

"What is death but a slumber from which one cannot be roused?" Madame Eldritch said, more gently than Sophie had learned to expect from her. "This woman is asleep. She need only be awoken." The woman placed a hand on Sophie's shoulder, drawing back her hair to expose the necklace around her throat.

Sophie looked down at the necklace. "The dispell bell . . ." she said.

Madame Eldritch smiled. "All charms guaranteed."

Sophie stared at the bell, hardly daring to believe what the woman was telling her. She reached behind her neck and unhooked the chain, then rolled the round bell between her fingers. Sophie turned back to the figure of her mother, resting so placidly atop the stone. She looked like a princess from a story, awaiting her prince. Sophie stepped toward her mother, the bell gripped tightly in her hand.

She raised the bell over her mother's face and rang it. This time, for the first time, the bell responded with a light chime.

The sound hung in the air for a moment, reverberating off the crypt walls. The next moment, the woman before Sophie opened her eyes. She did not gasp and sputter as one snatched back from death.

She opened them gently, blinking into the sunlight above her. She reached up an ink-stained hand to stifle a yawn. "Where . . . where am I?"

The woman sat up, staring at her tattered clothes. She looked at the crypt around her, rubbing her eyes as if unsure whether she was truly awake or still dreaming. And then she saw Sophie's father. "Augustus?"

Sophie's father let out a pained cry and very nearly staggered to the floor. "Coriander!" He ran toward her and swept her up in his arms, holding her tight. "My Coriander!"

That Sophie's mother was surprised by this reception was plain enough. "Augustus, what has happened to you?" she exclaimed, staring at his drawn face, his thin gray hair. "You look so very old." She could not, of course, see the streaks of gray in her own hair or the lines around her own eyes—for though Madame Eldritch's charms had protected her from death, they had not spared her the toll of time. "Where are we?" she said, pulling away to peer at the crypt. "And what am I doing in these rags?"

"You were asleep for a very long time, my love," Sophie's father said, still holding her close. "But it's over now. It's over."

It was clear that Coriander was beginning to remember more and more things. She let go of him, new panic in her face. She looked down at her chest, a jagged tear where Prigg's blade had pierced her body. "Where is the book?" she gasped, clutching her rags. "And Prigg?"

"The books are destroyed," Augustus said softly. "Prigg, too." He turned toward Sophie. "All thanks to her."

The woman's eyes finally found Sophie, who was watching very quietly in the shadows. Coriander was startled by the sight of this twelve-year-old girl, her dress charred and ragged, her face so much like her own. She let go of Augustus and stared into Sophie's eyes, blinking, confused. "But who is this girl?"

Sophie's chin quivered as if it might break. "Mama?" she said, tears welling in her eyes.

At this single word, the woman's expression bloomed into astonishment—for there are some things no mother can ever truly forget, and among them is the voice of her child. "Sophie?" she cried, and she rushed to her and took her in her arms. "My little baby." She pulled Sophie tight to her breast, rocking her back and forth.

Sophie Quire had spent her entire life imagining what it might feel like to be held by her mother—but no amount of imagining could ever have prepared her for the feeling now as this woman wrapped her up in her arms, squeezing her so tightly that it hurt, so tightly that all the pain and struggle and fear and doubt spilled out of her like water from a dam. "Mama," Sophie said, tears soaking her face and neck. "I thought I would never see you."

"I'm here now, child," her mother said. "I'm here now."

If Sophie's mother did not understand the exact circumstances of her being there in that cold crypt with her now-grown daughter and aged husband, she at least understood that it was no trivial thing that had brought them together in this place. Augustus joined in the embrace, and the three of them—father, mother, and child—held one another in the stillness of the crypt. Sophie looked toward the open door, remembering Madame Eldritch and Peter, but she found that they had been left alone.

Coriander pulled back from them, one hand on each of their shoulders. "My curiosity can only take so much," she said. "You must tell me how I came to be in this place, barefoot and bleary-eyed, with the two of you looking at me as though I'd returned from the dead—which, if my rags are any judge, I probably did."

Sophie sniffed, wiping her nose on her sleeve. "I'm afraid it's a rather nonsensical story."

The woman smiled, running her thumb along Sophie's cheek. "Those are my very favorite kind."

CHAPTER FORTY-FIVE

THE CITY *of* TALKING BOOKS

When the dust finally settled on Bustleburgh, the people emerged from the wreckage to treat those who had been injured by the Zeitgeist. Scrivener Behn and the remaining pilgrims—many of whom were versed in the secrets of old medicine—worked ceaselessly to tend to the wounded. Though many Bustleburghers were at first wary of these strange residents, they soon became grateful for their help.

Sophie's own burns from the Zeitgeist were not so easily treated, and she carried the scars on her neck and arms for the rest of her days. Over time, however, she developed a fondness for the places where the flesh rippled and twisted like dark mountain ranges. She had discovered for herself the truth known to adventurers the world over: The bigger the scar, the better the story.

Peter and Sir Tode decided to stay on to help rebuild the city. The fire that had spread so savagely managed to destroy almost every new building in Bustleburgh, leaving exposed the older stone towers and tunnels that had been buried and forgotten. Slowly, the people of Bustleburgh rediscovered the ancient city that they had worked so hard to forget.

Madame Eldritch did not remain long in the new city. Having seen the Last Resort rescued from the Uncannyon, she resolved to return to that place in search of Taro. Scrivener Behn and some of the pilgrims had offered to accompany her on this adventure, but she demurred, claiming that some journeys were meant to be made alone. By the following morning, she was gone. What Madame Eldritch encountered in those unknown depths, and whether she rescued Taro, is a story for another day.

But I would be remiss if I did not mention the *books*. You see, all of the above changes were nothing compared with what happened to the storybooks in Bustleburgh—a thing so curious that it has since made the city quite famous. Though the Four Questions had been completely destroyed, the other books in the Pyre had survived. When the Zeitgeist was at last vanquished, and its charred remains were scattered across the streets and rooftops, it was discovered that all the books had been changed in one small but remarkable way:

They were *alive.*

I mean this in the most literal sense possible. Imagine, if you will, tens of thousands of books all flopping about on the streets like beached fish. Some of the heavier volumes taught themselves to walk on the ends of their covers. A few smaller books managed to take flight like birds. This life was not limited to locomotion—for every one of the books, when opened, would also begin to *speak* its contents aloud to whoever would listen. The voice of each book was different, and (if accounts are to be believed) quite dramatic—complete with sound effects and colorful characterizations. By nightfall, the entire city was ringing with the voices of a thousand different stories.

At first, the people of Bustleburgh were understandably alarmed by this infestation of moving, talking nonsense. Many people tried to tear up or burn the books out of fear. But this revulsion soon gave way to a certain kind of fascination due to one immutable truth known the world over as Scheherazade's Law: It is impossible to kill someone who is in the middle of telling you a really wonderful story.

Men and women were suddenly reminded of the stories they had once loved as children. And soon people were bringing books back into their homes—caring for them as they would pets or even friends. As you might imagine, this did much to reinvigorate the book trade, and Quire & Quire soon found itself overflowing with customers, all eagerly searching for new books to read. Sophie's mother and father took to their work with clear delight—trading books back and forth, ceaselessly exchanging thoughts and ideas and opinions. Sophie thought she might be glimpsing what it had been like so many years before when her parents had first been in love.

"One thing that I cannot understand," Sophie said one afternoon while shelving books in her newly expanded work space, "if the Pyre was meant to destroy nonsense, why did it attack this city? Why these people?"

Sir Tode climbed onto a stool next to her. "I have seen my share of magic in my days, and if there's one thing I know, it's that it cannot be depended on to do anything one expects." He shook his shaggy head. "Perhaps there's more magic to these so-called common folk than we realize."

Sophie thought she might understand what he meant by this. For all the hours she had spent repairing books, she knew that stories were much more than words on a page. Stories lived inside those who read them. It was like Sophie with her mother: She might not have remembered her mother's face or voice or touch, but those things were a part of her all the same. "Maybe that was Prigg's real folly," she said, drawing a strand of hair behind her ear. "Magic cannot be removed from the world, because the world—every speck of it—is magical. It is simply a matter of whether or not we can see it."

✦   ✦   ✦

It was some months later when a new and wholly unexpected visitor came to the shop. It happened one quiet evening as Sophie was seated at the workbench, mending a book of limericks that had hurt its spine by leaping from a very tall height, Akrasia curled up at her feet. "Hold still," Sophie said to the protesting book. "I can't stitch your pages if they're flapping about."

There was a creaking behind her, and she turned to the bookshelf to see that it had been opened. Professor Cake was standing there, his hands atop his ostrich-spine cane, a pipe in his mouth. "Hello, Sophie," he said. "I trust I'm not intruding."

"Professor!" Sophie cried, leaping from her stool. She raced across the room and wrapped him in a great big hug. "I feared I might never see you again."

"There, there," he said, patting her on the back in a way that suggested he was not entirely accustomed to being greeted so informally. "I've been caught up with some important business."

"Greetings, Professor," Akrasia said, approaching and bowing her head. "I hoped we might meet once more."

The Professor knelt down and patted Akrasia's shoulders, his knotted fingers finding the scars where the beast had lost her wings. "Dear me," he said. "Feels like something's missing there. Perhaps we should do something about that?"

"Wait," Sophie said, stepping back. "Does Peter know you're here? We have to find him and—"

Before she could even finish her sentence, the door of the shop burst open. "I heard . . . the . . . Professor!" Peter cried, very out of breath.

"Indeed, you did!" Professor Cake said, laughing. "And you wasted no time coming to investigate." He peered at the boy, not unfondly. "I see you have dispensed with the blindfold."

Peter looked at the ground, then shrugged. "I guess I've found something worth looking at." His gaze darted to Sophie, and she felt a sort of shiver move down her spine. As the more astute readers among you might have observed, a special fondness had formed between the two of them—the sort of fondness that might one day grow into the stuff of legend and song.

Sir Tode appeared at the door a moment later. "Ah, Professor!" he said upon seeing the old man. "I was wondering when you might pay us a visit. A monster slain, a city restored. You'll have to admit, our Sophie's done quite well for herself."

"And why shouldn't she?" The Professor said warmly. "She is, after all, the Storyguard."

"Not anymore," Sophie said. "The books have been destroyed. There is no Storyguard."

The man drew his pipe from his mouth. "Is that what you think, child?" He took a heavy breath. "It is my duty to inform you that you are sorely mistaken. You cannot stop being the Storyguard any more than I can stop being Professor Cake. That the Four Questions were destroyed is immaterial. Those books were but a tool to help you in your task—a task that you executed with remarkable courage and unwavering determination. A task, I might also add, that is far from over." He waved his pipe like a wand. "Tell me, what do you know of the League of Maps?"

Sophie and the others looked at one another. "Er, afraid it doesn't ring a bell," Sir Tode said.

Professor Cake's face turned to scandal. "We must remedy that at once." He reached into his vest and removed a paper folded and marked with a blue wax seal. "Come. Your ship awaits."

Peter's eyes went wide. He started to reach for the paper but stopped himself short. "Professor, we can't go," he said, lowering his hand. He turned to Sir Tode. "I promised Sir Tode I would help him find a cure for his curse, and that's what we're going to do." He looked down at his friend. "It's time."

The old knight wrinkled his furry brow. "Yes, well . . . It's not every day the Professor asks for our help. Maybe one *small* digression couldn't hurt?"

Peter looked at Sir Tode, and a grin broke across his face. "One more adventure?"

Sir Tode nodded. "One more adventure."

"Excellent!" Professor Cake clapped his hands. "You will leave at once!"

"But, Professor?" Sophie said, looking back through the bookcase at the shop—its shelves and rafters and floors lined with books hopping and flitting about. "What about my parents?"

"What about them?" Professor Cake said in the tone of someone very unaccustomed to thinking of anyone's parents. He offered a warm smile. "Something tells me they should like some time alone. And haven't you grown a bit large for these four walls, Sophie Quire?"

Sophie did not say farewell to her parents before leaving the bookshop behind. Instead, she left a simple note on her workbench:

> *My tale is not yet told.*
> *I will return.*
> *Fondly,*
> *Sophie Quire,*
> *the Last Storyguard*

She knew they would understand.

✦   ✦   ✦

And so it went in Bustleburgh. The city that had set out to destroy stories had been transformed into a haven for books of all kinds. And as the population read more stories, the city itself began to change. At first the changes were small: a few sprites hovering over the dusky river, or a falling star on the horizon. But then more changes came. The Wassail lost its murky darkness and shone clear once more. The eyes of gargoyles shifted as one passed beneath them. Birds sang in three-part chorus. Mirrors reflected strange visions. Old, neglected wells started granting wishes. More than a few house pets took to uttering prophecies. As the city changed, so did the way people saw it: Old maids became crones, and naughty children became imps; the strongest men were hailed as giants and the fairest ladies called enchantresses. The once-level roads shifted and settled into twisting alleyways full of long shadows and narrow corridors—every one of them eventually leading to a small bookshop in the heart of the town.

I would like to tell you that Quire & Quire remains open to this day, but that would be untrue. The shop closed eventually, and its marvelous talking books soon made their way to other lands and other readers. Most of these books have grown shy in their old age, preferring to sit quietly on the shelf. But if ever you find a very dusty book on a very-out-of-the-way bookcase, put it to your ear and listen closely. *What do you hear?* The faint rustle of pages, the creak of an old spine, and the hushed song of a story waiting to be read.

✑ Author's Note ✑

Sophie Quire and the Last Storyguard was inspired by many things and many people, but none more than my mother. My mother grew up on a wheat farm on the plains of North Dakota—a place where books were few. She was a voracious reader, and she read everything she could find. When I was young, she would occasionally mention how, as a teenager, she ran out of novels to read—there were literally no more stories in her library. Anytime she mentioned this, I would think: What if she had found one last book hidden in the corner . . . and what if that book was more than just a story?

Both of my parents took pains to ensure that, even when we had little money, our home was never wanting for books. I was the only child I knew whose house included a "library." Virtually all of our books were used, which taught me at a very young age to see books as talismans that carried with them the memory of readers past. To this day, I prefer a tattered paperback to a shiny new hardcover.

It was in that home library that I discovered the stories that would one day provide the foundation for *Sophie Quire and the Last Storyguard*. Chief among them is *Matilda*, by Roald Dahl. *Matilda* was the first "long" book I ever read by myself. It remains my favorite children's book to this day. The image of little Matilda Wormwood lying on the floor with an oversized book was undeniably an inspiration for Sophie.

That library was also where I first discovered the stories of Charles Perrault—the author who single-handedly brought the fairy-tale tradition into the literary consciousness, some two hundred years before the Brothers Grimm. Those fairy tales soon led me to discover old bestiaries filled with strange descriptions of creatures at once both exotic and familiar. If you find yourself wanting to read such a book, I strongly recommend T. H. White's translation of *The Book of Beasts*, which puts *The Book of What* to shame. Finally, I owe a debt to Rudolf Raspe's *The Surprising Adventures of Baron Munchausen*, which sparked the hinterland empire. I think it would have found a home on Sophie's bookshelf.

This was without question the most challenging story I have ever undertaken, and I could not have written it without the help of fellow pilgrims: Sally Alexander, Jim Armstrong, Katherine Ayres, Chad W. Beckerman, Mary Burke, Caroline Carlson, Courtney Code, Orlando Dos Reis, Markus Hoffmann, Lynne Missen, Joe Regal, Bougie Sewell, Thomas Sweterlitsch, Jason Wells, and my friend and colleague Tamar Brazis—who bled for this book nearly as much as its author did. Thank you all.

✑ ABOUT THE AUTHOR ✐

JONATHAN AUXIER is the author of *Peter Nimble and His Fantastic Eyes* and *The Night Gardener*. He lives in Pittsburgh with his family. Visit him at TheScop.com.